Praise for *Dream Jungle*

"Jessica Hagedorn's intricate new novel boldly links a Manila millionaire's 'discovery' of a Stone Age tribe on Mindanao with a filmed re-creation of the Vietnam War on that same guerilla-plagued island six years later. . . . The result is her best book since *Dogeaters* . . . 'Performance or real life?' That is the crucial question posed by *Dream Jungle*. But the difference between the two, Hagedorn implies in this slippery, masterly novel, is a riddle better savored than solved."
　　　　　　　　　　　　　　　　—*The New York Times Book Review*

"With her flair for evoking place, her ability to construct strong, believable characters and a keen sense of both the political and the cultural impact of America on the Philippines, Hagedorn has woven a deft and complex tale of corruption, fealty and integrity."　　　—*The Baltimore Sun*

"A richly intriguing study of flamboyant ambition and the politics of corruption . . . Hagedorn's prose has the exciting ring of the new . . . she has the gift of making the surreal intimate, yet ringed in circles of strangeness, violence and beauty. . . . *Dream Jungle* creates a compelling symphony of voices and yet is one voice . . . delivering the emotional charge of politics race, and class."　　　—*The Seattle Times*

"Hagedorn offers a rich immediacy of detail and characters . . . [she] is a trustworthy guide, her navigation from the depths of the jungle to the seediest corners of Manila to the ostentatious mansions lining the city's so-called 'Hollywood Hills' is so assured that the juxtaposition of these places, however surreal, seems as perfectly rational as a dream."
　　　　　　　　　　　　　　　　—*San Francisco Chronicle*

ABOUT THE AUTHOR

Jessica Hagedorn is an acclaimed novelist, playwright, poet, and screenwriter. Born and raised in the Philippines, she moved to the United States in her teens. Hagedorn lives in New York City.

DREAM JUNGLE

Jessica Hagedorn

PENGUIN BOOKS

PENGUIN BOOKS

Published by the Penguin Group
Penguin Group (USA) Inc., 375 Hudson Street, New York, New York 10014, U.S.A.
Penguin Group (Canada), 10 Alcorn Avenue, Toronto,
Ontario, Canada M4V 3B2 (a division of Pearson Penguin Canada Inc.)
Penguin Books Ltd, 80 Strand, London WC2R 0RL, England
Penguin Ireland, 25 St Stephen's Green, Dublin 2, Ireland (a division of Penguin Books Ltd)
Penguin Group (Australia), 250 Camberwell Road, Camberwell,
Victoria 3124, Australia (a division of Pearson Australia Group Pty Ltd)
Penguin Books India Pvt Ltd, 11 Community Centre, Panchsheel Park, New Delhi – 110 017, India
Penguin Group (NZ), cnr Airborne and Rosedale Roads, Albany,
Auckland, New Zealand (a division of Pearson New Zealand Ltd)
Penguin Books (South Africa) (Pty) Ltd, 24 Sturdee Avenue, Rosebank,
Johannesburg 2196, South Africa

Penguin Books Ltd, Registered Offices: 80 Strand, London WC2R 0RL, England

First published in the United States of America by Viking Penguin,
a member of Penguin Group (USA) Inc. 2003
Published by Penguin Books 2004

1 3 5 7 9 10 8 6 4 2

PUBLISHER'S NOTE
Dream Jungle is a work of fiction inspired by events in the Philippines in the 1970s. While inspired by
actual events, the characters and narrative are the product of the author's imagination. Any dialogue
and action depicted are fictional and should not be attributed to any person, living or dead.

THE LIBRARY OF CONGRESS HAS CATALOGED THE HARDCOVER EDITION AS FOLLOWS:
Hagedorn, Jessica Tarahata, date.
Dream jungle / Jessica Hagedorn.
p. cm.
ISBN 0-670-88458-8 (hc.)
ISBN 0 14 20.0109 0 (pbk.)
1. Philippines—Fiction. 2. Motion picture industry—Fiction. 3. Indigenous peoples—Fiction.
4. Women journalists—Fiction. 5. Landowners—Fiction. 6. Actors—Fiction. I. Title.
PS3558.A3228D74 2003
813'.54—dc21   2003041080

Printed in the United States of America
Designed by Nancy Resnick

In memory of Santiago Bose (b. 1949, d. 2002)—
friend, visionary artist, and cultural provocateur.

And for John, Paloma, and Esther, always.

PART ONE

Discovery and Conquest

Primo Viaggio Intorno Al Mundo

excerpts from Antonio Pigafetta's account
of Magellan's expedition

E ach one of those people lives according to his own will, for they have no seignor. They go naked, and some are bearded and have black hair that reaches to the waist. They wear small palm-leaf hats, as do the Albanians. They are as tall as we, and well built. They have no worship. They are tawny, but are born white. Their teeth are red and black, for they think that is most beautiful. The women go naked except that they wear a narrow strip of bark as thin as paper, which grows between the tree and the bark of the palm, before their privies. They are goodlooking and delicately formed, and lighter complexioned than the men; and wear their hair which is exceedingly black, loose and hanging quite down to the ground. The women do not work in the fields but stay in the house, weaving mats, baskets (casse: literally, boxes), and other things needed in their houses, from palm leaves. They eat cocoanuts, camotes (batate), birds, figs one palmo in length (i.e., bananas), sugarcane, and flying fish, besides other things. They anoint the body and the hair with cocoanut and beneseed oil . . .

. . . They use no weapons, except a kind of spear pointed with a fishbone at the end. Those people are poor, but ingenious and very thievish, on account of which we called those three islands the islands of Ladroni (i.e., of thieves). Their amusement, men and women, is to plough the seas with those small boats of theirs.

Those boats resemble fucelere, but are narrower, and some are black, (some) white, and others red . . . and those boats resemble the dolphins which leap in the water from wave to wave. Those Ladroni (i.e., robbers) thought, according to the signs which they made, that there were no other people in the world but themselves.

Zamora: 1971

3rd person narr.

How to explain that moment when Zamora López de Legazpi first laid eyes on them? Zamora's gaze was steadfast and shameless. O they were beautiful, powerful, strange! Their fierce, wary eyes scrutinized him in return, taking in the brown, unruly curls on his head, the scraggly beard of his pale, unshaven face, the muscular arms and small, compact body that was, surprisingly, no taller than theirs. He had walked into a dream. Someone else's dream—perhaps Duan's—but now stolen and claimed by Zamora. The landscape of that dream—vast, ominous, shimmering blues and greens—was simply part of the loot.

The Himal people were not unfriendly; they could easily have killed him. One man demanded a cigarette, pointing to the Salems in Zamora's jean jacket. Zamora gave him the entire pack. Another pointed to the ornate collar of brass, glass beads, and bone hanging from his wife's neck, hoping Zamora would buy it. Zamora grinned and shook his head. Duan berated the man, who was crestfallen and backed away. The man's wife fingered her precious necklace, relieved not to have to part with it. Others offered wads of flat green leaves to Zamora as a test, a gift. Zamora crammed the rolled-up leaves into his mouth, chewing and spitting as he saw the old women around him chewing and spitting. His tongue and lips became numb, but his other senses grew more acute. It was almost unbearable. Everything he saw and heard filled him with love. The tips of his fingers tingled. His eyes were wet with tears.

Children hid behind the long, dazzling skirts of their mothers, stealing glances at the hairy stranger. The old women of the tribe were the only ones who acted indifferent. Squatting comfortably on bony haunches, they turned their brown, haughty faces toward the heat of the sun, away from where Zamora stood with a goofy smile. The old women smelled trouble; they were disgusted with Duan for bringing the hairy Spaniard to them. The old women spit at the dirt and muttered curses under their breath, hoping to drive the stranger away. Tiny bells jangled on their brass anklets as the splayed toes of their cracked, bare feet burrowed into the hard, red earth.

Zamora López de Legazpi had been traveling for days to Lake Ramayyah. The lake, once filled with crocodiles and considered sacred by the Himal people, was located in Cotabato del Sur, the southernmost tip of the Philippine archipelago. It was Duan's home, approximately 550 miles from Manila, as far from Zamora's mansions, cars, polo horses, and beauty queens as anyone could imagine. Zamora had traveled first by helicopter, then by jeep, then on foot. He was led by Duan into the heart of a remote Himal village at the base of Mount Taobo, a grand, forbidding mountain. In the Himal language, Mount Taobo literally meant "mountain of the human being." Zamora López de Legazpi stood in the shadow of the spectacular cordilleras surrounding Lake Ramayyah. Dense, rugged, green with trees, chains of dark mountains loomed in the clouds. That day he was a conquistador without an army, a rich man without his usual posse of bodyguards, photographers, doctors, PR flacks, cooks, and servants. That day his only friend was Duan, a man he did not trust. The thought was oddly liberating. Zamora kept chewing. The bitter, caustic juice of betel, tobacco, rock salt, and lime powder coated his tongue. *Bliss.*

Duan had repeatedly told him about the shy, mysterious people in the forest.

"Of course there are people in the forest! Why are you wasting my time with something I already know?" Zamora said, though he was intrigued. They were in a one-room shack made of cinder blocks and tin, what passed for a military outpost in the dusty, god-forsaken town of Sultan Ramayyah. Zamora kicked the back of Duan's leg. The older man grunted, taken by surprise. He was angry but did not dare show it. Duan was an elfin, toothless man of uncertain age who, while as poor as any Himal in this part of Mindanao, claimed to be a *datu*, a chieftain descended from a long, distinguished line of *datus*. Duan's reputation as a skilled hunter and guide was legendary. He was fluent in several obscure tribal languages and dialects, and he knew enough rudimentary English and Tagalog to be useful to Zamora. Duan boasted of having three wives and seventeen children, yet he was a loner perfectly at ease roaming the Muslim settlements and isolated Jesuit missions nestled in the lush valleys below the mountains. Duan had known Zamora's father, who once owned and controlled the profitable silver and copper mines in the region. But those days were long gone. Legazpi Mines now belonged to the government.

Duan rubbed the bruised calf of his leg where the Spaniard had kicked him. "These people are different," Duan kept insisting, glad no one was in the room to witness his humiliation. The soldiers were outside, joking with Zamora's bodyguard and pilot. "These people live in trees and caves. They are monkey people. Bat people."

Zamora chuckled. "Are they poorer than poor? Do they have tails?"

"No," Duan said. "They have no tails. But they climb and jump better than I can. I do not lie." Duan's voice grew whiny and higher as he became more agitated. "I am a *datu*," he kept saying. "I do not lie."

"Show me, prove it to me!" Zamora shouted. He lunged at Duan as if about to kick him again, then stopped himself. Both men stared at each other, breathing heavily. Zamora spoke after a long silence. "Lead me to them, Duan. Then you must promise to leave me alone with them. But if you are lying"—Zamora paused—"I will kill you."

❦

Duan's people, the people in the village by the lake, watched in silence as Duan and Zamora made their way up the mountain. The old women shook their heads and covered their eyes, amazed at the two men's foolishness. There were no trails, just clumps of thorny bush and vines, trickles of waterfall, walls of rocks and trees. The shrieking of birds and monkeys filled the air. The journey would take at least another four to six hours, Duan informed Zamora. Maybe ten. The thick mud made the going excruciatingly slow. It started to rain, gently at first. The steady patter of raindrops grew into a roar as the forest darkened. Zamora and Duan huddled together in the rotted-out cavity of a colossal tree trunk, forced to wait until the downpour ceased.

The rain stopped as abruptly as it had begun.

"We can go, boss," Duan finally said.

Zamora and Duan crept out of the makeshift shelter, carefully wending their way through the dense, thorny bush until they reached a small clearing. "Wait here. I will tell them you have come," Duan whispered before disappearing into the trees. Zamora collapsed on the muddy jungle floor and flung out his arms in joyful surrender. *All that green.* Humid, pulsating, unforgiving, alive with predators and scavengers. Zamora heard the triumphant screech of a monkey-eating eagle, imagined it pouncing on a startled tarsier. A yellow python uncoiled—swallowing an unsuspecting cloud rat, then a furious, screaming wild pig. Leeches dropped off jade vines in a sinister shower of welcome, slithering into Zamora's ear canals and the corners of his eyes. He blinked in wonder as they fattened and gorged on his blood. Trees towered two hundred feet above him—*Kekem, lunay, nabul, balete.* God's trees, so ancient and huge they obscured sky and sun. Such clichés he felt, such reverence and awe. A tingling in the loins, a fire in the belly you can only imagine. *Ilang-ilang, waling-waling.* Pungent perfume of wild, monstrous lilies and orchids in bloom. Pungent perfume of heaven, stink of fungus and mildew, bed of earth. Voracious green of dampness and rot. Green that lulled but also excited, green of exhaustion and thorns. Enchanted green of Lorca the poet. Ominous green of Mindanao rain forest.

Zamora would gladly die here, alone.

Just hours ago his knockout Teutonic goddess of a wife had sat up in bed and yelled out his name. ZAH-MO-RAH! She caught him just as he was about to sneak off in the gray light of dawn. "Why are you going to Mindanao? What is so important? Why? Why? Why?" The sounds of a car horn, honking once, twice. Sonny, his bodyguard, waited to drive him to the heliport. *Sorry, baby. Gotta go.* Ilse's mouth turned down in a grimace. His name uttered again. This time softly. "Zamora."

Come on, let's hear it, darling.

"Today is Dulce's birthday. Or have you forgotten? "

She turned away as he approached the bed. Zamora longed to reach out and kiss those parched lips, climb on top of that golden, clammy, perfect body and assure her that of course he had not forgotten his daughter's birthday. But instead he left the room and fled down the stairs. Celia stood by the front door, ready with his bag and a thermos of black coffee. *Good morning, sir.* Her face betrayed nothing—though surely she had heard it all, heard Ilse railing at him just moments ago.

"Good morning," Zamora said to Celia, who gazed at the floor. He raised his voice. "I said, 'Good morning,' Celia."

Hers was barely audible. "Good morning, sir."

"That's better," Zamora said.

Celia's blush deepened. Zamora did not regret intimidating her. Her discomfort and unease excited him. He owed her a visit. He had not visited her in a long time, and he missed her. Celia was the *yaya* in charge of his infant son. She belonged to him. She was ordinary-looking but young, with lovely, burnished skin and a taut body. At first Celia used to run and hide from him. It became a game with them, even after the night Zamora took her to the pool-house and deflowered her. Celia was seventeen then; she is nineteen now. She once made the mistake of daring to say she loved him. *Minamahal kita . . . po*, she had whispered in Tagalog. The *"po"* added as an afterthought, to signify respect.

Zamora's response had been brusque and chilly. "But, dear girl, I love my wife."

It amused Zamora to watch Celia, in her nervousness and haste, fumble with the lock on the front door. She finally got it open. The Mercedes idled in the driveway, Sonny at the wheel. Zamora stepped out into the rising heat. His arm brushed against Celia's swollen breasts, making her jump.

Ilse! If only you were here. Fire ants swarm across my face, minuscule spiders bite through the cloth of my pants, I feel eyes. Not animal or insect eyes, but human eyes peering through the leaves at me. I open my mouth and begin to sing, imagining you, imagining my secret audience hunkered down in the bushes, their amazement and surprise at the sound of my sonorous voice. "What a diff'rence a day makes." . . . A fluttering of wings. Your sigh. The rustling of leaves. The forest in an uproar as my voice booms and echoes. You run. I close my eyes and begin another random song, something I am sure my invisible audience would enjoy. "Cu cu rru cu cú, paloma . . . cu cu rru cu cú, no llores . . . las piedras jamás, Paloma, que van a saber de amores. . . ." I open my eyes. A boy with hair down to his waist—thin, naked—creeps out of the bush and stands there, gawking at me.

The boy's name, Zamora and the rest of the world would soon find out, was Bodabil. A born clown with a talent for mimicry, approximately ten years old. Maybe older, but none of the people in Bod-abil's tribe looked their age. The adults, by twenty-five, seemed as gnarled as the trees in their sacred forest.

Bodabil craned his neck to get a better view of Zamora. Duan had warned them all that the Spaniard was coming. A stranger so powerful that hair sprouted on his face; a stranger so powerful that he flew a whirling demon bird above the trees. Duan had spoken of the Spaniard with a certain proprietary air. "Be careful. The stranger carries anger inside him."

Zamora kept singing, but softly now. Bodabil hooted and warbled in response, either in appreciation or in mockery of his singing. The boy's reaction reassured Zamora. His singing faded down into quiet. Bodabil crept closer. Zamora lay still, did not dare move for fear the boy would bolt and run.

"Don't be afraid," Zamora whispered in English. He felt foolish—for why English? A twig snapped, but Zamora kept his eyes fixed on the canopy of dark trees above. "Don't be afraid, *mi hijito*," he continued in a low, gentle voice. Zamora added, in awkward Himal, "I am your Spirit Father, here to protect you." There were eyes and ears everywhere, watching and listening. Bodabil froze in his tracks, surprised by the familiar words the stranger was uttering.

"My language," Duan once said with pride to Zamora, "is understood by these cave people."

"But how is that possible?" Zamora asked, immediately suspicious.

"Because I taught them," Duan answered with a mischievous smile.

"How much time have you spent with them?"

Duan shrugged, feeling no need to offer the Spaniard any further explanation.

"All right," Zamora said, "then teach me your language."

Duan taught Zamora *bino-bino*, for "welcome"; *maladong*, for "companion"; *lagtuk*, which either meant "penis" or, with a slightly different intonation, "tree frog." Over and over Duan repeated the crucial phrase for Zamora to say: *Ago mong Amo Data*, for "I am your Spirit Father." Zamora had underestimated the wicked complexity of the Himal language. Nuance was everything. There were clicking words and gasping words, words that were quick intakes of breath, words that were harsh sighs of longing. One had to be careful about tone and inflection, to get it just right. Otherwise words could mean the exact opposite of what was intended. Just before he left Zamora alone in the clearing, Duan taught Zamora something else to say to the forest people, something important: *Laan-lan,* for "I mean you no harm."

language

Rizalina: 1972

Lina

Y ou don't know me, but that don't matter, because I gonna tell you. This all happened long ago, but not so long that I don't remember. My name is Rizalina, and when this story begins, I am ten years old. Is a beautiful name, *di ba?* I am the eldest and only daughter of the servant and cook, Candelaria Guzman, and the jack-of-all-trades-master-of-none, Sixto Cayabyab of Sultan Ramayyah, Cotabato del Sur. I am, I was, the big sister of the unlucky twins, Junior and Boy. They drowned, along with my father, when *The Mindanao Star*, the boat we took to visit my mother in Manila, capsized and sank during a sudden typhoon. As we approached Manila Bay, the sky went from dirty white to black. Just like that. The winds picked up as the sky cracked open and rain poured down on us. The boat rocked furiously from side to side. My brothers and the other children on board began to whimper and scream. The older people prayed—even my *tatay*, who never went to church and cursed at God when he was drunk. The prayers and screams grew louder and louder. *In the name of the Father, the Son and the Holy Ghost, in the name of the Blessed Virgin Mary, in the name of St. Jude and St. Christopher, Santa Barbara and San Martín de Porres.* I kept silent, holding on as best I could to the back of a bench that was bolted down. My brothers wrapped their arms around my neck. The wind and rain blew sideways, the waves gushed over decks packed with men, women, and children who could not swim. Imagine that. We who lived by the sea and lived off the sea—terrified by water. Packed into a poor-people's boat with no rubber rafts or life preservers to fight over and cling to for safety. My brothers lost their grip and slid away from me. I was blinded by water. Everyone—165 passengers and crew members—drowned.

Everyone, that is, except for me.

Me, Rizalina. Born into a life of shit, but nevertheless voted best number one elementary student in all of Sultan Ramayyah. Champion speller, speed reader, and secret keeper. Okeydokey fluent in English, as you can tell by now. Loves the word "nevertheless." Named after our beloved national hero, poet and novelist Dr. José Rizal. Voted "class comedian" in grade four. Voted "girl most likely to succeed" in grade five. Voted "most likely of anyone" to graduate from school, until that piece-of-shit boat was blown around by winds and toppled into the raging sea.

My mother—my *nanay*—used to say, "You are blessed with a strange intelligence, Rizalina. I will work hard as a *katulong* so you can finish school and become a something."

"Become a what?" I asked her.

"Not a *katulong*. Not a servant," Nanay said.

"Become not a servant? But how can that be?" I loved to tease my mother. "We are poor," I said. "Tatay says people born poor will die poor."

"Your father is bitter and stupid," Nanay said. "Don't listen to him. Your future is"—my mother paused, thinking hard—"*filled with hope.* You could become a nurse, Lina. Or a bank teller. There's a bank in the next town, *di ba?* Or maybe a teacher like that woman you admire so much . . . what's her name? Miss Angway."

Maybe, maybe, maybe. Too many maybes! I owned one soiled party dress and a pair of scratched-up patent-leather shoes, the latest castoffs from the rich man's daughter. The dress was too big, the shoes too tight and pointy toed for my feet, but I put them on whenever my father and brothers weren't home and pretended I was the town fiesta queen. In my stained organza gown, I chased after the desperate chickens that pecked at the barren patch of dirt in front of our little house. On my head was an imaginary rhinestone crown, gaudy and sparkling; I wielded the slim branch of a guava tree as my royal scepter. The starving chickens were my subjects. My future was set, all right. A future of shit.

I said to my mother, "Never mind Miss Angway. Miss Angway bites her nails and cries when she thinks no one is looking. I wanna be a servant like *you*, dressed in a crisp uniform, living in the rich man's big, beautiful house."

"Don't be stupid like your father," Nanay said.

My *nanay's nanay*, my Lola Isay, worked as a servant all her life. She keeled over dead while washing her master's dirty underwear. And my great-grandmother was a *yaya* who cared for rich people's children. And so on and so on. Washerwomen, *yayas*, cooks, house-cleaners, gardeners who toiled in Manila or Cebu, big cities far enough away from here that they hardly ever saw their own families or children. Just like my mother, they sent home every peso and centavo they earned for the education and betterment of . . .

Ha.

You see how far that got any of us.

I love my mother and always will.

I never liked my father and am happy he is dead.

My father—my *tatay*, Sixto Cayabyab—was a sometime fisherman, pedicab driver, ditchdigger, and carpenter. He was not particularly good at anything he did, except catching tilapia and women.

He drank and he beat me—usually because he had spent all the money my mother sent home every month and there was no more liquor or women to be had until she sent more. Mama could read and write just enough to get by, but my handsome father could not read or write at all—so he beat me for being able to do something he could not do, for reading and writing better than anyone at my school and probably all of Sultan Ramayyah, except, of course, the lonely and unhappy Miss Carmen Angway.

One night, when Papa was drunker than usual, he ordered me to read to him. *Read. Show me what you can do.*

"What do you want me to read?"

"I don't care. Just read!"

I picked up a tattered prayer book that once belonged to my Lola Isay and began reading the Gospel According to St. Luke. "At that time, Jesus said to His disciples: Ask, and it shall be given you: seek, and you shall find: knock, and it shall be opened to you—"

"Well, well. How nice. My daughter has a golden tongue. Read some more!" Papa shouted. I read psalms, Lenten prayers, whatever was on those pages. My father listened hard, red-faced and fuming. Then he fell asleep.

He beat me for burning the rice, for giving him the evil eye and making him lose at cards. "You are *malas*, Lina. Bad luck!" He beat me with a stick, with his belt, with his small callused hand. He never beat my brothers. Twins were considered a good omen, blessed and powerful, according to the townspeople. But Junior and Boy never brought Tatay any luck with his gambling, any extra food or money into our house or unexpected joy into our shitty lives. When my father beat me, they weren't any use at all. They either ran away and hid or huddled in a corner, their big, moist eyes staring at us in sick fascination. I did what I could to keep from crying out. I would never give my father or idiot brothers that satisfaction. Of course, my stubborn silence only made my father beat me harder.

I learned to endure, to clench my teeth and squeeze my eyes shut, lift myself outside myself and become other things. I was the invisible baboon, my ass the colors of a rainbow. My baboon self observed my father beating my girl self and listened calmly to the thump of his hand, the whoosh and slap of a thin strip of leather or tree branch whipping my flesh. I felt no pain. Was I not the powerful one? O the poetry and music in that room! Breathe, whoosh, slap. I counted from one to whatever it took inside my head, concentrated on remembering every detail of Miss Angway's pimply, kind face—anything to keep from thinking about what was happening to me. Until my father exhausted himself and fled from the room in . . . what? *Shame?* If I said shame, would that make you feel sorry for him? Fuck my father. He felt no shame.

Mama said I was cursed with my father's beauty. He was several years younger than my mother, a man with the slender body, delicate features, and long, curly lashes of a girl. If he hadn't been such a drunkard, he could have been a movie star. Women adored him. They didn't seem to care that he was a drunk and a gambler, burdened with a wife and too many children. Mama, who was not beautiful, won my father's heart mainly because she was fool enough to be willing to support him. She worked as head cook for Mister Boss Señor Zamora López de Legazpi's family in Manila. Mister Señor was rich—the son of an even richer man. He treated my *nanay* better than most rich people treated their servants. He never beat her, he paid her on time, and he gave her his children's castoff clothes and expensive toys with missing parts to pass on to her own children. This my mother mistook for genuine kindness. She was, like her mother—my Lola Isay—and Maximina, Apolinaria, and Concepción—all the women who came before my mother and grandmother—doomed to gratitude.

Square-jawed and stoic, perfumed by the faint scent of garlic and Johnson's Baby Powder, Mama visited us every three months and never came empty-handed. She brought bottles of Jōvan Musk cologne and tight, brightly patterned shirts for my father, gifts he would flaunt to his drinking buddies in town. We children always got food—flaky melon cakes and barbecued pork buns packed in pink boxes from the best Chinese bakeries in Manila. We gobbled everything up in one sitting, my brothers whining for more. "I am not made of money," my mother would say, exasperated. "Try to make it last." But how could we? We were always hungry. When Tatay finally stumbled home, his new shirt undone and his breath reeking of cane liquor, the fighting would begin. Mama spit out the usual accusations: *You're a weak man, a sinner! Hayop!* Papa flailed at her with his puny fists: *What did you say, Candelaria? What did you say?* But my mother was a strong woman with big arms, and sober besides.

Junior, Boy, and I feigned sleep, curled up on the floor on our *banigs*. Junior and Boy whimpered and peed on themselves, growing more upset as our parents fought through the night. Papa tried punching Mama again, lost his balance, and fell. I wanted to laugh. Suddenly he began to sob. "Forgive me, Candelaria. Please. You know how much I love you." Such lies! "Sixto!" my mother cried, feeling sorry for him. *Sixto, Sixto.* I hated her for loving him the way she did. My brothers and I lay facing the wall, but we heard every grunt and moan, every rhythmic, awful sound their bodies made as they slammed against each other, making violent love.

"Take me with you to Manila," I begged Nanay during one of her visits. We were outside in the dusty yard, under the scant shade of the lone guava tree. My mother sat on a low stool, picking lice from my long hair as I sat on the ground between her legs. "Take me with you," I said again. "Please, Nanay."

"Do you think you're going to heaven?" Mama laughed. "I do not want you to live the life of a servant, Lina."

"Mister Zamora owns a palace," I said. "You said so yourself. I want to go there."

Mama shrugged. "It may be a palace, but it has nothing to do with us. You have so much lice," she muttered. "We're going to have to cut off all your beautiful hair."

"I wish you would. I wish you'd cut it all off and leave me with a bald, shining head," I said. "See if I care." My mother stared at me for a moment, then took my hand and marched me two miles into town to see an old hag named Aling Belén.

"Is she a witch?" I asked Mama in a whisper.

"Do I look like a witch?" Aling Belén asked, smiling her toothless smile. She wore a long skirt wrapped around her waist and a turban made of colorful rags on her head.

"You are very old," I said. "Very, very, very old."

"Don't be rude!" Nanay hissed, pinching my arm to make her point.

"You mustn't hurt her," Aling Belén reminded my mother. She patted me on the head. "The child is right. I am indeed. Very, very old. Have you brought me a gift, Candelaria?" she asked my mother, who handed her a bag of betelnut, lime powder, and salt. Aling Belén seemed pleased.

Aling Belén rubbed a thick, kerosene-smelling ointment on my scalp and hair, then covered my tingling head with a towel and ordered me to sit still for what seemed an eternity. I imagined the lice on my head dying a slow, agonizing death, smothered by Aling Belén's greasy, lethal concoction. After she rinsed my hair clean, Aling Belén ran the comb through each strand to make sure there were no nits left. The sun had set hours ago, and it was dark outside.

"We have to go," my mother said.

"Let me read your daughter's palm," Aling Belén said.

Nanay was uneasy. "Why? She's just a child."

Aling Belén took my hand, turning it palm side up. "Look," she marveled, tracing the lines of my palm. "Such long, tangled life lines for one so young!"

"Is that good?" Mama asked, squinting at my hand.

"Very good," Aling Belén assured her. Apparently my life wasn't going to be as shitty as I thought. Mama thanked Aling Belén profusely, offering her a few pesos for her trouble, but the old hag refused to take her money.

"She's a nice witch," I said to my mother as we walked in the dark. The warm night smelled of ocean. In silence we marched back home, where my idiot brothers and drunk father waited, impatient for their dinner.

Candelaria. How I loved my mother, this terse woman I really did not know, how I felt safe only when she was near me! My heart broke every time I watched her repack the cardboard suitcase and get herself ready for the long journey back to Manila.

Please, Nanay. Don't leave without me.

"Don't cry," she said. "You must help your father and take care of your brothers. Finish school. Then maybe."

The harder I tried not to cry, the more my tears fell. "Maybe what?"

"Maybe you can come to Manila. Here—take my hanky. Wipe your eyes and blow your nose. Go on, Lina. Blow your nose."

"Can I live with you in Mister Zamora's house?"

My mother smiled one of her rare smiles. "Crazy girl," she said.

Once, just once, my father pulled up my dress and grasped between my legs. As if he wanted to catch something before it got away. He looked as stunned as I did, but he didn't stop—frantic fingers probing inside of me as if he had lost some precious object and was in a hurry to retrieve it. From time to time he paused to listen for anyone who might walk in the door. Then he would go back to probing, poking, making me wince and burn with shame. I stared at the torn calendar on the wall, wondered when he would stop. Questions rang in my head. *What is time? Who invented the calendar? What is God?* My brothers were outside playing. I could hear them shouting. My father stopped and pushed me away. Rinsed his fingers in one of the plastic gallon jugs of water I hauled daily from the town well. Unable to look at me, he went outside. I heard my idiot brothers yell. "Papa, Papa, come play with us!"

The sound of my father laughing.

I dreamed him dead, dreamed of stabbing him with the big, rusty knife on the kitchen shelf. Dreamed of scaling and gutting him like he had once taught me how to scale and gut a fish. Imagined the look of surprise on his face, the same stunned look when he first dared to touch me.

I never told my mother. Not even after he died. When the rescue workers later told us that my father had drowned—along with the twins and everyone else on that cursed boat—I became dizzy and confused. Mama said that my face became as white as the rich man's daughter and that I vomited until there was nothing left to vomit. And when the rescue workers explained that because of the sharks in the water, the bodies of my father and brothers would probably never be found, I was mute. My mother, lost in the depths of her own grief, mistook my fierce silence for sorrow.

I do not know how or why I survived the boat's sinking. I was not a particularly strong swimmer; maybe I was just too stubborn to die. "It's a miracle!" Nanay screamed, falling on her knees when she saw me pulled from the sea. "Santo Niño, the Virgin Mary of Antípolo, and St. Christopher must be watching over my baby!" Poor Mama. Such faith in the power of her Baby Jesus, her beloved Virgin Mary and saints. The truth was, a couple of fishermen in their *bangka* had spotted me flailing in the water. They hauled me in and dumped me on a dock at the Manila Yacht Club. A crowd, including rescue workers, policemen, and my astonished mother, was waiting.

"You'd better take the child to a hospital," a policeman said.

"I don't want to go to a hospital," I mumbled, trembling with cold. My teeth rattled in my head. A waiter from the yacht club ran up and draped a tablecloth over my shoulders. "Please, Nanay. I'm not sick," I moaned.

"The poor child's delirious," the waiter said.

To the hospital! To the hospital! people kept yelling.

A man took my picture, then another. "For the newspapers," the man said. My mother pushed him away and grabbed my hand. In the torrential rain, she led me past the growing crowd of gawkers and busybodies, through the yacht club's doors, and out to Roxas Boulevard. The streets were flooded, but somehow Mama managed to hail a taxi.

"Are we going to the hospital?" I asked, falling into the backseat. The tablecloth covering me was sopping wet, and I couldn't stop shaking.

"No, we are not," my mother answered, throwing her warm, plump arms around me. "Shh, Rizalina. Shh. You're safe now."

I closed my eyes. "Take us to Hollywood Hills," I heard her order the old man behind the wheel. "To the López de Legazpi compound."

"Hollywood Hills?" The old man clucked in disapproval. "In this storm? We'll never make it."

Mama's tone was sarcastic. "Shall I get another taxi?"

"No, no," the driver said. "It's just . . . well. It's *far*."

"I'll pay extra for your trouble. Hurry, old man. Can't you see my daughter needs help?"

"Shouldn't we take her to a hospital?"

"You will take us where I tell you to take us," Mama snapped.

I slipped in and out of a dream, noise and buildings so big, buildings on top of buildings, people on top of people, the zoom and rush of cars, jeepneys, *kalesas*, buses. Concrete. Thunderous noise of rain whipping against the roof of our taxi, radios blaring, men cursing and laughing, pretty girls in shocking dresses, broken umbrellas, the snake hiss of lust. Sounds I had never heard before, smells I had never smelled. Gasoline, cigarettes, perfume. The foul stench of the beautiful Pasig River.

Our slow taxi ride through underwater streets made me feel like I was back on that cursed boat. Finally the taxi pulled up in front of wrought-iron gates topped by the initials ZLL. My mother handed the driver all her money. Two armed guards, snug and dry in their sentry posts on either side of the main gate, peered down at us.

The fat one spoke first. "Is that child yours, Candelaria?"

My mother nodded.

"Everything all right?"

"She doesn't feel well," Mama answered.

"Better hurry inside, then," the thin one said, "or you'll both drown." The men laughed.

My mother seemed afraid to say too much. The skinny one pressed a button, and the gates of the fortress slowly swung open.

"*Maraming salamat,*" Mama said, opening her umbrella. I could feel their eyes on our backs as my mother and I trudged up the winding driveway toward the big white house, surrounded by other, smaller white houses. *Casas Blancas.* It seemed such a long way off. Two gray dogs with huge, square heads appeared in the rain, growling and barking. I froze.

"Caesar! Brutus!" My mother scolded the monster dogs in a sharp voice. The dogs fell silent, wagging their stubby tails. "Don't worry about them," she said. "They're ugly but harmless." The dogs didn't follow, but Mama kept a protective arm around me as we walked toward the back of the main house. Mama pushed a screen door open, revealing the largest, most amazing kitchen I had ever seen. All the lights were on in the middle of the afternoon. So much bright light, so many silver pots and pans, gleaming, filled with food! The servants who were busy washing rice and slicing vegetables glanced up, startled.

Their anxious voices cried out: *Candelaria! Candelaria's back with her daughter! We heard all about the accident on the radio. Poor Candelaria! Poor little girl! Ay, naku! She's a miracle child. Where's the rest of your family?*

"What's all this noise?" A tall, distracted-looking woman with yellow hair and green eyes glided into the kitchen. Green eyes! The servants immediately shut up. The woman wore a fancy dress and high-heeled shoes. *Where is my raincoat and umbrella?* Her voice was deep, her English harsh-sounding. *Sputnik, I need my umbrella.*

"Yes, ma'am," a girl smaller than I was mumbled. Sputnik ran out of the kitchen and returned, seconds later, brandishing a shiny coat and the loveliest and floweriest of umbrellas. She started to open it but was stopped by the green-eyed woman's screech. *Not in the house, Sputnik, it's bad luck!*

"Yes, ma'am. Sorry, ma'am," Sputnik said.

The green-eyed woman noticed my mother. "Candelaria, we weren't expecting you back this soon. Your family—"

Mama answered in English. "There was a terrible accident, Señora Ilse."

"Accident?"

"The boat capsized, ma'am. They're all dead, except for my daughter."

"What?" The green-eyed woman stared at me, trying to understand.

"It was on the radio just now, Señora Ilse," Sputnik said.

Señora Ilse continued to stare at me. "How terrible for you, Candelaria. Terrible, terrible."

"Yes, ma'am," my mother agreed. My knees started to buckle, and I felt dizzy again.

"This is your daughter?" Señora Ilse asked.

"Yes, ma'am. Her name is Rizalina."

"But this is so strange," Señora Ilse said. "You are both so calm."

"Yes, ma'am."

"Is your daughter all right?"

"Yes, Señora."

"She looks sick. Bring her a chair. *Ach, mein Gott.* How can you just stand there, Sputnik!"

I wanted to ask, *Sputnik. What kind of crazy name is that?* She slid a chair under me just as I was about to collapse.

Señora Ilse turned to my mother. "What about you, Candelaria? You don't look well."

"I am fine. Just tired and sad, Señora."

"Well," Señora Ilse sighed, "your daughter can stay here as long as she needs to, Candelaria. But she must work." Hastily she added, "When she feels better, of course."

"Of course, Señora," my mother said.

"What the hell is going on?" Mister Zamora López de Legazpi glared at us from the doorway of the kitchen. How long he'd been standing there was unclear. It seemed like Mister had just woken up, though it was late afternoon and the servants were in the midst of preparing dinner. He wore pajamas, his hair was frizzled and unkempt, his pale feet bare. Such pale people, such white feet, *Dios ko!* It was two Wednesdays before Christmas, I remember that much. Not as hot as usual but hot enough, though I was shaking and trembling with cold in the ugly dress I wore, the same ugly dress I had on when they pulled me out of the sea.

"Is she yours?" he asked Nanay.

"Yes, sir."

"Candelaria and her daughter have been through hell," Señora Ilse said. Candelaria's entire family ... well, except for this little girl—isn't she so pretty, *so wie ein Püppchen?*—drowned."

"Drowned?"

"Drowned," the señora repeated.

Mister Zamora was even more incredulous than his wife. "Candelaria, shouldn't you be at a hospital or a police station or something?" Then he announced, "I will, of course, pay for the funeral."

My mother's face crumpled up. She could barely get the words out. "No need. Thank you, but—there are no bodies, sir."

Señora Ilse shook her head slowly in pity and disbelief.

Mister Zamora was outraged. "What do you mean, *no bodies?*"

Mama's voice quivered. "Sir. The sharks—"

I slid off the chair in a faint and fell to the floor.

"Ah, son of a bitch!" Mister Zamora bent down and checked my pulse. He scooped me up in his arms and started to walk out of the room. I heard Mama gasp.

"Where are you taking that poor child?" Señora Ilse demanded to know.

"To Candelaria's room—where else?" Mister turned to a servant who was attempting to comfort my mother. "Gloria, get Dr. Ocampo on the phone." He glanced at his wife. "And where do you think you're going?"

"I have an appointment." Señora Ilse's voice was chilly.

"In this typhoon? What kind of appointment?"

Señora Ilse was silent.

The phones were not working because of the storm, so it was impossible to summon the doctor. I was wrapped in warm, scratchy blankets and forced to swallow Cortal tablets, which made me gag. Mister Zamora ordered my mother to make me drink glass after glass of water; he was very insistent and stayed in the room until at last I swallowed the aspirin. When he finally left, my mother sat by my side and watched me sleep. I woke close to midnight, not sure of where I was. In the dark, Mama leaned over to touch my forehead with the palm of her hand.

"You're still feverish," she whispered. Nearby someone snored softly.

"Where am I?" I asked, frightened. "Who's making that sound?"

"You're in the servants' quarters of Mister's compound in Manila," my mother answered. "Keep your voice down—everyone's trying to get some rest. It's been a long, terrible day. Do you remember what happened?"

"Yes."

"You're going to have to watch yourself, Lina. Remember who you are. Remember where you are. This is not your house, or my house. This is the López de Legazpi house. Your father is—your brothers are—"

She could not bear to say it, so I did.

"Dead." I whispered it for her in the dark, feeling a strange satisfaction. Life of shit, part one, was over. Maybe.

I closed my eyes, prayed for more sleep to quiet the questions in my head. The room, packed with all those bodies, was muggy and hot. I heard Mama move around, undressing carefully, trying not to wake me. She squeezed in beside me on the hard, narrow bed. I wondered if the pale man with strong arms who scooped me up off the floor was asleep now, too. I didn't think so. My mother began to weep again, her sobs muffled by the clatter of rain on the roof. Nevertheless, O nevertheless. Frogs croaked their gloomy lullaby in the gardens beyond these walls. *Sleep, Lina, sleep. Your father is dead and gone. Your brothers are dead and gone. You're in heaven now.*

A New Life

Lina

We servants never stopped cleaning. The grand house had too many things and too many rooms. I felt like my mother at the end of the day—ready to fall down and die from exhaustion. A blessed death, *di ba?* And that little Sputnik girl loved bossing me around. Always finding some new task for me to do.

"Time to feed the dogs, Rizalina. We feed them only once a day, okay? No extra treats. Those animals are ve-ry special, fancy-fancy."

"I don't like dogs."

Sputnik pursed her lips and crossed her arms, like she was some big-time Señora Lady Madam. "Too bad. If I say you have to feed the dogs, then you feed the dogs."

The dog pen was built under a shady old tamarind tree. A sturdy fence of heavy mesh surrounded two large kennels where the animals were housed. As we got closer to them, the dogs rushed the fence, banging their heads against it and barking at us. I clutched a pot of ground meat and rice with trembling hands. The meat was freshly cooked by Mama. Those animals ate better than most people did.

"Caesar! Brutus!" Sputnik called out in a clear, firm voice. The dogs made gruff, anxious sounds and ran in circles. Sputnik chuckled. "The poor beasts are brothers. Ugly, aren't they? It's fun watching them hump each other." She gave me a sly, searching look. "Are you a virgin, Rizalina?"

"*What?*"

"*Ay*, never mind. Play dumb all you want—I know you heard me." Sputnik unlatched the gate. "The one with the white star on his forehead is Brutus. That's the only way to tell them apart. Ready?" I nodded, cowering behind her. The one called Brutus growled. Sputnik held out her hand for the dog to sniff. I placed the pot of food on the ground and stepped back as quickly as I could. The dogs lunged at the food as if they were starving, which they obviously were not. It was disgusting and funny.

Work, work, and more work! My new life wasn't so different from my last one. Señora Ilse could be fussy to the point of madness. We were ordered to scrub the tiles in each bathroom with a toothbrush. Then we had to swab doorknobs with cotton pads soaked in alcohol. "What for?" I asked Sputnik.

"To kill germs," Sputnik said. "Rich people are always worried about germs."

Sputnik and I made sure there wasn't a particle of dust, not a smudge of grease or grime left anywhere. Otherwise Señora Ilse would ask us to start all over again. She always said "please." She tilted her head and spoke in a voice that was low and commanding. "Please, dear girls, I'd really appreciate it if you got down on your knees and did everything over again. Just one more time, only faster and better."

Faster and better, faster and better. My favorite job was killing cockroaches with the Flit gun. I loved watching the bugs slow down to a halt, intoxicated by the sweet-smelling poison. For such a grand house in such a grand city, there were enough snakes, bats, flies, lizards, moths, and mosquitoes to keep me and the other servants busy. The rats in the garden were another story—fair game for the master and his dogs. They were coaxed out of their nests by the master singing in his deep, dark voice, *Rats in the bushes, rats in the trees, rats in the mountains, rats in the seas* . . . He blew them to pieces with his gun, leaving bloody bits of fur and flesh for the dogs to clean up.

If you ask me, Señora Ilse spent too much time alone. Her maiden name, according to Sputnik, was Ilse von Himmel. A curt name, but like everything else about her, commanding—fit for a queen. I was fascinated by her presence and by those green eyes of hers that didn't seem human. Whenever I could, I studied her—dusting the furniture as I followed the señora from room to room, trailing far enough behind her so she wouldn't notice I was there.

Her two children didn't seem to be of much comfort. The baby boy, named after his father, was simply that. A baby—five months old, docile and plump. Dulce was my age, too clumsy and tall for her ten years. Born with none of her mother's grace or confidence. From the day I arrived, Dulce decided I was her sworn enemy. She made grotesque faces and cursed under her breath at every opportunity. "Why does she hate me so?" I asked Sputnik.

"I'm glad it's you and not me. Used to be me. Before me, there was Celia," Sputnik said.

"But what have I done? We've never even spoken a word to each other."

"You ask too many questions," Sputnik said.

"That new *achay* has no right to stick her tongue out at me," Dulce once said to her mother.

"Rizalina!" Señora Ilse called out. Barely a shout, but I heard it.

"Yes, ma'am?"

"Is it true you stuck your tongue out at Dulce?"

My baboon self stayed calm. "No, ma'am."

Señora Ilse smiled at her daughter. "You see? This little girl would never do that to you."

Dulce shot me a hateful look. "Liar! Liar, liar."

On a rainy afternoon after my first week in the house, Señora Ilse interrupted my cockroach extermination. "Come to the *sala* and tell me how you're doing."

"Yes, ma'am." She must have been lonelier than usual. I followed her into the living room. A song in a pretty language played on the stereo.

"Are you feeling any better?"

"Yes, ma'am."

"Your mother is a strong woman. But you—"

"I am fine, ma'am."

"Do you like this music?"

"Yes, señora."

"It's called bossa nova. From a country called Brazil. Do you know where Brazil is?"

I knew better than to act too smart around the master's wife, so I shook my head and answered in that meek voice Mama had encouraged me to use. "No, ma'am, I do not know at all about Brazil."

"Brazil is a country in South America. The capital is Rio de Janeiro," Señora Ilse said. "Did you know Brazilians invented the samba and the bossa nova?"

I wanted to correct her. *But, señora. According to Miss Angway, Brasilia is the capital of Brazil. Population: eighty million.* But I held my tongue. A moment passed.

"Shall I spray the room now, ma'am?" I asked.

"Of course." Señora Ilse drifted back to her music. A man crooned lovingly to an infectious rhythm. The señora knew the lyrics and sang along in Portuguese. I aimed my Flit gun behind the sofa, along the baseboards, in every nook and cranny I could find. The smell was overwhelming, but Señora Ilse was oblivious. The dreamy music kept playing, and she was lost. I stopped my work to gaze at her. Her eyes were closed, and her body swayed gently to the pretty melody. It was a broiling, wet afternoon. I felt a twinge of happiness, like we were the only two people left in the world.

Sputnik and I slowly became friends. She taught me how to swear and how to smoke. FUCK DAMN COÑO CABRON SHITTY-SHET SCREW PUTANG INA PUÑETA PUKI TITI MO! The harsh, ugly words made me giggle. We snuck behind the wall of the laundry area every day before noon, to puff on our stolen cigarettes.

"How old are you?" I asked her. I had been dying to ask since the day we met. Sputnik with her child's body, woman's breasts, and shrewd eyes. That plain, unforgiving face.

Sputnik bristled. "Sixteen. Why? Didn't your mother tell you?"

"No."

"You think I'm funny-looking?"

"Yes."

My answer made Sputnik laugh, though the laugh was hard and angry.

"Where did you get the name Sputnik?" I asked her.

"From Mister Boss. You know what a Sputnik is?" Sputnik's tone was challenging.

"No."

"It's a spaceship or something. From Russia. Boss said it's small and superior."

"Superior in what?" I asked.

"How should I know?" Sputnik whipped out a brown, gold-tipped cigarette from the pocket of her apron and held it under my nose. "See what I've got? Fancy-fancy Stateside and ve-ry ex-pen-sive."

"Did you steal it from Señora's purse?"

"Ko-rek, baby." Sputnik made a big deal of looking around furtively before lighting up. She passed the cigarette to me.

"Tastes like chocolate."

"You wanna kiss me?" Sputnik asked.

"No."

Sputnik grabbed the cigarette from between my lips and finished it off.

"Don't be so greedy," I said.

"Fuck you."

We passed a small white shed on our way back to the kitchen. I had seen Mister going in and out of the shed several times a day.

"Who lives there?" I asked.

"None of your business."

"But—"

Sputnik's eyes glinted with mischief. "But nothing. Why should I tell you?"

"Because I saw you kissing one of the security guards, " I said. "The skinny one. His hand was under your skirt. Ugh."

"So what? You're just jealous."

"If you tell me, I'll kiss you," I said.

"Ha."

I leaned toward her face, my lips grazing hers.

"You don't know how to kiss," Sputnik said with a snort of disdain. Then she said, "That's Bomba's house."

"Who's Bomba?"

"Bomba the jungle boy, *gaga!* That's not his name, but that's what I call him. He's a silly savage. Can't read or write. Can't talk anything you or I can understand. He's the boss's pet."

"Pet?"

"Stop repeating what I say. You're driving me crazy!"

"Can we visit him?"

"Why? You wanna see his big thing?"

"Maybe I do."

Sputnik cackled. "He's off-limits, Lina. No one but the boss is supposed to visit him."

"What about Señora Ilse?"

"Bomba thinks she's a bad spirit. Because of that white skin, that hair, and those eyes. He screams every time he sees her, so she stays away."

"But the master's skin is white."

"The boy loves him. Calls him something like 'Father.' Stupid, *di ba?*"

❦

I could stand it no longer. The next day, when I knew he was alone, I knocked softly on the door of Mister Señor's study. There was no response. I stayed in the hallway, trying to work up the nerve to knock again. Then I took a deep breath and banged on the door.

"*Entra!*" Mister shouted. The room was chilly and stank of cigars. Hundreds of books lined the shelves. There were lamps, paintings, photographs. Framed citations and awards hung on the walls. A stand held an illuminated globe. I longed to touch it. Mister sat behind a glass-topped desk, going through the piles of paper stacked before him. He glanced up, surprised to see me.

"What do you want? Can't you see I'm busy? Who told you to bang on the door like that?"

"I knocked first, but—"

"If there are visitors, tell them to go away! Don't just stand there with your mouth half open."

"Sir, I—I—"

"Speak!"

"The jungle boy, sir . . . that boy . . . in the little house?"

"What about him?"

"That boy . . . well . . ." I stammered, unable to get the right words in English out of my mouth. He was glaring at me. It seemed like everyone was always glaring at me.

Finally, he spoke. "He's a Taobo, Lina. Not a jungle boy. 'Tah-o-boh.' They're a lost tribe from the mountains around Lake Ramayyah. Right by where you used to live. Have you heard of the Taobo?"

"No, sir. Never mind, sir. I'm sorry to bother you." I stepped back, though my eyes stayed fixed on his face.

"Don't leave. Did I tell you it was time for you to leave?"

"No, sir."

"Your mother tells me you did very well in school. Is that true?"

"I think so, sir."

"Don't be ridiculous. You're either smart or not. Which is it?"

My ears were warm; so was my face. "Smart, sir."

"Good! That's the answer I want. When you've settled down a bit, I'll arrange for you to go back to school. How would you like that?"

"I like, sir. Thank you! Sir ... may I, can I ... ask? How"—I took another deep breath—"did the tribe lose its way?"

His laugh sounded like bursts of gunfire. "The Taobo aren't 'lost' in the way you are thinking, Lina. What I mean is, they were unknown to us until my recent ... uh, *discovery*. And therefore"—he cleared his throat—"they are lost."

"Oh."

He narrowed his eyes, looking more irritated than ever. "Don't you have any work to do? What do you really want, child?"

"To see him, sir. The boy."

"Why?"

"I don't know, sir."

He scratched idly at the tip of his nose with his forefinger, studying me.

"Does your mother know you are here?"

"No, sir."

"It's good to be curious and bold, but it can also get you in trouble."

I lowered my head, confused by what he was saying.

"I don't need trouble," Mister Señor said.

"I mean the boy no harm, sir."

He waved me away. "Enough! Go swat some flies and make yourself useful, before I start to get really angry."

The boy watched television. I stood on tiptoe and could see him through the screened window—a skinny boy with long hair hanging loosely down his back. Slim and pretty, like a girl. A skinny boy who crouched, enchanted, in front of the flickering TV screen. He wore nothing but a pair of hand-me-down shorts that were much too big for him.

"That's Bodabil," Sputnik whispered in my ear. I jumped back in surprise.

"I thought you said his name was Bomba."

"His real name is Bodabil." Sputnik pulled me by the arm. "Let's go. We're not supposed to bother him. If the master finds out—"

"He won't find out if we don't tell anyone."

Sputnik tightened her grip. "Fool," she muttered, dragging me away toward the house. *Fool, fool, fool.*

Mama waited in the doorway of the kitchen. "Where have you been?"

"Checking on the dogs," I answered.

My mother's hands rested on her hips, and she was frowning. "Since when have you grown so attached to those animals? I had to ask Sputnik to stop her work and go out and find you. You know I don't like having to do that. Now, tell me the truth: *Where were you?*"

I shot nervous glances first at Sputnik, then at Mama. "I wasn't doing anything bad."

Mama grabbed hold of my right ear and yanked. "Where were you?"

"Spying on the jungle boy," Sputnik said.

Mama gave my ear another twist.

"It was nothing," I mumbled, trying not to cry.

Mama twisted harder. "Don't . . . you ever . . . go . . . near that place . . . or that boy again. . . . You hear me?"

"I tried to warn her," Sputnik said. "But she did it anyway."

Three days later Sputnik found me in the music room. My Flit gun was aimed at an enormous *ipis* hiding underneath the piano. The wily cockroach played dead, its serrated legs and antennae motionless and stiff. I pushed in the handle, expelling a thick, rich puff of pesticide. *Boom.*

"Hoy, Lina. Hurry up. Boss wants you."

I ignored Sputnik. We had not spoken since the ear-boxing episode. The cockroach made a feeble attempt at motion. I sprayed a second time, then a third—finally killing it. Then I aimed the Flit gun at Sputnik. "I could kill you for what you did."

"You don't want to keep the boss waiting," Sputnik said.

We walked through the maze of hallways in heavy silence.

"How long are you going to stay mad at me?" Sputnik asked.

I answered with my own question. "What does the boss want?"

"You, I guess. Be thankful I haven't blabbed about this to your mother."

"You have a dirty mind," I said, without looking at her.

"And you have soft lips," Sputnik said. I couldn't help but giggle. We stood in front of the heavy door to his study. Though the door was shut, we could hear the drone of the air conditioner.

"Are we still friends?" Sputnik asked.

"You got me in a lot of trouble," I said.

"I know. It won't happen again," Sputnik murmured, walking away.

The jungle boy squatted by Mister Zamora's desk. He wore some sort of loincloth this time. I clasped a hand over my mouth, amazed to see him. The boy jumped up to imitate me, covering his mouth with one hand, his dark eyes gleeful.

"This is Bodabil," the master said. "You've been wanting to meet him, so . . ."

He turned and spoke to Bodabil in a fast, rattling language. I felt no fear, only excitement. I heard my name mentioned once, twice—wondered what the Spaniard was saying about me. Bodabil moved a few inches closer. I could smell his hair.

"He's about your size," the master observed with satisfaction. "You could be his sister."

Bodabil danced around me. "You shouldn't be frightened," the master said. "The Taobo are the gentlest people on earth. I am sending Bodabil back to his home in the forest. Manila isn't a healthy place for him. After all, he's not some animal in a zoo. Have you ever been to a zoo, Rizalina?"

I shook my head. Bodabil picked up the braid hanging down my back and held it up to his nose. I shuddered. "Please, sir. Make him stop."

Mister Zamora touched Bodabil lightly on the shoulder. He let go of my hair. "I admired your boldness and curiosity," Mister said to me in English. "That's why I decided to reward you by arranging this meeting. Bodabil's a treasure, isn't he? Pure, untainted. Do you know the word 'untainted'? Of course not. Don't be shy, Lina. Get your fill, for you will never see him again."

Bodabil chattered and cooed, tugging at the sleeve of Mister Zamora López de Legazpi's fine linen shirt. A shirt I had ironed just that morning. Bodabil pointed to me with his spidery fingers, then pointed to himself. Smiling and silly. I reached out with my hand, wanting to touch his sunken, hairless chest. Mister Zamora smacked my hand out of the way. Bodabil stopped smiling. The master reprimanded me in a stern voice. "That's enough for now, Lina."

"But, sir. You said—"

"Enough!"

Such a crazy man, with his bathrobes, wild hair, pale, bare feet, and not sleeping. Such a crazy man, ignoring his wife and children, fawning over those beasts in the garden, seeking me out and going on to me about things for too long. *Talking.* As if he had no one else to talk to in the world. I listened intently and nodded as if I understood. I learned fast while he boasted about being afraid of nothing and everything—including my mother, overzealous journalists, sly assassins, thieves, jealous husbands, jealous wives, even vampire *manananggals* who preyed on the fetuses of pregnant women while they slept. He confessed to being afraid of the president and the first lady, who were his friends.

"They want what I have," he said.

"And what is that, sir?" I dared to ask him.

"My history," the Spaniard answered, grinning.

There were those, like my mother, who believed that Mister Zamora was more important than the president. "Look at how the foreigners keep showing up, barging in on the boss, and demanding to be taken to see those forest people."

Mister Zamora obliged everyone at first, especially if the visitors were from Europe or America. He basked in the glow of their attention and flattery. There were endless parties on the terrace, feasts laid out on a long buffet table, plenty of rum and Coke to drink. I wore my new green uniform with pride, inching my way through the crowd with a tray of food.

Sputnik and I loved the master's parties. The loud music, the carefree dancing, the lewd remarks. We gawked at the perfumed women in their ostentatious dresses, at the fat, arrogant men chewing on cigars. One night the center of attention was a woman with a camera who never left Mister Zamora's side. "That's Gigi Fontaine, a French movie star," Sputnik whispered. Miss Gigi's name made me smile. She was, like so many others at the party, infatuated with the master. Maybe because he was famous, like she was. Miss Gigi arrived early and without her husband. I approached her with my tray.

"What is?" She peered at the appetizers with suspicion, then at me.

"Shrimpballs, ma'am."

"*Qu'elle est mignone!*" Miss Gigi cooed, pinching my cheek and staring at me as if I were some odd specimen of nature. She pointed her camera at my face. Click, click. I almost dropped the tray of food.

"You shouldn't have done that," Mister Zamora said to Miss Gigi in a curt voice. "Are you all right?" he asked me. Miss Gigi turned away from him, embarrassed and furious. I watched as Mister Zamora sighed, then ran his hand lightly against her bare back. Miss Gigi slowly turned toward him, grazing his hand lightly with her lips. I glanced around to see if anyone else had seen, my heart beating wildly. Where was Sputnik? Had I really seen what I thought I had seen? An act of blatant adultery, a sin punishable by eternal damnation! Señora Ilse was absent, as usual. I gazed at the glittering couple, entranced.

Miss Gigi leaned closer to Mister Zamora, entwining her arm in his. Confident again, her voice became husky and teasing. "I have wait so long, Zami. I can wait no more. When you will bring me to visit your forest people?"

Everyone came and everyone stayed. The guest rooms overflowed with visitors. We servants hardly slept—too busy changing sheets and pillowcases, emptying ashtrays and trash cans, mopping floors and spraying Lysol on toilet seats with a vengeance. Mama was delirious from all the cooking she had to do. Beads of sweat glistened on her forehead. She napped on her feet, in between grating and slicing, seasoning and stirring. She never had time to eat a proper meal, but she was getting swollen and huge. As if all the feasts Mama constantly prepared were being sucked into the pores of her flesh.

So many people. Coming and going, running through the house. Staying for weeks, months at a time. Miss Gigi—with her camera bags, stiletto eyes, and heavy perfume—stayed off and on for two months. Señora Ilse did nothing about it except hide in her room. Miss Gigi announced she was going to do a book about the Philippines. "My photographs of forest people, your words," she said to Mister Zamora. "You will write for me, Zami?"

"No," the master said. "Your book will be better without me."

The mute American transatlantic pilot, Charles—the tallest man I've ever seen—appeared without warning and flew to Mindanao for three days with the master and Miss Gigi.

Amado Cabrera—a young guy from the university—came and went. He claimed to have seen all of Miss Gigi's movies. She took his picture.

So many people. Famous and not. Dr. Eng, the linguist, spent two weeks in the jungle with the Taobo and Zamora. "Why does Dr. Eng talk funny?" I asked Sputnik.

"He's Australian," Sputnik said.

Señora Ilse seldom attended her husband's parties. She preferred staying in the bedroom with her television and her books. The children were never seen, tucked away in another wing of the house with their *yayas* and bodyguards while the parties raged on until morning. The señora sent the same hastily scribbled, apologetic message to her husband's guests. Mister Zamora made me read her message out loud:

> *Please excuse my absence, but I am not myself this evening.*
> *Mabuhay! Bon appétit! Alles Gute!*

"Never herself," the master snarled. I poured him more rum. He seemed tired and unhappy, as if all the noise and chatter had worn him down. I stuffed my mouth with morsels of chicken and balls of rice when I thought no one was looking. Sputnik and I laid out an array of desserts on the buffet table. Guava tarts, purple yam cakes, brazos de mercedes, leche flan. The guests swooped down on the sweets like hungry, vicious birds. More rum was consumed as the hour grew late—Flor de Manila, from Mister's own distillery. Miss Gigi leaned over the railing and vomited into the *gumamela* bushes. The master, with a look of disgust, gestured for us to help her. We half carried, half dragged the unconscious woman into the pool house to clean her up.

"Why do we have to do this?" Sputnik complained, roughly pulling off Miss Gigi's ruined dress. "Look at this. . . . No bra! No panties!" Sputnik snickered. She examined the thin gold chain around Miss Gigi's neck, the jeweled rings on her vomit-stained fingers. "I should steal this *puta's* shit," Sputnik muttered, "but the boss would cut off my hands."

"He would?"

Sputnik rolled her eyes. "*Gaga ka, talaga.*"

Miss Gigi's eyelids fluttered open. She heaved and retched, then passed out again. I wiped the runny vomit off her floppy breasts. "Maybe she's dead," I blurted out, suddenly worried. She was so still.

"You're a morbid one," Sputnik said. "Get closer—you'll hear the *puta* breathing. Go on."

I did as I was told. A sharp, sour smell emanated from the movie star's open mouth. "You're right," I said, making a face.

The heat rose off the ground in waves. The main house shone like an ornate wedding cake in the morning light. White swirls and curlicues, turrets and balconies, arched windows, massive doors carved from narra wood. A swimming pool shaped like a guitar. The garden ablaze with coral hibiscus, violet bougainvillea, white and yellow plumeria, red and orange bird-of-paradise. Santol trees. Acacia. Tamarind. Bamboo. The dogs barked. In the shed outside the kitchen, I turned on a faucet and carefully lowered my head to wet my hair. The water trickled out, rusty and tepid. Was the master spying on me from his bedroom window on the second floor? I felt his eyes peering at me from somewhere above, wondered if his golden wife lay snoring in the bed next to him. Sputnik said he spied on all the servants. According to Sputnik, the master had spied on Celia, fucked her and made her pregnant, then paid for some society doctor to take the baby out and kill it. Everyone knew it. Even Señora Ilse. Sputnik said Señora Ilse knew about everything when it came to her husband.

"You'd better watch out," Sputnik warned me. "Boss likes them young and stupid."

"I am not stupid!" I shouted. "I know the capital of Brazil, the capital of France, the capital of Japan, and the capital of California!"

My mother's baggy flower-print duster covered my spindly, slender body. Body of Sixto, my dead father. Was he watching me, too? I bathed as quickly as I could, but it was awkward because of my dress. I slipped a bar of coarse yellow laundry soap underneath it, rubbing across my chest and between my legs where Mama said I'd stink like fish gone bad if I didn't wash hard enough. I scrubbed hard. Hard hard, then up around my neck and shoulders, harder, then back down, between my pigeon toes in their sorry rubber slippers. When I was done, I smelled vaguely like bleach, not flowery and perfumey like the master's wife. I rubbed my hair vigorously with tree bark. Worked up a lather, rinsed off. Quick quick, before the water ran out. Quick quick, before the master and his family woke up with their whimpers and demands. I dried myself with a towel. My dress was completely drenched, nearly transparent. *Was he watching?* The heat rose in shimmering waves, almost visible. I turned off the faucet, slipped back into the kitchen, where Mama, awake since dawn, fried eggs and God-knows-what for Mister Zamora. Probably crocodile sausage. That's what they all said. The master lived on rum and crocodile sausage.

"*Hoy!* What the hell you think you doing, standing there practically naked?" Mama snapped. "Get dressed and start sweeping."

I have this dream. Where I hang from the thick branch of an acacia tree, peeping into the porthole of a cabin. I know Bodabil is inside— I feel his presence, I smell his hair. Light comes from a TV screen. Bodabil crouches in a shallow pool of water, watching TV with his back to me. He is naked, his hair wet and plastered to his skull. The pool of water grows bigger and deeper. Soon the entire room will be underwater. How can I warn him? I have lost my voice. Frantic, I bang on the porthole. Bodabil whirls around to confront me. His is not a boy's face, but a man's. Haggard and beautiful, the unhappy face of Sixto, my father.

The Great He-Goat

Mr. Zamora

Did he hate her enough to kill her? Zamora studied his wife while she slept. He could suffocate her right now with a pillow. He looked down at his pudgy hands, smooth and soft, an embarrassment. He liked to think of himself as a brooding poet or troubadour, lean and dangerous. Soft hands would never do. But of course Zamora López de Legazpi wrote neither poetry nor song lyrics. His wife, in a rare playful mood, once said he was a dead ringer for Bob Dylan. The nerve of her. *Coño! Qué barbaridad!* The bastard sounded like a baying calf, and besides, wasn't he Jewish? But Dylan was the current rage, Jewish or not; the young intellectuals worshipped him. Zamora was secretly flattered. Ilse raved—if a Teutonic goddess could be said to rave— about Dylan's "prophetic lyrics." Zamora used to wonder if the only reason she agreed to marry him was his uncanny resemblance to the singer. He wondered this until his father, Don Flaco, reminded him that the López de Legazpi fortune would be enough to win anyone over. *Legazpi Pacific International.* Rum, guns, rubber, logging, hemp, steel, silver, and copper. What in god's name didn't they own or control? Even a ball-busting snow queen like Ilse had to admit it was quite an empire. *Cunt.* That's what Zamora's father called his daughter-in-law. Not to her snow queen face, of course.

❧

Ilse loved one Dylan song in particular. *Coño*, that stupid one about "hard rain gonna fall"—with the nasal, whining chorus that Zamora found especially annoying. She played the record over and over, until the day Zamora ordered the gardener Peping to start a bonfire and threw Ilse's record collection into the flames. Zamora walked back into the house without saying a word. The servants huddled with the children underneath a mango tree. Baby Zamorito bounced in Celia's arms, cooing at the fiery spectacle. Dulce, bewildered and upset, started to cry. Bodabil crept out of his little cottage. Fire fascinated him. When he saw Ilse, he ran back inside. Ilse showed no emotion as the records melted and burned. The smoke grew black and thick, the stink toxic and faintly sweet. When it was over, Ilse calmly asked the driver, Benny, to take her to the biggest music store in Makati. Dulce insisted on accompanying her mother. She watched as Ilse bought thousands of pesos' worth of records, not even bothering to look at what she was buying. Bob Dylan, Pilita Corrales, Antonio Carlos Jobim, Diomedes Maturan, Johnny Mathis, and more Bob Dylan.

Zamora had to admire her for that. Her tenacity and ability to ignore him. On impulse, he kissed her gently on the forehead. Ilse snored. Lightly, softly. As only a Teutonic Goddess could snore. Even with her mouth agape, Ilse was unbearably beautiful. That's why he chose to marry her, didn't he? For her unbearable, alien beauty.

He could kill her with his bare hands. Smother her with a pillow. Arrange for a car accident or a kidnapping. Her melancholy vexed him. What was there to be melancholy about? Thanks to her marriage, Ilse was now richer and more powerful than her own family. Ilse called him crazy, but she was the crazy one. Unpredictable, paranoid, manic-depressive, hypochondriacal, frigid, melancholy woman. Don Flaco dubbed his daughter-in-law "my little Fraulein Ilse," pinching and touching her at every opportunity. Ilse would slap his hand away, muttering curses in German. Don Flaco was crude and shameless. But then, all López de Legazpi men were notorious for being crude and shameless. Short in stature, vain, fond of guns, and careless with women. Ilse found that out soon enough.

Zamora stifled a yawn and started to climb out of bed. He hesitated, gazing once more at his wife. Did he hate her enough to kill her? She slept so deeply, under the gauzy canopy of mosquito netting, lost in the huge and ostentatious Chinese wedding bed. Set high on a platform and carved out of teak, the bed—which once belonged to a decadent empress from some dynasty no one could remember—had been a rather embarrassing wedding gift from Don Flaco. Zamora observed, riveted, as Ilse curled into a fetal position, fingers of one hand crammed desperately into her mouth.

The sun burned through the curtains and shadows of their cavernous bedroom. The air conditioner hummed. Today was not the day to murder his wife. *Let her sleep all she wants.* Zamora headed for the master bathroom—another grand showroom with its his-and-hers sinks, marble tub, and imported bidet from France. He turned on the shower and started soaping himself. The water gushed forth, then gurgled and completely stopped. *Hijo de puta!* It was too early in the morning not to have any water. Zamora threw a robe over himself and went out to the hallway. The house was alive. He smelled something greasy frying, heard Candelaria barking orders in the kitchen. He padded down the stairs in his bare feet, startling Rizalina, who was in the foyer sweeping.

Magandang umaga, ho. The young girl averted her gaze from the pale man standing there, naked except for his loosely tied bathrobe.

Zamora's voice oozed with impatience. "What? Speak up, child!"

"Good morning, sir."

"There's no water, goddamn it!"

Rizalina trembled at the angry sound of Zamora's voice. Was he blaming her for the lack of water? He kept yelling:

"Why do I bother having my own tank installed when there's no fucking water? And when there *is* water, it's always fucking cold! *Que se joden!* I hate cold showers. Tell your mother to heat up some water. Hot, but not too hot. Hurry, quick! See all this soap on me? It's starting to itch! Hurry!" Rizalina started to run off, but his voice stopped her: "And I want *you* to bring the water to me. Understand?"

Zamora headed back upstairs. Rizalina hurried to the kitchen, where her mother's own sharp voice and equally sharp eyes awaited her.

"Why was the boss shouting? What have you done?" Candelaria asked.

"There's no water."

Candelaria led Rizalina to the pantry, where jugs of water were stored.

"He wants you to heat some up for his bath, Nanay," Rizalina said. "Hot, but not too—"

"I know, I know! Don't I have enough to do?" Candelaria grumbled. When she was done heating the water, Candelaria helped Rizalina pour it into two large buckets. "Can you manage?"

Rizalina nodded.

"Boss wants you to take it up to him, does he? These people," Candelaria muttered. "They think they can do anything." She studied her daughter. "Well, don't just stand there."

Rizalina didn't move. "It's not my fault if the master asks me to bring the water up to him."

"I never said it was."

"What if I don't want to go?"

Candelaria spread margarine on a warm pan de sal, sprinkled sugar on top, then handed it to Rizalina. "You haven't eaten yet, have you? Here. Hurry up before he starts shouting again. But be careful. Just do your job and get out of there as fast as you can. Don't let him touch you. You hear me?"

Rizalina wolfed down the sweetened bread. She climbed the stairs slowly, careful not to spill any of the water. A feeling of dread came over her as she approached the bathroom at the end of the hallway. How exactly did her mother expect her to defend herself? Rizalina set down the heavy buckets of water and knocked on the door.

"*Entra!*" Zamora, completely naked, sat on a footstool by the tub. His pale, hairy legs were crossed. He puffed on a cigar, relaxed and nonchalant. "Get my water ready," Zamora said. Rizalina poured the water into the tub. "Are you afraid?" Zamora asked. Rizalina pretended not to hear.

"I won't hurt you." Zamora climbed into the bath. "I'm used to more water than this," he complained. Zamora handed the cigar to her. His fingers were wet. "Take care of this, will you?"

Rizalina put out the smelly cigar in the marble sink. She wondered if she should flush the stub down the toilet but slipped it into one of her apron pockets instead. She had the sudden urge to pee. She started for the door.

"Don't go yet." Zamora chuckled softly. "Ever seen a naked man?"

Rizalina shook her head.

"No? Not even your father or brothers? Men's bodies are strange and rather ugly, don't you think? Nothing to be in awe of. Do you know the word 'awe'?"

"No, sir."

"Look at me—still young, but already such a paunch! Worse than my father's. Have you ever been told how pretty you are? No? You're quite a beauty."

Rizalina wondered if her mother was ever going to barge in and rescue her. Sputnik was right. Where was Sputnik?

The master was talking to himself again. "I had an interesting dream last night. Peculiar and interesting. There I was, a miniature goat nailed to a cross. The cross hung on the wall of an anonymous house. I entered the room as my real self, just as you see me now— except clothed, of course. I gazed at the crucified goat. Did I know I was actually that goat? I'm not sure. The male goat symbolizes the devil in certain cultures. Did you know that? But of course you don't. How could you? Do you miss your father and brothers, Rizalina?"

"Yes, sir."

"That's only natural," Mister said. "You and your mother have suffered an incredible loss. Do you know how much I admire you both? I don't know how well I would handle losing my father. And the funny thing is, I don't like the nasty sonuvabitch! What do you think, Rizalina? Is my father a nasty sonuvabitch?"

"I don't know, sir."

"Don't lie. I've seen the way you run from him. My mother is a saint, but my father . . ." Mister Zamora paused. "Never mind my fucking father. Let's talk about something profound. Do you like paintings, Rizalina?"

"Sir?"

"Paintings. Like the ones hanging on the walls of my house."

"Some of them, sir."

"Some of them what?"

"Are beautiful."

"Aha!" A moment passed, then Mister said, "My favorite paintings hang in the Prado museum. In Madrid. There's one in particular— *The Great He-Goat*, by Goya. In that painting a giant goat sits with these peasants around a campfire. The great beast seems to be telling them a story. The peasants listen to him in terror and awe. Except for this one young girl. She's the only one who doesn't seem impressed or scared of him. What do you think, Rizalina?"

"About what, sir?"

"Art."

Rizalina stared at the dark blue tiles on the wall. Moorish tiles from some place called Alhambra. She had gone over each and every one of them with a toothbrush just yesterday. Would she be asked to scrub them again today? If only Mister Boss Señor Zamora would shut up, get out of the bath, and get dressed. God, how he loved to hear himself talk! But he obviously had many amazing and important things to say. She must listen hard, like those peasants in the painting.

Zamora droned on. "There's another horrific painting that I love, called *Saturn Devouring One of His Sons*. It's about war. Goya was, is *great*. Don't let anyone tell you different. When someone asks you, 'Who's the greatest artist in the world?' answer this: 'Francisco Goya y Lucientes.' Fuck Picasso! Fuck El Greco and Velázquez! Fuck the French! Fuck Hieronymous what's-his-name!"

"Okay, sir."

"Do you enjoy your dreams?"

Again Rizalina was silent. Zamora leaned back in the tub and shut his eyes. "Enough about dreams. You'd better go, little girl. Or else your mother will think poorly of me. Or else my wife will wake up from her drug-induced sleep and accuse us both of dirty deeds. I've lived up to my promise, haven't I? Didn't touch you, didn't hurt you. You can stop trembling now. The lesson is over."

The Cave: 1971

3rd Person Narr.
Bodabil

"*Si Bo-da-bil ako.* Aaii yam Bo-da-bil."

"Not bad. Just repeat what I say, okay?"

Bodabil cocked his head, tried to understand. Father made him happy. Father came from a faraway forest called Manila. Duan had brought him to them. Father had come and gone a few times—always promising to come back. So far he had kept his promise.

Father touched a magic box and made things spin. Father had shown Bodabil and the other Taobo several magic boxes. There was a big, heavy one for capturing voices and smaller ones for capturing faces. The magic boxes frightened the Taobo, except for Bodabil.

"Now, say your name again," Father said, holding up a stick to Bodabil's mouth. "Talk into the mike."

"Bodabil!" The boy cackled, delighted with himself. Zamora rewound the bulky tape recorder and pressed "play." Bodabil gasped at the sound of his own voice coming back to him. He sniffed at the machine, wary but curious.

Father was speaking: "Bodabil are you listening? Now, say my name. Say it slowly into the mike. Zah-mo-rah."

Bodabil giggled, amazed by the bristly hair on Father's face. He reached out to touch it. Father let him. Bodabil sniffed Father's cheek. He smelled of wood, smoke, sweat. A strong smell. Zamora sat still as Bodabil continued to sniff and examine him. The boy ran his hands over Zamora's shirt, pants, shoes. Fingering colorful beads and bits of bone hanging from the strings around Zamora's neck. Gifts from Duan and the Himal people. Zamora took off one of his necklaces and draped it on Bodabil. Bodabil shrieked with pleasure.

Last night Father slept in the cave. Duan and the strangers Father brought with him slept outside in something Father called a tent. Bodabil stayed awake all night, staring at Father's sleeping figure. The other Taobo, shy and fearful of the strangers, chose to huddle in the farthest corner of the cave.

"Come on. Give it a try. Say my name," Father was saying. He had the same look on his face Bodabil's mother, Uleng, sometimes had when she was impatient and annoyed with him.

"Za—" Bodabil couldn't stop giggling. Why did Father need more names? He already had the name Duan had given him. *Amo Data*. Simple and powerful, it said everything.

"Mo—"

"Yes?" Father's eyebrows went up in anticipation.

"Rah!" Bodabil clapped a hand over his mouth.

Father bared his sharp little teeth in a friendly way, obviously pleased. "Excellent, Bodabil. That's very, very good."

The white giant with fire in his hair entered the cave. His name was Kenneth Forbes, a name that Bodabil found impossible to pronounce. Bodabil called him Kenit. Kenit had been sent for by Father. Father seemed to trust and love him. Duan said Father didn't love or trust many people.

"Good morning," Kenit said to Bodabil. A magic box dangled from straps around his neck. Kenit pointed the box at everyone and everything, infuriating Bodabil's mother.

Father pointed to the box. *Kah-meh-rah*.

Kenit aimed the camera at Bodabil, who puffed out his chest.

"Camera!" Bodabil shouted, making the strangers laugh.

Kenit mopped his forehead with a red bandanna. Bodabil pointed to the bright cloth and cooed. Kenit handed it to him. Bodabil mopped his forehead and pretended to take pictures. He ended by draping the bandanna around his neck and striking a coquettish pose. With his camera Kenneth Forbes captured Bodabil's performance. The Taobos woke up, confused by the commotion. Uleng chastised Bodabil in the rapid-fire Taobo language. *Stay away from those demons before we all die.*

Zamora listened carefully, the tape recorder on, trying to make sense of what Uleng was saying. He studied Bodabil's reactions. The boy, obviously intimidated, stopped clowning. Forbes kept snapping away, taking picture after picture until Uleng turned on him and made a terrible face.

"You're upsetting his mother," Zamora said.

Forbes put down the camera. "I got some great shit," he said.

Bodabil was the only one who didn't seem afraid. He was curious, eager to learn. But to learn what? Zamora wondered. Maybe Amado Cabrera was right. Bodabil's age made him the most susceptible and corruptible of the Taobo. So ready to please, so easily manipulated. Bodabil followed Zamora around, shyly touching and hugging him, calling Zamora *Amo Data*, or Spirit Father.

Amo = Taobo for "father." *Ama* = Tagalog for "father."

"Anyone with half a brain can recognize the similarities of these people's language with Tagalog," Cabrera said. But how was that possible?

Cabrera was a skeptic. Nevertheless, he was thrilled to be invited on this hush-hush expedition, the third one since Duan and Zamora's initial trip. It would be good for Cabrera's fledgling career as an anthropologist, no matter what. Zamora flattered the young man by pointedly addressing him as "Dr. Cabrera."

"Is our good doctor awake yet?" Zamora asked Forbes.

"I'll go out and see," Forbes said, grinning.

Bodabil interrupted his mother's tirade by walking over and rubbing his cheek against hers. Uleng visibly softened, though she pushed him away. She was a small, feisty woman with hair down to her hips—a young widow who was one of the more respected members of the tribe. She was unhappy with the strangers in their midst, especially Zamora.

"He is a bad spirit," Uleng whispered. "He will take our forest away."

"But he sleeps with us. He loves us," Bodabil argued.

The other Taobo tended to agree with Bodabil, though the big, clumsy strangers with their sinister-looking gear made them uneasy. *Amo Data sleeps with us in the cave. He loves us. He loves us.*

The sight of Forbes back inside the cave with Duan and the other two strangers made Bodabil anxious. What was happening? There was the slight young man with four eyes named Doctor and the fierce, quiet giant named Sonny. Doctor packed the magic box for capturing voices into a bag and went back outside to wait for the others. Bodabil, in a panic, ran to Zamora and threw his arms around him. Uleng snarled at her son and waved her arms in the air. *What are you doing, fool?* But she didn't dare come anywhere near Zamora or look him in the eye.

"We have to go," Zamora said to Bodabil in English. "But one day soon I promise to take you to Manila. In my helicopter."

Bodabil squinted at Duan, listening hard as Duan translated into Himal and Taobo.

The boy blinked back tears. *Why was Father abandoning them again?* He buried his face in Zamora's chest. It was one of those rare, Edenic moments Forbes couldn't resist. He pulled out his camera and took one last picture.

In the Palace:
Fritz, 1972

Fritz Magbantay

My name is unusual. Unforgettable. Fritz Magbantay, aka "Fritzie" or "Chino." I am the president's nothing of a nephew, illegitimate son of an illegitimate daughter of an illegitimate son. Who rose from nothing. Who came and went and did as he was told. A fly on the wall of history.

The president, my bastard liar of an uncle, was in a jovial mood. He greeted the Spaniard effusively in his study. He rose from behind that enormous hump of a desk and held out his hand. The Spaniard stood on tiptoe, reaching up to shake it. A burly man loomed behind him. "So good to have you here, Mr. Legazpi! At the dawn of a dark new day."

My uncle and Legazpi flashed teeth, pleased with themselves. How much longer was this ass kissing going to continue? It was midnight. The air con groaned like an old woman. I was wilting— my cheap *barong* shirt ruined by splotches of sweat. The president suddenly remembered that I existed. "Fritzie, say hello to Mr. Zamora López de Legazpi."

I spoke in English and bowed my head in deference to the hawk-nosed mestizo, the *Spaniard*. "Good evening, sir." Palace of lies, dungeon of polished molave and narra wood!

"Welcome to our humble abode," the president added. Legazpi smiled faintly at him, pretending to appreciate my uncle's corny humor.

"*Sigé*, Fritz. Show Mr. Legazpi's man where to wait outside," my uncle said to me.

"But—" Legazpi protested, glancing at his bodyguard.

"I would prefer a private conversation," my uncle said.

Sonny Limahan did not look pleased. "Please have a seat, sir." I called him "sir," though he was nothing but a hired goon, a hulking gorilla, obviously uneducated, much lowlier than I was. "Would you care for something to drink?" I asked, hoping he would say no.

"It's fucking midnight," the goon muttered, his voice like gravel, his eyes glued to the closed door. "Why was my boss made to come at fucking midnight?" Not pleased.

"I don't know, sir." I hurried back into the safety of my uncle's study.

"Sonny goes where I go," Legazpi was saying, "and that means right here, inside this room."

My uncle made the effort to smile. He was still handsome when he smiled. Smooth, confident, in spite of that bloated face. Not afraid of anyone, least of all the mestizo. "Come, come, Mr. Legazpi. We don't really need Lurch hovering over us, do we? You know Lurch? From *The Addams Family*."

Legazpi looked baffled, so I hastened to explain. "It's a TV show, sir. About a lovable family of ghouls and vampires. Lurch is a giant—the family's butler. Very much like your man Sonny."

"Ah," Legazpi said, scratching his nose. "Is it funny?"

"Very, sir."

My uncle, who did not approve of my talking out of turn, did not show his anger. "I love to laugh," he confessed to Legazpi. "But I was not amused when Frankie Salas dubbed my family 'the Addams Family of the Philippines' in that column of his. Did you read it?"

Legazpi had certainly read the article my uncle referred to—so had every other literate person in this country. But he said nothing.

My uncle's voice became louder, more heated. "My family was criticized for being greedy, corrupt, and vulgar. My wife, in particular, was described as an *aswang*, can you imagine that? A vampire preying on the poor and gullible masses, sucking the life out of them! It wounded her deeply. How do you think I should handle this, Mr. Legazpi? How would *you* handle it?"

"I would ignore it, Mr. President," Legazpi answered. Lies. All lies. I wanted to laugh, but I didn't.

"One thing politics has taught me is to forgive and forget," my uncle said. "I've developed a very thick hide. Insults and bullets bounce off me. I continue to enjoy my silly TV shows. I continue to believe in the democratic process, although in these lawless times it is getting more and more difficult to maintain. These press guys think they can say anything, write anything. *Talagang abusado!*"

The Spaniard couldn't resist opening his big mouth. "Is that why Salas has disappeared?"

Silence. My uncle kept smiling. The Spaniard was a Legazpi, after all.

"What are you insinuating, Mr. Legazpi?"

Legazpi shrugged. "I'm not insinuating anything, Mr. President. But you have to admit, the mysterious disappearance of Frankie Salas is big news. Everybody's talking. I hear you've even threatened to shut down the *Metro Manila Daily.*"

I stood with my arms behind me, back to the wall, ramrod straight. Waiting for my next cue. Grunt and groan of the palace air conditioner, buzz of a lone fly.

"My sources tell me Frankie's hiding out right here in Manila. This is nothing but a nasty joke—instigated by Salas and his leftist cronies to make me look bad," my uncle said. Again he remembered that I was in the room. "How about some coffee, Fritz? And please—change your shirt. "

I bowed, I scraped, I scampered off to the kitchen miles away. I ignored the dour-looking bodyguard in the foyer. Moments later I returned in a fresh shirt. I carried a silver tray, the one engraved with the presidential seal. The tray held a silver thermos of hot water, a jar of instant Taster's Choice, a silver bowl filled with sugar cubes, a pair of silver tongs, a small silver pitcher of condensed milk, and a silver platter—also engraved with the presidential seal—of a dozen Oreo cookies.

"We have Coffee-mate, sir, if you prefer," I said to Legazpi. Careful with my *p*s and *f*s, like my uncle had drummed into me.

Legazpi ignored me and glanced at the Rolex on his hairy wrist. "Surely you didn't summon me here at this hour just to have coffee with you, Mr. President."

"I have summoned you—" the president began. I could, of course, read his mind. My uncle, seated behind his desk on an elevated platform, looked down at Legazpi. He took pleasure in the Spaniard's unease, as I did. My uncle had had the special platform constructed to put Westerners—usually men much taller than he—in their proper place. I had supervised the building of it and made sure the platform was not so high off the ground as to call attention to itself. Then, in a stroke of genius, I'd had a glass cabinet installed to display my uncle's numerous awards and medals for bravery. A legacy of lies, deceit, and delusion! My uncle was pleased. In a rare gesture of generosity, he rewarded me with a bar of gold. I didn't know quite what to do and ended up stuffing it, in a fit of panic, between the mattress and the box spring of my bed.

My uncle cleared his throat. "I hear you've been poking around in the jungles of Mindanao, Mr. Legazpi. Helping our indigenous tribes and doing the world some good, I'm sure. "

Legazpi could no longer conceal his irritation. "You don't have to patronize me, Mr. President."

"I would never patronize you, Mr. Legazpi. I admire you, just as I admire your father. This unknown tribe you've stumbled upon—"

"I didn't exactly 'stumble' upon them, Mr. President."

"I'm sure you didn't," my uncle reassured him. "Weren't you trained in anthropology at that Ivy League school you went to? What was it—Harvard or Princeton?" My uncle uttered the names with relish.

"Yale."

My uncle made a sharp little noise and settled back in his chair. "I am truly impressed by your background and achievements, Mr. Legazpi. Which is why I called on you. I am here to offer my help."

Legazpi was taken aback. "Your *help?*"

"You heard me."

I felt Legazpi's cunning little mind attempting to process the layers and shades of meaning behind my uncle's carefully chosen words. Legazpi, too, chose his words carefully before he spoke. "The tribe needs your protection, Mr. President. They are forest people—unarmed, shy, and peaceful. They subsist on food they gather or pick with their bare hands. They are completely defenseless against the loggers and their private armies. You know how it is. The land and the resources are so rich—"

"Indeed."

After a pause Legazpi said, "I suppose the Taobo people could use your blessing. So could I."

My uncle was amused by Legazpi's arrogance. "You suppose?"

"Yes, Mr. President."

There. Legazpi had said it. Laid his cards out on the table and asked for a favor. Both his father and wife would later accuse him of being a fool, but no matter. Legazpi was not a stupid man. He was in the war room of the palace with my uncle, the president. The president listened to what Legazpi had to say. And I—the president's poor, forsaken, glorified gofer of a bastard nephew—also listened. Asking my uncle for a favor clearly pained the Spaniard.

My uncle's face remained inscrutable. As far as he was concerned, Legazpi's timing couldn't be better. My uncle's popularity had slipped at an alarming rate, something his shrew of a wife never hesitated to remind him on a daily basis. The mountains crawled with guerrillas; the military was paranoid and restless. Rowdy students demonstrated in the capital's streets, attracting the sympathy and support of second-rate intellectuals like Frankie Salas. Such an embarrassment! But my uncle had devised a plan. Tomorrow, martial law would be declared. Finally an end to chaos. For why not save ourselves from ourselves? Days of rot, days of futility, days of infinite possibilities!

My uncle studied the fair-skinned man before him. *Zamora López de Legazpi.* I could almost hear my uncle's brilliant, calculating mind clicking away—turning nothing into something, good into bad, loss into profit. I knew him as well as I knew myself. Surely there would be some way to turn this "discovery" of Zamora's into a public-relations coup. My uncle and his wife were avid believers in what they called "the power of PR." And I, too, in my short time here at the palace, have seen it with my own eyes. Legacy of lies, grandeur of delusions. Embellishments and manipulations. Sleights of hand. First a serpent, then a rabbit pulled out of a hat. A bearded woman sawed in half. Singing horses.

"Our helicopters, our soldiers and medical personnel are at your service, Mr. Legazpi," my uncle said. "Whatever you need. Whatever the tribe needs. Education, health programs, job skills, cottage industries! Are these people good at anything? Basket weaving? Pottery? Wood carving? Batik?"

Legazpi looked aghast, but my uncle, the president, was on a roll. His beady eyes glittered with excitement. Ideas flowed out of him. "We'll establish a special foundation, if necessary. You could be chairman. We'll call it the President's Indigenous Minority People's Foundation. PIMPF, for short."

"Thank you, sir," Legazpi said. "Sir," he called my uncle. Imagine that.

"You see, Mr. Legazpi? No need for bodyguards. Nothing to worry about."

"Yes, Mr. President."

They shook hands. Legazpi seemed resigned, but my uncle's smile was wide, heartfelt, and genuine. Tomorrow it begins. Dark miracles. Proclamations and decrees. Clarity, order, righteousness. Blood from a stone. Manna from heaven.

The First Voyage Around the World

Lina

Mister waited until his family and guests were passed out in their bedrooms; until we servants cleared the dishes, fed the security guards and ourselves; until we bolted the doors, latched the windows, set the alarms, turned off the lights; until we washed ourselves and recited our prayers; until with deep groans of exhaustion we finally dropped off to sleep. He would prowl through the gardens in his bare feet or lock himself in his study until the sun came up. What he did in there, no one knew. Maybe he wrote in his notebooks or got drunk on rum.

Sputnik and I spied on him once. Hid in the bushes and watched him scramble up a mango tree. He lay across a branch and howled softly at the moon, like some sad, weary animal. It made me giggle. Sputnik was too scared to spy on him after that. She swore Mister Señor was possessed by spirits.

Puwede ba. I'm not scared of him. Why should I be? The night Mister Señor caught me snooping in his library, for example. He didn't get angry. He just stood there dumbfounded—staring at me holding one of his precious books in my hands.

I slammed the book shut and slipped it back into its proper place on the shelf. "*Ay!* Sorry, sir!"

"What were you reading?"

"Uh . . . something by . . . It's called *The First Voyage Around the World,* I think, sir."

"Antonio Pigafetta."

"Yes, sir."

"Do you understand it? Does it excite you?"

"I don't know yet, sir."

My eyes swept over the messy room. So many books—stacked on the floor, arranged on shelves that reached all the way to the ceiling. I wanted to smell and read each and every one of them.

"I've had that book since college. Read and reread it, thousands of times. Scribbled notes all over the margins," Mister Zamora said with a little smile. I remembered how we never had enough books in school. The few books we had were tattered and out of date. But it didn't matter. The books were shared by everyone in the classroom, then passed on to the incoming students. Kind and gentle as she was, Miss Angway would've had no problem beating me for writing or drawing anything on those pages.

"Would you like to borrow it?" Mister asked.

I shook my head.

"Why not?"

"*Nakakahiya*, sir."

"Why should you be ashamed? Speak to me in English."

"Because, sir."

"Do you enjoy sneaking around my house late at night?"

Of course I did. I lowered my head. "Sorry, sir."

"Are you a thief?"

I shook my head. "No, sir!"

"I am going to see the president in the morning. You know why? Because I've been invited to teach him how to play pelota. The president is a pelota fan. And whether I like it or not, when the president calls . . ." Mister pulled the Pigafetta book off the shelf and handed it back to me. "Go to bed," he said in English before walking out of the room.

Said I to myself, Naku! You better hide that book somewhere before Nanay sees it and thinks the wrong thing, Lina. 'Nay said that Mister Señor talks to me too much. Said Mister like all men, like my father. Ha. If she only knew how true. 'Nay also said that Señora Ilse, with all her beauty and good thoughts, could never satisfy him. This I did not understand, but I kept all wonderings a secret.

Zamora

Señor Zamora

T he servants whispered. The servants always whispered. Sputnik, the sour-faced one, polished my living-room floor with a *bunot*. Her toes grasped the coconut husk, rubbing against the dark wood until it gleamed. Such a wide, splayed foot for such a tiny young girl. The charmless foot of an old peasant woman. Rizalina dusted the myriad objects that cluttered my *sala* without much energy or enthusiasm, though I could see that she took her job seriously—just look at her furrowed brow, that grave expression on her sublime face! If only she knew of my presence right behind the open door. I eavesdropped. Watched their every move. Laughed to myself.

"Sputnik, why is the señora's leg broken?"

"The señora's leg is not broken. It's her ankle, stupid."

"Okay, her ankle. But why?"

"But why, but why, but why?" Sputnik mocked Rizalina in a singsong voice, then proceeded to explain. "The señora was forced to accompany that crazy husband of hers to the jungle. And she had to walk and climb and walk and climb. She's not used to walking and climbing! Does that white ghost of a woman look like she's ever climbed a mountain?"

Hee-hee-hee. They giggled at the image of my wife scrambling up a steep mountain in her slingback Chanel pumps. An absurd joke at my darling Ilse's expense. But what do my silly servants know, or care? Sputnik danced around the room with her *bunot*— back and forth, back and forth.

Rizalina sighed. "I wish we could play some of the señora's bossah noh-vah."

Sputnik snatched the rag from her hand. "*Hoy*, Lina! You almost broke that thing! Are you working or dreaming? That thing is *anteek*. If you break it, we're both dead." Sputnik finished wiping the deceptively plain blue Ming vase just as I stepped into the room. Her jaw dropped open.

"Where are my wife and children?" I demanded to know, surprising even myself. For I am often indifferent to my family's whereabouts, much too preoccupied with other things.

"Ay! Good . . . g-good morning, sir," Sputnik stammered. Rizalina stood next to her, wide-eyed with fear.

I enjoyed making them squirm. "Where are they?"

"In . . . in the garden, sir," Sputnik answered.

I directed my gaze at Rizalina. "Is that ribbon new?" The child fidgeted with her hands, confused. Sputnik glanced at her with suspicion. "It's very pretty," I said.

The child kept fidgeting with her hands.

It was Saturday morning. My daughter, Dulce, sat at a table on the sun-drenched terrace and picked at her breakfast. My wife, Ilse, was ensconced in a rattan easy chair, squinting at one of her fucking novels in their original German: *Siddhartha*, by Hermann Hesse. Such a bookworm! She needed glasses—I'd told her so, but she never listened. Her swollen ankle, swaddled in an elastic bandage, was propped up on a stool. Our baby, Zamorito, lay in his portable rocking crib, watched over by Celia. Such a strong, big baby, blessed with that dark face that is not mine. But whose? I would know soon enough. But meanwhile the *chismosos* of Manila could keep gossiping—I didn't give a fuck.

Dulce's perennially unhappy face lit up when she saw me. "Oh, Papa—you're home. Will you play with me? I hate Saturdays. There's never anything to do!"

"Clearly a failure of your imagination, *Schatzi*," Ilse chided without looking up from her book.

"What? What did you say, Mama?" Dulce cried, stung by her mother's comment.

Celia pretended I was not there, which excited me. She rocked my son's crib with her delicate hands.

"Don't rock too hard," Ilse reminded her.

"Yes, ma'am," Celia murmured.

"Why don't you come with me to the Polo Club?" I asked Dulce.

"No." Dulce shoveled fried rice and eggs into her downturned mouth.

"Why not?"

"Because."

"Because why?"

Dulce shrugged.

"Not a good enough reason, darling." I struggled to conceal my irritation. My daughter gazed at me with worried eyes. She was not stupid; she knew she was a disappointment.

"I can smell your cologne." Ilse looked up from her book and wrinkled her nose at me.

I smiled. "Like it?"

She nodded, letting me kiss the top of her head without flinching. Celia glanced up from my son's crib, then quickly looked away.

"Go with Papa to the Polo Club," Ilse urged Dulce. "You can go swimming with your cousins. They'll all be there today. It's so nice and hot."

"We can ride horses," I said.

"No," Dulce said. "I can't swim that well. I'm scared of horses."

Ilse sighed. "Your attitude exhausts me, *Dulcelein*."

Dulce stared down at the now empty plate, her eyes welling with tears. She was about to explode, to rail against her strong, serene mother. My poor daughter. Implacable, unremarkable looking.

"All right, then. If you won't come . . ." I kissed Dulce's round, puffy cheek and turned to leave.

"Papa, please. Don't go." Her voice was small, imploring.

"But why should we stay cooped up at home on a beautiful Saturday morning?"

"Because!" Her eyes were shining now. "We can play with Bodabil—"

"Bodabil's sick."

"We'll play with the dogs, then. You can teach me to swim in our own pool, Papa."

"All right. Why not?"

"Really?" Dulce, stunned by my unexpected response, attempted a smile. I couldn't bear her desperation, those trembling lips.

The trees so high they blocked out the sky and sun. The forest world cool, dark and humid all at the same time. Bodabil prostrate on the ground, cowering and weeping. All of them cowered—Uleng, Ubut, Prit, the old man Bayam. The helicopter astonished and terrified them, the whirring, slicing sound of its huge blade magnified in the jungle silence. What dreadful futuristic bird was this, sent down by punitive forest spirits? And who could I be—with my week's growth of beard and pasty skin, the alien pistol strapped to my hip—but God Himself? In their eyes Sonny Limahan and my pilot, Buzz Ramos, were stone-faced guardian warriors, following close behind me with their long rifles.

"How long do you plan to be home this time?" Ilse asked.

"I'm not sure," I answered. "As soon as Bodabil feels better, I'd like to take him back to the mountains."

"Duty calls," Ilse said dryly.

"What is that supposed to mean?"

I ordered Bodabil to get up, but he didn't understand the words I was saying. Duan spoke to him in Himal, but Bodabil didn't seem to understand him either. Duan persisted in his rat-a-tat melodious language. Perhaps he said that we meant the Taobo no harm, or perhaps that we were shit-eating bas-tards from a faraway kingdom, not to be trusted . . . how would we ever know? At last Bodabil recognized a familiar word. He raised his head slowly and tentatively to look at us. I gave him what I hoped was a friendly smile, then made a motion with my hands for him to stand up. Uleng, the woman I would later find to be his mother, uttered something shrill to Bodabil, which I took to be a warning. Duan interrupted her in Himal and shook his head, as if saying, No, no, that's just not true. Bodabil gathered himself up and faced me, trembling. He was young. Like all the others in his motley tribe, he was thin and naked except for the orchid leaves and vines that they all wore to cover their loins. Why such modesty? The boy's wild mane of black hair hung down his back. Sonny, Buzz, and I stared at the tribe with joy and wonder. We, too, were trembling. Were there more of them hiding in the bushes? Sonny and Buzz thought so. I felt happy for the first time in my life. Yes, that is the exact word I must use: "happy."

"Do you love me?" Ilse asked. Celia, always discreet, picked up the baby and went for a stroll in the garden. Anxious and fascinated, Dulce stared—first at her mother, then at me.

"I love you, admire you, lust after you. I am proud of you." I sighed.

Ilse tore off a piece of Kleenex and marked her place in the book. She waited for me to continue speaking. When I didn't, she announced in a calm voice, "Zamora, I'm leaving you and taking the children with me back to Munich."

Dulce gasped. Her worst fears, confirmed.

"Mad whore." The words sputtered out of me.

"It's you who's the whore," Ilse retorted.

"Mama! Papa!" Dulce wailed. We ignored her, too absorbed in our own drama. Celia and Zamorito marveled at butterflies and flowers in the farthest reaches of the garden, safe from our fury.

"You married me for my face, my blood, my name, and—" Ilse hesitated.

"*And?*"

"My father's land." There was a directness and clarity about my wife that were new to me.

"Your beauty, absolutely, yes! But your *name*? Your *blood*? Your father's *land*? Come now, Ilse. Why would I need that worthless plot of German nothing? The hippies have taken it over, turned it to shit. You said so yourself. We Legazpis have more land and money than we know what to do with. We don't need yours."

Dulce meowed like a kitten. She got up from the table, sat down again.

"It doesn't matter," Ilse said. "You want what you want, even if you don't need it. You take it, because you can. You do it, because you can."

"What the fuck are you talking about?"

"I've done my job, Zamora. Borne you a daughter . . . and that most precious of commodities—a son."

"Mad woman. You are not taking my children."

"What are you going to do? Kill me?"

My wife so calm and confident, while my daughter whimpered. Lost, frantic, pulling at her hair. I would not, could not allow Ilse to take Dulce and Zamorito away from me! The children were mine, no matter what. Only I could provide the battalion of *yayas*, bodyguards, drivers, cooks, tutors, and doctors that they required. Had Ilse ever known how to change a diaper or boil an egg? Did she care? All she knew how to do was play those damn records of hers and read!

I lit a cigarette and held it out to the boy, who stepped back in fear. Pointing to the burning cigarette, Duan said, "Cigarilyo." The boy sniffed the burning smoke, made a face, and coughed.

In Himal, Duan asked, "Bagat maglam? Dabi amo." What is your name? Tell father.

The boy stared. Blank, perplexed.

Tapping his chest, Duan said, "Duan." He pointed to the trembling boy, repeating his question in Himal. "Bagat maglam?"

Suddenly the boy tapped his chest and scrunched up his face to look like Duan. "Bodabil!" the boy shouted. He covered his mouth with one hand, laughing. The others in the group covered their mouths and laughed, too, except for the scowling woman who would turn out to be the boy's mother. I pointed to myself, declared my name: "Zamora." They laughed even harder. I pointed to each one of them, but they were still too shy and fearful to speak. Bodabil then surprised us by stepping up and imitating my slightly bow-legged stance, the way my arms hung down, never relaxed—and my quizzical expression. He named his people for us: Prit, Uleng (his mother), Ubut, the old man Bayam. Then he warbled to the shadowy forest, perhaps to coax the rest of them out of hiding.

"There are more?" I asked no one in particular. My heart beating. Hoping.

Duan nodded sagely, answering in Tagalog, "Oo, po." There are more.

"I don't want to fight anymore," Ilse said.

"Neither do I," I said, which was a lie. I could see her resolve, the shimmer of steel beneath her fair, pampered skin. She was determined to leave me.

Dulce buried her head in her hands.

"Dulce," I murmured in a soothing voice. "Dulce, Dulce."

"Don't be sad," Ilse said to our daughter. "It's for the best, *Schatzi*."

Dulce wiped mucus and tears on the sleeve of her blouse and glared at us. "You are horrible, stupid people."

"How dare you—" I went to slap her but was stopped by Ilse. She blocked my arm with hers.

"Don't." Ilse's nostrils flared; she was breathing hard. "Zamora, *bitte*. She's a child. Control yourself. *Bitte*."

Dulce waited at the top of the stone steps that led down to the garden. Her eyes were swollen, red rimmed. For a brief moment a shadow of—what? eagerness, anticipation?—flitted across my daughter's solemn face. *Dulce*: Spanish for "sweet."

"Shall we let the dogs loose, Papa?" Dulce asked. Tremulous, quavering.

What I did next could be described as tender. A fatherly thing, uncharacteristic Zamora. But my daughter's pain necessitated that I rise to the occasion. I threw a protective arm around her rigid shoulders and drew her close. Her head rested on my chest. "*Si, hija.* Let's."

I felt Dulce start to relax. What a relief. Caesar and Brutus barked as we approached, distracting Dulce from her unhappiness. I spotted Rizalina through the wire-mesh fence of the dog pen. The white ribbon in her hair. She was busy feeding the animals. No longer in need of Sputnik's assistance, no longer afraid. My pulse quickened at the sight of her. Which was all wrong, I knew. Impulsively, I kissed the top of my daughter's head. Inhaled the strawberry-bubble-gum scent of her imported shampoo.

Birthday Girl

Lina

I should have told him the truth. That the ribbon was stolen
from the box on his daughter's dresser. Imagine that—a box
just for hair ribbons! Velvet, satin, all sorts of ribbons in every
color. There was also a box just for bobby pins, another for fancy
clips called "barrettes," another for hair bands. I helped myself.
While the brat was on her way downstairs to have breakfast on the
terrace. That's what the family did on Saturday mornings. They sat
around a table, under one of those big umbrellas. Reading, talking,
stuffing themselves with food, and doing nothing all day long. Mister Señor's father, that horny old man they call Don Flaco, would
show up sometimes with his wife, Mrs. Doña Mary. She was nice
enough—but all she ever did was talk about religion. When Doña
Mary wasn't there, a nurse in uniform would accompany the old
man. Why, I don't know. Even with that cane, he looked strong and
very much alive to me. His nurses were always shapely and always
young. I bet Don Flaco's never been sick a day in his life.

What would Mister Señor say if he knew that I was a thief? That I
snuck into his daughter's pink-and-white bedroom while she was at
school, sometimes just to gape at her things? Everything smelled so
flowery, crisp, and new. That morning I just couldn't help myself.
Sputnik was in the kitchen helping my mother, and I was by myself.

Finally! I tiptoed into the brat's bedroom and scooped up a handful of ribbons. Not many, mind you. Just three. Two white and a red. Plain, ordinary ribbons—made of the cheapest satin—which Miss Her Highness Dulce López de Legazpi would never miss.

This badness was new to me. A secret, one of many I did not share with Sputnik. My daring to steal from the master's daughter would've made her proud, but also jealous of me. As Miss Carmen Angway, my fifth-grade teacher, used to say, "Everything has a price. Even friendship." Nevertheless. I should have also explained the very specialness of that day, which was my birthday. I was eleven, almost twelve, almost a teenager! My mother had promised to take me to the new Dolphy–Nida Blanca comedy playing at the Miramar after I fed the dogs. Mister Señor had given us permission to take a day off for my birthday. I felt giddy-giddy-crazy. *Naku!* I had been in Manila for almost a month and had never been inside a movie theater, ever.

"We have to make sure we get home before curfew," Mama joked. Something called martial law had been recently imposed by the government. There were rules about everything. No spitting, no garbage throwing, no peeing in the street, no hippie-hippie boys with long hair. It was very confusing, because Bodabil had very long hair. And so did some of Mister Zamora's foreigner friends. There was also this curfew thing, which I didn't understand.

"What if we forget and stay out late?" I asked.

"Then off to Camp Crame we'd go," Mama answered.

"What's that?"

"A military jail."

"What happens there?"

"How should I know?"

"How long would we have to stay there?"

My mother shrugged. "Long enough to learn our lesson."

She was in a black mood when we started out that day. "Hmm. How pretty you look," Mama said. She didn't seem happy about it. What was she looking for? We waited at a street corner for the jeepney that would take us to Divisoria Market. Mama said it would be a long ride from the master's house in Hollywood Hills. We waited and waited until a jeepney packed with passengers finally pulled up—BURLESK QUEEN painted in yellow on a sign mounted on the jeepney's hood. We squeezed in and sat down, arriving at Divisoria forty minutes later.

I could hardly speak when I first caught sight of the sprawling *palengke*. The market went on for blocks and blocks. So big and wonderful, as if the whole world were for sale. Mosquito nets, feather dusters, brooms, shoes, shirts, palm-leaf fans, live chickens in cages, goldfish swimming in basins of water, nylon umbrellas, plastic handbags, rattan furniture, plants, burlap sacks, Scotch tape, Bic pens, and lined notebooks, their plastic covers embellished with the glossy faces of boyish pop stars and alluring starlets. With money I had saved from my first month's salary, I bought a Bic pen and a pink notebook with Nora Aunor's sweet, long-suffering face on the cover.

"What do you need that silly notebook for?" Mama asked.

"To write my life story," I answered, making Mama laugh in spite of her strange mood. I grasped her hand as we navigated the narrow, muddy corridors of the noisy, teeming market. We snaked past the butcher stalls, holding our breath as swarms of flies buzzed around the slabs of bloody meat. We passed the men and women selling rice, salt fish, and dried baby shrimp, the little boys hawking *balut*, the shops specializing in the gaudy and religious. Plaster statues of black Virgin Marys stood next to statues of the chubby Santo Niño—Baby Jesus with his blue marble eyes and yellow nylon curls, dressed in the red velvet robe and tin crown of a miniature Spanish king. Mama lingered to admire the colorful bolts of linen, cotton, satin, and silk fabrics on display in a tiny shop. An assortment of loose-fitting dusters swung from a rack.

"I wish I could buy you that." I pointed to a voluminous dress with flouncy butterfly sleeves.

Mama eyed it with suspicion. "You think I'm fat?"

"You're not fat, *Inay*. But when was the last time you bought yourself anything?"

"It's your birthday, Lina. Not mine. "

On hearing this the bored salesman perked up and smiled eagerly at us. "You need *tela?* I have many pretty *telas*, many pretty dresses. Cheap. Two for the price of one!"

"Go ahead, Lina. Take your pick," Mama urged.

The dusters were shapeless but colorful. I examined each one, my heart sinking. I finally chose two that I could live with. "Happy birthday," the salesman said, handing me the folded dresses in a plastic bag.

Going to Divisoria was not anything like market day back in Sultan Ramayyah. Market day began at dawn on Thursdays, while it was still chilly and the mountains were shrouded in mist. The merchants and traders who made the arduous journey from neighboring villages the night before set up their stalls in an open field next to our one-room schoolhouse. Under makeshift canopies of cloth or plastic, they hawked freshly caught tilapia, betel-nut leaves, rock salt, *kalamansi*, and yams. If the harvest was good, delicious upland rice—speckled red and white—would be available. When the Himal showed up, everything stopped. They were a strange and beautiful people who kept to themselves up in the mountains. So beautiful, in fact, that Christians and Muslims alike in the town of Sultan Ramayyah would gape in reluctant admiration as they walked down from the rugged hills in their bare feet, huge baskets of wares balanced on their heads. Some of the men rode on magnificent white stallions, which were prized and rare. My brothers and I loved to watch the horses prance around the town square, kicking up dust and snorting at anyone who came too close. My father was entranced by the Himal women. I often found him standing in front of the stalls where the women sold their beaded trinkets and weavings, gawking at them. The women ignored him, chattering quietly among themselves. They were a sight. Their arms tattooed with the letters and glyphs of some mysterious alphabet, their lips stained red with betel juice, their eyebrows exaggerated with sticks of charcoal, their ears elongated and pierced from top to bottom with brass hoops. "Just look at them," Papa murmured in a voice that shook with fear and longing.

The Himal women were known for their dazzling cloth. I remember the day I begged my father to buy me a kerchief of red, purple, and gold plaid. I don't know what came over me, for I had never asked my father to buy me anything in my life. The peddler was a young woman who was nursing a newborn infant. "I have no money," Papa muttered, riveted by the woman's bare breast. The woman glanced at me, indifferent to my father's lascivious gaze. Without warning she leaned forward and pressed the cloth into my hands. Confused by her generosity, I turned and ran all the way home, the cloth crumpled in my fist. Later that night Papa beat me for humiliating him "in front of that godless whore." Then he wept.

We arrived at the intersection of Santo Cristo and Claro M. Recto Streets. Mama pointed with her chin at the vegetable and fruit stands of Divisoria Market. "Look, Lina. See how beautiful?" I had never seen such an abundance of water spinach, okra, chayote, spindly string beans, and colossal yams, some still streaked with dirt. Bushels of garlic hung next to bunches of stubby finger bananas. Fragrant mangoes, red rambutan, and spiky, stinky brown durian. A gaunt, middle-aged woman with a pinched face scrutinized my mother as she picked through the piles of fruit.

"Please don't squeeze," the fruit seller said.

"I'm not," Mama retorted. A basket of *lanzones* caught her attention.

"They're all I have left," the fruit seller said. "I'll give you a good price if you buy them all."

"They're small and bruised. Crawling with ants." Mama paused, calculating the numbers in her head. "Five pesos."

"Five pesos?" The fruit seller crossed her arms, indignant. Would an argument ensue? I saw the familiar look of battle in my mother's eyes. Mama was a fierce haggler. So fierce, in fact, that she often went home empty-handed.

"*Aba!* Those ants are a sign of ripeness. You won't find fruit like this anywhere in Divisoria. You won't find *lanzones* anywhere else at this time of year, period!"

"Five pesos," Mama repeated.

"Twelve! Do you think I'm a fool? There's only one kilo left. One kilo of perfect, ripe *lanzones!* Look at this pitiful child staring at my luscious fruit! *Dios ko,* I should be charging at least fifteen pesos, but I've got a big heart."

"Six."

"Don't insult me, *manang.* Look at your daughter. Her eyes bugged out, her mouth watering—"

"My daughter is none of your business."

The fruit seller's voice grew shrill and loud. "*Hoy!* Don't forget, this is *my* fruit stand. If you don't want me talking about your pathetic little girl, then you'd better get the hell out before I—"

"Before you *what?*"

The fruit seller planted her hands on her hips. Mama did the same. Clearly the two women enjoyed making spectacles of themselves. A crowd formed, laughing and pointing. My birthday was turning into a disaster. If only I could leave Mama and flee this cruel, smelly place.

Mama remained calm. "Seven pesos. That's my best offer."

"You've insulted me enough!" the fruit seller responded. Mama and I started walking away. "Eight!" the fruit seller shouted after us.

Mama turned back with a look of triumph. She carefully

counted out the wrinkled peso bills kept in a cloth pouch pinned inside her blouse. The fruit seller, trying to get a rise out of my mother, counted the money again before putting it away. Mama was unfazed. The fruit seller scooped the *lanzones* into a large cone rolled out of newspaper. "Take it," she said, shoving the cone at me. "Before your bug eyes fall out of your damn head."

It was going to be a special day, after all. We stood waiting for the jeepney that would ferry us to another part of the city, where the Miramar Theater was located. The fruit seller was right. Her *lanzones* were ripe and unbearably sweet. Mama and I peeled off the tough outer skin and bit into the luscious, translucent fruit inside, spitting the bitter green seeds into the gutter as we ate. Mama's silence made me uneasy. "*Inay?*" I asked in a timid voice. "Is something wrong?" Ants streamed through my sticky fingers and danced up my arm.

"Who gave you this?" With one swift motion, Mama pulled the ribbon free from my head.

"I . . . I found it."

"Found it where? Don't lie to me, Lina."

"In the garden, lying in the grass. I didn't think anyone would care."

"It belongs to Señorita Dulce, doesn't it? I found the other ribbons stuffed inside your apron pocket. How long has this been going on?" Mama grasped my arm and squeezed, making me wince. A pair of preening teenage girls, loaded down with shopping bags, exchanged knowing glances.

"Ma, *please*."

Mama gave my arm another squeeze. "What else have you stolen? Answer me." She shook her head slowly in disgust. "I knew it was a mistake bringing you to that house. "

"I won't do it again. Promise."

"No one steals in our family," Mama said. "Your father may have been many things, but he was not a thief."

I wanted to shout, Tatay touched me, touched me there! He poked, prodded and excavated my insides, and may he burn in hell for it!

The teenage girls stared at us with sharp, unsympathetic eyes.

Mama let go of my arm. Her voice softened. "All right, *anak*. Never mind. We shall go and celebrate your birthday like I promised you."

"I don't want to celebrate," I said. "I want to go home."

"Don't be *maarte*, Lina. We are going to have a good time at the movies," Mama said, a look of grim determination on her face.

A jeepney pulled up, this one with a sign that read MIRAMAR— BINONDO. The teenage girls, playfully jostling each other, clambered on board in their fancy shoes. Mama and I followed, sitting directly across from them. My mother, spent by anger, dozed off as soon as the jeepney began moving. The teenage girls smirked as I struggled to ignore them. I wanted to throw the pitiful plastic bags filled with my pitiful new things out the window. Hateful day! I no longer cared if I ever saw a movie in a real theater. I no longer cared if I ever saw Miss Angway again, if my father and brothers were dead or alive, or any of it. The teenage girls climbed down from the jeepney as noisily as they had clambered on. Clack-clack went their fancy, clunky shoes. As soon as they were gone, I felt a surge of relief. All my shame and humiliation vanished with them. My spirits lifted—I was now really and truly eleven years old. Plus I owned two brand-new dusters, a Bic ballpen, and a shiny pink notebook with Nora Aunor—patron saint of all despairing birthday girls— on the cover. What more could I possibly want?

The jeepney zigzagged deeper into the heart of the city. Mama straightened up in the seat next to me, suddenly awake. She glanced out the window, yawning and rubbing her eyes. "Look, Lina!" she cried. "The movie theater's up ahead. See how grand? See how beautiful?"

The Enchanted Forest

3rd Person
Lina

The memory of Miss Angway's Uncle Agapito came to Rizalina. He was an old man with a shock of snow-white hair and slanted, twinkling eyes. He lived in Davao, had never married or had children. Miss Carmen Angway was his favorite niece. Agapito visited her at least once a year and always stayed for a week. No one knew exactly what he did for a living, but he seemed to have money and was well educated. He came with his ancient projector and private collection of vintage Tagalog movies, which he enjoyed screening for the townspeople. The movies were projected directly onto the cinder-block walls of the one-room schoolhouse—hard to see but not to hear, none of which mattered to Rizalina. Her favorite movie was *The Enchanted Forest*, starring Nida Blanca as Darna, a flying superheroine. The movie had been adapted from the popular "Darna" adventure *komiks*.

Agapito Angway tried to be helpful by giving impromptu performances before his screenings, which he wryly referred to as "lectures on the art of the *pelikula*." He began by describing the movie the audience was about to see, humming some of the music and reciting bits of dialogue. Agapito was a man possessed, gesturing dramatically as he narrated the action. "Trumpets blare, heralding the arrival of superwoman Darna. Darna soars in the sky! Tan-tarantan! Her silk cape billows behind her. Is it red? Yes, of course! All capes are red. Darna flies above erupting volcanoes and raging rivers, over steamy jungles and modern cities. She lands *splat!* somewhere in a clearing, right on her feet! Such effortless grace, *di ba?* Such co-ordination and balance! Will she find the lost child in time to save her? Dum-dee-dum-dum . . . Drums! Bass! Violins! 'Is that you, Darna dear?' a little girl's plaintive voice asks. But we can't see the child. It is so dark. Sooo terrifying! *Dios ko!* Where is the poor, lost child hiding? Are we in an enchanted forest? Is the child really a child, or possessed by a sly and cunning witch? *Ay, naku!* Of course the child is possessed! But Darna can't be fooled. . . . Her powerful X-ray vision—a thousand guitars, strummed simultaneously—slashes and burns through the glittering trees. *Voilà!* The witch is discovered, cowering inside the hollow trunk of a balete tree. Darna vaporizes her with a single, searing glance! *Voilà!* The wicked witch is dead! The grateful, weeping child—a pure, beautiful little girl— lives!"

Enthralled. Rizalina and the townspeople were swept up and enthralled. They listened to Agapito's narration and gasped softly in appreciation. They applauded enthusiastically at the end of Agapito's screenings. But as the years went by, they grew tired of the same old movies and began to complain. Rizalina's father was the rudest among them:

"Can't you bring us something new? Something in color?"

"No," Agapito answered, and that was that. He visited less and less. Miss Carmen said he had grown frail and sickly; the long journey from Davao City to Sultan Ramayyah was now too much for him. When he managed to show up, Agapito projected the same black-and-white movies onto the cinder-block walls of the school-house. Hardly anyone ever bothered going inside to watch anymore, except for Rizalina. Her tenth birthday was the last time she would encounter Agapito Angway. Upon hearing that it was her birthday, Agapito decided to screen *The Enchanted Forest* especially for Rizalina.

"Thank you for being my loyal audience, my *only* audience after all these years," Agapito said, patting her gently on the shoulder.

Waving good-bye, Agapito hobbled away on the arm of his niece. The images on the wall were grainy and blurred, as always, the classroom unbearably stifling. Rizalina went outside for air. The skittish white stallions belonging to the Himal people grazed on the grassy fields. Beyond the mountains Lake Ramayyah shimmered in the blinding sunlight. Beckoning and deep, vast as an ocean. The movie blared from the open windows of the desolate schoolhouse. Rizalina closed her eyes and listened to the soothing, mellifluous voice of Nida Blanca: "I, Darna, have finally come to save you."

Kenneth Forbes:
1971

Kenneth Forbes

Zamora summoned me from Saigon, where I was working as a photojournalist. "Stop trying to get yourself killed for nothing, Ken. Come to the Philippines and document my expeditions. I promise you'll be paid real money," he said on the phone. He had figured out how to track me down through his sources at the American embassy. Zamora was the kind of man who always had sources with access to certain information. Like how to find me.

"Expeditions? What's this all about?" I hadn't seen him in at least ten years. I had heard that he was married to some great beauty, which didn't surprise me.

Zamora's tone turned confidential. "I've discovered a tribe."

"A what?"

"A tribe, *pendejo*. A Stone Age tribe."

"Yeah, okay, sure. And I've got Fred Flintstone right here in Saigon. His leg's blown off, and he's anxious to meet you."

"Listen, *pendejo*—I'm not kidding! I need someone good, like you, to photograph what's going on."

"Why don't you hire a local?" I asked. "There's gotta be plenty of good photographers in Manila."

"You're one of the best, *di ba*? I've been keeping up with your work, and I'm very impressed. Plus, you're my college buddy. I need someone trustworthy by my side, Ken. This is an incredible opportunity. You'll be paid well. I'll make the arrangements—get you on a plane out here as soon as possible. We'll make history together," Zamora said.

"I don't know about history, Z. But your timing couldn't be better, and your bullshit is as seductive as ever."

Zamora laughed. I was burned out and broke. Zamora knew it.

Mindanao. "The Wild, Wild South," as Sonny Limahan put it. Zamora knew that no helicopter could possibly land in this unbroken jungle of trees and mountains, but didn't let it stop him. Our helicopter flew low, then ascended at an angle. Zamora sat next to the pilot. Sunglasses shielded his bloodshot eyes. He chewed on an unlit cigar. I sat behind him, next to Sonny and a Himal elder named Aket. Tattoos crawled up and down Aket's withered arms and the back of his long, goitered neck. I counted eleven brass rings hanging from each drooping earlobe. Aket had his eyes squeezed shut. Clearly the poor man thought he was doomed.

Concentric patterns of brown earth. Bursts of emerald green and searing blue. Wisps of white cloud. The helicopter whizzed over thatched huts, muddy rivers, fish ponds, the tops of coconut trees. Buzz Ramos, our dapper Philippine air force pilot, seemed undaunted by flying in uncertain weather. Buzz was useful in other ways, too, fluent in several languages and dialects, including Himal and a bit of Manobo, which we'd been told the forest people might recognize. Plus, as Zamora informed me with a hint of pride, Buzz was the president's favorite pilot—a good omen in these tricky times.

There had been warnings about a possible typhoon. Buzz and Zamora were unfazed, but I was nervous. I felt Aket next to me, shaking with fear. "How much farther, Aket?" Zamora asked in English. He turned to the pilot when there was no response. "Buzz?"

Buzz spoke to Aket slowly in Himal. Aket answered in a whisper, but his eyes remained shut. The language was nasal, high pitched at times. I could only imagine what the two men were saying.

"Aket says Father has to wait," Buzz said to Zamora in English. "But he also says we are almost there. I'm on the lookout for the landing perch."

"Tell him Father says fuck you," Zamora said, dryly. Buzz and Sonny chuckled. Zamora shouted at Aket. "Goddamn it. Open your eyes, old man!"

Aket ignored him.

There it was: a treetop perch, barely visible from the air, erected by Duan and a small crew of Himal tribesmen in the midst of the jungle. It had been Zamora's idea to have the perch built, enabling the helicopter to hover long enough for each of us to dump our gear and jump onto the platform. Aket's eyes flew open, and he became agitated, muttering to himself.

"Looks like the old man is afraid to jump," Sonny said.

"It's going to be okay, Aket," Zamora said in English. "Okay. Okay?"

Aket moaned. Zamora glanced at the old man with a mixture of sympathy and irritation.

"We mustn't stay long, sir," Buzz reminded Zamora. "The weather—"

"We'll see what happens," Zamora replied. "Are we ready, gentlemen?"

Sonny Limahan slid the door open. I tried helping Aket undo his seat belt, but he cringed when I touched him. He could barely look at me—repelled, I'm sure, by my red hair and the freckles on my face. Aket gave a little cry as Zamora jumped out first, almost staggering off the edge of the platform. There was a crude ladder fashioned out of sticks and saplings leading down from the platform to the ground, roughly eighty feet below. Duan, a grizzled man carrying an AK-47, waited at the bottom of the ladder. When Aket saw him, he gave another cry—this time one of relief and recognition—and slowly climbed down.

"What's with the gun?" I asked Zamora.

"Necessary," Zamora said with a shrug. "Around here you've got a little bit of everything—bandits, insurgent guerrillas, goon squads hired by greedy logging companies—all sorts of nasty intruders. After Vietnam you should be used to this."

Duan made a sweeping gesture toward the green surrounding us. He addressed Zamora in a mixture of Tagalog and English. "The forest people refuse to come out of hiding. You have brought too many strangers with you. The sound of your flying machine terrifies them."

"Tell them they are safe," Zamora said. "*Amo Data* has come back with his friends. They should know we are not here to harm them."

Duan pointed at me with his chin. "They say the stranger with fire in his hair is a demon."

"Ken is Father's brother. A good man," Zamora said. "Tell them he is here to help them, too."

Duan went off into the bush while Aket reluctantly stayed behind. We heard the rustling of bodies and leaves, Duan speaking another language in an urgent voice. Zamora asked Aket a question in a mishmash of Tagalog and Himal. Aket shook his head. Zamora looked at me. "I'm asking the old man to translate," he explained in English.

Aket responded in Himal. He mentioned Duan by name many times.

"What's he saying?" I asked Zamora.

"Beats me. Something about not being like Duan, who can speak many ways."

Duan emerged from the bush with a woman, three men, and a boy of about ten. All cowered behind Duan. They were naked except for loincloths fashioned out of leaves and strips of what looked like bark. They carried no weapons or tools. As soon as they set eyes on me, they threw themselves on the ground and began to wail. I aimed my Nikon at them.

"Put the camera away for now," Zamora said in a low voice.

"But—" I clicked away at the marvelous, prostrate people. Click, click.

"Get up, for God's sake, all of you!" Zamora barked in English. I snapped his picture. The boy scrambled to his feet, glanced at me in terror, then ran back into the forest. The woman and the three men remained on the ground, facedown and still. "Up, up!" Zamora shouted at them, to no avail.

"You brought rice?" Duan asked him.

Zamora nodded. "Rice, blankets, some other things. I don't want to overwhelm them."

"It's all right. Overwhelm them, give them everything," Duan said with a mocking smile.

Aket, clearly angry at Duan, started railing at him. Duan tried to walk away, but the old man kept after him, yelling. Zamora grabbed Duan's AK-47 and aimed it at Aket. "Shut up, *viejo*, or you're dead." Zamora spoke harshly, in an alien language—but the old man clearly understood.

Enraged, Zamora turned on Duan. "What's the matter with Aket? You said it was a good idea to bring him along. That Aket knows this land as well as you do. But he's been nothing but a whiny, helpless *woman*—no good to me at all!"

Duan gazed back at him, stone-faced and calm. One hand rested lightly on his weapon. Sonny kept both eyes on Duan and one hand on the .45 inside his jacket. Ready to lay down his life for Zamora at any time, I supposed.

Days, months, years later, I would replay my first encounter in all its endless variations. Bodabil creeping out of the forest, unable to contain his curiosity, Zamora handing Bodabil a guava-jelly sandwich, which the boy warily sniffs and flings to the ground, Duan and Aket making some sort of uneasy peace between themselves. Was my memory dependable? Who else was actually present that wondrous day? Maybe the anthropologist, Amado Cabrera. Though as I remember it, the good doctor was invited along on another, later expedition. Maybe it was an impetuous tribal beauty from somewhere else, invited along by Zamora at the last minute. He loved impressing pretty women. She might've gasped as the helicopter ascended, holding her breath as we flew over clouds and valleys, shrieking as she leaped from the helicopter on to the treetop perch with astonishing grace. It didn't really matter. Buzz Ramos was later killed when Moro National Liberation Front guerrillas shot down his helicopter during a military skirmish. Irony of ironies, Buzz crashed into the very same mountainous jungle of trees where the Taobo lived. Aket and Duan survived well into their nineties. They told and retold their elaborate versions of the Taobo story to anyone who cared to listen, in exchange for provisions and a modest fee. In 1986 Sonny Limahan emigrated to my part of the world and settled into anonymity in San Diego. And I, still haunted by the ghosts of the Mindanao rain forest, am writing my own book on the Taobo people. Discovery and aftermath, discovery and ensuing controversy, the aftermath of the aftermath. They tell me no one really gives a shit these days, but that's beside the point.

Primo Viaggio Intorno Al Mundo

*excerpts from Antonio Pigafetta's account
of Magellan's expedition*

A t dawn on Saturday, March sixteen, 1521, we came upon a high land at a distance of three hundred leguas from the islands of Ladroni, an island named Zamal (i.e., Samar). The following day, the captain-general desired to land on another island which was uninhabited and lay to the right of the above-mentioned island, in order to be more secure, and to get water and have some rest. He had two tents set up on the shore for the sick and had a sow killed for them. On Monday afternoon, March 18, after eating, we saw a boat coming toward us with nine men in it. Therefore, the captain-general ordered that no one should move or say a word without his permission. When those men reached the shore, their chief went immediately to the captain-general, giving signs of joy because of our arrival. Five of the most ornately adorned of them remained with us, while the rest went to get some others who were fishing, and so they all came. The captain-general seeing that they were reasonable men, ordered food to be set before them, and gave them red caps, mirrors, combs, bells, ivory, bocasine, and other things. When they saw the captain's courtesy, they presented fish, a jar of palm wine, which they call uraca (i.e., arrack), figs more than one palmo long (i.e., bananas), and others which were smaller and more delicate, and two cocoanuts. . . .

Zamora

The Taobo were bewildered by the sacks of rice we offered them. They didn't understand when Aket and Duan tried to explain how rice needed to be cooked. The concept of cooked food . . . well. We brought bolo knives, tin pots, matches, wool army blankets. I struck a match. The flame made them scream.

"Ask them what else they want or need," I ordered Duan and Aket.

No one responded at first. Then the oldest-looking man in the group, who could have been anywhere from thirty to sixty, shook his head vigorously and made outward motions with his arms.

"He wants your protection," Duan said to me.

"Are you sure that's what he's saying?"

Duan nodded.

"Tell them all they will always have it."

It was time. The helicopter hovered above us. I draped strands of colorful beads around the men's necks, which seemed to please them. The woman named Uleng, who refused to come anywhere near me, was intrigued by this gift in spite of herself. She held out her hand and turned her head away. I passed the necklace on to Duan to give to her. Uleng did not allow him to drape it around her neck. Instead she cupped the necklace in her hands, rubbing the blue and yellow beads gently against her cheek.

I scrambled up the ladder leading to the treetop perch. "Tell them we'll be back!" I kept shouting to Duan in broken Himal and Manobo. What I literally said translated into something ridiculous, like "Say I am come." Duan gave me a perplexed smile and held up his gun in a farewell gesture.

"That was amazing," Forbes said once we were inside the helicopter.

"What?"

"The people. Your language skills."

"The people, yes. But my language skills?"

"Boss is a connoisseur," Sonny said to Forbes in a joking mood. "He know French, he know Spanish, German, Tagalog, little bit Ilocano, and Bisayan. *Di ba*, boss? And don't forget what else."

"What?" I asked, playing along.

"He know English real goood."

We all laughed, except for Aket.

Once again Aket squeezed his eyes shut and muttered to himself. I tapped him lightly on the shoulder. He stiffened. "Why didn't you just stay back there with Duan?" I questioned him in a language he did not speak. Aket muttered and gnashed his teeth, spooking me out.

"The *viejo's* getting on my nerves," I said to Sonny.

"Want me to throw him out of the helicopter, boss?"

Forbes was genuinely alarmed. "Good God, man. You don't mean that, do you?"

I told Rizalina later about my recurring dream. Where it was always night, the ocean black and inky. I am the pilot of a helicopter spinning out of control, headed straight for the water. I throw my hands up in front of my face in a futile, protective gesture.

"Do you crash, sir?"

"I haven't yet. I always wake up right before—"

"You die." Dear little blunt Rizalina. Who sweeps dead leaves and insects off my terrace each morning. When the wind blows everything back, she sweeps again.

"Are you finished with my book?" I asked her.

"I am a slow reader, sir. Because—"

"Because what?"

"I stop to read all your messy notes." She glanced at my face, perhaps wondering if she had offended me by speaking too freely. I smiled, hoping to ease her mind.

"I won't break my promise, Rizalina."

"Sir?" A flicker in her soft brown eyes. A pause in her sweeping.

"To send you to school."

"*Salamat.* I mean, thank you, sir." She blushed and started sweeping.

Her mother appeared on the terrace. Anxious, busily wiping her hands on her apron. "Good morning, Candelaria," I greeted her. What I really wanted to say: *Go away, woman. Leave us alone.*

"Good morning, sir." Candelaria frowned at her daughter. "Lina, aren't you finished with that yet? I need you in the kitchen."

The child stopped sweeping and started to follow her mother into the house.

"Keep the book if you want," I said. But Rizalina refused to turn around. It was Candelaria who gave me one last hard, questioning look.

Multi-lang.

Primo Viaggio Intorno Al Mundo

excerpts from Antonio Pigafetta's account
of Magellan's expedition

Those people became very familiar with us. They told us many things, their names and those of some of the islands that could be seen from that place. Their own island was called Zuluan and it is not very large. We took great pleasure with them, for they were very pleasant and conversable. In order to show them greater honor, the captain-general took them to his ship and showed them all his merchandise—cloves, cinnamon, pepper, ginger, nutmeg, mace, gold, and all the things in the ship. He had some mortars fired for them, whereat they exhibited great fear, and tried to jump out of the ship. They made signs to us that the abovesaid articles grew in that place where we were going. When they were about to retire they took their leave very gracefully and neatly, saying that they would return according to their promise. The island where we were is called Humunu; but inasmuch as we found two springs there of the clearest water, we called it Acquada da li buoni Segnialli (i.e., "the Watering-place of good signs"), for there were the first signs of gold which we found in those districts. . . . There are many islands in that district, and therefore we called them the archipelago of San Lazaro, as they were discovered on the Sabbath of St. Lazarus. They lie in X degrees of latitude toward the Arctic Pole, and in a longitude of . . .

DeeDee and the Boys:
1960

3rd Person
  Zamora & Forbes
    Zamora loves DeeDee

February in New York. The bitterest cold Zamora had ever experienced. Clumps of white snow fell briskly and blanketed the city. Pristine and beautiful. Zamora laughed with delight, sticking his tongue out to taste the powdery snow. His friend Kenny Forbes was bitching. His friend Forbes was always bitching—not in the least bit thrilled at the idea of flagging down a cab in the middle of a blizzard and journeying up to Harlem in search of jazz. It was two o' clock in the morning.

"At this hour?" Forbes was incredulous, apprehensive. He was unprepared for the weather, shivering in his cheap wool coat. A pale, freckled redhead from Sacramento, California, Forbes was Zamora's roommate at Yale.

"I know this place," Zamora said.

"What kind of place, exactly?"

"Great live music. Cozy." A cab appeared—a mirage in the freezing desert of whiteness. Forbes hesitated. "You don't have to come if it makes you nervous," Zamora said, climbing in.

Forbes took a deep breath. "Who says I'm nervous?"

The Do-Drop In was a basement club at the bottom of steep, narrow stairs that led down from 126th Street. The atmosphere was thick with cigarette smoke, the buzz and feel of too many people crammed too close at rickety tables. Everyone seemed to be having a good time. A sad-sack piano player hunched over a scarred baby grand. The piano and its player had seen better days, but the music had bite. The player's fingers danced over the keys, teasing the audience with a fragmented, staccato introduction to a song that seemed terribly familiar and yet elusive. Forbes pricked up his ears. Something about the song. He caught Zamora staring at the singer onstage, a voluptuous, middle-aged woman poured into a tight, beaded crepe gown. Hers was a tough, unforgiving kind of beauty. The warning in her hazel eyes was clear: *I'll fuck you over first.*

She glanced at the piano player, impatient. He bobbed his head and grunted as he played, oblivious. Tinkle, tinkle. Jag-jag-jaga-ram-ram. Brrrom!

Anticipating her cue. Was he here tonight? Her lover boy, with the soft, smooth, manicured hands.

"That's DeeDee," Zamora murmured, "DeeDee Wright."

"No kidding." Forbes was impressed. What was a legend like that doing in a dump like this? Not quite a dump, perhaps. But so out-of-the-way, so seedy and claustrophobic.

"You've heard of her?" Zamora was pleased.

DeeDee stepped up to the microphone, her voice cracking just a little. "What a diff'rence a day makes. . . ."

Uh-oh. Of course. She was better than Dinah Washington, Forbes thought, thrilled. Zamora and Forbes lingered at the bottom of the stairs, looking for somewhere to sit. The place was packed. An old man with the air of an undertaker made his way toward them. He shook Zamora's hand. Money was exchanged.

"Very nice to see you again, Mr. Z."

"Likewise, Otis."

"Why don't you and your friend follow me." Otis led them to an empty table that appeared, as if by magic, right by the stage. A waiter set down glasses and a bottle of Flor de Manila rum.

"I don't drink," Forbes said.

Zamora poured two healthy shots. "Now you do."

Forbes took tiny, careful sips. "My family's rum," Zamora announced with pride. "This is the only place in New York you can get it." He refilled his glass. "This is the best. Better than that Cuban or Jamaican stuff."

"I wouldn't know," Forbes said. The rum had gone straight to his head. His face was flushed.

"Now you do."

DeeDee struggled through the final bars of the song, her face shiny with makeup and sweat. She scolded the pianist, forgot lyrics, scatted instead. Was that why her once promising career had stalled? The crowd applauded as she took a bow, smiling unhappily. She stepped off the stage and glided toward them. A man at one of the tables dared to touch her arm and make conversation, but DeeDee shook him off with a withering look of contempt.

She towered over Zamora. "Hey, baby. It's rough out there. I didn't think you'd make it." The waiter reappeared with an extra glass and a chair for her. "Goddamn. I was lousy tonight."

"Oh, I don't think so," Forbes blurted out, immediately regretting it.

"Why thank you, darlin'," DeeDee drawled. "And . . . who are you?"

"My roommate," Zamora answered. "Ken Forbes. A country bumpkin on scholarship to Yale." Zamora laughed. DeeDee and Forbes were silent.

Forbes held out his hand.

"You're the first friend of Z's I've met." DeeDee shook his hand, then turned to Zamora, her voice softening. "You stayin' for the last set and hangin' with me later?"

"I am, yes." Zamora grinned with pleasure.

It was clear to Forbes from the way DeeDee cuddled with Zamora that his presence was unwelcome. Aside from a drunk blonde at the bar, Forbes was aware that he and Zamora were the only white men in the room. No one seemed to give a shit, but he had no idea where he was or how to get to Grand Central. It was later than ever—almost four in the morning. Should he leave them to their romance and take his chances in a snowstorm?

He stood up from the table.

"Leaving so soon?" DeeDee asked sweetly.

"I think so."

Zamora frowned, annoyed. "I'm not ready to go."

"I didn't think you were," Forbes said. "But I thought it was time for me—"

Zamora gestured for Forbes to sit back down. "You think too much, Kenny."

The bottle of rum was half full. Zamora poured another round. "I can't drink any more," Forbes said.

"Where you from, Kenny?" DeeDee asked.

"Out west."

"I got people out west. Utah. California. I got people all over the damn place," DeeDee said.

"I didn't know there were Negroes in Utah," Zamora said.

DeeDee laughed. "Didn't know I had some Filipino in me either, did you? My grandma was from someplace called . . ." DeeDee made a show of trying to remember some arcane fact, some marvelous detail about her exotic ancestry. Forbes was sure she was as drunk as, if not drunker than, Zamora, but her gaze remained steely and focused. "Davao!" DeeDee declared. "Granny came from someplace called Davao."

"Makes sense," Forbes said.

Her tone was hostile. "What does *that* mean?"

"The war," Forbes answered.

Zamora snorted with disdain. "Which one?"

"The Philippine-American War—1899 until 1902 or three, depending on who you're talking to. Was that when your grandfather was over there?" he asked DeeDee, who shrugged.

"I wouldn't know," she said. "He never talked about it."

"You should ask him," Forbes said, warming up now. His major was history. "My grandfather—"

"*My* grampa's dead," DeeDee snapped. "So is my *lola*."

It was Zamora's turn. "*Lola?* You called her *lola?*"

"That's right."

Later Zamora said to Forbes, "Imagine that. *Una negra filipina.*" He shook his head in wonder.

"Makes sense. No big deal."

"*Coño* it's no big deal!"

"When you colonize the world . . ." Forbes began, his voice trailing off.

"You bring back a wife," Zamora finished the sentence for him. "You love her?"

"Something like that. She's a little old, but—"

Forbes couldn't help himself. "She's a gorgeous woman. Majestic."

Zamora was both amused and taken aback by his friend's unabashed enthusiasm. "Majestic?"

"What would your father do if you married her? Disown you?"

There was a silence. Forbes knew he was treading on dangerous ground. He was gentle but insistent. "I said, what would happen if you brought DeeDee back to the Philippines as your wife?"

Zamora sighed. "I'd never do that."

"I see."

"You see?" Zamora's mood switched from pensive to imperious. "This is actually none of your business, Kenny."

"I'm your friend."

"Sometimes," Zamora agreed. "When I let you."

She was drinking more than he was.

"What's wrong?" Zamora asked, impatient. He wanted her to hurry up and get into bed with him. They were in her apartment. Forbes was long gone, sent off in a private taxi that had been summoned by the dependable Otis.

"I got troubles," DeeDee said.

"We all do," Zamora said. He held out his arms. "Come here."

She threw back her head and laughed. Her tone was affectionate, but he knew she was angry. "You spoiled little sonuvabitch!
How dare you? How dare you talk down to me?"

"I don't know what you mean."

"Of course you don't. You don't live in the real world."

Zamora wrapped his arms around her. He smelled the musky
Shalimar scent on her hair and body. Her signature perfume.
Something he'd brought her from his last trip to . . . was it Hong
Kong or Paris? "I love you," he mumbled, aroused.

But she was tougher than he was. "This is never going to work,"
she said, pushing him away. "I knew that from the giddyup. You'd
better go, baby."

Zamora was stunned. "What?"

"I'm too old for this shit. You should've left with your buddy. Go
back to Yale. Or Manila. Or wherever the fuck you come from."

"But, Dee—" He was a bewildered, petulant child. DeeDee almost caved in. But being drunk helped. Fogged her up and brought
out the razor blades.

"You'd better go," DeeDee repeated, gazing at him coolly. She
took her time lighting the Pall Mall. Blew smoke in his face, languid
and sexy—like a gangster's moll in some old movie. Cardinal rule:
Always be the first to say good-bye. There was no turning back,
once she got started.

Uleng and Bodabil, 1971:
Some Observations on the Taobo[*]

by Amado Cabrera

fake field observations

U familiar with fire, but it is she who screams loudest when the match is struck by Z. Her screams not out of fear, but of fury.

U cunning and smart. Aware of settlements beyond the jungle, from what D has told her. D a chatterer and braggart—dispenser of dubious but often useful information.

D claims to have taught the Taobo many things. Exactly what? I ask. D chuckles. How to plant yams, how to use a blade. Chop, chop.

Is D to be trusted? Z patronizes him but depends on D as facilitator. Also D is good with languages.

D convinces U to allow us to follow her down to the stream, where she and B fish for tadpoles. I am asked not to bring the tape

---

[*]*Field notes:* The Taobo, though shy and wary with strangers at first, are affectionate with each other and physically demonstrative in general. A peaceful, cave-dwelling tribe of twenty-five people discovered by Zamora López de Legazpi in the rain forest of Mindanao, the Taobo survive on a diet of wild fruits, berries, yams, grubs, and tadpoles. Possibly paleolithic??? The oldest member of the tribe is a man named Dakay. The youngest are the infant Tiking, a boy of about six months, a girl of four or five named Suryam, and a preadolescent male named Bodabil.

recorder, which U considers an "evil box." I bring notebook instead. Mother/son sit on haunches, side by side on flat boulder overlooking trickling stream. Fishing for tadpoles with bare hands, but in no big hurry. When she finally (thank God!) forgets that we are there, U scolds B. Translation by D (is it reliable?) goes something like: "Do not be foolish, my son. I am the only one who can protect you since your father was taken by the sleeping sickness. You are light in spirit, too easily swayed. Easily distracted by everything from a grub to a deer to that demon bird. Like your father, you are too eager for praise!"

B rolls his eyes (typical preadolescent).

"I see you are not listening."

"I am always listening, *Ana*."

U yanks B's hair in a playful gesture. Disapproval? B chews on orchid stem, trying not to show agitation or excitement. His mother watchful.

U's mantra to her son: "Take care, or you will be caught and eaten."

B's response: "I know, but . . ."

I know, Ana.

I know, Ana, but . . .

("Amo" = father; "Ana" = mother?)

U's way of disciplining B consists of yanking a fistful of his hair—hard, to make her point. She clucks at him as a warning, a signal. Sometimes she looks like she is about to swat him with the palm of her open hand, but she never does.

No slapping or hitting of any children by adults has been witnessed. Actually, no physical abuse of any kind, between adults or with adults and children, has been witnessed. Not counting grabbing of hair, of course.

B likes to play rough, which bothers his mother and some of the older Taobo. But B so charming he is tolerated.

A dry day in the forest. Sunlight filters through trees. Beautiful. U finally speaks, her voice shrill and urgent. "Smell danger. Know when it is near. Use your snout like the black pig, or you will be caught and eaten. Scream like the monkey. Pierce the air with your screams to warn others. Sharp eyes, my son. Sharp eyes and ears. Limber arms and legs to swing from vines high up in the trees. Be like the black pig. Root around the bottom of trees with your snout. Find food where no one else can find it. Scurry through the shadowy forest, grunting softly. So no one can hear, so no one can find you. For they would if they could. For they will if you are not careful. Bewitch you, for you are easily bewitched. Pounce and grab you with their bare hands. Capture you with their wily traps. Wound you with their slingshots and their arrows. Tie you up and carry you away. String you up. Build a fire and dance around you. Singe the coarse hair off your flesh. Slash your throat. Turn a deaf ear to your squeals for mercy." (Translation by D from Taobo to Himal to Bisayan. D becomes more poetic and eloquent as he goes along. D pulling my leg?)

Boy seems exhausted by mother's grim lessons. She nags at him every chance she gets, as if fearful that at any moment he will make a fatal error. Endanger himself and them all. B scoops up a handful of tadpoles, drops them into small sack woven from leaves. His gaze fixed on the trickling stream. Shutting out mother?

D whispers story about B. He pulls out a small mirror from his pouch, which he had once shown B. What made you do that? I ask. To scare him, D says, cackling. B fascinated, of course. On the back of the mirror is painted image of Jesus / Sacred Heart. D says B gasped in amazement as he turned the mirror over and over in his hands, trying to comprehend its power.

"That's you in the mirror, Bodabil," D said. "And that's Gee-soos on the other side."

D likes saying *Gee-soos*, makes a thing out of it. Someone had given the mirror and a plastic comb to him as payment or exchange for something. For what, exactly, D no longer remembers. The comb lost during his travels, but Duan plans to give the mirror as gift to Himal woman he's spotted in Sultan Ramayyah market. *Herinaya.* A ripe young woman, D says. Maybe my new wife. Ha-ha.

D sighs. Mirrors, Jesus, pretty women! Too complicated to explain to someone like B.

B rubbed mirror against his cheek, according to D. As if to say, *This is mine now.*

I told him better give it back to me! D says.

B jumped up and down, waving mirror and calling to mother in Taobo. *"Ana! Ana!* Look what Duan gave me!"

D snatched mirror away from him. Instantly regretted losing his temper. B ran away. Boy acts very different around him now, D says.

D quite imaginative at spinning tales.

"Are you listening?" U nags B.

"Yes, *Ana.* Always listening."

"No, you are not."

U nudges B. B nudges back. Great affection/play between them.

"Ana," B teases, "Dakay thinks you are pretty. Dakay's eyes *see* you."

"Dakay can keep his eyes," U retorts. "Dakay is too old and ugly for me." U scrunches up face / narrows eyes. Approximation of ancient Dakay's features?

"But, *Ana,"* B protests, laughing, "you ARE alone."

"I am not alone. There is you. There are many of us."

"Yes," B agrees, "but Dakay is a wise man."

"No, he is not! He is old and foolish. And ugly."

"What about Duan? Duan is strong and kind. Duan's eyes see you—"

D giggles at the mention of his name.

U snorts, unimpressed. Her playful mood vanishes. "Duan's eyes see too many things. Duan is a stranger to us."

"But we call him brother," B insists.

"I do not call him brother." U glowers at D. Glowers at me. Makes her point. Fearless bitch.

Primo Viaggio Inforno Al Mundo

*excerpts from Antonio Pigafetta's account
of Magellan's expedition*

There are many villages in that island. Their names, those of their inhabitants, and of their chiefs is as follows: Cinghapola, and its chiefs, Cilaton, Ciguibucan, Cimaningha, Cimatichat, and Cicanbul; one, Mandaui, and its chief, Apanoaan; one Lalan, and its chief, Theteu; one Lalutan, and its chief, Tapan; one Cilumai; and one, Lubucun. All those villages rendered obedience to us, and gave us food and tribute. Near that island of Zubu was an island called Matan, which formed the port where we were anchored. The name of its village was Matan, and its chiefs were Zula and Cilapulapu. That city which we burned was in that island and was called Bulaia.

Those people go naked, wearing but one piece of palm-tree cloth about their privies. The males, large and small, have their penis pierced from one side to the other near the head, with a gold or tin bolt as large as a goose quill. In both ends of the same bolt, some have what resembles a spur, with points upon the ends; others are like the head of a cart nail. I very often asked many, both old and young, to see their penis, because I could not credit it. In the middle of the bolt is a hole, through which they urinate. The bolt and the spurs always hold firm. They say that their women wish it so, and that if they did otherwise they would not have communication with them. When the men wish to have communication with their women, the latter themselves take the penis, not in the regular way and commence very gently to introduce it (into their vagina), with the spur on top first, and then the other part. When it is inside it takes its regular position; and thus the penis always stays inside until it gets soft, for otherwise they could not pull it out. Those people make use of that device because they are of a weak nature. They have as many wives as they wish, but one of them is the principal wife. . . .

Every night about midnight in the city, a jet black bird as large as a crow was wont to come, and no sooner had it thus reached the houses than it began to screech, so that all the dogs began to howl; and that screeching and howling would last for four or five hours, but those people would never tell us the reason of it.

On Friday, April twenty-six, Zula, a chief of the island of Matan, sent one of his sons to present two goats to the captain-general, and to say that he would send him all that he had promised, but that he had not been able to send it to him because of the other chief Cilapulapu, who refused to obey the king of Spagnia. He requested the captain to send him only one boatload of men on the next night, so that they might help him and fight against the other chief. The captain-general decided to go thither with three boatloads. We begged him repeatedly not to go, but he, like a good shepherd, refused to abandon his flock. At midnight, sixty men of us set out armed with corselets and helmets, together with the Christian king, the prince, some of the chief men, and twenty or thirty balanguais. We reached Matan three hours before dawn. The captain did not wish to fight then, but sent a message to the natives by the Moro to the effect that if they would obey the king of Spagnia, recognize the Christian king as their sovereign, and pay us our tribute, he would be their friend; but that if they wished otherwise, they should wait to see how our lances wounded. They replied that if we had lances they had lances of bamboo and stakes hardened with fire. (They asked us) not to proceed to attack them at once, but to wait until morning, so that they might have more men. They said that in order to induce us to go in search of them; for they had dug certain pitholes between the houses in order that we might fall into them. When morning came forty-nine of us leaped into the water up to our thighs, and walked through water for more than two crossbow flights before we could reach the shore. The boats could not approach nearer because of certain rocks in the water. The other eleven men remained behind to guard the boats. When they saw us, they charged down upon us with exceeding loud cries, two divisions on our flanks and the other on our front. When the captain saw that, he formed us into two divisions, and thus did we begin to fight. The musketeers and crossbowmen shot from a distance for about a half-hour, but uselessly; for the shots only passed through the shields which were made of thin wood and struck the arms (of the bearers). The captain cried to them, "Cease firing! cease firing!" but his order was not at all heeded. When the natives saw that we were shooting our muskets to no purpose, crying out they determined to stand firm, but they redoubled their shouts. When our muskets were discharged, the natives would never stand still, but leaped hither and thither, covering themselves with their shields. They shot so many arrows at us and hurled so many bamboo spears (some of them tipped with iron) at the captain-general, besides pointed stakes hardened with fire, stones, and mud, that we could scarcely defend ourselves. Seeing that, the captain-general sent some men to burn their houses in order to terrify them. When they saw their houses burning, they were roused to greater fury. Two of our men were killed near the houses, while we burned twenty or thirty houses. So many of them charged down upon us that they shot the captain through the right leg with a poisoned arrow. On that account, he ordered us to retire slowly, but the men took to flight, except six or eight of us who remained with the captain. The natives shot only at our legs, for the latter were bare; and so many were the spears and stones that they hurled at us, that we could offer no resistance. . . . Recognizing the captain, so many turned upon him that they knocked his helmet off his head twice, but he always stood firmly like a good knight, together with some others. Thus did we fight for more than one hour, refusing to retire further. An Indian hurled a bamboo spear into the captain's face, but the latter immediately killed him with his lance, which he left in the Indian's body. Then, trying to lay hand on sword, he could draw it out but half-way, because he had been wounded in the arm with a bamboo spear. When the natives saw that, they all hurled themselves upon him. One of them wounded him on the left leg with a large cutlass, which resembles a scimitar, only being larger. That caused the captain to fall face downward, when immediately they rushed upon him with iron and bamboo spears and with their cutlasses, until they killed our mirror, our light, our comfort, and our true guide.

True Romance: 1973

"If you don't run away soon, you are really gaga," Sputnik said. "I've seen how he looks at you."

"But the master is—" I stopped myself from saying what I wanted to say because of that look of scorn on her face.

"Go on, admit it. You've fallen under his spell—just like that other gaga, Celia. A man who sleeps in a coffin! A man who fucks savages! A man who promises to send you to school but doesn't."

"Mister Señor lets me read all his books. I don't need to go to school," I said with a perfectly straight face. I wanted to say, *He thinks I'm smarter than all of you.* But I didn't. I scratched at a wart on the back of my neck until it started to bleed.

Lina has a crush! Lina has a crush! Sputnik taunted me in singsong. We were on our way to the Hollywood Hills Plaza Supermarket, where Mister had a special account. So special that Sputnik and I didn't need to pay for the groceries with money. I just signed Mister's name on a little piece of paper. *Zamora López de Legazpi.* I did all the signing because—even Sputnik had to admit—my handwriting was better than hers. Benny usually drove us to the Plaza in one of Mister's cars, but neither Benny nor the cars were available today. We were forced to wait on the corner for a taxi or a jeepney, whichever came first. Sputnik forgot to bring an umbrella, which made her crabbier than ever. The blazing noon sun beat down on our heads.

"Can I have one of your lemon drops?" I asked.

Sputnik reached into her pocket. "It's the last one you're getting for free. You owe me five pesos for all the ones you've eaten."

"What?"

"*Five pesos.* Let's see, at five centavos each . . . that means you've eaten exactly five hundred lemon drops! Or is it five thousand?"

Not a taxi in sight. Jeepneys whizzed by, crammed with too many people. I held up a hand to shield my eyes from the sun and sucked slowly on the sour lemon drop, trying to make it last. "Why do you think Señora Ilse ran off with the children?"

"*Kasi*, she got tired of finding Celia in her bed," Sputnik said. "But don't you worry—Boss will get his children back. Whatever Boss wants, Boss gets."

My eyes widened. "She found Celia in her bed? Really?"

Sputnik shook her head in disbelief. "You're so childish and gaga, always asking stupid questions."

"And you—you're mean!"

Sputnik laughed. That nasty laugh I knew so well. I turned away from her, defeated. Sick of her mockery.

The loud, persistent honking of horns broke our ugly mood. A brightly painted jeepney appeared alongside us. "*Hoy*, Lilibet!" The driver called out to Sputnik. "Long time no see." Sputnik gasped in surprise. A rare smile on her face. The driver slouched behind the wheel, cigarette lodged behind one ear. Dark and handsome, not much older than she was. Sputnik plopped down in the passenger seat next to him. I climbed in back, next to a plump woman holding a bag of fresh fish wrapped in bloody newspaper. I held my breath. The driver's twinkling eyes met mine in the rearview mirror.

"Boy, am I lucky today! Where are you beauty queens headed?"

"*Sa* Hollywood Plaza," Sputnik answered, in a giggly voice I had never heard her use before.

"Who's your friend, Lilibet?" the driver asked.

"Are you trying to make me jealous?" Sputnik made the driver laugh. The woman next to me shifted and made a noise. "She's a little young for you, don't you think?" Sputnik teased.

"You aren't."

To my amazement the driver leaned over and boldly kissed Sputnik's neck. She pushed him away, giggling. The woman crossed herself and clutched the bag of raw fish closer to her ample chest.

"Come on, Lilibet. Bet your friend's got a pretty name to match that face of hers," the driver said.

I opened my mouth to speak, but Sputnik beat me to it. "Chito, say hello to Lina."

His voice was low, a caress. "Hello, Lina."

I glanced away. "Hello, Chito," I said to the wind.

The jeepney pulled up by the plaza. I climbed out. "How much do we owe you?" I asked Chito, refusing to meet his eyes.

"On the house," Chito answered. He whispered something in Sputnik's ear. They both laughed. With a sigh Sputnik waved goodbye as Chito drove off into traffic.

"You never said you had a boyfriend. Or that your real name was Lilibet," I said.

Sputnik rolled her eyes. "So what? You never bothered to ask what my real name was. As for boyfriends . . . *puwede ba*. Chito's my cousin."

"*He kissed your neck.*"

"Just playing," Sputnik said with a shrug.

Like magic the glass doors of the grand supermarket slid open as we came near. A blast of cold air greeted us. Pretty music played in the background. The aisles were spacious and clean. The food didn't smell. The salespeople were dressed like doctors. We pushed our cart slowly, stopping to stare at the colorful jars of Tang and Kraft Cheez Whiz, in no big hurry to get back to the master's house.

"Love at first sight," Sputnik said.

"What?"

"My cousin Chito has fallen for you."

"Me?"

"Don't pretend. Are you interested?"

"I don't know," I said.

Mama cornered me in the kitchen a few days later. She grabbed me by the arm and waved an envelope in my face. She had found the letter while snooping through my underwear. She'd been snooping since my last birthday. She asked if the bleeding had started, if my *regla* had come yet. "You will tell me as soon as it happens, won't you? It can happen anytime. You're at that age. The age of trouble."

I knew better than to hide Chito's letter in my folded panties. I should have torn it up and thrown it away. Or better yet burned it. But how could I? It was a love letter. *My first.*

"Who is this Chito, and why is he writing you dirty things?"

"I don't know, 'Nay. I don't know!" I tried to pull away, but her grip was powerful.

"You don't know? How did this letter get to you?"

I could not betray Sputnik. I bit down on my lower lip and refused to answer. Mama twisted my arm until I could hold it in no longer and screamed. Gloria and Celia came running in, crying out when they saw what was happening. "Go away!" Mama shouted at them. "This is none of your business!"

Sonny appeared in the doorway. "What the hell is going on, Candelaria?"

"Nothing," Mama answered, letting go of me.

"Boss wants to see your daughter," Sonny said.

Mama looked frightened. "But Lina has work to do."

"Boss wants to see her," Sonny said.

I followed him down the hallway, dreading every step I took. I tried to swallow the pain, but tears kept streaming down my face.

Mister Señor stood by the door, waiting.

"Show the boss your arm," Sonny ordered. I stared at the floor and lifted my left arm, filled with shame.

"Your mother did this?" Mister Señor's voice gruff and gentle. He wiped a tear from my cheek with his fingers, making me even more ashamed. Nevertheless.

"Sir. I *was* bad." In the crack between the floorboards, a procession of ants made its way toward my feet.

"What do you mean?"

Nevertheless. "She . . . found a letter, sir."

"What kind of letter?"

My voice barely a whisper. "From someone."

"You mean a boyfriend? You have a boyfriend, Rizalina?" Mister Señor smiled. Was he making fun of me? I shook my head, confused by my sudden hate for him.

He reached out and lightly touched my arm. I winced. He turned to Sonny. "See that? Her arm is broken. See how it hangs?"

Mama in the brightly lit kitchen, frantic with worry. Probably wondering if she had really hurt me this time. Wondering if she should bother cooking. It was time for dinner. Sometimes the master forgot to eat, but my mother insisted on preparing elaborate dishes as if nothing were wrong. Whatever he didn't eat, we got to eat. Grilled fish, tender steaks, enough rice to silence the pangs in our bellies. There was no one left in the house, except for Mister Señor and his servants. We were his family now: Mama and me. Sonny. Peping the gardener, Benny the driver. Skinny and Fatso, the guards. Sputnik, Gloria. And Celia, who crept off to the master's bedroom when she thought the rest of us were all asleep.

Rizalina. Mister's gruff voice.

Yes yes yessir.

"Don't be afraid. Sonny will take you to the hospital," he said.

Pink-faced, balding Dr. Ocampo was indignant about being called away from a banquet at his country club. He poked roughly at my limp arm, reeking of whiskey and indifferent to my cries of pain. We were in the emergency wing of Our Lady of Grace Sanatorium, a poor people's hospital built by Doña Mary, Mister Zamora's mother.

"The arm is fractured, not broken," Dr. Ocampo said to Sonny. "Nothing to worry about. I'll put her arm in a partial cast. That's about all I can do." He chuckled. "By the way, is this one pregnant, too?" When he saw the grim look on Sonny's face, Dr. Ocampo shrugged and said, "Joke, Sonny."

I glared at the floor, wished the pink-faced doctor dead. All around us people waited to be seen. They coughed and hacked, delirious with fevers. They bled from knife wounds, patient and resigned. They were there when we came. Still there when we left.

Mister Señor decided to teach my mother a lesson. He pretended to slap her across the face while Sonny, the other servants, and I were forced to watch. This he did exactly three times. "You are not to hurt your child in this house," he murmured, lifting his hand as if to strike her. Mama flinched. He let his hand drop suddenly, then raised it again. Mama uttered a sharp sound. His hand stopped an inch before her face. "See? See how it feels? You have so much power over your child, Candelaria." He stepped back, lifted his arm. Mama covered her face with her hands.

How I wished he had simply hit her and been done with it. Blinded by tears, I threw myself at him. "Stop doing that to my mother!"

Sonny pulled me away. "He isn't really hurting her," he said, trying to reassure me.

"Yes he is!" I shrieked. I broke free from Sonny's grasp and kicked at the master's shins with my bare feet, hurting myself more than anything. The master said nothing and finally left the room. Sonny and the other servants left with him, leaving Mama and me alone with our shame and humiliation. My mother stroked the cast on my arm, begging my forgiveness. I begged her forgiveness in return, promised never to be bad again, which was a joke, of course, because how could I ever agree to such a thing?

It was sad how we wept together, making promises meant to be broken. I will not lie I will not lust I will not be lazy I will not steal I will not envy I will not take the name of the Lord in vain I will not I will not! Every night for the next couple of weeks, my mother sprinkled talcum powder inside the cast to soothe where my healing arm itched.

"Who is this Chito?" Mama kept asking. "How did you meet?"

"Nobody important," I answered. "It won't happen again."

There was a look in her eyes. Half crazy. "Promise me you won't do anything foolish. Not with him. Not with the master."

I threw my good arm over her shoulders and laid my head on her chest, hoping to comfort her. Promise, my mother whispered. Promise, promise.

Her Last Night

The plaster cast stank when it came off. The flesh on her left arm had turned pale and blotchy, hidden from the sun all those weeks. Another letter came from Chito. Sputnik slipped it into Rizalina's apron pocket as she unlatched the gate to the dog pen. Feeding time. Brutus and Caesar almost knocked over the large bowls of food set down before them. Sputnik peered over Rizalina's shoulder as she read the letter:

> Dear Lina,
>
> Hope your arm is better! I am sorry for causing you so much trouble, esp. with your mother. A Mother's Love is so precious— I wish you both true happiness. NO MORE TROUBLE OR PAIN. "Life is too short." Is it true your heart already belongs to a lucky someone? (Lilibet told me. Sigh!) Can we still be friends? If you ever change your mind, you know where to find me. I eat lunch at the carinderia next to the Caltex station—one o' clock every day!
>
> God bless you.
> Ramón "Chito" Dizón
> P.S. I will never stop hoping

His handwriting was small, careful, and neat. The blue ink of a Bic ballpen on lined paper. "My cousin made it to second year high school," Sputnik said with pride. "But, *kawawa naman*, he had to drop out when his father died. Chito works hard. He takes care of Auntie Ludy, who's always sick. Plus his three younger brothers and two sisters. But one day he wants to go back and finish school. He'll be the first in our family." Sputnik's mouth fell open as Rizalina tore the letter into little pieces and fed the scraps of paper to the dogs. "*Bagsak ka ba?* What the hell you think you're doing, Lina?"

"Why did you tell Chito that my heart belongs to someone?"

"Isn't it true?" A smirk on Sputnik's face.

"You're crazy!" Rizalina shouted, flushed and amazed at the depths of her own anger.

"Am I?" Sputnik was unfazed.

"Tell your cousin not to send me any more letters," Rizalina said.

She wanted to see Zamora one more time. Maybe to return his book, maybe not. Maybe just to talk. She was tired of listening; it was her turn to tell him stories and ask questions. Maybe. She waited until three in the morning, when she was sure her mother was truly asleep. When she was sure Celia was too exhausted to sneak off to be with him. She waited until all the bodies in the room were finally still, their breathing soft, steady, and peaceful. Rizalina tiptoed down the hall in her bare feet. The dim glow of light from under the door of his study meant that he was there. Maybe drunk, maybe not. She knocked softly. There was no answer. She opened the door and tiptoed in. Surprising him. He looked up from his desk, bleary eyed. He had been writing in that little brown notebook of his, the one he kept locked in a drawer. The room was a mess. Papers scattered on his desk. A half-empty bottle of rum, an ashtray overflowing with cigarette butts and cigar stubs next to the unplugged phone. Everything coated with dust. The room a mess. The whole fucking house a mess, since the wife and children had left. "Don't touch a thing," he would say whenever Rizalina attempted to clean. "Can't you see I'm busy?" Visitors still came, but not like in the old days. The few who did seem moved by a strange curiosity or pity, which made Zamora angry.

"What are you doing here?" he asked. She placed the Pigafetta book on top of his desk. He barely glanced at it.

"Your book, sir. I'm finished with it."

"I told you it was yours."

"*Salamat*, sir. I mean, thank you."

Zamora gestured for her to sit down. "Does your mother know where you are?" Rizalina shook her head. She arranged herself primly in the chair by his desk, pulling at the hem of her mother's old dress, the one she always wore to bed.

"You want to borrow another book?" Zamora asked, looking hard at her now. A moment passed before she dared to meet his punishing gaze. His unshaven face seemed ravaged and older than usual. She had no desire to, but she knew she should leave the room immediately.

"Have I told you about the time I accidentally killed a man? Not a man, but a boy, actually. I was alone, driving my Alfa back to Manila from Baguio. Driving too fast, but then that's what sports cars are for, aren't they?" Zamora paused, studying the young girl before him. She had taken him completely by surprise. "I've totaled four cars in my time. Twice when I was a student. I walked away from each collision, each accident, unscathed. Oh, a bloody gash here and there, a bruise. Nothing serious. Whereas my cars were mangled to bits. My father threatened to disown me, but he kept buying me more cars. But this time with the Alfa, it was different. I killed someone. A barefoot boy walking by the side of the road. You know how the road zigzags to Baguio, Rizalina? How it zigzags past waterfalls and rice terraces up the side of mountains, how steep the drop is down the unprotected side of the road, how there is nothing between you and God and the jungles of trees?"

"I have never been to Baguio. I don't know about those things, sir," she answered. His family owned a vacation home in Baguio, that much she knew. And that Baguio was a beautiful city high up in the mountains, where it was cold.

Zamora lit a Salem. "There was fog. I didn't think there'd be anyone out so damn early in the morning. I wasn't drunk. The boy had a basket of something on his head—papayas and mangoes that flew all over the road and made a big nasty mess when I hit him."

"Why are you telling me this? *Sir,*" she quickly added.

Zamora took a swig of rum. "The point is, the boy was small. Scrawny, like you. When he got hit, he flew up in the air like a rag doll. He landed in a ravine, thirty or so feet below. I paid for his body to be hauled up and sent home to his family. Paid for his burial. Paid for his sister's schooling. Paid off his family's debts." He saw how her eyelids fluttered from the need to sleep. *Brown angels. Glory of saints.* "I wasn't even drunk," he said. "He was not the first person I've killed, of course. Nor my last." She sat up, curious. Her eyes luminous, wide open now. "Why are you here, Rizalina?"

Zamora realizes he's dangerous [margin note]

It was cold in the room. Rizalina wrapped her arms around herself.

"What? What is it?" he demanded in Spanish.

Rizalina reached out and placed her hand on his bristly cheek. He closed his eyes, turned his head so his mouth touched her palm. She pulled her hand back, horrified. She had touched him, done the unthinkable. *Nevertheless.* She balled her hand into a fist. Pressed it against her mouth. He hadn't moved from his seat, drifting now. Idly scratching the tip of his nose, thinking about something or someone more important than she was—that dead boy in the ravine, maybe. Hot tears trickled down over her fist. Did he love her the way Chito did? This longing she felt, this aching, inexplicable confusion whenever Mister Zamora was near—was it love?

"What day is this, Rizalina?"

"Thursday, sir."

"That's perfect," he crowed. "We'll go to Baguio for the weekend. Would you like that?"

"Sir?" Rizalina, uncomprehending. Still stunned by the surprise of his skin, its coarse texture.

"You said you've never been. Don't you want to see Baguio?"

"But my mother—"

"I'll take care of her. Don't worry about that. And on Monday you'll start school. Just as I promised, Rizalina."

Rizalina shook her head.

Zamora felt ridiculous saying it. "I want you to be happy."

No, she murmured. No, no, no.

He came over to where she sat, cowering in the chair. He knelt before her. Waited until they had both calmed down a little. He could hear her shallow breathing. Had he walked into another dream? *Brown angels. Waling-waling. Glory of saints.* Zamora picked up her left arm as if it were made of fragile glass. He stroked the underside, where the cast had been. Splotchy and pale, belly of a fish. Would a kiss be too obscene? He moved her small fist—wet with tears and saliva—away from her mouth. She would not stop trembling. Her gaze met his—steady and defiant. There was something else—did she also despise him? Zamora lifted her chin, drank in the sly sweetness of her face before reluctantly letting her go. He had read too much into it. She was a child, after all. A child no older than his own daughter. Even he had his limits. Zamora stood up and went to the door. Had she locked it from the inside by accident? He stifled an urge to laugh as he undid the lock and held the door open for her. "Get out," he whispered hoarsely in English.

The day she ran away, Rizalina wore one of the dusters her mother had bought a year ago, for her eleventh birthday. It was one she hadn't quite outgrown, her favorite—blue cotton sprinkled with tiny orange flowers. Rubber slippers were on her feet. A size too big, which meant they would last a little longer. Two thousand pesos were stuffed into her pocket, half of which she had stolen from her mother. The other half from Zamora. The Pigafetta book was still on the desk in his study, where she had left it.

She waved to Fatso and Skinny in their sentry posts.

"Where you off to?" Fatso asked, leering down at her.

"The *botica*," Rizalina answered.

"My head hurts," Fatso moaned. "Hurry. Bring me back some aspirin, Lina."

"That's not all that hurts," Skinny teased. As usual, the guards laughed at their own pathetic joke. Rizalina felt their lustful eyes following her as she walked out the gates of the compound. She was careful not to walk too fast, not to seem in too much of a hurry. There had been no good-byes, not even to Sputnik. Rizalina crossed the wide street and disappeared from view. It was exactly one o'clock in the afternoon.

The Conquistador's Lament

Zamora - multiple tenses

She's gone. Gone! Would you believe the nerve? The courage. *Puñeta!* Her mother broken, runs through the halls of my house, lamenting her lost, darling daughter. Gone, gone, gone, Candelaria! They're all gone. My wife, my son, my daughter, yours, . . . I try to shake, rattle, and roll her, snap Candelaria out of that useless fog of misery that threatens to suffocate her. And me. It's for her own damn good! I shout. Rizalina has gone away for her own damn good! If Mama only knew. But her poor, fat, sweaty mama has no idea what I'm shouting about. Blinded by a broken heart. What she doesn't know is, so am I.

Please, boss. Can't you send Mister Sonny to find her? Fatso and Skinny? Maybe the police and the army?

You're a great cook, Candelaria. A loyal servant. The best I've ever had.

If you let me use the driver and car, I'll find her myself. She blithers in Tagalog and Bisayan—I can barely comprehend what she is saying. But she's a true Filipina. The tears keep coming, flooding out of her. *Please, boss. Send the navy! Find my beloved Lina and bring her back! I have no one left! No one!*

You will always have a home here with me, Candelaria. You never have to worry.

God bless you, sir.

Exhausted by her grief, I wander outside with my gun. Take a walk around the desolate garden. End up by the dog pen, shooting at the damn dogs.

Puñeta. And where is my father now? The jungle floor a damp pile of fallen leaves and bits of broken trees. I stare up at the green darkness, trees that seem to go on forever, obscuring the sky and whatever sun is left. I am alone, finally alone with myself, the silence not a silence but humming, wired, alive, all eyes on me now, bats parrots monkeys flying squirrels, beautiful black unblinking eyes darting over the floor of coiled serpents and dead monarch butterflies on which I lie, dreaming of my father.

He yells and curses at me: *Junior, Junior, what the fuck are you trying to prove, sonuvagun sonuvabitch* mi hijito? Huge distended Mandarin ears flap like an elephant's. Papa glares at me, arthritic fingers grasping at the carved dragon's head on his cane. Angry and disappointed with me as usual. Because I refuse to cave in and become who he is—Zamora López de Legazpi el Primero—conniving, wily, cunning, lecherous, tight-fisted, covetous businessman with a capital *B*, Mr. Mercenary who loves and understands money, so damn good at making it, who would think nothing of selling his own mother— no, his one and only son—down the river.

O Papa. *Supreme macho tightwad patriarch shithead. Bacalao eater, empire builder, hawk-faced man of few regrets. I hear your voice like a broken record. Scolding, nagging, grating. Wearing me down. Mi hijito, that wife of yours—a beauty, but she's got you by the—*mi hijito, be careful— *empires crumble just like that—look at those shit-eating Romans and Brits—never expected their niggers and Indios and coolies to—don't roll your eyes at me—think with your brains not with your* pititing—*no son of mine can afford to be—we're barely forty years away from the jungle—* coño—cabrón—puñeta—pendejo—*don't waste my time with your dreaming—listen to this cough—the cough of a dying man*

❧

Did I love money, did I love anyone or anything? *I loved the jungle.* I lay dreaming on the jungle floor—dreaming of my pious mother and sisters, determined martyrs from the day they were born. I had lived up to their expectations as only son and brother, fulfilled some of my destiny, married and impregnated a woman more golden and uattainable than my mother or sisters could ever be. Ilse, Ilse of heaven. And what of my mixed blood, what of it? Basque, Negrense, a dash of North American Irish from my mother, Mary. Curdled, diseased, robust, and volatile, my blood runs hot and cold like a faucet. Does it explain anything?

God waited with me in that forest. We were alone, swallowed up by trees. I rested on the ground, my feet in their muddy motorcycle boots propped up on a grub-infested log. How I remember it! How I remember it as if it were . . . what? Yesterday, today, tomorrow. Spiders and ants swarmed over my face, leeches feasted on my arms. I was indifferent. There were too many eyes watching me. Not animal or insect eyes but the human eyes of forest people.

I sat up without warning, startling the boy.

Sigé, hijo. Tayo na. I am ready to see your home. As if the boy and his people could understand my language. I made shooing gestures, urging the boy to lead the way.

The boy—I did not know his name yet—flitted off into the bush, moving fast where there were no trails or clearings, gliding, not really walking, through thorny bush, skipping nimbly from rock to fallen tree trunk. I tried not to fall behind, grasping at vines with my cut and bleeding hands. I groaned with the excruciating effort of finding my foothold on the slippery slopes leading up to the caves. Overcome by a macabre onslaught of giggles, I toyed briefly with the idea of letting go of whatever root or sapling I clutched onto for dear life. It would be so beautiful. Falling down the steep slope into the terrible, dark ravine hundreds of feet below. I forced myself to look up. I was almost there. The boy had nearly reached the top of the mountain, waiting for me with a look of amusement and concern. Some other men appeared, small and slender like him, but older and less amused. The forest boy held out his arm. I crawled up the side of the mountain, toward him. Random images flashed in my mind. Ilse sitting on the terrace lost in one of her books. Dulce trudging behind Celia and the baby in the garden. The firmness of Celia's thighs. The terrace and garden and the servant's thighs hundreds of miles and light-years away. I smelled the red earth of the mountain's side, felt it scraping against my face. I could die here, alone among these people. Ta-o-bo. An abrupt name that didn't quite do them justice. Perhaps I misheard what Duan originally said to me. "They call themselves *Tao, po.*" Human beings. Nevertheless, I wrote it down. *Taobo.* Leaked the information, however dubious, to the anthropologists and the press. *Did you say "Stone Age," sir? Paleolithic?* Yes, yes! That's exactly what I said.

The publicity, the absurd headlines in Manila that screamed: EX-PLAYBOY SAVES OUR CAVEMEN! Ilse was horrified. But I loved it. Journalists clamored for interviews. It all happened fast, much too fast. I agreed to be interviewed by everyone. Such fun.

The boy pulled me to safety, laughing softly. In a sudden burst of affection, he rested his head on my shoulder. *What is your name, mi hijito?* The boy scurried away. I saw two caves up ahead, one on top of another. The larger one, with a wider, deeper chamber, was on the bottom ridge of the mountain. An impossibly steep and narrow trail led from behind a boulder at the mouth of the cave up toward the smaller cave on the upper ridge. I sat on my haunches—let the Taobo gaze down at me for what seemed like hours. *Laan-lan,* I said. *I mean you no harm.* There were a dozen or so people gathered at the mouth of the larger cave. A chubby baby boy with long, coppery hair wailed at the sight of me. An albino? I smiled in the baby's direction, but he kept screaming. The young woman carrying him did not return my smile. I was aware of more faces crowding the mouth of the upper cave. How many Taobo were there? I shifted my weight to prevent my legs from cramping. From out of the corner of my eye, I saw the forest boy take an old man by the hand and lead him slowly and carefully toward me. Wearing a skirt of leaves, the old man squatted down beside me. He pointed to my beard and clasped a hand over his mouth. The old man's solemn expression never changed, but I knew the fact that he remained by my side was a good sign. The forest grew noticeably cooler, and the light began to fade. Even the baby grew silent. I slept, delirious with happiness. In my dream Papa sat in the middle of the forest, on a stool carved of bone. A gnome with elephant's ears. Long live the king. Long live the Jesuit pimp, the brilliant navigator, the cosmic tycoon! In my dream Papa was kind. In my dream Papa called out to me. His voice crackled in the wind. An old man's voice, tremulous and thin—a scratchy record. *Junior! My sonuvagun! My sonuvabitch! Mi hijito! Finally, something of your own.*

It was the beginning of everything.

PART TWO

Napalm Sunset
1977

Vincent Moody

3rd person (handwritten)

Moody (handwritten)

The phone call about the movie came from his agent, Ross Fox. "It's a war thing," Ross said, sounding excited. Ross never got excited. "It's definitely going to be *big*. Tony Pierce is directing. Risky, but the buzz is unbelievable." Ross took a deep breath. "Now, listen—I don't know why, but Big Man wants *you*."

Vincent Moody swallowed hard. A moment passed.

"You've ninety-nine percent got the part," Ross said, trying to sound upbeat.

"What's it called?"

"Pierce hasn't thought up a title yet."

"World War Two?"

"Vietnam. A really bad idea, if you ask me. That war's barely over—but who the fuck am I to complain? I'm just an agent."

"You're my pimp."

"If I'm your pimp, then I must really be a dumb one, because you make a lousy whore, Vince."

Moody chuckled. "Does Pierce know you call him 'Big Man'?"

"Everyone calls him that," Ross said.

"I've never worked with a boy genius," Moody said.

Ross gave a little snort. "Get ready for this. Pierce is writing the script and investing his own money. He wants to shoot in Vietnam, but the studio threatened to pull out if he did. So you're going to the Philippines. The terrain is similar, apparently."

"I can vouch for that."

"How the fuck would you know? You've never been to 'Nam or the Philippines. Don't you have flat feet or something?"

"I was deemed psychologically unfit," Moody said. "The army didn't want guys like me."

"I don't blame them. Anyway, I'm sending you the script."

"Am I the lead?"

"No, but this is a meaty role. Please, Vince—pretty please—don't fuck up. Pierce wants you for the part of Cowboy—a lovable kook who rides off into the napalm sunset."

Moody's voice was flat. "Ha-ha."

"It's a great part. You'll make it great."

"I was a child star. Nominated for an Academy Award when I was ten."

"Right." Then, not unkindly, Ross reminded him, "And you haven't worked since . . . when?"

"Right."

Several days later Moody paid a visit to Sandy Watanabe's travel agency on Main Street, a few blocks from where he lived in Santa Monica. A sign on the door read PARADISE GETAWAY ~ ADVENTURES IN TRAVEL. Sandy puffed angrily on a Kool. "I am not in a very good mood," she greeted him.

"Business bad?" Moody asked.

Sandy nodded. "My girl just quit. Don't know if I can afford to hire another one. Maybe I should take my parents up on their offer to send me to law school."

"I need a vacation. Can you help me?"

"What?"

"A getaway." Moody grinned. He placed his forefinger on the map tacked to the wall. "That's where I wanna go."

Sandy got up from her seat, walked over to where Moody stood, and squinted at the map. "The Philippines?"

"Yup."

"If you need a little R&R, I can offer you a great discount to London. Hotel included. C'mon, Vince. Lighten up. Have you ever been to swinging London?"

"Brits are pompous and boring. Brits can't cook." Moody pulled a tiny, folded square of aluminum foil from his shirt pocket. "Wanna toot?" He rolled up a twenty-dollar bill and spread the coke on Sandy's desk. She leaned over and snorted up two quick hits, ever efficient, grunting with pleasure. She looked up at Moody, teary eyed and grateful.

"Wow," Sandy moaned. "That was wicked. . . ." After a brief pause she went right back to her sales pitch. "What about Paris? I can get you there for the same price. And you've got that ex-girlfriend over there to stay with, don't you? What was her name? Fifi, Mimi—"

"Clotilde."

"Yeah, right. Paris is never boring."

Moody shook his head.

"Spain? You've never been."

Moody was unrelenting. "So—what do flights to Manila cost these days?"

"Are you taking Lori and Alex?"

"No."

"Interesting," Sandy murmured. She had gone to high school with Lori. A loyal friend. Moody had never regretted sleeping with her.

"I've landed a job in this movie," Moody said.

"So I heard. Good for you," Sandy said.

"We're shooting in the Philippines."

"So I heard. Why are you paying your own way?"

"I wanna go early," Moody said. "Get the lay of the land."

"You're nuts."

"Am I in the wrong place? Aren't you the purveyor of obscure, sexy, and somewhat sinister destinations?" Moody teased.

"Fuck you, Vinnie." Sandy Watanabe pulled up her chic, clingy

T-shirt and flashed him small, perfect tits. She liked shocking people.

"You'd better watch it. Your receptionist could walk back in at any minute."

"I doubt it, babe." Sandy pulled down her shirt and snorted another line. "I can't believe you're running out on Lori and the kid. Just when things are looking up and you've landed a part in a big movie. What the fuck's going on?"

"You're a magnificent woman," Moody said. "Magnificent tits and a brain to match." Then he said, "I need some time alone. Please—don't say anything to Lori."

Sandy took a deep breath. "Why are you doing this? Lori's been so good to you. *So supportive.* This is crazy, Vince. Irrational. Are you strung out again? You need me to loan you money or something? This is goddamn crazy—"

Moody held up his hand. "You sound like a broken record. Like all of them. My agent. My mother. My wife. Scolding. Nagging. Bitches."

"Misogynist motherfucker."

"I didn't know you were such a feminist."

She dabbed the filter end of a Kool in the coke dust on her desk, then lit up. "Get out of my office," she said, purposely blowing smoke in his direction.

Moody pulled out his American Express card. "They haven't canceled this yet, so let's try it. I need economy class, no special meals required, an aisle seat. Preferably near the toilets, but not all the way in the back. I hate how it starts to stink on those long flights, don't you?"

She shot him a hateful look. "You've always been an asshole, but I can't believe you're abandoning—"

"I'm doing them a favor. Gimme a break, Sandy."

"Apologize first."

Moody started to laugh, but it came out cracked and bitter, all wrong. "Oh, Sandy. Dear Sandy. Why are you putting me through this unnecessary shit?"

"Shit begets shit."

"I should marry you," Moody said. "You're the only one who understands me."

"More shit," Sandy said, taking his credit card.

On a Saturday afternoon Moody left Los Angeles. Lori, his girlfriend, was on location in the desert and wouldn't be home until
late Sunday night. Their three-year-old son, Alex, was staying with
Lori's parents in Glendale for the weekend. Sandy was right. Moody
was a shit. It was sickening, Moody thought, how easy it was for
him to leave them. The only witness was his dog, Duchess—an ex-
pert in abandonment. She was an old, half-blind, white Labrador
that Moody had found wandering on the Santa Monica Pier early
one morning. The day of Moody's departure, Duchess followed him
around from room to room. As if she knew. She wagged her tail,
farted, made sorrowful, grunting sounds, as if to chastise him. *You
dumb fuck, how could you leave us?* With her one good eye, Duchess
watched Moody cram his things into a huge backpack. Moody did
his best to ignore her. He set two large bowls filled with food and
water on the kitchen floor, then called for a cab to take him to
LAX. He would leave his beloved Porsche behind for Lori to sell—
the least he could do. The car was dented and badly in need of a
paint job, but still amphibious-looking and beautiful, still fast, still
worth something.

Whatever guilt Moody felt melted slowly as he boarded the Philippine Airlines jet, packed with Filipino families on their way home.
The atmosphere was festive. Moody made his way down the aisle.
A few passengers recognized him and whispered among themselves. Moody nodded at them and smiled. He settled into the aisle
seat, which he had specifically requested so he could have access to
the toilets and get high in private. The old man in the seat next to
him was already asleep. Sandy had warned Moody that it would be

a long, tedious flight—at least twenty hours. He drank vodka. A mystery meal drenched in brown sauce was served, which he ignored. The first of many unfunny comedies was screened. Moody locked himself in the toilet. He licked a dab of windowpane off a piece of paper—a going-away gift from Sandy—then went back to his seat and waited for the acid to take effect. He tried reading a spy thriller by some Englishman, but the words on the page wouldn't keep still. Except for a distant hum, the plane grew dark and silent. The head flight attendant, a wistful beauty, tentatively approached. "Mr. Moody," she said, in a low voice, "perhaps you'd feel more comfortable in our first-class cabin?" Her face cracked open. Pieces of it fell away from her skull, revealing layers of tissue and bone. Her teeth were towering architectural monuments—glistening, infinite.

"*Are you all right, sir?*"

Moody, transfixed by his hallucination, said nothing.

"There's a seat available."

"M-m-my ticket's coach." Blood coursed through her veins. Tunnels of red, throbbing worms. Moody was awestruck.

"Yes, I know, Mr. Moody."

He tried to make out the name tag pinned to her blouse, but it was on fire.

"Call me Vince. Wh-what's your name?"

"Linda Torre, sir. Please come with me."

"Linda m-m-means 'pretty' in Spanish, right?"

She blinked. Electric sparks flew in the air. Moody stumbled down the aisle behind her, forcing himself to act calm, though the floor was a tangle of vicious moray eels. They snapped at his heels. Linda pulled back a heavy curtain. There it was. *First class.* A hushed chamber of privilege. Tycoons whistled and snored in their sleep, wrapped in blankets of cashmere.

"You're very kind," Moody said to Linda. Her face was back. "Are you my angel? You must be an angel." His new seat was plush, big as a boat.

"Shh. Please, sir. Keep your voice down." Linda smiling, relentless. She disappeared behind the curtain. Moody felt a terrible lone-liness, a terrible urge to laugh and weep. The acid made everything throb and pulsate. High-pitched moans emanated from the plane's engine. The night never seemed to end. There were movies pro-jected that no one watched, a three-hour stopover in Hawaii that seemed like a hellish dream—all glaring sunshine and tedious wait-ing. Back on the plane Moody longed for real sleep. But the acid lin-gered and wouldn't let him rest. "Good morning, sir." Linda handed him a heated face towel scented with cologne. Moody stared at his breakfast, afraid to eat. The plane descended slowly. Babies wailed in pain as the pressure built. Moody's ears popped. Faster and faster, the plane plummeted, landing with a thud.

"Welcome to Manila International Airport. *Mabuhay!*" Linda Torre's cheerful announcement came through the speakers. Passen-gers burst into applause.

Moody stumbled off the plane into the thick, sweltering heat of Manila. A lopsided smile was fixed on his face. People stared at his unkempt hair, bloodshot eyes, and greasy jeans, horrified and amused. *Are you here on holiday or business, sir?* The customs agent snickered. Another asked for his autograph. The insides of Moody's head felt soft and scrambled. Somehow he managed to maintain his composure as he walked through the customs area, past the soldiers with guns. Maintain, maintain. It was important to keep cool and alert no matter what. He congratulated himself for remembering to change his dollars into pesos before exiting the busy terminal. Packs of dusty children swooped down on him as soon as he stepped out-side. The heat felt good. *Carry your bags, Joe?* Moody marveled at the children—stunning in their sad-eyed beauty, skinny, anxious, hun-gry. Little hands flapped in his face. Moody gave the children money. They demanded more, shoving and pushing to get closer to him. *Me, me, gimme, Joe!* A taxicab pulled up in the nick of time. Moody climbed in, relieved to escape the children's grasping hands. A young man sat behind the wheel. A rosary and several scapulars dangled from his rearview mirror. "Someplace fun, please," Moody mumbled. The cabbie turned to give Moody a hard, appraising look before driving off. Moody rolled the windows down as far as they would go. Hot air blew in his face. Ocean, raw sewage, the fragrance of flowers. The cabbie stole glances at Moody in the mirror, laughing softly to himself when he finally recognized the actor.

Manila astonished Moody. The cabbie drove past swamplands and crumbling colonial ruins, past jazzy discotheques, grand hotels, and haunted cathedrals. Past squatters' shacks on vacant lots, past brand-new skyscrapers made of smoky glass and steel. Billboards advertised kung-fu movies, Camay soap, and Kikkoman soy sauce. Less familiar products and names fascinated him. *Aji-No-Moto, Magnolia, Cortal, Rufina Patis, Eye-Mo.* Red-and-white Coca-Cola signs shimmered in the sunlight.

The cabbie turned onto Mabini Street and stopped in front of a go-go bar called the Love Connection. "Here is your fun." The cabbie grinned, taking Moody's money. It was noon. A man with stringy hair and gold teeth hovered by the doorway. "You want girls? We got plenty nice girls." Moody shook his head and peered inside. A couple of cops in uniform were at the bar talking—their faces made ghoulish by the glow of black light. They turned to stare at Moody as he walked in. Teenage girls in transparent baby-doll nighties lounged about, looking bored. An extremely tall and sun-burned white man in bermuda shorts, flip-flops, and a T-shirt that read MISSING IN ACTION sat brooding in a corner. The bartender, whom Moody at first mistook for a man, gave him a curt nod. A few of the girls perked up, recognizing Moody from movies they'd seen. Moody parked himself at the bar, next to a speaker. Some disco thing was blaring. A bubbly replica of the Bee Gees, except sung in Tagalog. The language was percussive, new to Moody's ears. One of the girls tapped him boldly on the shoulder. She was a scrawny, feline beauty. The prettiest one, unbearably young. Moody was instantly smitten.

"Buy me a drink, Mister?" Her smile, practiced and hopeful.

"Sure," Moody said. "What's your name?"

"Jinx," the girl answered.

"You should try our San Miguel," the bartender said to Moody. "Best beer in the world." She was a colossus of a woman, her hair cut and styled in a flamboyant ducktail pompadour.

"Sure," Moody said.

"I want champagne," Jinx said.

"No." The bartender glared at her. "Too early for you."

Jinx said something incomprehensible to the bartender. Something that to Moody sounded very much like a complaint. The bartender retorted in an angry voice. Jinx stormed off to her shadowy station by the stage, where she huddled with the other girls, pouting. The bartender turned her wrathful gaze on Moody. "You wanna beer or what?"

"Sure. Is this your place?"

"You bet."

Moody held out his hand in a friendly gesture. "Vince." The bartender contemplated his hand for a moment. With great reluctance she shook it. "Peaches."

"I didn't mean to cause trouble," Moody said.

"That's good," Peaches said.

The man with stringy hair and gold teeth suddenly appeared and claimed the stool next to Moody. Peaches introduced him as Bong. "I am your number-one fan," Bong said to Moody. "I recognize you when you got out of the taxi."

Moody bought a round of drinks for Bong, Peaches, and himself. Peaches, softening, offered him a taste of the local rum. *Flor de Manila.* "Very strong," Peaches warned him. Moody, delighted, ordered doubles for himself and Bong.

"To Manila!" Moody shouted, holding up his glass in a toast.

"*Mabuhay!*" Bong shouted.

The cops at the other end of the bar kept staring.

Night fell. Moody had not moved from his seat, except to stagger to the toilet once or twice. The other men were long gone, including the tall, sunburned white man. Only Bong—Moody's new best friend—stayed behind.

"Let's go eat, Vince."

"Not hungry." Moody sniffed under his arm and made a face. "I need a shower."

"First you eat. Come on—I will take care of you," Bong said.

Moody slid off the stool and followed Bong across the room to a door marked KEEP OUT. Jinx stood by the door, smoking a cigarette. "Where you going?" she asked Moody in English.

"Bong's taking me somewhere to eat. Wanna come along?"

Jinx smiled. God, she was glorious when she smiled, Moody thought.

"No," she said, "better not."

"Why not?" Moody asked, impatient.

She exchanged glances with Bong.

"Peaches will get mad," Bong explained. "Let's go, Vince."

Bong led Moody outside, to an alley reeking of garbage and urine. They walked for several blocks. Bong pointed to a home-made sign. MELVIE'S CANTEEN.

"My wife's place." Bong beamed with pride. "We can eat good. You like Pilipino food?"

"I don't know," Moody replied. "Never had it."

MELvie's was a hole-in-the-wall lit by a blue-white fluorescent bulb swarming with gnats and mosquitoes. The food was delicious. The two men devoured oxtails in golden peanut sauce, eggplant and bittermelon, mounds of rice. Salty and satisfying, like nothing Moody had ever eaten before.

"Are you here to make a movie?" Bong asked, sucking on a toothpick.

"Nah. I'm a tourist."

"Bullshit, man. Can I be an extra?"

"It's not up to me."

"Aha! So you *are* making a movie?"

"Sort of."

Bong's eyebrows moved up and down, speaking a language all their own. "Sort of? You crazy, man. Don't make no sense." After a pause he called to his wife, a frazzled woman stirring pots in the tiny, makeshift kitchen behind the counter. "Melvie! When you gonna stop cooking and come meet our new friend? He was in that movie you liked, that one about the shark."

Melvie flashed Moody a strained smile and kept stirring. "Get me his autograph!" she shouted in Tagalog.

"What? What did she say?" Moody asked.

Bong made a dismissive gesture. "Always working," he grumbled. "Always working, never wanna stop."

"Well," Moody said, "someone's gotta do it."

A young man with a shag hairdo walked in. Bong introduced him as his cousin, Ziggy. Moody was introduced as "the star of that shark movie" to Ziggy, who looked only slightly impressed. Ziggy responded to Bong brusquely in Tagalog. Both men laughed. Moody understood he was the butt of some mysterious joke but decided to blow it off, knowing that Bong's friendship would turn out useful in the end. All the drugs and initial excitement had worn off. Moody was suddenly overcome by a feverish exhaustion.

"I gotta get going," Moody said.

"Where you staying, boss?" Ziggy asked.

"Nowhere."

Bong was incredulous. "*Nowhere?* You wanna go Hilton Hotel? Right down the street. I got connections. I can get you discount. Forty percent."

"No, no thanks. Nothing fancy for me," Moody said.

"My mother runs a *pensión* nearby," Ziggy offered.

"Sounds good to me," Moody said.

"Fuck the *pensión*!" Bong, irate now. "What about air-con or swimming pool? Room service?"

Ziggy shot Bong an irritated glance. "My mother has a very nice place," Ziggy said to Moody. "Not the Hilton, but clean. Cheap. Safe."

"Let's go," Moody said.

The three men started walking down the street. Bong refused to let up. "Wow, man. What kind of movie star are you? You don't want *air-con*? You don't have money?"

The Pensión Belén was a ramshackle wooden house off Remedios Circle, protected from the busy street by a bamboo fence crawling with vines of purple bougainvillea flowers. The house had withstood most of the horrors of the Japanese occupation, according to Mrs. Dava, Ziggy's formidable mother. "To hell and back," she muttered, walking Moody through the available vacant rooms. *Oh, yes, Mr. Moody. We have been to hell and back.* Moody rented a single on the second floor and crashed off and on for a day and a half. His nightmares flew by in blurry fragments. What he would remember later was one particular dream. He and his son, Alex, dangled upside down from a Ferris wheel on the Santa Monica Pier. They seemed to be the only people left in the world. The pier below them was a vast cemetery of white headstones, neatly arranged in rows. Alex kept laughing. Joyous, unafraid. "Vincent, Vincent," he called to his father, holding out his arms.

Moody woke in a pool of sweat. Where was he? The room—clean and spare except for a painting on velvet of a Moro *vinta* sailing into a tropical sunset—gave off no clues. Frantic, Moody checked his knapsack for his wallet and passport. He was in Manila. Manila! The money was all there, stuffed into the wallet. Everything intact in the knapsack. The first draft of Pierce's script, still in its big brown envelope. Sealed and unread. Which meant that Bong and cousin Ziggy could be trusted. Moody washed himself, using water from a metal drum kept in one of the nonfunctioning shower stalls in the pensión's communal bathroom. He slipped on a fresh T-shirt over the same greasy jeans he'd been wearing since he left L.A. His gray, puffy face in the mirror belonged to a stranger. Moody resisted the familiar pang of guilt and self-pity gnawing at him. He should've left Lori and Alex a note on the kitchen table—one of those "I'm sorry, I just have to go away for a little while and clear my head" kind of notes. For Alex's sake, at least. But instead he'd acted like a coward—incapable of articulating what exactly he was running from. He imagined hearing Lori's voice, crackling with despair from thousands of miles away. *Weak self-indulgent asshole why do I love you?*

Moody welcomed the noise of the streets. The heat was breathtaking, the sounds of traffic and people jarring and loud. His skin hurt. *Gotta find my Love Connection.* Moody wondered if he could find his way back to the bar. He brushed past rowdy American soldiers on leave, strolling with their girls. *Hey, man. Don't I know you?* a soldier yelled at him. The sidewalks were slivers of cement, hardly sidewalks at all. Where was MELvie's? If he could just find MELvie's. He passed stalls of moneychangers, their signs written in English and Arabic script. One souvenir shop after another displayed the same array of painted fans, capiz-shell place mats, intricately embroidered shirts, obscene ashtrays. Moody panicked. Was he headed in the right direction? The grand, moss-covered church loomed up ahead. Another relic of history that Bong had proudly pointed out to him two nights ago. Moody rejoiced. The Love Connection had to be just around the corner.

Peaches greeted him with a grim smile. "*Kumusta*, Pretty Boy?"

"Couldn't be better," Moody answered. His eyes scanned the shadows for Jinx the beautiful, but she was nowhere to be found.

Moody decided that the Love Connection, as unwelcoming as it was, would be his home away from home. At least until the cast and crew arrived and the movie began shooting. Moody lusted after Jinx, felt an aching need to be around her. She no longer spoke to him and moved away whenever he came near her. Moody knew that Peaches was behind this; Peaches with her burning, possessive gaze. He fantasized wooing Jinx away from Peaches and bringing her to New York. He would introduce her to his mother, Marian. Jinx was a made-up name; all the girls had names like that. *Jinx, Zsa Zsa, Melody, Boots.* Sweet and ironic, like the girls themselves. Marian Moody would enjoy Jinx's company. She had endured poverty, war, and years of marriage to a liar and cheat. She could love and accept anyone and anything. She certainly loved and accepted her only child. Moody imagined his mother escorting Jinx to the Museum of Natural History, his favorite haunt as a kid. Jinx and Marian would go to Mass at St. Patrick's Cathedral. Marian was a lapsed Catholic, but she loved the spectacle of High Mass and savored the sacred mysteries of Latin. Jinx would probably be baffled and enchanted by his mother. Inevitably, the grandeur and filth of New York would make her homesick for Manila; she would flee. Moody sometimes fantasized a rosy ending to his sordid, unrequited romance— marriage, bouncing halfbreed babies, the whole bit. But the reality of Peaches, the reality of Lori and his son back in Los Angeles always sobered him up.

Moody didn't care if the movie was ever made at all. Days crawled by at a pace where nothing seemed to matter. The regulars—hard-eyed men who conducted their business discreetly—considered Moody a curious fool but soon grew bored with him and let him be. From Bong, Moody learned to swear in Tagalog and say *"putang ina."* Things were absurdly cheap. Some days on the black market, it was fourteen pesos to the dollar. Moody felt like a rich man. His friendship with Bong gave him access to what he needed and desired—things he'd never even dreamed of. There were places in the city Bong took him to, at night. Places hidden behind the staid monuments and the five-star hotels on the seafront boulevard. Ziggy, a devoted family man, always refused their invitations to come along on these nocturnal expeditions.

The places Bong and Moody frequented were not easy to find. There were no landmark signs, no streetlights, no numbers on the shacks and lean-tos made of broken planks and corrugated tin. Muddy passageways led to subterranean worlds, concrete bunkers guarded by men with guns. Ghostly men and women lurked in the shadows, ready to be summoned, willing to do anything. For the right price, orgiastic spectacles and private shows could be arranged. Cane liquor was sold, along with rum and beer, spicy things to eat. The places catering to rich people and foreigners offered even more sumptuous delicacies. Imported Scotch. Spanish brandy. Heroin from Pakistan via Thailand, cocaine from Bolivia via Amsterdam, opium from China via Spain. The marijuana was homegrown and powerful, smelling of dirt.

On Moody's twenty-sixth birthday, Bong promised a unique celebration. "Something you will never forget," Bong said. First they rode a taxi, then walked on unlit, unpaved roads for what seemed like miles. "I don't like this," Moody complained, suddenly paranoid. Bong shushed him into silence. Moody wondered if this was the night Bong would decide to murder him. Over some imagined slight, or maybe for his money. Or to become famous. "Where the fuck are we going?" Moody asked. Bong chuckled. The only light came from the burning tip of his cigarette. Moody looked over his shoulder to make sure they weren't being stalked by bandits or zealous military cops. Mosquitoes feasted on his face and bare arms. They hurried past several squatters' shacks before they came to a field of cogon grass. A crowd of men was gathered; some held flashlights. A middle-aged woman with bleached-blond hair down to her ass walked up to them, gnawing on an ear of roasted corn. She scrutinized Moody while exchanging friendly words with Bong in Tagalog. *Kumusta, Bong? Sino iyan?*

"My friend," Bong boasted in Tagalog. "He's a movie star."

The woman pointed the ear of corn at Moody and spoke in English. "You know me? I am famous, too." She went back to chewing her corn and walked away.

"Her name is Rapunzel," Bong said.

A bar was set up in the field. Portable coolers overflowed with bottles of beer and rum. A kerosene lamp emitted soft, dim light. The men stood around in a loose circle, smoking and drinking, waiting for something. Bong and Moody waited with them. "What's happening?" Moody whispered anxiously to Bong. "What are we waiting for?"

Bong put a finger to his lips.

A boy of twelve and a girl about seven years old emerged out of the thick darkness, shooed into the middle of the circle by Rapunzel. She stood aside, gnawing idly on a fresh ear of corn, as the boy unceremoniously pulled down his pants. He began jacking off. "Wait a minute," Moody said, a little too loudly. The boy froze, his tiny penis lost in his hand.

"Wha's da problem?" Rapunzel asked Moody, waving the ear of corn in his face.

She signaled with a nod of her head. The boy began to jack off again.

"Fuck this," Moody said. He wanted to run, but instead he started walking away, as far from the center of the open field as possible. He had no idea where he was or where he was going.

"Hey, you! *Amerikano!*" Moody heard the woman's distant taunting, her jeering laugh. Moody turned and saw Bong, out of breath, trying to catch up with him.

"You can stay back there if you want," Moody said.

"You almost got us killed," Bong said.

They continued walking in angry silence. It was almost sunrise. Even the squatters' shacks along the banks of the brackish river were bathed in a luminous glow.

"Don't ever take me to see shit like that again," Moody said.

"Never bother you before."

"Bothers me now."

"Why? You got children?"

"Yeah. You?"

"I got plenty children. And those children you saw—"

"Yeah?"

"Rapunzel pay them good. And when she pay them good, they eat."

Moody gave Bong a hard, searching look. "Were they your children?"

Bong's tone was contemptuous. "They nobody's children, man."

Back on Mabini Street, the men parted ways. Moody headed in the direction of the *pensión*, while Bong crossed the street and kept walking. Moody realized that after all these weeks, he had never bothered to ask Bong where he and Melvie lived. Resisting the impulse to run after his friend and attempt some form of reconciliation, Moody unlatched the gate to the *pensión*'s small front yard instead. He climbed up the stairs to his room, each step heavier than the last. He felt dirty and tired. Moody fell across the bed and shut his eyes. Images, sounds, and sensations kept coming back to him. The drone of cicadas, the sharp blades of cogon grass brushing against his skin, Rapunzel's derisive laugh, the forlorn children poised in the middle of the field, ready to perform.

It was a slow night at the Love Connection. His pride wounded, Bong now purposely stayed away from the bar and Moody. It had been a week since the encounter with Rapunzel. Moody realized how much he missed Bong and how much their uneasy friendship actually mattered to him. He watched Jinx and the other girls dance listlessly to Fleetwood Mac. Naked except for high heels, pasties, and fringed G-strings, the girls pranced and posed, impassive. Moody locked eyes with Jinx, then looked away. The phone on the counter started ringing. Peaches grunted into the receiver, looked surprised, then handed Moody the phone.

"Person-to-person from L.A., *daw*."

Moody was annoyed. "Is this some kind of joke?"

"I don't think so, Pretty Boy."

Moody took the phone and heard Ross on the other end, practically frothing at the mouth. "Goddamn it, Vince—what the fuck are you doing in Manila? You were supposed to be in rehearsals in L.A. ! This is *suicide* for you and your career—which, by the way, as you may already know, is going nowhere fast!"

"How did you find me?"

"You can run, but you can't hide, " Ross snapped. "You know I have my ways. My reliable underground network of moles and clandestine informants."

Moody chuckled. "God, it's good to hear your voice. How are ya, Ross?"

"We all thought you were dead. Pierce is shitting bricks. Thinks he may have made a mistake by casting you."

"Fix it. Tell him how dedicated I am. I got here early to do my research. Even paid for my own ticket."

Ross groaned. "Lori came by the office looking for you. Had the kid with her. Not nice, Vincent."

"What? I can't hear you."

"Fuck, I know you can hear me fine! How could you leave them like that? She's pretty pissed off. Wants to sue your ass—"

"She should. She can have it all. She deserves it all. The car. The dog. The house—"

"Lori doesn't want your house. Hates it, apparently. She took the dog and the car and is staying with Alex temporarily at her folks' place."

"That's good," Moody said. "Good for my boy."

Ross was silent for a moment. "Hey, Vince. Guess what? They caught that Son of Sam guy in New York."

"No shit."

"And guess who died today?"

"Nixon."

"It hasn't even hit the papers yet."

"Ross, I'm running low on cash."

"I'll wire you some money. And if you promise to act like a good boy and nail this part like I know you are perfectly capable of doing, you don't even have to pay me back. Now, don't you have the slightest bit of curiosity about who just died?"

"Okay, okay. Who the fuck died in your time zone, Ross?"

His agent's voice was solemn. "Elvis Presley."

Moody burst out laughing. "Did he choke on a peanut-butter sandwich?"

Ross sounded genuinely offended. "Presley might've been a sorry fat fuck in the end, but I don't think death is really that funny, Vince."

"Well, I do."

Moody hung up the phone. A few minutes passed. The phone rang again. Moody shook his head as Peaches reached over to answer it. The phone stopped ringing. Jinx stepped off the tiny stage.

"You wanna buy me a drink?" she asked Moody.

"Jinx don't drink," Peaches said.

"Yes Jinx do!" Jinx retorted, giggling.

"*Landi! Puta ka, talaga!*" Peaches yelled in a fury.

Their bickering continued in several languages and dialects. On the sound system, Stevie Wonder crooned "Superwoman." The Love Connection felt like a sad party waiting to happen. The nostalgia was getting to him. Moody gulped down a double shot of Flor de Manila. He shouldn't have hung up like that on Ross. But surely, Ross would call again. Maybe even show up in Manila waving contracts and revised scripts. He was that kind of agent, fond of the grand gesture—pushy and thick skinned, loyal to Moody in spite of everything. Good ol' Ross. Moody chided himself for not asking if the movie had a title yet. Oh, well. Titles were the least of it. He needed another drink. He could feel the eyes of the beautiful Jinx from across the room—questioning, imploring. Fuck Tony Pierce and box-office disasters waiting to happen. Moody tapped his empty shot glass on the counter. Peaches glanced his way, irritated. She and Jinx huddled in a corner, arguing softly. Jinx was in tears. He tapped his glass again. Peaches took her time coming over to pour him another drink.

"Everything okay, Peach?"

"Everything always okay with me, Pretty Boy. As long as you leave my girl alone. Maybe you need to go away for a little while, like Bong."

"I like it here, Peach."

"You act right, then. Respect me. You know about respect, Pretty Boy?"

"You bet."

"You a drunk sonuvagun. I don't like drunk sonuvaguns."

Moody held out his empty glass.

Peaches shook her head. "Who call you just now?"

"My agent."

"This goddamn movie ever gonna happen?"

"Who the fuck knows?" Moody chuckled. "Guess who just died?"

"Who?"

"Elvis."

"*Presley?*"

Moody tried not to slur his words. "You're a big fan, right?"

"No."

"But what about that hairdo, Peach? It's very Elvis."

"Just a hairdo, Pretty Boy. Just a hairdo."

Paz Marlowe

1st person woman

My older brother, Ricky, called to say our mother's condition was deteriorating rapidly.

"Take the next flight out or else."

"Or else what?"

"You should be here," he said, his voice flat. He hated being the messenger of any kind of news, especially bad. Bad meant that he would be forced to deal with people up close, in those clammy, messy, teary situations he'd dreaded since the day he was born. Messenger was the role my father, Enrique, expected him to play, and my thirty-two-year-old brother never said no to him. My father, like all the men in my family, was a master of passing the emotional buck. It wouldn't surprise me if Ricky just snapped one day and shot him dead.

All that pent-up rage.

"Okay," I said to him, "I'll get there as soon as I can. I was coming anyway. I got a writing assignment."

Ricky was silent, so I went on. "Ever heard of *Groove Rocket?*"

He was still silent. "It's primarily a music magazine," I explained. "But they also do pop-culture stuff. I pitched them a story on Zamora and the Taobo tribe. There's an investigation going on about some kind of hoax—"

"Yeah, I know." Ricky snorted in disdain. "I don't think Zamora's doing any more interviews these days."

"Yeah, but I thought that since our families knew each other, he might make an exception."

"Just get here as soon as you can," Ricky said. He hung up without saying good-bye.

I had no idea how I was supposed to pay for this trip. I didn't have enough cash for a round-trip ticket and no credit cards to my name. My freebasing, soon-to-be-ex-husband had emptied our joint account and run off to Belize with a Playboy Bunny named Desiree.

I bit my lip and called Ricky right back, person-to-person collect, to borrow money.

My brother, a lawyer whose wife owned a string of popular seafood restaurants, was *not* pleased.

"I thought you were working for that *Rocket* magazine."

"The magazine's brand-new and without resources," I said. "I'm working on spec."

Ricky sighed. "You mean, for free."

"Not exactly."

"Doesn't whatever-his-name-is have any money?"

"Well," I said, feeling more humiliated than ever, "he ran away with all of it . . . and a Playboy Bunny."

"*Coño*," Ricky muttered. "You never should've married that foreigner, Paz. Want me to find him for you and teach him a lesson?"

I laughed. "The fucker's not worth it. Just loan me money for the plane ticket, okay? I'll pay you back, Ricky. Promise."

"Do you mind not calling me Ricky? The name's Enrique. You can call me Rick."

"Sure," I said, "Enrique."

The plane landed at exactly 7:38 in the morning, Manila time. *Where's Papa? Where's Ricky?*

Mrs. Locsin, my father's secretary, was the only one there to meet me. "We have to hurry back to the hospital," she said, steering me through a maze of customs agents and inspectors. *Passport, passport. Show them your passport.*

"Is Mama dead?"

"Show your passport," Mrs. Locsin repeated, even louder.

The agent scrutinized my U.S. passport carefully, then my face. "You are Pilipina?"

"Yup."

Mrs. Locsin pursed her lips in haughty disapproval. *"Bakit? May problema ba?* Your supervisor, Mrs. Gómez, is my cousin."

The agent handed my passport back to me with a melancholy smile. "No problem, miss. Welcome home."

"Paz." My father stood in the doorway of my mother's room in the intensive-care unit of San Juan de Dios Hospital, the same hospital where Ricky and I had been born. I didn't recognize Papa at first. I'd been gone for seven years, since I married Stefan and moved to L.A. The change in my father was profound. His head of thick, wavy, black hair had thinned and gone completely gray. His posture was stooped and defeated, and he had lost a lot of weight. I threw my arms around his neck, smelled the familiar whiff of aftershave and cigars. The sound of a woman softly sobbing came from inside the room. Probably Chari, my brother's wife.

"I'm sorry, Paz," Papa said. "But she's gone."

Mrs. Locsin held on to my arm. She anticipated some sort of dramatic reaction from me, like a fainting spell or something.

"What?"

"Your mother passed away at exactly 7:38 A.M.," Papa said.

"Ay naku!" Mrs. Locsin moaned.

The louder Chari and Mrs. Locsin wailed, the more the feeling of helplessness mounted up inside me. My brother was stoic, as usual. He sat by my mother's empty bed, staring at the mattress that had already been stripped of its sheets as if he were waiting for a sign. Everything in the room was beige—the walls, the metal bed, the TV set, the air conditioner. I put a hand on Ricky's shoulder to comfort him, but he stiffened and pulled away. I began to weep. They all stared at me: my father, my brother, Chari, Mrs. Locsin. My sobs turned into words. *Where's her body, damn it? Where's Mama?*

My mother's memorial Mass was held in San Agustín Church. A huge crowd of mourners—my mother's friends, family, her collectors, doctors, and nurses—came to pay their respects. I found myself sitting between my childhood friend, Pepito Ponce de León, and Ruby, my father's mistress.

"Your mother was such a good woman," Ruby whispered. "I hope you don't mind my saying so, Paz. She was fair to me, fair to your father."

I turned away, wishing I had sat somewhere else.

"Are you all right? You look a little—" Ruby hesitated. "Maybe it's jet lag."

"I'm fine," I said, unable to look her in the eye and show her how much I detested her. "Thank you."

Ruby didn't know when to stop. "*Dios mío,* how can you sit here so calmly, with your poor mother dead and gone! She suffered so—"

"Ruby, please. I want to hear what the fucking priest is saying," I hissed. Pepito and I exchanged glances.

"Wanna get some air?" Pepito asked in a low voice.

The priest droned on, spouting platitudes. How well had he known my mother? I caught a glimpse of my father weeping quietly in the front row. Ricky had his arm around him. "Let us not grieve, but let us celebrate the remarkable life of the artist, wife, and loving mother, Pilar de los Santos Marlowe. . . ."

Pepito mumbled "excuse, excuse" as we made our way through the crowd and out the doors of the magnificent old church. My mother's favorite place of worship. So much history, Paz, she used to marvel. So much history! The humid courtyard smelled of stone and algae. Pepito offered me his pack of Gauloises. We smoked in silence for a brief moment.

"I'm glad you're back," Pepito said. "It's been too long."

"I want to scream," I said.

"Go ahead," Pepito said with a sympathetic smile. The service was interminable. We hovered by the doorway, watching everyone line up for Holy Communion. My father, Ruby, Mrs. Locsin. Ricky and his family. They all knelt before the altar, squeezing their eyes shut and sticking their tongues out in anticipation. "Aren't you going to receive the sacrament?" Pepito asked.

"I haven't been to church in years," I replied. "What about you?" Pepito rolled his eyes. We watched the priest place flat white wafers on each person's tongue, careful not to let his fingers make contact. I remembered the familiar bread taste, the thin hardness of the Communion wafer. The first time I had dared to take a bite was when I was eight years old. I then waited for God personally to step down from His throne in heaven and punish me for committing sacrilege. *Dominus vobiscum, et cum spiritu tuo.*

"Look who's here," Pepito muttered through clenched teeth. He cocked his head in the direction of a short, scruffy man who sat alone in a back pew—a stiff, erect figure whom everyone, except for Pepito and me, took great pains to ignore. I immediately recognized Zamora López de Legazpi.

"They say his great-great-great-great-great-great-grandfather is buried right here in this church," Pepito said.

"Conquistador of conquistadors," I murmured.

Two weeks later I found myself sitting on a terrace overlooking the lush gardens of Casas Blancas, attempting to interview Zamora López de Legazpi. He stared off into space and chain-smoked Salems, looking bored and impatient. We had played cat-and-mouse games for the past two weeks—my initial request for an interview having been declined by a polite but firm man who answered the phone.

"Sorry, miss. Mr. Legazpi is, uh, not doing any more press."

"But this is different. Tell him that—"

"He is away."

"Is he in Mindanao? When is he coming back?"

"It's very hard to say, miss."

"Who am I speaking to?"

"Sonny Limahan."

I kept bugging Sonny anyway, calling daily and leaving messages. It was almost fun. "Sonny," I'd say, "guess what? It's me again."

"Yes, Miss Marlowe. How are you today?" Sonny never lost his patience with me. His tone remained polite and deferential.

"Is he there? Have you heard from him?"

"Sorry, miss."

When I finally decided to give up and get on the next plane back to Los Angeles, Sonny surprised me by showing up at my father's house. He was a tall, brawny man. The Mercedes he stepped out of seemed too small for him.

"Miss Marlowe, Boss says he can see you now. I will take you to him."

"What? But I—"

"Now or never, miss."

Casas Blancas, Hollywood Hills, Metro Manila. A grand pair of evil-looking macaws was chained to a perch nearby. A diminutive female servant came and went, bearing trays of drinks and sweets. Zamora called her Sputnik. I repeated my question: "What do you think about the allegations that your discovery of the Taobo was nothing but a hoax?"

Zamora sipped Coke through a straw. Smiled a little. I waited, then asked him another question: "Are you planning to attend the symposium on the Taobo controversy that will be held at the University of Hawaii in October? The organizers have invited some of your former colleagues to speak." He refused to meet my gaze. I sat frozen in my chair, wondering why he had bothered to see me.

"I was not invited," Zamora López de Legazpi said.

More silence. "Would you rather I leave, Mr. Legazpi?" I finally asked.

"Of course not. I said I would do this, didn't I?"

"But you haven't dealt with any of my questions."

"I know your family well."

"Is that why you agreed to this meeting? To be polite?"

"You are quite blunt. Very much your mother's daughter," he said. He became agitated. "But I must tell you I think this whole thing's pointless. There's nothing new you can say about me or the Taobo. The world is sick of us."

"I don't believe that. The symposium—"

"Fuck the symposium. How do you like living in the States?" Zamora suddenly asked. It was the first time he actually looked at me. "I spent a lot of time there."

I had read all the articles about him, of course. "You mean when you were a student at Yale?"

Zamora chuckled. "Ask me another question, Paz."

A high-pitched, warbling sound broke the heavy stillness, rousing the blue-and-red macaws from their stupor. A lithe teenage boy loped across the lawn toward us. He was barefoot and wore baggy shorts. He whistled and whooped, causing the macaws to flap their massive, clipped wings in impotent fury. The birds screeched at him, bobbing and weaving on their perch, lifting their talons and clawing at the air in response. The boy's smile was blinding. A red hibiscus behind his ear enhanced the deep mahogany brown of his skin. Was it a setup—the boy an actor or dancer hired by Zamora to play noble, beautiful savage for my benefit? As he came closer, I recognized him from the *National Geographic* articles on the Taobo. My heart jumped.

"Bodabil," Zamora called out in English, "come meet Miss Marlowe."

Bodabil waved at me but kept running. He disappeared from view behind a grove of bamboo.

"I guess Bodabil's not in the mood today," Zamora said.

"He understands English?"

"I've been sending him to school. He's highly intelligent, eager and curious. What he doesn't understand, he figures out by the tone of my voice. Sometimes I talk with my face or hands. He definitely understands that."

"I thought you sent him back to the forest long ago."

"I did. But then he wanted to come back here, to me." Zamora scratched the tip of his nose lightly with his finger. "My children consider Bodabil their adopted brother. Did you know that? You should see them together."

"Where are your children?"

"Away at boarding school," Zamora answered.

My tape recorder was running. I scribbled everything down in a notebook anyway, in the shorthand I had devised for myself. Maybe there was a story after all. The birds gurgled as they settled back down into their grouchy stupor.

"Manila must be so strange for Bodabil," I said.

"Of course it is. But he's used to it, by now. What is it you want to know, exactly?" Zamora asked, hostile again. "Are you here to expose me, like all the others?"

I decided to be honest. "I'm not sure."

"You're wasting your time," Zamora said.

"That was kind of you, to attend my mother's funeral Mass," I said, after a pause.

Zamora was surprised. "How did you know I was there?"

"My friend pointed you out."

"One of your mother's paintings is in my collection," he said.

"I'd love to see it."

"Sonny will show you. On your way out."

"Is that a hint?"

"I really have nothing more to say. I knew your mother and admired her, Paz. You were right. That's the only reason I agreed to see you. I don't do interviews."

"You used to. There were so many articles. I watched that documentary about you on American TV."

Zamora grimaced. "*Pero no más.*"

I pressed on, hoping for some sort of revelation. "Were the Taobo nothing more than members of the Himal tribe, made to look primitive and coached by you and your staff to speak gibberish?"

"Of course not!" Zamora's eyes flashed with anger. He was no longer indifferent. "I know what you want. You want proof. You want permission to visit the caves. To see for yourself. But it's too late, Paz. You met your one authentic Taobo when you met Bodabil. The most famous and photogenic of them all. You're lucky. Not many people have been as fortunate. Relatively painless and easy, wasn't it? No difficult trek up into the mountains, no hostile insurgents or military, no bloodsucking leeches and malarial mosquitoes. You can still write your story." He stood up and held out his hand. My first impulse was to refuse it, but I didn't. Zamora had made a fool of me. "Sonny will take you home. He'll show you my collection on the way out, if you like. I think you'll enjoy it. There are two Amorsolos and a Luna. One tiny Gauguin."

Sonny Limahan waited in the hallway, his broad, handsome Malay face a genial mask. I'd heard from Pepito that Sonny was the only man Zamora trusted, a combination confidant, bodyguard, and drinking buddy—although from what I'd also heard, Sonny didn't drink.

"Boss said to show you the paintings before I take you home, miss."

"Thank you."

He unlocked the door into a huge, stuffy room. It was clear no one had been in there for a long time. "Used to be Señora Ilse's favorite room," Sonny blurted out.

"Where is she now?" I dared to ask him.

Sonny, aware of his indiscretion, frowned and said nothing. He turned on a light switch. We were surrounded by paintings. Some leaned against a wall, others were hung haphazardly—without regard to style or subject. I felt like I had walked into some crazy person's private museum. The tiny Gauguin was actually a charcoal study of a bare-breasted, bored-looking Tahitian woman holding a mango in one hand. Next to it hung Mama's 4-by-4-foot oil painting of a fighting rooster and an old man. Her deft imitation of an Amorsolo painting. I remember how she had once dismissed her early work as her "soft Amorsolo period."

"That's my mother's," I couldn't help saying to Sonny.

"Yes, I know. Very nice, miss," Sonny murmured kindly.

My attention was caught by a huge painting that took up most of one wall. On a beach, Spanish soldiers decked out in medieval armor were gathered next to a group of wary-looking natives with faces like Sonny's. A balding Spanish priest offered up a chalice to the sky. The smell of blood and betrayal was in the air. Or so I imagined.

"Is that an Amorsolo?" I asked.

Sonny beamed with pride. "Yes, miss. *Galing, ano?* Boss is thinking of donating it to the Manila Metropolitan Museum."

He navigated the Mercedes through traffic-clogged streets while I slumped in the backseat, my brain roiling with questions. Was this story worth it? Zamora had humored me, but now what? At a red light a gaunt young woman dashed up to my window. A dirty towel lay draped across her head. She was a solemn Madonna, cradling a listless infant wrapped in rags. As I dug into my bag for money, the light suddenly changed. The Madonna darted back to the safety of the traffic median, hugging the limp baby close to her chest. Sonny kept driving.

The Love Connection

1st person Moody

My father, Joseph Vincent Moody, was killed in a car accident the year I turned ten. He was a charming, irresponsible man who had blown most of my mother's inheritance on bad investments and younger women. Eight months before he died, my mother, Marian, decided she'd had enough and kicked him out of our West Village apartment. I never saw my father again.

I was an only child. Anxious, overweight, prone to bad dreams. I worshipped my father. Blindly, as my mother once observed with a tinge of bitterness. I told myself I didn't, couldn't hate her for throwing him out. I was ten years old, a precocious actor. Skilled at appearing brave and nonchalant. I sleepwalked through most of my classes at the Manhattan School for the Performing Arts. On the way home, I'd stuff myself with all things salty, gooey, and soothing. *Potato chips, pizza slices, ice-cream sandwiches.* I turned into a cuddly teddy bear, a fat little pretty boy with a wounded look on his face. Endearing for a kid actor, so I kept getting work. My mother grew thin, too sad to be alarmed by anything I did or did not do. I never spoke of my father's absence to her or to anyone else.

No one knows exactly where my father was headed on the night he died. The accident occurred on a desolate stretch of highway leading to Taos, New Mexico. I've pieced together bits of information from the folder of yellowed newspaper clippings my mother gave me on my sixteenth birthday. "Here you go, Vincent," she

truth by writing

chirped. *Here I go.* Apparently, Papa was speeding. It had started to
rain; the road was probably slippery. He crashed his Lincoln Conti-
nental into a battered pickup truck driven by a pregnant Mexican
woman named Angelita Chávez. Her five-year-old twins, Circe and
Cielo, were riding with her. Angelita and her children flew right
through the windshield and landed in a ditch.

Everyone died. My father was decapitated.

My mother and I moved uptown to one of those gloomy prewar
buildings on Central Park West and hid from the world. I stopped
eating. Our incessant visits to the Museum of Natural History,
which Mama referred to as the "Mausoleum of Dead Animals and
Looted Things," provided us with respite from our self-imposed
isolation. The low lights and musty grandeur suited us fine. We
wandered from floor to floor in a fog of grief and devastation, mar-
veling at the eerie, kitschy dioramas, barely able to speak. Birds of
the World. Hall of Gems and Minerals. Hall of Asian Peoples. Hall
of African Mammals. Hall of Meteorites.

What I can't forget: the closed coffin at my father's wake. How I
didn't, couldn't weep. My mother was stoic, though I saw the tears
well up in the corners of her eyes. They never fell, though. Mama
was tough, just like Jinx was tough. Dancing onstage at the go-go
bar in Manila, Jinx moved in resistance to the funky, pulsating music. She took cautious steps in those high-heeled, fuck-me slip-ons
they all wore, like she was afraid her ankles would give out and she'd
fall. Pasties on her tiny breasts, G-string stretched across her bony
hips, Jinx exuded the blank-faced glow of a saint. When I told her I
was in love with her, she laughed and called me stupid.

"Why you act so hard all the time?" I asked her.

"Why you ask so many questions, Pretty Boy? *Sigé, naman.* Buy
Jinx champagne—only da best for da best, *di ba?*"

Peaches took care of Jinx. From Peaches I learned that Jinx had
a kid somewhere, that before her job at the Love Connection, she'd

been dancing and turning tricks at an even worse place down the street.

"Jinx a baby with a baby. Too young for you," Peaches said.

"Then what's she doing dancing half naked at your place?" I asked.

"Even babies got to earn a living."

"She's . . . what? Fourteen or fifteen years old? I could have you arrested."

Peaches burst out laughing. "By who? Marcos secret police? You think they care about poor girls like her?"

"No."

"You better believe it, Pretty Boy."

But of course I couldn't, wouldn't leave Jinx alone. Early one night I simply stood outside the bar and waited for her to show up for work. Danny, the old peddler who hung out by the curb, kept trying to sell me things. Cigarettes, Bic lighters, Chiclets, glow-in-the-dark yo-yos made in Taiwan. Jinx was late; Jinx was always late. I spotted her sashaying across the street with her buddy, Zsa Zsa. Their arms were linked; they seemed confident of the power of their beauty. Zsa Zsa saw me first and nudged Jinx with her elbow. "You waiting for us?" Jinx's tone was a challenge.

"Actually, I wanted to talk to you about something."

Jinx murmured in Tagalog to Zsa Zsa, who snickered and went inside the bar. Jinx turned to me. "Okay . . . what you want to talk about?"

"Let's go somewhere."

"What?" Jinx clasped a hand over her mouth, trying not to laugh. Her fingernails were bitten, unpainted.

"I want to get to know you, that's all," I blithered. Scared, not wanting to scare her off. "We don't have to do *anything*. We can just talk. Maybe go to a movie. Wanna go to a movie? Whatever you want."

Jinx smiled. "You wanna die?"

"No."

"Then stop bothering me. Or else Peaches gonna shoot you."

A prosperous-looking Chinese man and his two beautifully dressed children stepped out of a chauffeur-driven sedan. Danny began demonstrating one of his glow-in-the-dark yo-yos. "Made in Taiwan! Lifetime guarantee!" The children were sullen and unresponsive, but their father bought each of them a yo-yo anyway. He led them away to a fancy seafood restaurant a couple of doors down the block.

"Please," I begged Jinx. I wanted to say, I am drawn to you, for some strange reason. Fucking intoxicated by your smell. Dear fucking God. Dear fucking Jesus.

"Later," Jinx said.

"Later?" I didn't think she'd suddenly be so agreeable. I was in a mild state of shock.

"I'll act sick and tell Peaches I need to go home early. Meet me at the Hobbit around midnight." She paused. "You know the Hobbit?"

I nodded. She hurried past me and disappeared into the Love Connection. Take it or leave it. Tonight or nothing. I wondered how many times in the past she'd betrayed Peaches. I didn't know why she decided to risk everything and meet me. Maybe she suffered from some sort of suicidal streak—or maybe she thought I was her only ticket out. *Oh, baby, I am. Your ticket out.* I thought this deluded shit as Marvin Gaye's "Got to Give It Up" drifted out into the street. Sex music. Had she already stripped down to her pasties and G-string, slipped on her high heels, started dancing?

"You got Stateside Marlboros?" I asked Danny.

"Stateside, local . . . ebree-ting, boss."

I bought a pack of blue-seal Marlboros, a Bic lighter, one glow-in-the-dark yo-yo. Love offerings.

The Hobbit House was a popular club with a gimmick—the waiters were dwarfs. Cheerful, helpful, gracious male and female dwarfs. I got there around twelve-fifteen. "Welcome, sir," the head dwarf greeted me. His handsome face and shag haircut reminded me of Ziggy. The club was steeped in darkness, which I was thankful for. No one recognized me at first. "Psst," the head dwarf hissed to another dwarf, this one a waiter who was much older and not so handsome. He waddled over and gestured for me to follow him to a table directly in front of the stage. A spotlight shone on a Filipino man who strummed a guitar and wailed "Blowin' in the Wind." It was weird, but he sounded just like Dylan.

"Can you gimme something more private?" I asked the waiter, who gave me a puzzled look. "Something in the back of the room." He guided me to a corner table with a perfect view of the door. "Perfect," I said. I tried slipping him a tip, but he waved it away with a shy smile. I waited and waited, nursing my San Miguel, wondering if I'd been made a fool. The Hobbit House attracted tourists and antigovernment, hippie student types—a crowd that was an odd mix of the gentle, the earnest, and the curious. A young woman and man sitting nearby stared at me. They looked vaguely Spanish or Italian. The man's long, bushy hair was tied back in a ponytail. He wore eyeglasses and sported a goatee. The woman's hair was long and straight. Silver hoops dangled from her wrists and ears. Were they tourists or mestizo locals? They looked too at ease to be foreigners. The man scribbled something on a napkin and asked a waiter to bring it to me. The note read

Are you Vincent Moody?

If I nodded, would that give them permission to pester me? If I shook my head and acted as if they were mistaken, would that piss them off and cause a scene? I decided to do nothing. After conferring with the man, the woman boldly sauntered over. "Excuse me," she said, "I apologize for bothering you, but . . . you are who we think you are, right?" Her English was clear, unaccented.

"I'm afraid so."

"I made a bet with my friend. He's a filmmaker, you know."

"Uh-huh." Uh-oh.

"You were on my flight coming here," the woman said. "Are you going to be in that Vietnam movie?"

"What're you? A CIA agent?" She wasn't bad looking. I glanced at the door. No sign of Jinx.

"Everybody knows. All the filmmakers in Manila are talking about it," she said with a smile. "Do you mind giving my friend your autograph? He's too shy to ask you himself."

I signed the napkin. "Thanks," she said. "Sorry if we bothered you." She started walking away.

"Hey," I said. "You know my name, but I don't know yours."

"Paz. Paz Marlowe." She nodded toward the man at her table. "And that's my friend, Pepito. Pepito Ponce de León."

We had caused a scene. People turned their heads to gawk at me. It was time to leave. I got up from the table and noticed Jinx lurking in the doorway of the Hobbit House. I walked over and took her hand. "I thought you'd never show up." She extricated herself from my clammy grasp but didn't run.

"Are you drunk again, Pretty Boy?" Her gaze met mine. Wary and hostile. I wondered why she'd agreed to meet me at all.

"I am not drunk."

Her voice dropped to a whisper. "Jinx wants to get out of here, Vincent."

"Groovy," I said. "Groovy, groovy."

Here, I said. Handing her the cigarettes, the lighter, and the yo-yo. Surprising her. Making her laugh, for real. She lit a Marlboro, threw everything else into her bag. Took my arm. A few more heads turned. I'm sure we made quite a pair: the depraved foreigner with his underage *puta*. We fled into the streets. Children with beseeching, woeful expressions swarmed all over us. I couldn't stand it anymore and reached into my pocket, but Jinx shook her head and tried to shoo them away. An older boy made obscene gestures at her. Jinx gave him the finger. The children scurried away, yelling *"Puta!"* at her. "*Putang ina kayong lahat!*" Jinx yelled back. A light rain fell, cooling down the steamy streets. Jinx was preoccupied and upset. I wanted to put my arm around her shoulders to comfort her, but I knew better. "You wanna duck into Rosie's and have a bite to eat?" Rosie's Rendezvous was a popular hangout in the neighborhood—a haven for off-duty cops, whores, drag queens, and the drunken after-disco crowd. The food was ghastly, but nobody went there for the food.

Jinx hesitated, then shook her head again. "Rosie is Peaches' friend. If Rosie sees Jinx with you—"

"Did you tell Peaches you were sick?"

Jinx shrugged. "*Bahala na* what Jinx told her. *Basta*, Peaches believes whatever Jinx says." *Bahala na* seemed to be everyone's favorite fatalistic saying, quaintly and absurdly translated in my *Tagalog for Tourists* handbook as "leaving it up to Lady Luck."

I found Jinx's habit of talking about herself in the third person disconcerting, but I quickly got used to it. "You'll take Jinx to your place?" she asked me.

"If you like." I wondered how I was going to get her past Mrs. Dava. Lightning flashed across the sky. The rain came down harder, soaking through our clothes. In the dimly lit foyer, Mrs. Dava sat behind the reception desk, absorbed in her beloved movie magazines. She glanced up as we entered. "*Naku!* Mr. Vincent, your shoes!" Dismayed, she shouted for the houseboy. "Tikoy!"

I looked down at the mud tracks on the floor. Tikoy appeared, sleepily rubbing his eyes. "Take their shoes and clean them," Mrs. Dava ordered. She scrutinized Jinx coolly, then me. "How are you, Mr. Vincent?"

"Never been better." I untied my sneakers and handed them to Tikoy. Pursing her lips in disapproval, Mrs. Dava watched as I knelt to take off Jinx's ruined sandals, something Jinx could've easily done for herself. Jinx stood in a trance, shivering.

"We don't want mud inside," Mrs. Dava said.

"Of course not." I took Jinx by the elbow and started up the stairs toward my room.

Mrs. Dava's grating voice stopped me. "Uh, uh, uh, Mr. Vincent. You know the rules. Absolutely no visitors after 10 P.M."

"You've never enforced those rules before."

Mrs. Dava was not amused. "Mr. Vincent. *Puwede ba.*"

"She's a relative."

"Is that so? You think me a fool, Mr. Vincent?"

"Never, Mrs. Dava."

"My son Ziggy has told you. I run a respectable *pensión*—"

"I'm aware of that, Mrs. Dava."

"Are you?"

A moment of tense silence passed between us. Tikoy emerged from the kitchen, triumphant. He held up our now spotless shoes. I thanked him and handed him all the change in my pocket, the sorry equivalent of about ten pesos.

"That's way too much." Mrs. Dava made clicking sounds with her tongue against her teeth. "You're going to spoil him."

Once again I started up the stairs with Jinx.

"Just remember your room is billed as a single," Mrs. Dava said.

I groaned, worn down by all the endless negotiating that seemed to be going on—a dance of ambivalence between Jinx and myself, between myself and myself, and now with my bull-necked landlady. "I'm thrilled to pay extra for the inconvenience, ma'am. Now, if you don't mind, my cousin seems to have the chills."

Mrs. Dava gave me one last withering glance, then went back to her movie magazines.

I undressed Jinx and wrapped her in the threadbare chenille bedspread. My unmade cot was actually an old hospital bed, one of many that Mrs. Dava had salvaged from a recently closed-down TB sanatorium. My room was just big enough to turn around in, with a night table and one lamp. There were no closets. Everything I owned was scattered on the floor.

"Your room is *mabaho*," Jinx said, wrinking her nose in distaste. She fell back against the graying, sweat-stained pillow and shut her eyes. Embarrassed, I slid open the shutters to air out the room. The wind and rain blew in.

"I am cold," Jinx whimpered. I felt her forehead.

"You've got a fever," I said. "I'll go get some aspirin—"

"Jinx don't want you to go."

I hurried back downstairs. "Mrs. Dava, my cousin's got a high fever. Can you help me?"

Mrs. Dava kept her eyes on the movie magazine.

"Mrs. Dava, please."

"Tikoy!" Mrs. Dava shouted without looking at me. Tikoy stumbled out once again from behind the flowered curtain that separated the foyer from the kitchen. "Get Mr. Vincent some Cortal," Mrs. Dava said. Tikoy returned with a couple of white tablets and a plastic glass of cloudy water.

I thanked him profusely. "*Maraming salamat,* Tikoy."

"I'll have to charge you extra for the Cortal, Mr. Vincent," Mrs. Dava said.

"Of course," I said.

Jinx kept spitting up the white tablets until the Cortal disintegrated on her tongue and she could finally wash it down. I kissed her bitter aspirin mouth. She didn't resist. I wondered about Peaches and what she might do if and when she found out, though I knew there really was no "if" when it came to Peaches. She would definitely find out, sooner rather than later. I couldn't stop kissing Jinx, who weighed nothing in my arms. Her hair smelled of coconut oil. I licked the feverish hollow of her neck, then moved down slowly, tasting the sunken hollow of her small breasts. I buried my face in the stretch marks that creased and scarred the lower half of her belly. She stared at the moth-covered bulb on the ceiling. A tiny lizard darted across the wall behind our heads. I left the bed and pulled at the cord dangling from the lightbulb. The room plunged into darkness. In bed with her again, I slipped a hand between her legs. Rested it there and closed my eyes, pretending she was mine. Jinx pushed me away.

"Tell me about your child," I whispered.

"No."

"I have a son."

"So what?"

Desire made me sweat. I loathed myself yet couldn't stop—crawling on top of her, kissing and mauling every inch of her salty flesh. She lay there limply, making no move to escape. "Don't you know how much I love you, Jinx?"

The chenille bedspread fell to the floor. With a sigh of resignation, Jinx spread her legs farther apart. "Jinx don't care," she murmured. And neither did I. My brutal thrusts made her cry out. Then there was a terrible silence. I kept it up for as long as I could, fucking her in a joyless frenzy. I longed for her to make a sound, any sound at all. To surrender and utter the word "love." In English, in Tagalog, in Bisayan, in whatever goddamn language she chose to speak. The night engulfed us, deeper and blacker than anything I had ever known. I was on the verge of tears.

Snipes

Paz 1st pers. (handwritten)

No one answered the phone at Casas Blancas. The phone kept ringing—long, forlorn trills that echoed through the abandoned white mansions and neglected gardens of my imagination. No one had any idea where or why Zamora and Sonny had gone, though of course there were plenty of theories flying around. My favorite was Pepito's: "The *cabrón's* been deported to Paraguay by none other than Madame Marcos. It's the same old song. She was in love, but he wouldn't put out."

"Keep trying to get to the bottom of it," Annie Scardino, my editor at *Groove Rocket*, urged during one of our long-distance conversations. "I like this angle with Imelda."

"I think it's trivial and irrelevant," I said.

"Oh, yeah? Lemme tell you, Paz—the only thing most of our readers know about that wacky country *is* Imelda."

" 'That wacky country' happens to be where I was born."

"Yeah," Annie said, "I know."

I made a list. *Find K. Forbes. Talk to Amado Cabrera.* Pepito offered to help. He prided himself on knowing everyone in the country. "If I don't know them personally, I'll know someone who'll know someone." He showed up at my papa's house early one morning. "Get your clothes on, *mujer.* We're going to UP." He was referring to the

University of the Philippines, which was way the hell out in Quezon City. It would take us over an hour by car. Pepito had located
the elusive anthropologist by simply looking him up in the phone
book. Amado Cabrera agreed to see us that very day.

"Should I call him 'doctor,' 'professor,' or what?" Papa overheard
me ask Pepito.

"You're in the Philippines, Paz. 'Doctor' carries more weight." It
was the first time my father had smiled since my mother's death.
Papa moped around the house and office like a grieving zombie, refusing to return calls or answer his mail. The stalwart Mrs. Locsin,
Papa's secretary of twenty years, fended off a growing list of anxious
clients and irate creditors. Papa spent most nights at his girlfriend
Ruby's apartment, slumped in front of the TV with a highball in
his hands. I didn't know how Ruby could stand it.

"Okay, Papa. We're off to see the eminent doctor professor," I
said when I was dressed, kissing the top of his head. His hair
smelled of pomade. "See you later?"

My father gave a little shrug. Ho-hum. The bags under his eyes
sagged more than ever. I persisted. "Shall we plan to have dinner
out? Maybe Ricky and his family can join us."

Papa made a supreme effort to sit up straight and look interested.
His gray eyes zeroed in on me. "*Sigé*, Paz. That . . . would be . . . nice."

I climbed in the front passenger seat of Pepito's beat-up Karmann-
Ghia.

"I told Cabrera we would treat him to lunch," Pepito announced.
"Your magazine will reimburse you, I assume."

I explained the shaky nature of *Groove Rocket*'s finances. Pepito
sighed. It was a loud, disgruntled *ugh*. . . . After a pause he offered to
foot the bill. "*Pero dios mío*, Paz. Why are you wasting your time?"

"It's a good magazine. Don't worry. I'll pay you back."

"Yeah, yeah, yeah."

Cabrera's office was on the third floor of the Social Sciences
Building—a hot, dusty cubicle at the end of a dark corridor. An an-

cient Underwood typewriter sat in the middle of his heavy desk, which took up all the room. Pepito and I hovered in the doorway, hoping he would notice we were there. Cabrera finally took a break from his rapid, two-finger typing and glanced over at us. "You are Miss Marlowe and Mr. Ponce de León? A historic name, *ano?* Is your family related to the famous explorer?" Pepito grinned devilishly in response. Cabrera grinned right back. They seemed to be flirting. Cabrera got up from his seat and squeezed around the monstrous desk to shake our hands. He was a total surprise— younger looking than I had expected, decked out in a wild Hawaiian shirt and stone-washed jeans. His horn-rimmed glasses were held together by gaffer's tape. He had a distracted, mischievous air about him. "Thank you for agreeing to see us on such short notice, Dr. Cabrera," I said. His handshake was sweaty but firm.

"But of course. This is all so very interesting! Your magazine— what is it called again?"

"*Groove Rocket.*"

"Cute." Cabrera only had eyes for Pepito. "You are writing this article together?"

"I'm just the driver," Pepito replied.

At Cabrera's suggestion Pepito drove us to Cocina Alma, a cozy restaurant specializing in Spanish food. It was close to the university. "But far enough away," Cabrera said, "so I can escape from my darling students." He had taken over the front passenger seat next to Pepito, while I was crammed into the back of the car. Cabrera adjusted his glasses, which kept slipping down his nose. "Are you related to Ricky Marlowe?" he asked me. When I nodded, Cabrera brightened. "I went to school with him at Ateneo." I smiled and made a mental note to grill Ricky later. We rode in happy silence to "The Waters of March" on Pepito's eight-track, sung in melancholy Portugese by gravel-voiced Jobim himself. *Sticks, stones, guns in the night. . . .*

"A perfect song," Cabrera said, "for a perfect day." He brimmed with enthusiasm and curiosity. "Where does your father's family come from, Paz?"

"Havana and Ireland," I answered. "My father was the first Marlowe to be born in Manila."

"*Dios ko!* How exotic. And your mother?" Cabrera's gaze was intense.

"She was a de los Santos, from Cotabato. She just passed away."

"My condolences to you and your brother, then."

There it was. A bungalow in the middle of nowhere, painted a welcoming pastel pink. We pulled into the graveled driveway. Cabrera led us up the rickety stairs to the plant-filled dining room—empty except for the proprietor, a stout, cheery woman in black. She smiled widely at the sight of Cabrera, who kissed her effusively on both cheeks. They were obviously fond of each other. "Dr. Cabrera is my best customer," the woman said. Cabrera introduced her as Señora Alma, aka the Widow Alma—a native of Málaga who had married a rich Filipino and settled down in Manila. Then the war came. "Ah, the war! There was before the war, and there was after," Señora Alma sighed, slowly shaking her head. Her smile was gone. "I lose my husband, my babies, and my money, but I no want to go back to Spain. I love this country too much. Don't I, Amado?"

Cabrera nodded in agreement. "Yes, you do," he murmured.

Señora Alma shrugged. "So I bury my husband and babies, paint my house pink, and start cooking!"

A ceiling fan twirled. Screened windows kept most of the flies out, though a couple of giant *bangaw* managed to sneak in and buzz around our heads. Señora Alma ushered us to a table directly beneath the twirling fan, but it made no difference. The room was an oven. We sat down. Pepito mopped his brow with a hanky and looked unhappy, but Cabrera was oblivious to the stifling heat.

"We'll have *agachonas*, señora. Those little snipes you Spaniards are so fond of."

The Widow Alma fluttered into the kitchen. Cabrera turned to me with an aggressive smile. "Well, Miss Marlowe? What do you wish to know? I am *ready*." He was amused by all of it. Our presence, my curiosity, the promise of so many tiny, delicious birds heaped on a plate.

I turned on the portable recorder. "You don't mind?" I asked Cabrera.

"Not at all."

"Your involvement with Zamora and the Taobo goes back to 1971. Can you talk about it?"

"Of course I can talk about it. And why shouldn't I? Why shouldn't I talk about it? I give speeches on the subject. Lost tribe of X. Kingdom of X. Were the Taobo real or not? Let me tell you, Miss Marlowe—"

"Paz."

"The Taobo are real, Paz. Real people who live in the rain forest. Never mind about Stone Age anything. That isn't really the point."

"But how can you say that?"

"What do you mean, how can I say that? I can say anything. *I was there.*"

A solemn little boy brought glasses of water and utensils to our table. Cabrera continued. "My dream is to one day organize a conference right here, at the University of the Philippines. Anthropologists from all over the world can come to the actual scene of the crime and discuss what really happened. I am not afraid of a healthy debate. In my field controversy is a positive thing."

"Would you invite Zamora to your conference?"

"Of course! If we can find him." Cabrera laughed.

"Are you going to speak at the upcoming Hawaii symposium?"

Cabrera shrugged. "Depends. One gets tired of being constantly put on the defensive, Paz."

"What are your feelings about Zamora?"

That bemused look again. "My feelings? You mean my *personal* feelings?"

"Professional, personal. However you choose to answer, Dr. Cabrera."

"He's a rich man who made things possible," Cabrera said after a pause.

And then came the birds. Delicate things, charred brown, their tiny heads and beaks smothered in oily garlic, served over rice. The boy set down platters for each of us. "They're so small," I marveled, staring at my plate.

Cabrera and Pepito dug in with their forks and spoons. "This is the widow's best dish. You can eat each bird in one bite. Their bones are soft and edible," Cabrera said, chewing away. "Aren't you hungry? *Kain na.*"

"Do you mind if we continue our interview while you're eating?" I asked.

"How does that saying go? We all have to dance for our supper, *di ba? Alam mo,* Paz—Zamora Legazpi had a lot of enemies. But I wasn't one of them. I was young and too easily impressed. But other people were envious. They resented his wealth, his arrogance, his"— Cabrera paused—"mestizo sense of entitlement. You speak Tagalog, *di ba?*"

"Yes."

"Good. Knowing the language helps to understand the complexities of our situation. Don't misunderstand me—Zamora was also loved by the people. I don't mean the people of Manila or the urban *masa.* I mean the *indígenos*—the tribes up in the mountains no one in Manila gives a damn about. They worshipped him. I saw it with my own eyes."

The birds grew cool on my plate. "I've heard some nasty allegations, Dr. Cabrera."

Cabrera nudged Pepito with his elbow. "Your friend has turned into such an *Amerikana, ano?*" We all laughed. He grew serious, once again. "What sort of allegations?"

"That the entire time Zamora was pretending to help the Mindanao tribes, he was actually gathering information about the leftist rebels hiding in the mountains. That guides and translators like Duan and Aket were nothing but spies. That the information they gathered was then passed on to government-sanctioned hit squads. That many people were targeted and killed."

Cabrera didn't miss a beat. "Wow. I feel like I'm on trial, Paz." He chuckled softly. "We live in difficult times, *di ba?* But if any of these allegations are true—" He glanced at each of us. "I had nothing to do with any of it. I was invited along on Zamora's expeditions because of my professional expertise. I collected data as an anthropologist, not as a government agent." He noticed the untouched birds on my plate. "You can't stomach the food?"

I decided to lie and be gracious. "Sorry. I had a late breakfast. Would you know how I could find Kenneth Forbes, Dr. Cabrera?"

"He's back in the States. Probably San Francisco." Cabrera squinted at his watch. "*Naku!* I have a class to teach." He got up from the table.

I wanted to say, *You can't leave. I'm not finished.* Instead I said, "We'll be happy to give you a ride back."

"Never mind, I'll take a taxi. You must stay and try Señora's special coconut flan. *Talagang* heavenly." We shook hands. My head throbbed. The meeting with Cabrera had left me even more confused. "*Salamat* for lunch. Regards to your brother, Paz." Cabrera waved good-bye as he ran out the door.

Pepito shook his head in disbelief. "Where the fuck was that guy coming from?"

I put the tape recorder away. "He was flirting with you. Too bad I scared him off."

"Not my type," Pepito said, making a dismissive gesture. He eyed my uneaten snipes. "Can I have your *agachonas?*"

"Knock yourself out," I said, pushing the plate of birds in his direction.

Lake Ramayyah

The first day of shooting, Tony Pierce asked everyone to make a circle, hold hands, and improvise some kind of hipster prayer. The Filipino crew members stood on the periphery, unsure of what to do. The ritual felt silly and insincere—an embarrassment to Moody. He stood between Franco Broussard, the director of photography, and Caleb Brook, the production designer. Both men looked just as embarrassed as Moody did.

"May the gods bless this movie, which is gonna be a great fucking movie, you better believe it, guys. . . . It took blood, sweat, guts, tears, and my own goddamn money to move this fucking mountain and get all the way here . . . but we finally made it and *we're going to do a helluva job . . . yeah!*" Pierce raised a fist in a Black Panther–style salute. The Americans and Europeans dressed in fashionable jungle gear cheered and saluted back. Everyone was more than ready. The crew flitted about in a blaze of nervous energy. Moody counted the small number of white women present—wives and girlfriends of crew members and actors, or part of the production itself. A few worked as set dressers or in the costume and makeup departments. He was reminded of Lori. He had not heard from her at all, but Ross had assured him that she had just been hired to do makeup for a TV sitcom and was getting paid a lot of money. The news assuaged Moody's guilt somewhat.

Scantily dressed party girls with predatory eyes floated about, driving the men to distraction. Moody wasn't sure if they were hookers or starlets flown in from L.A. by Gary Givens. Givens was a notorious womanizer. He was also the star of the movie. One of them anyway. Sebastian Claiborne hadn't arrived yet. Claiborne was the bigger star, the legendary class act, the reclusive weirdo prince who had agreed, for $2 million, to appear in a tiny but crucial cameo.

The movie's working title was *Napalm Sunset*. Ross Fox had sent Moody the latest version of the script through some bureaucrat friend of his who worked at the American embassy in Manila. The embassy happened to be located four blocks from the Love Connection. The bureaucrat, on his lunch break, found Moody at the bar. He handed him the script in a diplomatic pouch and left without saying a word. Attached to the script was a note from Ross:

> *Give the Big Man's latest a chance.*
> *This draft is pretty terrific shit. Plus, he still wants you!*

Moody read the whole thing straight through in one night. He hated to admit it, but his agent was right. The script was too long, but it was good. Exciting good. Unsettling good. Pretentious in places, but meaty, ambitious, and complicated. Funny in a fatalistic, ironic, Filipino kind of way. No clear-cut heroes or villains, no simplistic, black-and-white notions of justice. Just murk and mud. That was the Big Man's vision, and Moody loved it. It was six in the morning by the time he finished reading. He couldn't wait. Moody threw on his jeans and went downstairs to the lobby, where Mrs. Dava sat eating her breakfast of salt fish, green mango slices, and fried rice.

"Mr. Vincent, you are up very early! You want coffee?"

"I need to use your phone, ma'am."

Mrs. Dava studied the young man standing before her. She couldn't get over the fact that an American movie star, no matter how troubled or broke, had chosen to stay at her humble *pensión* all these months. Mr. Vincent was a strange man, *talaga*. Not obnoxious and disgusting like those other horny foreigners wandering up and down Mabini, looking for *putas*. This one was wan as a ghost, kind and strangely sweet, even when he was high or drunk. Mrs. Dava gave a weary sigh.

"A local call, I hope?"

"Person-to-person collect, ma'am," Moody answered.

Mrs. Dava reached under the counter for her rotary phone and went back to eating her breakfast.

Moody tried his agent at home. "I'm fucking excited, Ross! I also wanna thank you. For, uh—"

Ross laughed. "You weren't put off by that hokey title?"

"It's beautiful," Moody said.

It took hours to set up the first shot, which involved a hundred extras, a helicopter, a boat, and plenty of explosives. Then the rain came pouring down. The actors ended up waiting for nothing. The second day of shooting, the mood was less enthusiastic. The Americans and Europeans were wilting from the intense heat, grumbling about some kind of dysentery that was going around. It would be another wasted day, as far as Moody was concerned. Pierce was setting up the same helicopter shot, which had been rewritten to involve only Gary Givens and the Filipino extras playing assorted villagers and Vietcong. Moody clearly wasn't needed, but he'd been summoned to stand by, "just in case."

"We've only just begun . . ." Pierce warbled the Karen Carpenter song, acting the fool to keep the cast and crew's spirits up. A bearish, bearded man in his mid-thirties, Pierce was a bundle of contradictions. Cocky and surefooted one minute, anxious and insecure the next. He ran hot and cold. Moody chose to stay out of his way but loved watching Pierce work. Meeting Pierce on the first day of read-throughs in Manila had been a thrill. As he shook Pierce's hand that day, Moody had felt the intensity of the director's gaze. Detached yet curious, dissecting him.

"Y'know," Pierce said with a disdainful smile, "we could've used you at those rehearsals in L.A."

"I'm sorry. By the time I found out," Moody said, "I was already in Manila."

"Do you make a habit of leaving town whenever you get a job? I was all set to fire you, but your agent talked me out of it." When Moody didn't respond, Pierce said, "I like your agent, Vince. He claims you're worth the trouble."

Fuck you, Moody wanted to say. But he didn't.

The read-throughs of the ever-evolving script were held in a suite at the Manila Hotel. The actors sat around a table and read their dialogue, while Pierce paced back and forth listening. Pierce's assistant director read the scene settings and the descriptions of the action. Another assistant took notes. Moody sat next to Billy Hernandez. Hernandez was a stage actor from the Bronx, who described himself as "the only Nuyorican ever hired to play Othello." He was a warm, friendly, middle-aged man with a distinctive voice and a leonine, pockmarked face. The character he'd been cast to play was a sympathetic sergeant named Driver, who would be killed and beheaded in the movie's grisly final scenes.

Moody and the other actors were pumped up by the audacious material. Moody still couldn't quite believe he was part of Pierce's team. Plus, he wasn't sure if he or anyone else in the room totally understood the script. What, ultimately, was this damn movie about? That war made men crazy? What the hell. Pierce was the genius auteur, the highbrow intellectual. Not he.

Long days passed. Pierce was short tempered. "Will you please take that fucking camera out of my face?" Pierce whirled around to confront his wife, Janet. She had been following him around with a sixteen-millimeter camera since the first day of read-throughs. Everything stopped. "I'm sorry, Jan—" Pierce called out, groaning as his wife stormed away.

Moody couldn't bear the tension in the air and headed for the huge tent that served as a mess hall for the cast and crew. He needed something badly. He wasn't sure what—maybe a glimpse of her face. Inside the tent was the usual setup for assembly-line eating—chafing dishes, Sterno cans, folding tables and chairs. The drone of generators was constant. They were all going to get fed whether they liked it or not, though it was too hot to eat. So much food! The villagers had never seen anything like it. Refrigerated trucks delivering hundreds of fancy steaks and plump chickens, all the way from God-knows-where. Workers hired from nearby towns stood behind counters, ready to ladle out whatever was on today's menu. Jinx was one of them.

"Want something, sir?" she asked shyly, playing with him.

Moody smiled. He couldn't believe that he had managed to pull it off. That she was there, with him. "Just came by to say hey."

"Hey."

"Lina!" Came the sharp sound of a woman's voice from the kitchen area.

"I must go," Jinx said, quickly moving away. Her long, glossy black hair hung down her back in a single braid.

Moody reluctantly went back outside. There was nothing for him to do except go down by the lake to watch them filming. "Look out!" he heard Pierce yelling. Something exploded. Water and pieces of a boat flew up in the sky. The ground shook.

"Cut!" Pierce shouted. He seemed pleased. *Cut, cut, cut.*

Lunch was announced. Moody made his way to the head of the line. He was still not hungry, but it did not matter. Jinx stood next to an old woman.

"Chicken, sir?" she asked. "Beef, rice, or noodles?"

"Hi, again," Moody said. "I'll take a little bit of everything."

Jinx piled the food high on his plate. The old woman, her white hair hidden in a head wrap of faded cloth, gazed at Moody with suspicion.

"Are you Aling Belén?" Moody asked.

The old woman looked hard at him. She spoke to Jinx in a rattling, high-pitched language, gesticulating furiously with her hand. "Aling Belén does not speak English," Jinx said to Moody.

"What did she say to you?" Moody asked.

"She wonders why you can't see that we are too busy to talk to you."

"I wouldn't wanna fuck with that girl's *abuela,*" murmured a familiar raspy voice behind him. Moody turned and grinned at Billy Hernandez. "You gonna eat all that?" Hernandez asked, incredulous.

"No."

"Lemme have it, then." Hernandez took the plate from Moody and led him to an empty table. They sat down. "You look strung out, man." Hernandez glanced at Jinx behind the counter, then at Moody. "I can see why." Hernandez chuckled to himself as he started in on Moody's food. "This is one of the most beautiful places on earth. Sacred land, man. Can you feel it?"

"Sure."

"No need to bullshit me, Vince. You see the way the cast and crew walk around here like they own the place? Pierce is the worst. Thinks this country's nothing but a backdrop for his movie. The people don't matter, except when they service him and his family. They serve us, they feed us, they fuck us—"

Moody frowned. "Whoa, Billy."

" 'Whoa Billy,' what?" Hernandez said. "Come on, man. You know I speak the truth. That's why the old lady is so pissed."

Pierce had his own tent, his own cook, and a personal waiter. His wife and two children sometimes ate with him while he was working, but today they chose to be driven back to the house Pierce had rented in Sultan Ramayyah, a town on the other side of the mountain. Pierce had invited his leading man and his director of cinematography to join him for lunch. The men were in the midst of laughing at a dirty joke Franco Broussard had made in broken English when Pierce spotted Moody and Hernandez walking by, outside the tent.

"Would you care to join us, gentlemen?" Pierce called out. Moody and Hernandez peered inside. Platters of steaming linguine and grilled prawns were set in the center of a large, round table. A distinguished-looking, silver-haired Filipino man was uncorking bottles of Chianti and pouring the wine into crystal goblets. The scent of marijuana was in the air. There was a young woman present—a brunette wearing jeans and a midriff halter top. She was flat bellied, stoned, and smiling.

"Hey," she said. "Hey, Mr. Moody."

"Hey." Moody was cautious but not unfriendly.

"I gotta go," Hernandez murmured to Moody. "You stayin' or what?" He didn't bother waiting for a response and gave Pierce a little wave. "Thanks, but I already ate. See you later, boss."

Pierce waved back. "What about you, Vince?" Pierce gestured for him to sit down.

Moody sat next to the young woman. She was loose and friendly—reeking of patchouli oil and sex, no older than eighteen. Givens watched her like a hawk. Moody was reminded of Peaches.

"What a small world," the girl said. "You really don't remember me, do you? I'm Claire. Claire Jenks. I used to baby-sit for you and Lori." She held out her hand. Silver and turquoise rings adorned every finger. Her tanned arms were covered with multicolored glass bangles from India. A turquoise stud pierced her nose. "I used to live two doors down from you."

Moody grinned, suddenly remembering. He didn't know what else to do, so he shook her hand. She had been heavy at fifteen, luscious and round and infinitely more desirable, shamelessly flirting with him whenever Lori wasn't around. He almost gave in and fucked her one night, but Lori came home early. "That little slut sure wants you bad," Lori had said after Claire left. Lori was smiling as she said it, but she never hired Claire again.

"Another glass for our guest, Cirilo," Pierce said to the silver-haired man. "I borrowed Cirilo from the Manila Hotel," Pierce explained to Moody. "He's one of their best waiters."

Cirilo set down a goblet, another plate, and some silverware for Moody.

"No paper plates or plastic cups?" Moody asked.

"Are you mocking me, Vince?" Pierce's tone was mild, but he was clearly not amused.

"Not at all," Moody said.

Gary Givens laughed. "Of course you are. You are a funny man, my friend." He was fortyish, with an amazing head of fluffy blond hair and the trim, muscular body, square jaw, and chiseled good looks required of male movie stars. His real name was George Kuvacich. He addressed Pierce: "My God, Tony. What a long morning! I don't think I've recovered from all those fucking explosions. My ears."

"Don't get too comfortable," Pierce said. "There's more to come."

The wine was aged and delicious; Moody tried not to drink too fast. He avoided Claire's adoring gaze and turned to Givens. "You're one of my favorite actors, man."

"That so," Givens said, exchanging glances with Pierce.

"*Good Cop, Bad Cop* was in-fucking-credible. Your performance was great. In-fucking-great! You should've won the Oscar."

"Definitely," Claire agreed. "Baby was robbed."

Givens shot her a warning look but warmed up to Moody. "You'll have to credit Tony here. He pushed me beyond the limit." He said to Pierce, "I swore I'd never work with you again. Didn't I?"

Pierce smiled coolly. "We were meant for each other."

Moody kept his focus on the preening actor. "It's an honor to finally work with you."

"Well, well, well," Givens said. "*Thank you.*"

"How's Lori and Alex?" Claire suddenly asked Moody. "Alex must be . . . how old now?"

"Lori and I aren't together anymore."

"Sorry." Claire didn't look sorry at all.

"It's okay," Moody said.

"Claire-bear. What am I always telling you? Think, then speak!" Givens said.

"Yeah, yeah," Claire said.

They were all drinking hard. Claire rolled a perfect joint, lit up, and passed it to Pierce. He waved it away, drank more wine, leaned back, and closed his eyes. Moody wondered how the shoot would go this afternoon.

Pierce opened his eyes. "I worked with your wife on *Islands of Thieves*," he said to Moody.

"We have a son, but we're not married," Moody said.

"Oh. Well, uh . . . Lori's a nice girl," Pierce said. He helped himself to another plate of linguine.

"What is this Lori everybody talk about?" Broussard asked.

"Hair and makeup," Pierce said. "You remember, Franco. She worked with us in Mexico."

"No," Broussard said.

"I remember," Givens said.

Cirilo poured Moody more wine.

"This is mellow," Moody said to Pierce, a silly grin on his face. He felt queasy. *I should eat*, Moody thought.

"Aren't you going to partake of my sumptuous bounty?" Pierce asked, as if reading his mind. "You know, I have a chef who travels with me everywhere, but today's meal is a spur-of-the-moment creation by Franco. Franco's amazing."

"Where do you find the energy to cook?" Givens asked Franco Broussard. "This place is so damn hot, it takes it right out of me."

Claire passed Givens the joint. He took one toke, winced, then passed it to Broussard, who refused it. Givens passed the joint to Moody. Moody took several deep drags and promptly forgot he was holding on to it.

"I find it because, how you say, it helps me—" Broussard

searched for the right word in English. He turned to Pierce for help. "Tony. How you say?"

"Unwind," Pierce said.

"Ahhh, *si*. Unwind. Cooking good for relax, play with mind, think about next shot. "

"Jesus-fucking-Christ," Givens muttered, sighing. He rubbed his stomach. "It's too hot. I shouldn't have eaten so much."

"I think I'd better go." Moody rose unsteadily to his feet.

"Then gimme back my spliff," Claire said, taking it from him with a laugh.

"You are okay, Vincenzo?" Broussard was genuinely concerned.

"Yeah."

"Drunk as a skunk," Givens said. "Higher than high."

"Oh, me, oh, my," Claire said.

"Thanks for the hospitality," Moody said to Pierce.

"*De nada*," Pierce said.

Givens waited until Moody left and was out of earshot. "So how about it, Claire-bear? Did you fuck the guy or what?"

"Fortunately for you," Claire snapped, "we never got around to it."

"I love you, too," Givens said.

Pierce savored the last of the garlicky prawns while Broussard showed Cirilo how to make espresso. Broussard always brought his own coffee beans, grinder, and well-used espresso pot along on location. Cirilo, who had been taught the art of brewing a perfect espresso by the Swiss chef at the Manila Hotel, acted appropriately baffled and listened patiently. Claire perched on Givens's lap. She finished the rest of her joint, sullen and furious. Givens had a hard-on. "I think it's time for a little siesta," he whispered. He kissed the nape of Claire's sunburned neck.

"Stop," Claire said, squirming uncomfortably. She slid off Givens's lap and went back to her chair.

"Time for coffee, not pussy," Pierce said.

Broussard insisted on pouring the espresso himself. "Sorry we not have the right cups."

Pierce pushed his plate away, burping loudly.

"You know, I'd watch it if I were you, Tony," Givens said. "Moody's a loose cannon. Has a problem with authority or father figures or something. He punched out Chuck on that movie, remember?" Givens turned to Broussard. "Weren't you the DP on that?" Broussard shook his head. "I coulda sworn you were the DP on that," Givens said, disappointed.

"Chuck who?" Claire's eyes were heavy. Givens ignored her.

"Moody's trouble," Givens said.

"Moody's gonna be fine. It's Sebastian Claiborne I should be worried about," Pierce said. "Ah, fuck it. Fuck 'em all. I love trouble. I invite trouble. Isn't that what making art is all about?"

Moody managed to get out of the tent without heaving his guts. He refused to give them that satisfaction. He was surprised to find Jinx waiting for him outside. They started walking down the hill, toward the lake. "Where's your grandma?" Moody asked.

"Aling Belén is not my grandma."

"Well, whatever her name is—she doesn't like me, Jinx."

"My real name is Lina."

The path was steep and rocky. Moody lost his footing and was about to fall when Lina grabbed him by the arm, steadying him.

"You are drunk," she said, in a disapproving tone.

"Sorry," Moody said, meaning it. "Shameful, isn't it?"

Lina nodded. "Nevertheless," she said.

"Nevertheless," Moody agreed.

She did not let go of his arm; they made their way cautiously down to the water's edge. Lake Ramayyah, choked with snarls of pink and purple lotus blossoms, was once again peaceful and still. The foreigners with their explosives, gadgets, and props were gone for the moment. Moody gazed at the body of water before him. The dark, jagged peaks of Mount Taobo loomed in the distance. Pierce had said something about the mountainous forest's being perfect for his jungle location. Moody felt a chill run through him. Billy Hernandez was right. This was sacred ground, swarming with restless spirits. Los Angeles and New York were irrelevant, inconsequential abstractions, other worlds and galaxies away.

"Everything is gone," Lina said. "The schoolhouse. Miss Angway."

"Who's Miss Angway?"

Silent, Lina stared at the water, as if waiting for something to reveal itself to her. Moody was humbled by her sorrow. Was this love? It had crept up without warning, hit him right where it hurt. An ache in the belly, something caught in his throat. Instantaneous, overwhelming, ridiculous. The real deal, as his mother used to call it. You'll know when you get there, Vincent. All right, then, Moody thought. *I am here, Mother. Awash, awash with love!* Should he run the risk of losing her by declaring it out loud? *I love you, Jinx Lina. Whoever you are.* He heard rustling sounds, the flapping of wings as birds flew high above them. Higher and higher they flew, toward the green, forbidding mountains.

"I have to go back," Lina said.

"See you later?"

"I miss Yeye. Maybe I go stay with Aling Belén tonight. I really do not know."

Moody understood that she was not being coy or evasive with him, but blunt and truthful. Lina had given Yeye, her two-year-old daughter, to the old woman to care for—believing that it would be a better life for the child. But she visited Yeye as often as she could, sleeping curled up next to her on the old woman's bamboo floor. Lina walked briskly up the hill, away from him. She did not look back. Moody remained at the water's edge, watching her disappear around a bend. Wonder of the world, heartbreaker. Love surely existed, and God was everywhere.

Zoom

[handwritten: 3rd person / Janet Pierce]

There he was—pacing back and forth, struggling not to lose his temper. Problem solving. Janet Cattaneo Pierce aimed the Bolex at her husband. *Zoom.* Tony God—Tony G, or TG for short—was her secret name for him. Tony God hated having to wait for anything, even if the delays were his fault. In his various roles as executive producer, director, and screenwriter of *Napalm Sunset,* Tony God hadn't calculated on the combination of paralyzing heat and wicked typhoon season in the Philippines. It had been raining off and on, making the shoot next to impossible. But today—day whatever-it-was—the sun snuck out from behind the clouds. *Hallelujah,* Janet thought. Maybe TG would actually accomplish something and feel good. Some small thing, she didn't give a fuck what it was.

The crew was scrambling to reset the scene for the umpteenth time. Janet panned to Franco Broussard—a harried, physically expressive man. He gestured wildly and yelled in Italian at some cringing young man. Probably one of the electricians. Janet whipped the camera back to her restless, pacing husband and once again zoomed in. Tony God was sweating, thinking hard. Something needed to change. Some action, some dialogue needed to be improvised to take the scene in another direction, to another level . . . *but then what?* Janet sensed that the actors were tiring of her husband's capricious demands. She saw it in their tight, guarded expressions. Especially that one—Vincent Moody. An apt name.

They were the best. Brave, intelligent, generous actors—beautiful to watch. It would all make for a compelling documentary. She knew that much. "An inside look at the making of . . ." Ha. Since that first awful day, Janet had learned how important it was to be invisible. To stay out of Tony God's way, out of everyone's way—yet get what she needed for the film. *Her film*. Financed out of her own pocket, with a little help from hubby. She even managed to pull together a small crew. Brad Wong was her everything guy—additional camera, editing, whatever else needed to be done. Diane, his wife, did sound. They had flown in from San Francisco; Janet knew she was lucky to have them. The film of the film was going to be good. No one knew it yet. No one paid attention to the slender, smiling, unobtrusive woman and her discreet crew of two. Wife of director. Mother of director's sons. Who was she, really—and why should anyone on the set care? They were all too busy, too preoccupied with the immense task of pleasing her husband. In their eyes Janet was being indulged—her documentary nothing more than a glorified home movie. The day she'd approached Tony God with her idea, he'd been in a generous mood. She felt his vibes, she read his mind: What the hell, Jan. If it makes you happy. But of course that's not what Tony God had said. What he said was actually more mundane and clipped than usual: *Why not?* He even gave her his Bolex, which he'd had since film school. TG urged her to start using the sixteen-millimeter camera immediately. *To practice. Get used to it, Jan.*

She had free rein.

What she loved best was wandering around on her own, finding things to shoot. Janet ambled down toward the lake, where Moody, in costume and makeup, stood smoking a cigarette during a break. The teenage Filipina girl—Janet didn't know her name—was with him. They were laughing about something. She aimed the camera at them. Moody shook his head, held a hand up to shield his face. The girl turned away. Janet kept walking and stumbled on a shirtless Gary Givens, sitting under an enormous tree with Claire. Claire wore a bikini top and the flimsiest of denim cutoffs. She waved gaily to the camera. Boyet, a village kid who hung around the set and sometimes ran errands for the crew, wandered into the frame. He stared at the hunky movie star and his provocative girlfriend. They were clearly uncomfortable. After a moment Givens tried shooing Boyet away. "Get the fuck outta here," Givens said. Boyet refused to budge. Janet kept the camera on them. Boyet finally lost interest and wandered away. Claire looked back at the camera and giggled. "Horny little devil," she said. Givens reached into a cooler for a bottle of mineral water. Cases of it had been sent by air freight from California at his request. Givens drank. He opened another bottle and kept drinking. Zoom. Givens smiled into the camera, displaying a mouthful of bleached, capped teeth. His handsomeness was unreal. "You gotta keep hydrated in this heat," Givens said. Zoom out. The camera panned to Claire, who reached into a straw bag and pulled out a bottle of Bain de Soleil lotion. She squeezed the lotion into her hand and rubbed it all over Givens's bronzed body, taking her time. At one point she leaned over to kiss him. It was a long, showy, far-too-intimate kiss. Janet zoomed in.

Janet went back to the set. The next scene called for Moody to be wounded by a sniper and collapse, screaming, "Jesusfuck, I've been hit!" The other actors—Kevin Cassells, Isaiah Waters, and Billy Hernandez—were to rush over to Moody and act appropriately distressed and concerned. Take after take was shot from every angle and POV imaginable, but Tony God wasn't satisfied. Janet's camera took in the frustration on his face. She stayed on him.

Tony God took Franco Broussard and Julie Boyd aside. Boyd was the hulking, six-foot Irish Amazon who headed the props and special effects department.

"It's too clean," Tony God complained.

"What do you mean?" Boyd asked.

"Don't be stingy with the blood packs, Julie," Tony God said. "I need to see blood. Vince gets hit in the stomach, on his left thigh and left foot. We've got to see it and *feel* it."

"Hmm." Julie Boyd crossed her arms, defensive and wary. She was formidable on camera. "Yeah. Well."

Now it was Tony G's turn to blow up. "Don't gimme me this noncommittal shit! Can you do it, or not?"

Julie Boyd was livid. "Of course I can do it!"

Janet panned to Franco Broussard, trying to placate everyone. "I can help, Tony. I'll shoot slow-mo. One after the other. Ka-ping! How you say, *excruciation*. Very beautiful."

"But the foot," Tony God said to Julie. "I want it to be a surprise."

"His foot? Where on his foot?" Boyd asked.

"Through the sole of his boot. Right as he falls."

"Boom!" Broussard said. "Ka-ping! Blood spurting up, down, slow-mo."

"Yes, Franco, yes." Tony God smiled. The tension eased.

"That's a lot of boots you're talking about," Boyd said.

"Whatever it takes," Tony God said.

Another break. The girl sauntered up to Moody. "Hey, Lina," Moody greeted her. He glanced over at Janet's camera, annoyed by the intrusion, but said nothing.

"How come your boss makes his movie when the weather's bad?" Lina asked.

"He's nuts," Moody said, "like the rest of us."

"*Nuts?*" Lina seemed amused by the word. "Are you going to do that falling-down thing again?"

"You must be so bored." Moody chuckled.

"I like it."

"You like it?"

"How you do it a little different but the same every time."

Tony God came up to them. He wore his usual uniform—a grimy sweatshirt with cutoff sleeves and khaki shorts. Moody nodded in greeting, noting the director's sun-browned skin and the enormous amount of weight he'd lost since they'd begun shooting.

With his hair longer and his paunch diminished, Tony God looked his age. Almost handsome.

"How's it going, Vince?"

Moody was taken aback by Pierce's buddy-buddy, jocular mood. "Are you going to introduce me to this ravishing beauty, or do you plan to keep her tucked away for the entire shoot?"

"I work in the food tent," Lina said. "Every day."

"Oh." Tony God looked flustered. "Of course." I didn't recognize—"

"You don't eat in the food tent," Moody reminded him. "Lina, meet Tony Pierce. Our, my—the director."

TG held out his hand. Lina, blushing, took it. "Call me Tony," TG said, trying not to leer. Janet couldn't believe what an ass her husband was making of himself—and with his own wife just a few feet away, pointing the damn camera at all of them. *Poor baby*, Janet thought. *Poor, needy baby.*

"Well," Tony God continued, finally letting go of Lina's hand, "you and Vince should join me for dinner later." He turned to Moody. "How about it, *amigo*? Franco and the boys are cooking up another feast."

"We've made other plans," Moody said.

"Other plans? You're in the middle of nowhere, man. You can't be serious."

"But I am."

"You like Italian food?" Tony God asked Lina.

Lina shrugged. "Spaghetti. Okay *naman*."

"Okay *naman*! There you go. See what I mean, Vince? If you don't come to my party, you'll be denying this lovely girl an authentic experience." TG spoke directly to the camera. "It's been a difficult week, so we're having a little party tonight. A much-needed culinary fiesta. To loosen us all up."

"Are we going?" Lina asked Moody.

Tony God hammed it up, laying it on real thick for her. "You know Franco? He's that skinny Italian over there. A great cinematographer, a genius in the kitchen! Garlic, cheap white wine, a rotten tomato or two—you name it, he'll transform it. Who knows what tricks he's got up his sleeve for tonight? But I promise you, lovely Lina, the result will be absolutely satisfying."

"Okay," Lina said.

Tony God gave a little bow and made his exit. Janet followed close behind, with her camera.

Lina and Vincent

3rd Person
Lina & Moody

"Your boss is strange but nice," Lina said.

"I don't want to go to his damn party," Moody said.

Lina smiled. "But I do, Pretty Boy."

They shot the scene of Moody getting hit by a sniper a few more times, but by three o'clock the sun had disappeared and the rain came down hard again. Pierce called it quits. The extras—locals, mostly—were left to fend for themselves, while the foreigners were driven to their rented houses in nearby towns.

"You are angry with me?" Lina climbed into a Volkswagen van with Moody.

"Forget it." Moody put his arm around her as they settled into their seats. Lina sighed.

Billy Hernandez sat in the back of the van with Moody and Lina. Cassells and Waters sat up front. The rain pelted against the windows as they all watched a Filipino driver hold open the passenger door of an ostentatious Cadillac parked across the way. Next to the driver stood Boyet, holding open a golf umbrella. Pierce, Janet, Franco Broussard, Gary Givens, and Claire Jenks climbed into the limousine. "Will you check out that shit," Kevin Cassells sneered. Car and driver seemed ridiculously out of place, rented by the production company from the enterprising mayor, whose name was Fritz Magbantay. Magbantay was a jovial little gangster, rumored to be yet another illegitimate relation and confidant of the president's. A powerful man, in other words.

Lina snuggled close to Moody, which surprised him. It wasn't like her to be demonstrative or affectionate in public. Moody suspected that she was trying to appease him about the dinner invitation. Billy Hernandez leaned his head back and pretended to fall asleep. Moody saw the Cadillac start to pull away from the lone, wistful figure of Boyet. Maybe he was hoping for a tip. His by-now-useless umbrella was turned inside out with the force of hurricane winds and driving rain. Moody wondered if Pierce or Givens would have the decency to offer the kid a ride home—if the kid even had a home. An image of his son, Alex, flashed before him. Standing in a corner of the front yard, back to the world, thumb in his mouth. Alex could stare at anything—the fence, a tree trunk, pebbles on the ground—for hours. He was indifferent to other children. Refused to deal with anyone, really, except for Moody. Marian, Moody's mother, had written him about a special school in New York for kids like Alex. *When he's old enough,* Marian Moody wrote, *just send Alex to his grandma. I'll take care of it.*

The car drove off, leaving Boyet standing in the pouring rain, ankle-deep in mud.

"Hey, Ernie," Moody called out to the van's driver, "let's give Boyet a ride."

"Sir?"

"Pull over," Moody said.

Billy Hernandez opened one eye and stared with some curiosity at Moody. "That's very kind of you, brother."

Kevin Cassells groaned. "Oh, man. Puh-leeze. That kid's a pest. Always hustlin'—"

"So what?" Moody retorted. "He's liable to get pneumonia standing out there like an idiot."

"Not my problem," Cassells snapped. "It's been a long fucking day. I just wanna get back to the crib and crawl into bed."

Moody slid open the van door and motioned for Boyet to climb in. Boyet huddled on the floor by Moody's feet, shivering. Moody pointed to the empty seat in front of him, but the kid shook his head.

"Try not to drip water all over the place," Cassells said.

"Shut up and take it easy, Kevin," Moody said. They rode the rest of the way in silence. Moody had no real problem with Cassells. He'd once worked with him on a TV pilot that never went anywhere and found Cassells to be the kind of guy who was jolly and generous when he was among men and felt secure. Cassells had a reputation as a gifted character actor—volatile and quirky like Moody. Directors like Pierce loved to cast him. Cassells and the rest of the ensemble had been carefully chosen by Pierce for his Vietnam boogie-woogie war epic. In fact, all of them, except for Moody and Isaiah Waters, had worked with Pierce many times before. The latest version of the script called for Cassells to be mauled and eaten by a tiger in the jungle. Cassells, usually cast as either a fiendish psychopath or a comedic foil, was rightfully nervous. The tiger was scheduled to be flown in from some fancy animal farm in California in the next couple of days. Pierce planned to shoot the death scene by the end of the week.

"Soon I'll be outta this shithole, man," Cassells announced.

"Yeah, either that or dead." Isaiah Waters chuckled. He and Cassells loathed each other. Waters was a lanky, doe-eyed, sixteen-year-old from Brooklyn. Pierce had personally discovered him in Times Square, hustling for change by playing Isley Brothers tunes with an old Stratocaster plugged into a sorry little amp.

"Buried with the roaches and the lizards," Hernandez teased Cassells, who didn't respond. Hernandez went on. "Nothing to be afraid of, my brother. Nothing to despise. Just look around you. Look beyond the material and the physical."

Cassells rolled his eyes. "Please, Billy. Don't bore me with that hippie-dippy mumbo jumbo."

Hernandez cackled good-naturedly. He was the veteran of the group, having played every imaginable ethnic type in movies, on television, and onstage. Pierce was beefing up his role in the movie, rewriting the script daily.

"Billy's the man in the black hat," Pierce once said with unabashed admiration.

Isaiah Waters had insinuated himself into becoming Hernandez's protégé, following him around and studying his moves in every scene. Tonight Hernandez was in a preaching mood; Waters was all eyes and ears. "Look beyond the shit," Hernandez rambled on, "and I guarantee you'll see just how much beauty and power there is."

"Maybe I need glasses," Cassells said.

"Ha-ha," Waters said in a flat, contemptuous tone.

"I'm getting real sick of you," Cassells said to him.

Hernandez lit a thick joint. "We all need glasses, man."

Boyet sneezed several times. Lina offered him Moody's denim shirt, which she wore over her T-shirt. Boyet shook his head again. Lina draped the shirt over his shoulders.

"He is sick," Lina said to Moody. Thunder crackled in the distance. The boy hunched his shoulders, miserable.

"Damn! Can't this guy drive any faster?" Cassells whined.

"We're in the middle of a typhoon, muthafucka," Waters reminded him.

"I love this country, I really do. I can relate to it," Hernandez went on to no one in particular. On his Taino face was a look of bliss. "The roaches, the lizards, the bats, the heat, the rain"—he gave Lina a nod of acknowledgment—"the unforgettable women, the grinding poverty. I know this place like I know my own heart." He passed the joint to Moody, who took a deep drag.

"Beauty," Moody murmured, exhaling clouds of smoke.

"Yes, brother. Seek and you shall find," Hernandez said.

Lina

1st Person, Lina

Still, Lina is an observer

We drop Boyet off in front of Aling Nora's sari-sari store near the plaza. "Sure you don't want to spend the night at our place?" Pretty Boy asks him. Boyet shakes his head no, as I knew he would. Nevertheless.

"Jeez-us, man, " the angry one named Kevin says, "next thing I know, you'll be offering to adopt the poor bastard."

The van stops in front of the house owned by Mayor Magbantay, who owns almost everything in Ligaya and Sultan Ramayyah. My Pretty Boy has claimed the smallest room for himself, in the back. The sun is long gone. Only rain, darkness, and more rain.

Angry Kevin begins complaining loudly as soon as he gets out of the van. "Shit! No electricity again. And the friggin' house is probably flooded!" Mang Pablo, the *bantay-bahay*, peers down at us from the top of the steps. He carries a kerosene lamp.

"Aren't you and Lina coming in?" The black one named Isaiah asks. I like Isaiah. I don't know why, but I like him. He avoids my eyes, but I feel that he likes me looking at him, that when he talks to Vincent, he's really talking to me.

"We've been summoned by the Big Man," Vincent answers.

Isaiah makes one of his faces. I am never sure if he is making fun or he is irritated. "Say what?"

"Pierce is having one of his dinner parties, and we aren't invited," Angry Kevin says. *Naku. Sobra talaga.* Always in a rotten mood! He disappears into the house without saying good-bye.

"Rude muthafucka," Isaiah mutters, making me giggle.

"Don't waste your time on negative energy, kid. Let's go smoke some more weed." Old Billy's smile is crooked. His eyes droop, and he walks like a drunk. Isaiah takes him by the arm and guides him gently up the stairs. Billy starts to sing in a beautiful, low voice; he seems very happy. Something in Spanish? Isaiah joins in. He whispers—something dirty or loving—in Billy's ear. Billy stops his singing to laugh.

"See you guys later," my darling Pretty Boy shouts as the van drives away. He asks Ernie to turn on the radio. Nothing but static. Ernie fumbles around in the glove compartment for a cassette to slip into the tape deck. Something familiar comes on, sweet and sad, sung by a man.

"I don't like this song," I say.

"You don't like bossa nova? Everyone likes bossa nova." Vincent rests his head on my shoulder. His hair smells like gasoline.

"You must be very tired," I say.

"This movie's kickin' my ass."

"Kicking everybody's ass," I say.

Suddenly he says in a broken voice, "I miss my son, Lina."

The van pulls up in front of a big, welcoming house, lit up by hundreds of flickering candles and kerosene lamps. Finally we are here.

The Dinner Party

The power was out in the entire valley, but it didn't seem to matter. The party was in full swing, and the tantalizing smells of Franco's cooking wafted through the house. Fresh basil and garlic, lemon, the purest of olive oils. Everyone looked warm and radiant in the flattering glow of flickering candlelight. Mayor Magbantay—whom everyone referred to as Mayor Fritz—smiled genially from his seat at the head of the table. He was young, for a politician. Next to him sat a forlorn beauty who never said a word. Pierce later whispered to Moody that she was Dolly, the mayor's common-law wife, a former starlet and the mother of his children. According to Pierce, there were many other children by many other women, but Dolly was Mayor Fritz's official main squeeze. Flushed and high from wine and who-knew-what, Pierce introduced Moody and Lina to Mayor Fritz, "our guest of honor." Pierce, who was seated at the other end of the table, also made sure that Lina sat next to him. Moody was annoyed but tried not to show it.

"I have seen your movies," Mayor Fritz said, vigorously shaking Moody's hand. He glanced at Lina.

"I pity you," Moody said, beaming back at him.

Mayor Fritz frowned, offended—but only for a second. His smile reappeared, infinitely more dangerous. "You are a joker, Mr. Moody?"

"Call me Vincent."

"You are a joker, Vince?"

"Yeah, I guess you could say that."

"Here, here," Claire Jenks said.

"Good! I like a man with a sense of humor." Mayor Fritz addressed Pierce. "You like a man with a sense of humor, Tony?"

"Sure," Pierce said, "but that doesn't mean I trust them."

Claire raised her glass in a toast. "I second that emotion."

"How long are you staying?" Moody asked her.

"*Quién sabe?*" Claire answered, with a shrug.

"You're all jokers." Mayor Fritz's smile widened. His teeth were more beautiful and intimidating than Gary Givens's.

The cluster of votive candles adorning the center of the long, spartan mahogany table gave the party a slightly religious or funereal air—Moody wasn't sure which. He sat beside Janet, Pierce's slender, boyish wife.

"No camera tonight?" Moody asked.

Janet tried not to smile. Moody noticed how attractive she actually was. "I've decided to give you all a break," she said. She got up from the table and went to check on her two young sons, already asleep in an upstairs bedroom.

"For God's sake, Jan," Pierce said when she returned.

"Our son Jesse has a fever," she explained to everyone as she sat back down.

"I can send for my doctor in Ligaya," Mayor Fritz said.

"Thank you, Mayor. But he'll be fine," Pierce said.

"He has a fucking fever," Janet muttered softly to herself, but only Moody heard her.

Pierce turned to Lina. "I bet you eat like a bird."

"Tony—" Janet said.

"I don't," Lina said to Pierce.

"Tony, I'm talking to you," Janet said.

Pierce gave her an ugly look. "What now?"

Mayor Fritz whispered something in Dolly's ear. He was not pleased.

"Would you care for some wine?" Moody asked Janet.

Janet thrust her empty wineglass out to him. "Sure. What the hell."

"There you go," Pierce said.

Moody poured her the red. She drank most of it down. Moody poured again.

"Take it easy, Jan," Pierce said.

"Do you play golf, Vince?" Mayor Fritz asked.

"No."

"Then you must learn. I will invite you and Gary—"

"Golf in the jungle?" Moody grinned.

"I have my own little golf course," Mayor Fritz said.

"I'm there," Givens said.

"A little girl like you needs fattening up," Pierce said to Lina. Lina looked uneasy.

"I'm fucked up," Janet Pierce said very quietly to Moody.

"It's okay," Moody said.

"Let's go smoke," Janet said. They got up from the table.

"Now where the hell are you two going?" Pierce asked.

Janet mimed puffing on a cigarette.

"You can smoke right here," Pierce said. They sat back down. Moody felt Janet seething across from him. She signaled one of the maids to bring over her pack of Players. As she lit one, Moody noticed that her hand was trembling. "Want one of these?" she asked him. "I bought them in Hong Kong. They're not bad."

"Thanks," Moody said.

Franco swept in from the kitchen, brandishing silver tongs and a pot of noodles. Sweat streamed down his face. Cirilo followed behind him with a saucepan and a ladle. Franco set the pot on the table and dabbed his forehead with a corner of his stained apron.

"At last," Mayor Fritz said.

"Sorry this has taken so long, my friends," Franco apologized. "Is very hard, cooking by candlelight. Is my own version of marinara linguine. Hope you enjoy. I use plenty Chianti. These typhoon nights are an improvisation, no? Hard without electricity, but is fun. Is all very very good, I promise you." He kissed the tips of his fingers for emphasis and collapsed into a chair. The sounds of rain falling and people eating were oddly comforting—sighs and murmurs, noodles being slurped, the tinkle of glass and silverware. "My God, isn't this rain ever going to stop?" Givens asked at one point.

"It will end as suddenly as it began," Mayor Fritz said. "Maybe as soon as tomorrow."

The servants—a trio of resigned women with Cirilo in charge—danced around the room, anticipating every need. Everyone ate heartily, except for Janet Pierce.

"I don't want to be here," she murmured to Moody.

"Neither do I," he said.

"My husband's making a fool of himself. You should go soon." Janet glanced in Lina's direction. "She's your girlfriend?" Moody nodded. "A bit too young for you, isn't she?"

"I want to see you again."

The corners of her eyes crinkled in amusement. Moody wondered how old she was. Thirty-five? She had one of those faces. Raw and compelling. Like Lina's. "Why? Do you feel sorry for me?"

"You turn me on."

Janet tossed her head back and burst out laughing.

Pierce looked up from his food. "What's so funny?"

Janet's eyes, frantic. "He was telling me about—"

"All your damn takes," Moody said, rescuing her. "How I got shot over and over again today. What a madman you are."

Pierce resumed eating.

"I would like to visit the set," Mayor Fritz said to him.

"We'd be honored," Pierce said. Moody wondered why Pierce kept kissing the mayor's ass.

"Come on tiger day," Givens said. "We're expecting a movie-star tiger at the end of the week, all the way from Hollywood—no, actually, the tiger's being flown in from some wild animal farm in *Tarzana*, California. Isn't that a gas?" Givens paused. "Tiger, Tarzana—get it?" Mayor Fritz was silent. "Well, anyway. Tony here's written a brilliant scene featuring said tiger suddenly jumping out of the bush and attacking one of the soldiers—no, actually, 'mauling' is a much more precise way of putting it—wouldn't you say so, Tony?"

Pierce burped, then called Cirilo over and helped himself to the last of the linguine. Janet Pierce grimaced. Moody felt Lina's eyes pleading with him, but he ignored her. She was ready to go home, but Moody was just starting to enjoy himself. He was going to punish Lina for dragging him to this dinner party, for being naive and stupid enough to be flattered by Pierce's attention.

"I have never seen a tiger," Mayor Fritz said.

"Don't they have tigers in the Philippines?" Claire asked.

"You know," Moody suddenly said, "the weirdest stuff has been plaguing this production. First the weather. I mean, this is a storm of biblical proportions! Then the helicopters. I mean, talk about setbacks."

"No big deal," Pierce said. "I can handle it."

"It's a big movie. Big movies are often complicated. Haven't you ever worked on a big movie, Vince?" Givens asked, his voice dripping with sarcasm.

"I know it's none of my business," Moody said, his gaze fixed on Pierce. "I mean, I'm just an actor, right? But is it true you made some kind of deal with the Philippine government so you could use their helicopters?"

"You do what you gotta do," Pierce said.

Moody turned to Mayor Fritz. "Yesterday, right in the middle of a take, the helicopters were suddenly called away by the military."

"Here we go," Givens muttered.

Mayor Fritz, amused. "Is that so?"

"Yeah. Apparently, there were reports of guerrilla sightings," Moody said. "What do you call your guys? NPA. Yeah, that's it. There were NPA sightings up in the mountains. Not too far from here. And the helicopters were called away."

"It happens," Mayor Fritz said. "MNLF, NPA—"

"How many people were killed? Would you happen to know, Mayor Fritz? It happened right around here—"

"You're out of control," Givens said.

"Are you interested in politics, Vince?" Mayor Fritz asked.

"I'm a history buff," Moody answered.

"So am I. We must talk again, soon." Mayor Fritz stood up from the table, and Dolly quickly followed suit. "It's been a very entertaining evening, but we must go. My wife does not feel well." Mayor Fritz gave a nod in Franco's direction. "The food was exceptional." He shook Pierce's hand. "Next time you will all come to my house for dinner."

"I'll see you on the set," Pierce said.

"Tiger day," Mayor Fritz said.

An armed man carrying an umbrella appeared in the doorway as if on cue. He escorted Mayor Fritz and Dolly outside to their waiting car. Givens turned to Moody, furious. "What the fuck were you getting at?"

"Nothing."

"Nothing my ass. You are one strange sonuvabitch, and you're going to get us in a lot of trouble."

"It's okay, Gary," Pierce said. "Mayor Fritz is cool."

"Mayor Fritz is cool? Mayor Fritz does not strike me that way, Tony. Mayor Fritz strikes me as very very hot," Givens said.

"Spooky," Claire said.

"I can handle it," Pierce said.

"I want to go now," Lina said to Moody.

"But that would be very rude," Pierce said. "It's one thing for our little mayor to be rude. He's the *jefe* of the jungle, so I can't really argue with the man, now, can I? We haven't had dessert yet."

"Lovely fruits," Franco added. "Mangoes and things."

"I think you should be a gentleman and take her home," Janet Pierce said to Moody. She looked around the table. "Actually, I think it's time for everyone to go. Big workday tomorrow, isn't it?"

"Jan," Pierce said.

"The missus has spoken," Givens said. One of the servants helped him on with his rain jacket. "Well, Tony. It's been a swell evening, as usual."

"You really don't have to go," Pierce said.

"No, darling. They do," Janet said. Her tone was quiet but firm. She called over another servant. "Tell the driver that our guests are ready to go home."

Moody, Lina, Claire, and Gary stood by the door. Franco undid his apron and followed them, a hangdog look on his face. "It was lovely," Janet said. "Thank you so much, Franco."

Franco smiled at her. "Was okay? Was really okay?"

They could hear a child whimpering upstairs. *Mommy.* Crystal clear, in spite of the pounding rain. Janet hurried back up the stairs.

"You can't jump every time—" Pierce said, but she was gone. He noticed them staring at him. "The kid's got nightmares. Bad ones."

"Why don't you go to him?" Claire asked.

"Yes," Lina agreed.

"What?" Pierce seemed bewildered by their suggestion. Moody took Lina and Claire by their arms and steered them quickly out the door. Everyone else was already in the car.

"Well, that was fun," Claire said. She fished a joint out of a fringed silk pouch she wore around her neck and lit up.

Givens, irritated, said, "Jeezus, Claire-bear. Can't you make it through one damn day without getting stoned?" The sweet smell of burning marijuana filled the van. Moody and Lina sat in the back next to Franco, Lina resting her head on Moody's shoulder. She was asleep in a few seconds.

"What was all that crap with Janet?" Givens asked Moody.

"What crap?"

"I was watching you. Having a little flirtation with the boss's wife, are we?" Claire started coughing. When Moody didn't respond, Givens continued. "I wouldn't, if I were you. Tony may look like a patsy, but . . . Wouldn't you say Tony has a dark side, Franco?"

Franco looked more unhappy than ever.

"A *very* dark side," Givens repeated.

"Stay out of my fucking business," Moody said, "and I promise to stay out of yours."

Givens did an exaggerated double take. "My, my. Have I offended you, Mistuh Moody?"

Mayor Fritz

3rd person (handwritten)

Mayor Fritz was indeed a fan of history. As a young man, he had toyed briefly with the idea of becoming one of those stodgy academics at the University of the Philippines in Diliman, or at the more elitist Ateneo de Manila. A good Jesuit university, but one he could never afford. Not in those days anyway. But now things were different. Mayor Fritz's fortune had changed. His father was dead. Finally dead, and all that hate in Mayor Fritz's heart, all that hate gnawing at him since the day he was born, was gone with him.

Mayor Fritz's own history was quite complicated. And yet, as things go in the Philippines, not surprising. He was the illegitimate son of Lucio "Lucky" Lim, a shady, prosperous lawyer, and Rosa Magbantay, the unlucky laundress who worked at Lim's seaside estate. Lucio Lim was known for molesting his female servants and fathering numerous bastard children. Rosa, barely fourteen when she was raped by the then fifty-year-old Lim, gave birth to Fritz nine months later. She was immediately thrown out of the house by Lim's enraged wife. After his mother committed suicide, Fritz was left to be raised by Lolo Pablo, Rosa's widower father, a fisherman who had lost part of one arm to a shark. *Fritz Juan Pablo Magbantay.* Who knows what possessed Rosa to name her son Fritz? He was a joke in the fishing village, the object of bullying by other children. Pigeon-toed, small, his nose perennially crusted with mucus. Pathetic. Fritz brought out the worst in people. Instead of pity, he inspired contempt. "*Pritz, Pritz, anak ng puta, anak ng Intchik!*" The village children, led by the popular bully, Totoy Robles, chanted in cruel singsong. *Son of the dreaded Chinaman, son of a whore.*

To protect himself Fritz retreated into a stoic silence, performing whatever task was demanded of him at home and at school, but doing only what was asked and no more. He became a master of setting limits: never giving anyone trouble or cause to remember him. He blended humbly into the background with cunning and ease. All that changed when Fritz turned twelve and Lolo Pablo brought home a dog-eared copy of José Rizal's *El Filibusterismo.*

"You might find this interesting," Lolo Pablo said. "Someone left it behind in the jeepney I rode this morning."

On the cover page, a name was written in faded ink but scratched out. "I'm sure it's no one from around here," Lolo Pablo assured him.

Fritz plowed through Rizal's novel—an uninspired translation into English from the original Spanish—in two days.

"Is what this book says about the church true?" he asked his grandfather.

"José Rizal was a martyr who died for our country," Lolo Pablo replied. "It must be true."

"They teach us about him in school," Fritz said, unimpressed. "Rizal this, Rizal that."

"Aha. And you are obviously sick of it." Lolo Pablo's tone was sarcastic.

"I am."

"You are a smart boy. The first one to read and write in our family."

Fritz's eyes widened in amazement. "Is that so?"

The old man nodded. "You should know that Rizal wouldn't lie. Priests are corrupt shits. It's the ugly truth. Just ask your mother."

"Mama's dead, remember?"

With his one good hand, Lolo Pablo reached for the cigarette tucked behind his ear. Fritz lit it for him. "Lucky Lim wasn't the first man to rape your mother. There was a priest in town. Fat mestizo priest. He got all the little girls going to confession. He got your mother. She was stupid and trusting, just like the rest of us." Lolo Pablo exhaled smoke, staring at Fritz with cloudy eyes. A battle-weary dragon. "The church sent him away before I could kill him."

"Shut up, Lolo."

Lolo Pablo grabbed Fritz's wrist with his good hand. "I will never shut up about your mother. She was my only child, you stupid son of a—"

"Chinaman," Fritz finished for him. "Chinaman and a whore."

Fritz buried himself in whatever books he could beg, borrow, or steal. *A History of the Philippines, Ancient Greek Mythology, Children's Bible Stories.* Rizal's *Noli Me Tangere.* Plato's *Republic.* He was determined to graduate from high school. The nearest college was in Davao City, but there was no money to get there and no chance of a scholarship. But in a strange way, Fritz didn't care. He had all this knowledge burning in his head, and that was what mattered. There was also his uncle, a popular and rising politician in Manila. If Fritz graduated from high school with honors, then maybe his powerful uncle could be persuaded to help him.

Fritz started working at the high school as a janitor and all-around handyman, forced to endure a new wave of taunts and snide remarks from Totoy Robles. One night, as Totoy was crossing a dark field on his way home, he was ambushed by Fritz. Fritz jumped on Totoy's back and pummeled the bigger boy with his fists. Totoy fell to the ground. Fritz threatened to bash Totoy's head in with a sharp rock. Fritz was small and slender, but his rage made a lasting impression. Totoy Robles promised that he would never pick on Fritz again, and he kept his word.

Shortly after his grandfather died, Fritz was haunted by a recurring dream in which he and Lolo Pablo rowed their *bangka* on Lake Ramayyah. There seemed to be no real purpose to their journey, except to enjoy the warmth of the sun and the extraordinary beauty of the day. As they rounded a bend, the lake—its surface choked with lily pads, vines, and fallen trees—became suddenly treacherous to maneuver. The *bangka* was stuck in mud and rocks. Lolo Pablo and Fritz climbed out and found themselves on an unfamiliar, uninhabited island overgrown with trees. Fritz glimpsed a broken, winding staircase through the foliage. The stairway led up to nowhere. Tarsiers leaped up and down the stone steps, gnashing their teeth. Farther on were the ruins of a great temple. Fritz and his grandfather exchanged glances, terrified and excited. Was this temple some sort of secret library hidden in the jungle? The dream always ended as the tarsiers fell silent and the men approached the ruins.

Fritz would wake, vexed and bewildered.

He killed his father shortly after his sixteenth birthday. Years later Mayor Fritz told the story to the American actor who reluctantly accepted his invitation to dinner. "I waited for that moment all my life. I never knew the man personally, you understand. But he was pointed out to me. 'There,' they would say. 'There goes your father. A coarse man. A terrifying man.' Everyone said I looked just like him. I was brown like my mother, but I inherited his Chinese eyes." Mayor Fritz paused for effect. "Do you think I look Chinese, Mr. Moody?" He did not wait for an answer. "I couldn't escape it. His—how do you call it?—his *legend* haunted me. As I grew older, my father went away to the big city and involved himself in politics." Here Mayor Fritz chuckled. "We heard stories. How Lucky Lim was behind the kidnapping and assassination of this man or that. A couple of pesky lawyers and policemen with their hands out, nothing too awful, you understand?"

Moody nodded. *I understand.*

Mayor Fritz nodded. *Do you?*

The mayor poured another round of Chivas on the rocks. They were alone in the *sala* of the mayor's fine house. A ceiling fan blew hot air around the room. Dinner was over, Dolly was asleep upstairs, and the bats, moths, lizards, cicadas, and mosquitoes were out in force.

"My father's seaside house stood empty all those years, watched over by a caretaker couple. But suddenly we heard that Lucky was back in Ligaya. Ready to retire to a peaceful life, *daw*. Can you imagine? Like any other old sonuvabitch might do."

"You saw your chance," Moody said.

"Indeed. It was now or never. My Lolo Pablo was dead, and I had nothing to lose. I went to Lucky's house one night—it was as simple as that. I had a stolen gun. It was raining lightly, as it is now. Lucky was on the veranda, brushing his teeth after dinner. I hid behind a banana tree and watched him for a while. After all, he was my father. Then I shot him. His house is my house now. This very house! That very veranda! That grove of banana trees outside in the garden, wet with rain . . . a setting very much like it was that night, many years ago. Do you have any children, Mr. Moody?"

Moody found it disconcerting to be addressed so formally, but he knew better than to argue with the mayor. "I have a son, Alex. He's turning four."

"A beautiful age," Mayor Fritz observed. "So what are you doing with that poor young girl?"

"You mean Lina?"

"I mean Lina."

"I'm in love with her."

"But you are a married man. Much too old for her."

"I'm not married," Moody said.

"Ah."

"I'm not taking advantage of Lina, if that's what you mean."

"I was watching you the other night, at Mr. Pierce's party. You were also interested in his wife, *di ba*? You were in a reckless mood. Even those things you said to me—"

"I apologize, Mayor Fritz."

Mayor Fritz held up his hand. "No, no. Nothing to apologize for! You know, Mr. Moody, it all comes down to this. I believe in loyalty and everlasting love. God has forgiven me for the sins of my youth. God has given me another chance by giving me Dolly and my children." Mayor Fritz beamed with drunken pride. "When they grow up, we're going to send them to the best schools in Manila. I am determined to give them what I never had. God forgave me, Mr. Moody. And so it is easy for me to forgive you."

Jesus Christ, Moody thought. *Jesus fucking Christ get me the fuck out of here tonight, alive.*

Mayor Fritz gestured for Moody to follow him over to the baby grand by the window. Photographs in ornate silver frames were arranged on top of the piano.

"Is there a musician in the family?" Moody asked, curious.

"No." Mayor Fritz pointed his chin toward a photo of a stern young man wearing glasses. "That was me, when I worked as an aide to the president. He is my uncle, you know." Moody nodded. Mayor Fritz then pointed his chin to an official photo of the president and first lady, signed, *With love from your Tiyo and Tiya.* Then to a young girl in a long white lace dress. "Our daughter, Rosa, in her First Holy Communion gown. She is named after my mother."

Moody managed a weak smile. "Cute."

"My only regret is that Lolo Pablo did not live long enough to see all this happen. I am a successful man. A very happy man, Vince."

They sat back down on the plastic-covered sofa and resumed drinking. Moody wasn't sure why he was still here. Dinner had been forced and drawn out, although the food was exceptional. Lechón of suckling pig, prawns in coconut milk, grilled tilapia. Mayor Fritz had pulled out all the stops. His children had made an appearance, dressed in frilly party clothes—then were whisked away to god-knows-where by their no-nonsense *yayas.* Moody wondered, as he kept eating and drinking, what the mayor was really thinking. Gary, Franco, Tony Pierce, and the missus had been invited but backed out at the last minute. The mayor seemed unfazed by their rudeness, but Moody had been in the Philippines long enough to know better.

"You are a drinking man," Mayor Fritz observed, pleased.

"Most people disapprove," Moody said.

"I don't. Let he who is without sin, blah-blah-blah."

They were finished with the Chivas by now. Mayor Fritz was getting ready to open a bottle of Fundador brandy. "A gift," he explained, "from one of my constituents."

An armed man stuck his head in the doorway. "The driver wants to know if he should wait, boss." Mayor Fritz glared at him and answered harshly in another language. Tagalog? Bisayan? The man lowered his eyes. "Yes, Boss." Mayor Fritz dismissed him with a wave of his hand.

"I should go," Moody said.

"Have some brandy first."

"It's late. I don't want to keep you and your men—"

"You are not keeping me. I am having a very good time. As for my men . . . well, that's what they are paid to do. Stay awake until I say something different."

"Tomorrow—I mean, *today* is a workday for me," Moody said.

"You movie people are all drinkers," Mayor Fritz said, ignoring his comment. "I like that."

"Except for Gary. He's a health nut."

Mayor Fritz sighed. "Ah, Gary. I am disappointed in him. And in your director and that Italian man. Dolly worked so hard to prepare this feast for them."

"I know. They were sorry they couldn't make it, but everyone is down with either the flu or diarrhea or something."

"Except you."

"Yeah. I'm pretty tough." Moody felt queasy. *Uh-oh. Time to go*, he thought, his ass sinking deeper into the plastic sofa.

"Why did you ask me about the NPA and the helicopters the other night?"

"I don't remember."

"I don't believe you. Are you fascinated by our troubles, Vince?"

"Actually, I find your entire country fascinating."

"Ah. Not just our women, then?"

"No. But you'll have to admit—"

Mayor Fritz waited.

"Your country has the most beautiful women in the world."

"So they say."

"You don't agree?"

"Whether I agree or not is really beside the point. But I actually expected more of you than these tired clichés." The surprised look on Moody's face made the mayor laugh. "You think you're talking to some peasant ID-JOT, Vince?"

"Not at all."

"I don't like Americans, especially American men. But I find you interesting. Just like you do me." The mayor paused. "Is that not so, Vince?"

"Yup."

"Mutual respect, *di ba?*"

"Grudging, but mutual."

"I know what that word 'grudging' means. It's a good English word. Precise. Do you know how to speak any of our languages?"

"Which one?"

"Ilocano, Tagalog, Illongo, Bisayan—"

"I can cuss in Tagalog."

The mayor grunted in contempt. "Of course you can."

Moody forced himself up from the sofa. He was drunk, but he would walk home if he had to. "*Magandang gabi,* Mayor Fritz. Thanks to you and Dolly for everything."

"Good night to you too, Vince. My driver will take you home."

"No thanks. I'll find my way."

"It's raining."

"The rain's let up," Moody said. "I need to walk off the alcohol."

"Nonsense. Pssst! Get the car, Napoleon," Mayor Fritz called out to the man waiting outside.

A fresh wave of fatigue washed over Moody. He had no choice but to be a good boy and do what Mayor Fritz wanted him to do.

American Movie

3rd Person.
Paz

Paz got the assignment to profile Tony Pierce when the story of Zamora and the Taobo looked like it wasn't going to pan out. Pierce's Vietnam epic, shrouded in conflict and mystery, would make a colorful, sexy, and more accessible story, according to Annie Scardino. Paz had to agree.

"Rumble in the Jungle, Thrilla in Manila, and all that sort of thing. Much better than some phony Stone Age tribe," the editor said on the phone. "This might be a cover story. I'll try to get you a little more money, Paz."

Yeah, sure, Paz thought, rolling her eyes. "Gee, Annie. Thanks," Paz said.

As soon as he found out she was now doing the article on Pierce and his movie, Pepito invited himself to Mindanao. "We can stay at my family's summer home near Lake Ramayyah," he said. "I guarantee you'll love it."

They flew to Cotabato del Sur in a small, creaky plane. Paz was glad to have Pepito along for company. She was nervous about flying, nervous about meeting the notoriously difficult director, nervous about fucking up the assignment. She'd heard the usual contradictory shit about Pierce. He was a genius. A hack. A nice guy. An asshole. A womanizer. A faithful husband, a loving father.

Perhaps it was all true. She was reminded of the legends that pre-
ceded Zamora.

The movie was forty-one days into shooting. Gary Givens, the
Nordic Adonis, had suddenly been replaced by the swarthy and intense Michael Barone. An amicable parting of the ways, Pierce's
publicist insisted. *Gary's health was an issue. The jungle didn't agree with
him.* There had been a young girl who'd disappeared, some friend of
Gary's from L.A. who dealt dope. Rumors were flying. The actor
claimed she'd simply left one day to go sightseeing and never came
back. The girl wasn't quite eighteen yet; her parents were threatening to sue the production company and have Givens arrested. There
was another, equally damaging tidbit known as "Gary's nineteenth
nervous breakdown"—a crack-up supposedly documented on camera by Tony Pierce's wife. Poor, fastidious Gary. All those hours of
pumping iron and gulping crates of imported mineral water hadn't
been of much use to him. *An amicable parting of the ways,* the publicist
repeated in another press release. But no one believed anything
could be amicable, not when it came to Pierce or his troubled movie.

The interview took place at Pierce's rented house. A servant
ushered Paz into the dining room. Pierce sat at the long mahogany
table—hunched over a typewriter, working on rewrites. He stood
up to shake hands. Paz felt the director's eyes move from her face to
her breasts and back again, dissecting her swiftly. "Let's get going,
shall we?" Pierce said, not bothering to conceal his impatience. "I
don't have all day." They sat back down. The table was strewn with
scripts, storyboards, half-empty coffee mugs, crumbs of food. *The
great director's beautiful mess,* Paz thought, fascinated. She set up the
tape recorder and microphone, keenly aware that Pierce was eager
for her to leave as soon as possible. She hoped he hadn't seen that
her hands were shaking. "Let's start with an obvious question, but
one that needs to be asked. What exactly made you want to tackle
the Vietnam War?"

"Because no one else has," Pierce snapped. "Because war fasci-
nates me. And this particular war . . . well, it's so very intimate and
ambiguous—wouldn't you agree?"

"What do you mean, exactly?"

"Oh, come on. First of all, Miss Marlowe, there is no 'exactly' in this situation. And speaking of 'exactly'—why is *Groove Rocket* so fucking interested in me, anyway? It's a music magazine, isn't it, exactly?"

"They've branched out. Movies, politics—"

"That last question of yours was tiresome."

"It's the heart of this story."

"But the answer's so obvious."

Paz glared back at him. "And it needs to be articulated by you, Mr. Pierce."

Pierce grinned. "The Vietnam War makes us uneasy. It's a dirty little war, full of dirty little secrets. Do you know anyone personally who got drafted, Miss Marlowe? Anyone who died or went mad? This particular war is not heroic, not simple, and that's why I'm obsessed by it."

"Drugs, rock and roll, the unknown."

Pierce gave a little snort of amusement. "Good God. Did you get all that out of reading the first draft of my script?"

"Yes. It's a wonderful script," Paz added, meaning it.

"I'm into draft number ninety-nine now, you know. You might want to take a look at it before you write anything final."

"Where exactly did your sympathies lie? In terms of the war, I mean."

"I don't have a political agenda." Pierce sighed. Why did he agree to this? He was tired of interviews, tired of the endless ass kissing with the press, tired of being cautious with his words. Most of all he was tired of these smug, self-righteous women with their misplaced aggression, these scruffy proponents of so-called new journalism, who were, in the end, really only writing about themselves. Though this one was attractive and feisty enough to be interesting. Not his type, but . . . Pierce yawned. He'd been up all night rewriting and was in an evil mood. Black hole: an ending still eluded him.

"Why was Gary Givens fired?"

"Gary was *not* fired," Pierce said. "How many times do I have to say this? I needed a different kind of energy, that's all. It wasn't Gary's fault. My vision changed. The script changed. Michael Barone's energy is opposite from Gary's. He embodies the character much more fully."

"What do you mean?"

"Detachment isn't useful to me right now. I need heat. Gary played detachment. He was great, but—"

recognize imp. of tense

"I notice you're referring to him in the past tense."

"Of course I'm referring to him in the past tense. You don't see Gary in the room, do you?"

"No, but—"

"But what?"

"Something. You talk like he's dead."

Pierce rubbed his chest absentmindedly. A nervous gesture, Paz determined, when he was caught off guard.

"Gary isn't dead to me," Pierce said. "You might say he's dead to this project."

Paz took a deep breath. *Here we go*, she thought, dreading her own question. "There are ugly rumors floating around. The girl, Claire—Claire Jenks?—has been missing for over—"

Pierce slowly shook his head. "I don't know anything about Miss Jenks's disappearance, Miss Marlowe. She was Gary's guest, not mine. Are we here to talk about my movie or what?"

A servant girl carrying a heavy platter loaded with food entered the room. Prosciutto, slivers of melon, a ball of cheese, a loaf of crusty peasant bread. She froze before the pile of papers on the table, unsure of what to do.

"Just put the damn thing down," Pierce said in a sharp voice.

"Where, sir?"

"Anywhere!"

The girl carefully set the platter down on a pile of papers and hurriedly left the room.

"Have some," Pierce said, suddenly expansive and cordial. "I get homesick and cranky, so I have these goodies flown in. My goodies appease me." Pierce tore off a piece of bread, added the prosciutto and cheese, stuffed the whole thing into his mouth. Bread crumbs dotted his chest, but he didn't seem to care. "Would you like some wine? I have that flown in, too."

"No thanks," Paz said.

"You don't drink?"

"Not until the sun goes down."

A moment passed. "Are we done?" Pierce asked. "I have work to do."

Paz smiled. "Not quite. I wanted to ask: Now that all your actors are in place—"

Pierce raised his eyebrows. "My actors are in place? Sebastian Claiborne hasn't arrived yet."

"Does that worry you?"

"Of course it worries me! I'm not just the director—I'm one of the producers on this movie. Until Claiborne actually sets foot on this soil, I'll worry. I worry all the time. That's my job. I worry, for example, that this movie may ultimately prove to be a pretentious piece of nothing. There's no middle ground for a movie like this. It's either gonna end up a colossal piece of shit, or great."

"And why is that?"

Pierce shrugged. "Every artist's nightmare, I suppose."

"I talked to Vincent Moody on the set yesterday," Paz said. "He claims you tend to improvise a lot and veer off the script. Do you enjoy taking risks?"

Pierce chuckled. "I trust actors and their instincts. What I can offer is a challenging setup. The rest is up to them."

"Is that how you always work? *Underdog* seemed tightly written. And so did *Good Cop, Bad Cop.*"

"But would you know if a script was tightly written just by looking at the finished product? Some people swear even a convoluted piece of shit can be fixed in the editing."

Paz was silent.

"Did you go to film school?" Pierce asked with a hint of scorn.

"Nope."

"I did. It was good for me, in the long run. Most of what I was taught I learned to throw out the window." Pierce tore off another piece of bread. "You wanna be a filmmaker?"

"Doesn't everyone? But actually, no."

A tanned woman with cropped brown hair swept into the room, followed by two equally tanned, beautiful little boys.

"Oh, there you are," the woman said merrily to Pierce.

"Oh, there you are," Pierce said to the woman. The smaller and younger of the boys climbed on to Pierce's lap.

"I saw a lot of Indians today, Papa."

The woman corrected him. "They're not *Indian*, Jesse. They're *Himal*."

"But they look like Indians."

The older boy rolled his eyes. "You are such a dummy."

"Shush, Dante! Don't talk like that to your brother." The woman nodded at Paz and held out her hand. "Hello. I'm—"

Pierce finished the sentence for her. "My wife, Janet. And our sons, Dante and Jesse. Everybody, meet Pascal Marlowe."

"You can call me Paz," Paz said to Pierce's wife and children.

"Who are you?" Jesse Pierce asked, staring at Paz with great curiosity.

"I'm here to interview your father," Paz answered, smiling.

"What's an interview?" Jesse asked.

"Jesse, please. Sorry if we've interrupted—" Janet said.

"Not at all," Paz said.

"I'm tired of talking," Pierce said to Paz.

Paz turned off the tape recorder and started packing up. "Can we continue this tomorrow, Mr. Pierce? I'm on a deadline."

Pierce shook his head. "Tomorrow's tough. We're shooting up in the mountains, at another location."

"May I come along just to observe?"

Pierce was clearly unhappy with the idea. He exchanged glances with his wife, who seemed sympathetic to Paz. "Just don't get underfoot," he finally said, after several moments had passed.

"You'll never have to worry about that," Paz said, relieved. "Thanks for your time, Mr. Pierce." She waved good-bye and left the room.

"Good riddance to another ingenue," Pierce murmured.

Janet's laugh was thin and nervous. "She seemed perfectly capable. Do you have to be so fucking rude, Tony?"

"Ma," Jesse whined in horror, "you said the f-word!"

"Ma," Dante mimicked his younger brother, "the f-word!"

"Sorry, darlings. But sometimes I just have to," Janet said.

Mayor Fritz had rented Pierce and his family the two-story house on the edge of town, which had a patch of cement lined by potted plants passing for a front yard. Here Paz stood and waited for Pepito. Pepito was always late. The rain had stopped temporarily; it was dreary and humid outside. Paz inhaled the stink of dying fish washed ashore, stunned by all the explosives the movie people were using. They were always blowing things up. Building elaborate sets only to blow them all up. Paz had observed two days straight of a simulated Vietcong hamlet's being bombed, coconut trees on the shoreline of Lake Ramayyah ablaze with fire and smoke. The noise had been deafening. Paz borrowed earplugs from a gaffer named Bob, who later kept trying to hit on her.

The older townspeople of Ligaya and Sultan Ramayyah kept their distance, but the young were thrilled by the flash and commotion. They hung around the edges of the closed set, awestruck by the lavish audiovisual feasts of destruction. Futuristic helicopters swooped down from the sky in a sinister ballet set to loud, pompous music. Movie stars were shot and stabbed, their wounds rendered in loving detail by sweating makeup artists with clenched teeth.

"How much do you think this cost?" Paz overheard one teenage boy ask another in Tagalog.

"Who cares, 'pare? Basta, realistic talaga," the other boy replied.

Sometimes the children were tapped for the spontaneous scenes Pierce was fond of creating. They played fallen, bloody corpses or extras in crowd scenes with humor and enthusiasm.

"Hey, Franco, I've got an idea I'd like to try," Pierce would say.

"Why not," Franco Broussard would answer, always game for

anything. More statement than question, really. Because whatever Pierce wanted to try was a given; that much was clearly understood by everyone.

"You don't mind?" Pierce would always ask. A show of concern and consideration; that was key.

And of course, no one did.

Broussard had been around Pierce long enough to know that what Pierce often came up with—on a whim, or after mulling it over many nights—would be brilliant. "He is great American director," Franco Broussard later said, when interviewed by Paz. "The most demanding and—how you say?—*crazy*."

"Why do you qualify it by calling him 'American'?" Paz asked. "Does it matter what nationality he is?"

"I don't know," Broussard said after a long moment of silence. Then he laughed. "I don't know."

Pepito drove up in his parents' Datsun—the one they kept stashed away in the garage of their lakeside retreat—just as Paz had given up and started walking toward the center of town. There was one main road that zigzagged over the mountains and eventually connected to the highway. The sky darkened, and Paz anticipated more rain. She hoped to reach the plaza before any drops fell. "Toot, toot!" Pepito yelled, pulling over.

"It's about time." Paz got in the car, annoyed. "I've been waiting for nearly an hour."

"*Ay!*" Pepito seemed genuinely appalled. "Am I that late, *ba?*"

"You're chronic. I think you should see a doctor."

Pepito laughed. Paz wondered if he was high. Something by Boz Scaggs was blaring a little too loudly from his eight-track. "The whole country should see a doctor," Pepito said. "You've been in the States too long, Paz. Time has become too important to you. So tell me. How did your interview with the great man go?"

"Like pulling teeth."

Pepito drove cautiously on the rutted roads. A boy riding a *carabao* waved to them from a rice field. "I wish I had been in the room with you. Pierce is one of the reasons I want to make movies."

Paz was fuming. "For fuck's sake. Who cares about Pierce? Can't you be more considerate?"

"About what?"

"About me. Didn't you hear what I said? I waited for—"

"*Sigé*. I apologize from the bottom of my heart, Paz."

"What happened? Did you have car trouble or something?"

"I have no excuses."

"No excuses," Paz repeated slowly.

"None."

"You keep everyone waiting. At the domestic airport, for example. I waited for hours. We almost missed the flight to get down here."

"*Dios ko*, Paz. What's eating you? Was the interview that unpleasant?"

"Do you remember how I used to cry whenever I visited your house on San Gregorio Street?" Paz suddenly asked.

Pepito smiled. "You thought it was haunted. You claimed you saw ghosts."

"I did."

"It made you unhappy, but you kept accepting my invitations to come over and play. You even agreed to spend the night once," Pepito said, swerving to avoid a woman carrying a bundle of laundry on her head. "But our parents wouldn't allow it. So what's all this nostalgia about? Don't you want to talk about your glamorous interview?"

"No. When we get back to Manila, let's go see your old house," Paz said.

Pepito gave her a quizzical look. "Didn't you get my letter? The house burned down a year ago. We never found out what caused it, but we weren't surprised. That house was so damn old."

"It was a beautiful—"

"It was *old*. Prewar. All that rotting wood. A firetrap, *talaga*. We were lucky we were on vacation when it happened, or we might all have perished."

They drove the rest of the way without speaking, past the mayor's huge house, past fields of cogon grass and wild lilies, then down to the end of a narrow, sandy road. A hand-painted sign hung off the barbed-wire fence:

PRIVATE PROPERTY
Mga Trespass Beware!
Bawal Umihi Dito!!!

No trespassing, no pissing.

Designed by Pepito's architect mother, the house was a rich person's version of a native hut, with a two-car garage, wraparound bamboo veranda, and thatched roof. Next door was a shack, home to the caretaker, Rufino, and his mongrel dogs. Rufino emerged to greet them, hurriedly wiping his mouth with the back of his hand. He unlatched the gate, shooing the dogs away.

"I cook your dinner already, sir," he said to Pepito.

"Great. Now you can put the car away," Pepito said.

The old man left. From high up in the trees, a gecko lizard clucked its ritual night song in the gathering darkness. Pepito and Paz entered the stylish showplace of a house. Pepito removed his shoes, then immediately began puttering around the kitchen.

"How long are we staying here?" Pepito asked.

"As long as it takes to finish my interviews," Paz answered. "You don't mind, do you?"

"Don't be silly. *Mi casa es su casa, di ba?* I'd better go with Rufino to the market tomorrow and get some more supplies."

"I really appreciate this," Paz said.

Pepito smiled. "You're going to introduce me to the production manager, aren't you? I'll do anything, just to watch Pierce direct."

Paz laughed at the thought of Pepito actually doing grunt work. "I don't have any clout with those people. And like I said, Mr. Director isn't too fond of me."

Pepito was unfazed. "So what? If you really want to, you can charm the pants off most people, *di ba*? You almost charmed the pants off me, once. I just happened to prefer boys."

"I don't have the energy to flirt right now."

"*Puwede ba*," Pepito scoffed, rolling his eyes. "Is this the result of your disastrous marriage?"

"Speaking of disaster, did you bring any dope?" Paz asked.

"Did you?"

Paz was irritated by Pepito's coyness. She watched him stir the broth in a pot.

"Hmmm. Yummy. Rufino cooked his special *sinigang*." Pepito made smacking sounds with his lips. "Let's eat."

"Need help?"

"There's nothing to do. See? The table's already been set. Rufino prepared everything ahead of time."

"I can't get used to being spoiled by that sweet old man," Paz said.

"Rufino makes a nice living compared to most people around here," Pepito said. "But if it makes you feel better, you can wash dishes later."

After dinner Paz lingered on the damp veranda, enjoying one of Pepito's Gauloises. How in God's name did he manage to obtain French cigarettes on a regular basis? It was an amusing affectation. Pepito was a mystery to Paz, though she considered him her oldest friend. They had been in and out of touch ever since she married Stefan and left for the States. As the eldest son from a large, prominent family, Pepito had been groomed to follow in his father's footsteps—attend some prestigious law school abroad, marry a debutante, spawn at least ten children, and eventually end up in politics. But Pepito made no secret of his sexual preferences, nor of his lifelong dream of making movies. His father threatened to disown him, but Pepito held his ground. For if an overpopulated, complicated, postcolonial India could produce a glorious filmmaker like Satyajit Ray, why couldn't an overpopulated, complicated, postcolonial Philippines produce an artist of equal stature in Pepito Ponce de León? Pepito once wrote to Paz, "Some of my early work is so *pompous!* But what can you expect from a self-taught auteur? When it's good, it's really really good . . . but when it's bad—ayayay! P.S. I don't think Godard or Kurosawa ever went to film school. Do you?"

Paz was eager to see his work. Pepito promised to arrange a screening for her, but somehow things kept getting in the way. Paz wondered if Pepito was just another poseur.

A few stars were out. Paz hoped the bad weather had come to an end. She looked forward to Pierce's shoot in the mountains. It was a long way up some very tricky, winding dirt roads. The call was for 5:00 A.M. Maybe Pepito could drive her there. After all, he desperately wanted to meet Pierce and Sebastian Claiborne. It was to be a big scene—one they had all been waiting for. As if summoned by her thoughts, Pepito emerged from the house and joined her on the veranda. He had thrown a flowing caftan over his jeans and wore his long, frizzy hair loose—very much the grand, barefoot, chunky mama-san. Paz was happy to see him. "Pepito, have I told you that my mother's family was originally from this region?"

"That explains it, then, " Pepito said.

"Explains what?"

"Your fucked-up-ness. This is *aswang* country, Paz. You must've grown up hearing those vampire stories." He unearthed a ball of hash and a small clay pipe from some secret pocket. "Nightcap?"

"Thought you didn't have any," Paz said.

Pepito ignored her comment. He packed the pipe and lit it, taking a deep toke before passing it to Paz. While she smoked, he peered into the blackness. "*Mira*. It's so clear, you can almost make out Mount Taobo."

Paz strained to see, but it was too dark. She sighed, disappointed. "You think any of it's true, Pepito?"

Pepito shrugged. "Who knows. Vampire *aswang*s are probably nothing more than giant fruit bats."

Paz giggled. "No. I mean the stuff about the Stone Age tribe. Zamora's discovery."

Pepito was indignant. "*Puwede ba!* My family's been coming here for years. How come we never knew that such a tribe existed?"

"But—"

"But nothing. Pass the peace pipe."

A piercing howl shattered the heavy silence. Paz gasped. The anguished cry came again. It made her skin crawl.

"What the fuck was that? It sounds like a woman screaming."

"*Haribon*," Pepito replied.

"What?"

"King bird. Nothing to worry about, Paz. Just another mournful eagle hunting for monkeys to eat."

Flashback

The sporadic screeching and howling persisted, the unseen eagle growing more desperate as the night wore on, determined to find his prey. Pepito and I stayed out on the veranda for hours, listening to the *haribon*'s spooky cry. Pepito finally had enough and gave me a good-night peck on the cheek. "Don't forget we have to get up at the crack of dawn," he said before disappearing back into the house. "Try to get some sleep, Paz."

But how could I? The shadowy outline of what I imagined was Mount Taobo loomed in the darkness, reminding me of my unfinished story.

I had gone back a second time to see Zamora before he disappeared. Without bothering to call ahead, I simply showed up one day at Casas Blancas. I didn't really expect him to be there, but I felt good about trying. I never shared this bit of information with Pepito. Was I afraid he'd consider me a fool for going back? Persistence was not in my nature. But in the matter of Zamora, I was determined to persevere. To sit down with him again and get answers to my questions: *Who are you, anyway? What made you do what they say you did?*

In a statement issued to the press before he disappeared, Zamora claimed to have arranged the relocation of the Taobo to an even more remote region of the rain forest. "We must save them from being permanently damaged or destroyed," he wrote. Did anyone give a damn about Zamora or the Taobo anymore? Bodabil then injured himself by falling from the fence surrounding Zamora's compound, in one of his frequent attempts to sneak out and go "exploring." Pictures of Bodabil being hauled off on a stretcher, his tiny face contorted in pain, barely made the newspapers. Zamora was blamed for the accident. Rumors that the first lady had been laundering dirty money through the President's Indigenous Minority People's Foundation (PIMPF)—of which Zamora was chairman—didn't help any. Zamora's days as a benevolent savior were over.

Why did I care so much? To this day I do not know. He was not related by blood, yet he felt like blood.

Persistence.

When I told Papa I wanted to try talking to Zamora again, he shook his head in disbelief. "Why bother, Paz? Zamora will never tell the truth. He doesn't know how. All that crap about some phony tribe! You think it's more profound and complicated than it actually is. Those people were not from the Stone Age! They were nothing but actors! Zamora is so rich he thinks he can fool the world. What about those children and that poor wife of his? *Pobrecita, talaga!* He drove her crazy, I'm sure of it. Ilse used to be such a sweet, smart, beautiful girl." My father seemed to have snapped out of his grief, if only for a moment. I loved seeing him so outraged and animated. "It's all just a game with him! Zamora's worse than his father. You remember how the two of them would come to our house when you and Ricky were little kids?"

"No," I lied.

"I once tried to broker a deal with Don Flaco. I wanted to import Swiss tractors to this country, and I needed his help to get past all the bribes and bureaucracy. It didn't work out—the old man wanted too much in return for his cooperation. Don't get me wrong—I respect him. He's straightforward, unlike his son. The old man never tried to screw me—not directly, at least." Papa chuckled. "Guess I'm too small-time. Zamora Junior used to tag along, whenever Don Flaco came to our house. While I talked business with the old man, Junior would flirt with your mother."

I was stunned but tried not to show it. My father went on, "Zamora was twenty-something. Your mother was thirty-something—beautiful, bored, and frisky."

"Didn't it bother you, Papa?"

"It was just a flirtation."

My father worked all his life managing the Manila branch of Zoltan Incorporated, an international trading company owned by a Hungarian Jew from Shanghai. He did business with the López de Legazpis and the other handful of powerful families who controlled shipping and commerce in the Philippines. After martial law was declared in 1972, my father was forced to do business with the president and his cronies. The president and first lady were greedy and became greedier. Everyone who could, everyone who was not poor and powerless, followed suit, grabbing at whatever piece of pie was available. There were, of course, those who remained uncorrupted, who were angered and troubled by the insane feeding frenzy that seemed to have gripped the nation. Many had already left, including me. My parents chose to stay, a bit more guarded and grim, but determined to stick it out. I went back and forth from L.A. to New York, staying for extended periods of time in each place until my unease became too overwhelming. I looked to my husband for answers, which was a big mistake. He was as perplexed and annoyed by my vague yearnings as I was.

Persistence.

I convinced Papa to let me borrow his car and drove to Casas Blancas one afternoon. I parked right outside the front gate.

"*Hoy!*" I shouted up to the sentry posts.

The guards were jolted from their naps. "*Sino po kayo?*" The skinny one rested his hand on a sawed-off shotgun.

"Paz Marlowe to see Mr. Legazpi," I said in English.

He rubbed the sleep from his eyes. "Boss is not here."

"How could that be? We have an appointment."

The fat one picked up a phone and spoke into it. He never once took his eyes off me. He hung up. A few moments passed.

"Well?" I asked, crossing my arms at my chest.

"You wait, miss," the skinny one said. More agonizing minutes went by until the phone finally rang. "Okay, okay. *Sigé.* Roger, over and out." The fat one jerked his head in the direction of the main house.

"*Salamat,*" I thanked him.

Sonny Limahan waited for me by the front door. "We were not expecting you, miss."

"I need to see Mr. Legazpi again."

"He is away on business," Sonny replied, then added, "for a while."

"Strange."

"Strange?"

"That you're here and not there, with him. Wherever he is."

Sonny grinned. "I'm sorry you waste your time, miss."

"Will you tell Mr. Legazpi I came by? That I need to meet with him again? Please, Sonny."

"Yes, ma'am," Sonny said.

The scent of rotting *kalachuchi* hit me as I headed back to the car. My father's parting words came back to haunt me: *Whatever you do, don't go there and make a fool of yourself.* A wispy young girl suddenly crossed my path, running toward a cluster of banana trees. Was she a ghost? She wore a faded blue dress, much too big for her skinny frame. Rubber slippers on her dusty feet. The girl returned my smile. "Psst," I called out softly, but she was gone. *Kalachuchi* blossoms rained down from the flowering trees and rotted as soon as they hit the ground. Their cloying perfume, perfume of death, filled my nostrils.

Why had I lied to my father? My childhood memories of Zamora and his father were vivid and powerful. There was one Saturday morning in particular. Don Flaco's green-and-white Cadillac—big and imposing as a battleship—pulled up in the driveway. Zamora strutted into the *sala* of our house, and lagging a few paces behind was his hawk-eyed father. My father greeted them warmly. He and Don Flaco sat down on the sofa while Zamora wandered out into the garden. I hid behind a clump of bamboo and weeds that grew right outside the living-room window, spying on everyone.

My mother floated on her back in the small, murky swimming pool. Her eyes were closed. Dragonflies darted around her. The water was strewn with fallen leaves, flailing bumblebees, a dead caterpillar or two. Zamora walked to the edge of the pool and glanced down at her.

"Pilar, I don't understand how you can lay in that water."

"We can't afford to have the pool cleaned," Mama snapped. Her eyes remained closed, but she was smiling.

Zamora repeated her name. "*Pilar.*"

In the *sala* Papa listened intently as Don Flaco pontificated over God-knows-what. The mysteries of making money, I supposed. And though I was only eight years old, it was obvious to me that while my father desperately needed Don Flaco, Don Flaco needed no one. Papa looked more unhappy as Don Flaco droned on. At one point both men turned their heads toward the window. I crouched down low to avoid being seen. Zamora lingered by the pool. Mosquitoes attacked me; my calf muscles cramped from sitting on my haunches for so long.

"You haven't been by," Zamora complained to my mother, a slight trace of irritation in his voice. "Are you playing dead?"

"Did you know your father has commissioned me to do a family portrait?" Mama asked.

"*Qué?*"

"A portrait of your father, your mother, your sisters, you."

"My sisters live in Spain."

"I'll work from a photograph, then. I don't usually paint portraits," Mama continued. "But your father has convinced me to try it. He can be very persuasive."

"Get out of that filthy water." Zamora's voice shook. "That *swamp*."

My mother floated away.

The silence and heat were heavy and delicious. Papa and Don Flaco got up from the sofa, finished with their business. Don Flaco patted my father on the back in a consoling gesture. My father's smile was small and tight. They moved outdoors.

"Pilar," my father called, "Don Flaco wants to see you."

Rubber slippers. A faded blue dress that I'd outgrown. Terrified of being discovered, I became totally still. Tiny red ants swarmed over my bare feet, biting as they went. I stopped breathing.

"Pilar?" my father called out. "Pilar?"

"Where's my favorite artist?" Don Flaco cackled. The sun-soaked garden shimmered before him. His son stood at the edge of the pool, looking down at my floating mother.

My brother's chubby face peered through the thicket of bamboo. "What are you doing?"

"Nothing."

"Mama! Papa!" Ricky cried out, triumphant. "Paz is spying on you!"

He had returned from another afternoon spent proselytizing to unbelievers and teaching English to the children of Barangay Pagibig, a squatter settlement along the Pasig River. Ricky's weekly missionary expedition was part of the extracurricular activity expected of an honor student at the all-boys Ateneo de Manila.

It was a privilege and a blessing to teach the poor to love and obey God, the Jesuit priests had constantly drummed into him. *For the meek shall inherit the earth. So Jesus has taught us.*

Suffer the little children to come unto me, Ricky would respond. *So Jesus has taught us.*

My mother once went to observe Ricky at work and forced me to go with her. We stood in the sun while he took roll call, solemn and imperious in his Catholic-school uniform. I was embarrassed by the vulgar size of the silver Sacred Heart medallion Ricky wore around his neck. I winced as he shouted out the children's names, railing at them in English: BOY FRANCISCO! BOY GAMBING! JEN-JEN ALEJANDRO! ARE YOU PRESENT AND ACCOUNTED FOR? LOVEY FERNÁNDEZ, WHY WERE YOU ABSENT LAST WEEK? The children, for the most part, didn't understand most of what Ricky was saying but endured him with grace and good humor. They sucked contentedly on the lemon drops Ricky brought as a reward for parroting the catechism lessons back to him:

Who made you? God made me.
Who is God? All-seeing, all-hearing, all-powerful.
Who made the world? God made the world.
Who is Jesus? The son of God, who died for our sins.
Who is Mary? Blessed mother to Jesus.
Who are you? An instrument of God's love.
Very good, Jen-Jen. Very good, Boy.
What is sin?

———

What is sin?

———

Jen-Jen?
Ha?

"Spying!"
    "Shut up, Ricky."

"You little brat," Ricky hissed. I emerged from my hiding place, furious.

Don Flaco, Papa, Ricky, and I watched as Zamora extended his hand and pulled my mother out of the pool. She was laughing. I was embarrassed and intrigued by their display, aware that something wasn't right. My brother was oblivious, but I wondered what Papa and Don Flaco were thinking.

"I'm ready to go," Don Flaco announced curtly to his son.

"*Sí, Papa.*"

"*Ay, Paz,*" Mama said to me, exasperated. "What mischief have you been up to?"

"Nothing," I said.

"Little brat," Ricky hissed.

"I'm going to kill you!" I shouted.

"You're going to burn in hell for saying that," Ricky said.

"You kids better stop, or you'll both burn in hell." Mama's tone was light and teasing. She seemed in a playful mood.

"*La niña es muy maldita.*" Don Flaco glanced at me disapprovingly.

"Go to your room, Paz," Papa said, "while I consider the appropriate punishment."

"But I promise . . . I won't do it again."

"No more buts, Pascal."

"Paz is a spy and a sneak," Ricky taunted.

"That's enough, Ricky," Papa warned.

"A troublemaker! A spy and a sneak!" Ricky kept taunting. I burst into tears. My father grabbed my brother by the arm and dragged him back into the house.

Don Flaco glared at his own son. "Are we going or what?"

Mama took me in her arms and attempted to comfort me. Utterly humiliated, I hid my teary face in her damp bosom. Her skin smelled of chlorine and perfume.

I heard Zamora murmur, "*Hasta luego, Pilar.*"

My mother didn't respond. I felt the pressure of her arms around me. There was a silence. I imagined Zamora flashing her a bitter, melancholy smile before finally waving good-bye.

Flashback Redux

3rd Person Zamora

It was quiet. Sonny watched Paz walk down the winding driveway, pausing for a brief moment by some bushes. The mestiza had seen something—he wasn't sure what. She walked at a brisk pace past the guardhouse and disappeared into the street. Sonny went back into the house.

"She's gone, sir," Sonny said.

"Funny girl."

"*Oo nga, ano?*" Sonny agreed, grinning.

Night crept up, blurring the edges of things. Flowers—blooming blood-red in the harsh light of day—now drooped with exhaustion in the creeping gloom.

"Are you hungry?" Sonny asked. When Zamora didn't respond, he said, "Boss, you have to eat—"

"What a stupid thing to say," Zamora said. "Why? Why should I eat?"

"Sorry, boss."

"Do I look like I'm starving?"

"No."

"Do you think I'm going to die?"

The lights in the house were off. Sonny longed for the rain to fall, for lightning and thunder to crackle and break the silence. The gloom seemed to swallow them up. *Tu-ko*, the gecko called from the trees. A sad, clucking sound that always got under Sonny's skin. He thought of his wife, Dely, back in Bacolod. How he missed her and the children he barely knew. How the thought of loving them with the same pure, earnest passion of the pop songs he cherished comforted him. And yet he refused to quit his free-floating job with Zamora (aide, bodyguard, last-minute golfing partner, a job without titles) and go home to his family. The two men stood on the terrace for a long time. The distant, tinny sound of a transistor radio drifted from the guardhouse.

"Do you miss my wife?"

"Sir?"

"You heard me."

Sonny dreamed of turning the tables. Asking, *Do you miss your wife?* In the dark he listened to Zamora breathe. "Your wife was very kind to me. We all miss her, sir."

"My wife was born to be a nun. She would've been better off in a convent."

"Maybe, sir," Sonny said. Zamora gazed at him for a long moment, then turned away.

"That Marlowe girl," Zamora said. "You think she'll come back?"

"No, sir. I think she got the message," Sonny assured him.

The Emperor of the Jungle

3rd Person.
script

The chunky, bespectacled man with Jesus Christ hair and the haughty, craggy face of a Spanish conquistador was introduced to Tony Pierce as Pepito Ponce de León, a rising local film director. "Your movies are my inspiration," Pepito said in earnest, as Pierce shook his hand.

Pierce was harried, but in an affable mood. "Film director, huh? Have I seen anything?"

"I doubt it," Pepito replied. He was nervous about being in the famous man's presence but tried not to show it.

"Well," Pierce said, turning his attention to Paz, "gotta get to work. Just try to stay out of the way, okay?"

"Of course," Paz said.

"*Que se joden,*" Pepito muttered to Paz as Pierce walked off.

Paz giggled. "Say wha'?"

"I said fuck him," Pepito whispered.

Sebastian Claiborne had finally arrived and was scheduled to shoot his first scene. Though no one had actually seen him yet, everyone was excited and almost giddy with anticipation. It was six-thirty in the morning, but Pierce was on overdrive, barking orders to everyone on the set. "It's very important to me that Commander X's jungle fortress be exactly right. His hideout is practically a world unto itself—know what I mean?" Pierce scowled at Caleb Brook, the production designer.

Brook nodded, muttering "time, time" under his breath as he hurried away.

"Who's he?" Pepito whispered to Paz, observing Brook. "He's got a nice ass."

"My God, Pepito. Is that all you ever think about?"

"Sorry, but I haven't been laid in a while."

"Well, neither have I," Paz said.

"Where's Menching?" Pierce yelled to no one in particular. "Somebody fucking get me Menching and a cup of coffee!"

"*Qué barbaridad!* I had no idea Pierce was sooo evil!" Pepito gushed in mock horror.

"Control yourself," Paz said.

Where was Sebastian Claiborne? Pepito wondered, eyes scanning the busy set. Pierce in the midst of it, shouting, a worried look on his sunburned face. Pepito fantasized having chummy conversations with the director about the day-to-day headaches of making movies. Those terrible, trivial details that you had to pay attention to, or else. . . . He fantasized standing next to Pierce, observing him shoot take after take of a particular scene, then being asked by him to critique it. Pepito had spent one semester, after all, at UCLA film school. He had never told Paz he was in L.A. while she was there. Pepito had enrolled in the same program Pierce had attended for a semester and a half, before dropping out to make *Who Killed Jimi Hendrix?*—an animated, surrealistic short that went on to win several awards and jump-start Pierce's career. It seemed to Pepito that even from the beginning, Pierce could do no wrong.

Pepito and Paz watched Pierce rehearse Michael Barone with Isaiah Waters, Billy Hernandez, and Vincent Moody. It was a new scene, which Pierce had written that very morning. Barone kept blowing his lines. "They should never have fired that Gary guy," Pepito said.

A middle-aged Filipina woman appeared, holding a Styrofoam cup of steaming coffee. "Menching, I've been looking for you," Pierce said to the harried production manager.

"Yes, sir. Here—" She handed him the cup.

"I've been warned by our friendly mayor that we're getting a few unfriendly visitors sometime today or tomorrow."

"*Dios ko.*" Menching glanced at Paz and Pepito.

"You know what this means." Pierce took her aside, whispering to her in a low voice. Menching's face collapsed into a frown. Pierce started to walk away, then remembered that Pepito and Paz were standing there. "Oh, Menching—"

"Yes, sir."

"You've met Paz. And this is—" Pierce had already forgotten his name.

"Pepito," Pepito said. "Pepito Ponce de León."

"*Ay!*" Menching exclaimed in recognition.

"You know me?" Pepito asked, puzzled.

"I worked on your movie," Menching replied. "That Magellan thing. What was it called? *Circum*-something?"

"*Circumnavigation,*" Pepito said. Paz wondered why he seemed uncomfortable.

"Did you ever finish it? " Menching asked.

"It's on hold. Until I find some more money," Pepito said, clearing his throat.

Pierce chuckled. "Sounds familiar."

"Speaking of— Are there any jobs available? Any way I can work on this production?" Pepito was trying hard not to beg. His eyes darted from Menching to Pierce.

"Everything's taken," Pierce said.

Pierce turned to Menching. "About our problem . . ."

"Yes, sir."

"Take care of it," Pierce said. He went back to rehearsing the actors.

"*Ayyy,*" Menching sighed again. The heavy weight of Pierce's demands pressed down on her.

"Something wrong?" Paz asked.

Menching was lost in thought. "Aren't you working on a new movie?" she suddenly asked Pepito, perking up.

"*D.O.A.,*" Pepito answered with pride. *Dead on Arrival.* It would be his first feature. No half-hour arty stuff like *Circumnavigation*, but a big vehicle for some action star, with a title boldly appropriated from a Hollywood classic.

Menching gestured for Pepito to come with her. As Paz started to follow, Menching held up her hand. "Sorry, Miss. But—"

Paz, annoyed. "But what? He's *my* guest."

Menching shrugged. "No reporters allowed. Don't worry. I'll bring him right back."

They walked toward a hangarlike warehouse that housed costumes, props, and equipment. Several vans were parked nearby. A tall, sandy-haired man emerged from the building. "Our production designer, Caleb Brook," Menching announced.

Pepito grinned. Brook scrutinized Pepito closely. "Who's this?"

"One of our local movie directors," Menching said.

"No kidding," Brook said.

Pepito kept smiling. The patrician Brook with the great ass was definitely his type.

"You know our problem," Menching said to Brook.

"Yeah."

"Well, sir. It just occurred to me that Mr. Ponce de León here is also making a movie."

Brook frowned. "I don't quite follow you, Menching."

"Excuse me?" Pepito interrupted. "Could someone please explain?"

"We've got bodies in the warehouse," Brook said. "Unclaimed bodies from the local morgue."

"D.O.A." Menching giggled.

"Excuse me?" Pepito repeated, baffled now.

"Pierce requested dead bodies," Brook said. "He never specified that he wanted *props*."

"A Filipino misunderstanding," Menching murmured.

"I understand," Pepito said, not understanding at all. Was he dreaming all this?

"Somebody told somebody," Menching said. "According to Mayor Fritz, the authorities are threatening to close down the set."

"It's a bit awkward," Brook said.

"Maybe you could use them," Menching said to Pepito. "For your movie?"

"But we haven't started shooting," Pepito said.

"*Bahala na. Basta*, if you help us, we will help you." She turned to the production designer. "*Di ba*, Mr. Brook?"

"Sure," Brook said.

Ruthless, scheming Menching. Pepito wondered why he couldn't remember her from the movie. Menching. Menching. And this thing with the giveaway corpses—Pepito felt a mixture of disgust and admiration at the sheer *cojones* of it all.

"Where are the bodies?" Pepito asked.

"In there," Brook said, nodding toward the warehouse. Pepito stared in disbelief. "It's air-conditioned," Brook added with a smile.

Pepito, Menching Lázaro, and Caleb Brook stood outside the building contemplating what was inside. Menching, recently separated from her philandering husband and now responsible for feeding five children on her production manager's salary, knew exactly what it would mean to take care of this particular situation. Pierce would reward her with a raise and a hefty bonus. Caleb Brook, who worked on all of Pierce's movies and would continue to do so, was simply being loyal by trying to help Pierce out. But Pepito Ponce de León, hungover and consumed with dread, wasn't sure how he felt.

Pepito spoke first. "No," he said.

"No?" Menching looked stunned.

"No," Pepito repeated.

"I guess the shit's gonna hit the fan," Brook said before disappearing back inside to where the frozen bodies lay waiting.

Pepito couldn't get away fast enough, his heart racing at the thought of what gruesome gifts had just been offered him. Menching called his name, but he pretended not to hear, mumbling "excuse me excuse me *lang*" as he made his way back to Paz.

"What's going on?" Paz asked.

"I've had enough," Pepito said, shaking. "Let's get out of here."

"I can't leave. They haven't even started shooting."

"Fuck that. I thought I was crazy, but these people . . ." Pepito shook his head.

"There you are!" From out of nowhere, Menching appeared, panting and out of breath. She grabbed Pepito by the arm. "I've been looking all over for you—" She became aware of Paz staring and stopped herself.

"I told you no," Pepito said to Menching.

"Please." Menching tightened her hold on his arm.

"Sorry." Pepito extricated himself from her grasp.

Menching sounded resigned. "*Sigé.* I understand. But remember that what happened today is strictly off the record."

Pepito nodded. Menching gave him one last imploring look before leaving.

"Wow," Paz said. "Heavy drama."

"There goes my career," Pepito said.

"When are you going to tell me what this is all about?"

"Off the record?"

"Off the record."

"You can never ever write about this," Pepito said. "Promise?"

"Cross my heart and hope to die," Paz said.

What the hell, Pepito thought. *Tell her.* "They have actual corpses stored in a freezer to use as props, Paz. Corpses no one has claimed.

Someone squealed, and the authorities are coming out tomorrow for a full-scale inspection."

"What's your role in this?" Paz asked, stifling a laugh.

"Nothing. I'm just the fool they saw coming toward them. They tried to pawn the corpses off on me." Pepito paused. "You're laughing?" Paz laughed harder. "You don't think this is terrible?"

Paz didn't respond, lost in some dark joke of her own. She wiped a tear from the corner of her eye. Her laughter trailed off into a sigh. "What a great story. Wish I could use it."

"But don't you think it's—" Pepito searched for the right word— "blasphemous?"

"If you're a Catholic, probably yes."

Pepito studied his friend with renewed interest. "You're something, Paz."

Paz smiled. "We can't leave, Pepito. Sebastian Claiborne is finally here. Finally, really, really here."

A huge crowd had gathered on the periphery of the set. Claiborne's bulky six-foot-four-inch frame towered over the actors, extras, and crew. He listened intently to something Pierce was saying, Pierce who squinted up at him and gestured with his hands. Claiborne's head, shaved for the role of Commander X, glinted in the hot morning sun.

"*Dios mío*," Pepito uttered in a low voice. "He's fatter than me."

Paz stood on tiptoe to get a better look. "I'm still in love with him. Wish I'd met Claiborne when he was my age."

They inched their way through the crowd. Mayor Fritz was ensconced in a canvas chair up front, wearing wraparound sunglasses. A well-dressed little boy sat on the mayor's lap sipping a Coke.

"Well, well," Pepito murmured. "Looks like a lot of VIPs here today."

Pierce and Claiborne stayed huddled in an intense tête-à-tête, much to everyone's consternation. Claiborne, clad in voluminous drawstring pants and kimono-style jacket, was doing most of the talking. He and Pierce were oblivious to the waiting actors, the growing crowd of fans and onlookers. Janet Pierce and two other people were all over them with their cameras and microphones.

"Who's that woman?" Pepito asked.

"Pierce's wife," Paz answered. "She's making some kind of a documentary."

"Wow."

"The way I see it," Claiborne was saying, "my character is essentially a good man—"

"Gone wrong," Pierce reminded him.

"No," Claiborne said, "I'd have to disagree. The world just isn't ready for him. Blood is spilled in the name of beauty, love, that sense of connection to self. Primal self. That's why he—the commander— created his kingdom in the jungle. When you finally understand what it means to kill—to take away someone's precious life—well, then. The commander's madness comes out of a kind of stoic purity, a great sadness. That's why the tribesmen worship him. They are the only ones, ironically, who can appreciate—"

"You're right. But I still insist. He's in over his head," Pierce said, interrupting once again. "Way in. And that's all you have to know to nail the character in this particular scene."

Claiborne was cool and serene. "We're beyond that, Tony."

Pierce stifled the urge to scream. It was close to noon, and they hadn't shot one fucking scene yet. All because of Claiborne, who'd finally arrived last night on a private jet. Months of convoluted negotiations, broken promises, and endless demands finally over. And now this. Claiborne wasting everyone's time with his rambling analysis of the role he was to play. Pierce had been warned repeatedly by Claiborne's personal manager not to interrupt the actor when he was off on one of his stream-of-consciousness tangents. "It's all part of his creative process—dissecting his character to bits until he's comfortable with himself and with you. Sebastian's a very sensitive man," the manager said. "One of a kind." To be interrupted while he was talking was apparently something Sebastian Claiborne could not, would not, tolerate. "He might walk out on you," the manager continued. "I've seen him do it. Walk off the set and never look back."

Pierce wondered if he'd blown it. Claiborne kept staring at him. "Did you find my references helpful?" Pierce asked after a long silence.

"Of course," Claiborne answered. His cherubic face broke into a smile. He was obese and no longer handsome, but his smile was still dazzling and powerful. "*Heart of Darkness, Lord Jim, Tarzan.* That's what got me thinking, Tony."

"Shall we try it, then?" Pierce smiling back, gentler now.

"Try what?" Claiborne seemed genuinely puzzled.

"A take."

"Ah," Claiborne said. "Why not?"

"I want to go home," the well-dressed little boy whined.

"Soon," Mayor Fritz promised, patting his son affectionately on the shoulder. The boy sulked. "When are they going to start, Papa?"

"I warned you," Mayor Fritz said. "Movies are a tedious business."

"That man is *mataba*," the boy complained. "What kind of movie star is he?"

Too fat and too arrogant—that's what they were all thinking and whispering, except for Mayor Fritz. "That man is the greatest actor in the world," Mayor Fritz said to his son.

The bored child began picking his nose and squirmed on his father's lap. "Can we go now?" he whined again. Mayor Fritz swatted his son's hand and shot him a threatening look. The stunned child was about to cry but, after assessing the murderous gleam in his father's eye, didn't.

81. EXT. BORDER BETWEEN LAOS AND CAMBODIA—LATE AFTERNOON

CAPT. FLINT, COWBOY, MONK, and DRIVER approach the jungle hideout. The four soldiers are on a secret mission to terminate the renegade COMMANDER X. Cowboy, his face and naked

torso smeared with mud and camouflage paint, seems most
at home in the jungle. His eyes are bright with morbid anticipation. Monk, the youngest and most inexperienced of the
three, is jittery and tense, jumping at the sound of every
twig breaking, every bird and monkey screeching. A look of
confusion and terror on Monk's face. Flint and Driver, sea-
soned warriors, lead the expedition.

The scene had no scripted dialogue and the actors were on their
eighth or ninth take. Moody was in trance mode and had stopped
caring or counting. Claiborne as Commander X stood on a hill
looking down at him, surrounded by loincloth-wearing Filipino extras playing mountain tribesmen. The extras took their roles seriously, brandishing fake spears and cutlass *bolos* with gusto. Their
eerie, masklike faces were painted white and streaked with slashes of
red. The scene—the way Claiborne as Commander X was framed
with his menacing army against a chilling backdrop of mutilated
corpses, their hands and feet bound, hanging from trees like ghastly
Christmas ornaments—had an ominous grandeur to it. Pepito wondered if the realistic-looking corpses were actually dummies or part
of Menching's macabre loot. Paz nudged Pepito with her elbow,
wondering the same thing. *Where was Menching?* Pepito saw no sign
of her in the crowd. From the sidelines even Mayor Fritz and his
restless son fell silent.

On a bamboo platform fifteen feet off the ground, a shirtless,
sweating Tony Pierce observed the action being filmed. He took a
series of slow, deep breaths to calm himself down. Gary Givens was
gone, and now his replacement was threatening to quit, but Sebastian Claiborne was finally here. Perhaps his movie wasn't jinxed, after all. Pierce glanced down at the crowd. Who the fuck were all
these people? He had to talk to somebody about it. Security was
getting much too lax. Lately things were starting to disappear. Nothing too valuable yet—just beer and some canned goods, a few props
left lying around. Billy Hernandez's Rolex. Minor bullshit, really. But
still.

As scripted, Claiborne made a small, graceful gesture with his hand. Some sort of clandestine signal to his native troops. In response the extras lifted their spears. As scripted, Barone, Hernandez, Waters, and Moody froze in their tracks. Not sure of what to do next, or if they were about to die. The silence was broken as the extras roared in unison, bringing their spears back down to the ground with a definitive thud. End of scene as scripted. The cameras continued to roll. Claiborne's presence had worked its magic.

"Well, well. What the fuck do we have here?" Billy Hernandez (as Driver) improvised.

Isaiah Waters (Monk), not to be outdone, started to cry. Vincent Moody (Cowboy) aimed his weapon at Claiborne and his men.

"It's over," Waters whimpered. "Fucking over." His knees buckled, and he fell to the ground slobbering. In a flash of inspiration, Moody aimed his weapon at Waters. At the exact same moment, Claiborne lifted his head toward the sky. The bald head and massive girth added to his majesty. Claiborne smiled his dazzling smile at the sun, at God, at no one in particular. He repeated the cryptic hand gesture.

"Cut!" Pierce yelled, thrilled. You had to hand it to the actors. There it was—a gift. One of those incredible, instinctive moments that Pierce lived for. He was pleased. Profoundly pleased. You could practically see the joyous light radiating from his pores. "Shall we do one more?" Pierce asked, beaming.

The Final Interview

3rd Person
Paz & Pierce

"The beauty of a location like this is that it offers you everything you need. Beach, ocean, jungle, lake, mountains, waterfalls, cheap labor—"

"And of course there's Mayor Fritz, your protector, your fixer, your landlord, your biggest fan," Paz added.

"The earth seemed unearthly." Pierce smiled.

"Have you heard of a man named Zamora López de Legazpi?"

"Uh . . . what was that name again?"

"Legazpi. Zamora. He claimed to have discovered a Stone Age tribe right around here, on Mount Taobo."

"Sounds familiar."

"He's not quite as famous as you."

"Is that right?"

"To us he is. But to the outside world—"

"Hmm. The earth seemed unearthly."

"That's what you say, Mr. Pierce."

"No, that's what Conrad says, Miss Marlowe. 'We could not understand because we were too far and could not remember because we were travelling in the night of first ages, of those ages that are gone, leaving hardly a sign—and no memories.'"

"Thanks for letting me read your new script, by the way."

"You sure you have the right version? It's a wonder the actors can keep up."

"They're extraordinary. Even that really young one."

"Isaiah. I discovered him—"

"He's very cute."

"—at Port Authority."

"I thought it was Times Square."

"You know the difference?"

"I've lived in New York. Okay, so you spotted him . . ." Paz waited for Pierce to finish her sentence.

"Playing the guitar. His guitar case open so people could throw money in it, the whole bit. He wasn't making much. His guitar was out of tune, and his little amp kept feeding back. It was awful." Pierce chuckled.

"But he was it. What you were looking for."

"He was fresh. He had chutzpah. You know chutzpah?"

"Balls."

"I'd been auditioning lots of black actors for the role of Monk. They could do Shakespeare, all that shit. But they were all too old. Too *trained*. I needed a kid. A raw, vulnerable type. So . . ." Pierce shrugged.

"He blew me away. That thing yesterday?"

"Isaiah's a natural. Totally instinctive."

"Falling to the ground, scared and crying? I was speechless. Is Cowboy going to kill him?"

"What?"

"Vince Moody's character. You know how he aimed his gun at the kid because the kid pisses him off? Then you yelled 'Cut!' How does the scene resolve?"

"It wasn't scripted. I don't know."

"You don't know?"

"I haven't made up my mind. I mean, what would have more impact for an audience? The kid being shown mercy or having his head blown off?"

"Depends."

"It always does, doesn't it? How it's played out, and by whom. A kiss is never just a kiss. I get high just thinking about it. Tickled at the insane possibilities. Which way does my story go? Everyone's waiting, on edge, and I am high." Pierce was smiling at her again. A smile full of heat, big and terrifying.

"The night of first ages. Into the heart of darkness," Paz murmured.

Pierce nodded. "Something like that. Did you get everything you need for your story?"

More than I bargained for, Paz thought. "Yes, thank you," she replied. "I go back to the States in a few days to finish working on it. My editor says it's going to be the cover story. You'll get copies as soon as it's published."

"Can't wait," Pierce said.

Rizalina and Yeye

Yeye, baby girl—are you still asleep? My Yeye's had a bad night. My Yeye's sick. The weather is at fault. So much rain, you catch a chill. Aling Belén blames it on the movie people. "They bring typhoon and sickness with them," she says. The old witch crushes herbs with camphor oil and rubs the paste all over your chest. She sings and chants to you all night long, orders me to sing and chant with her. "What a shame you don't know these songs," the old witch sighs. But I do my best.

Yeye, my Yeye.

I remember the morning I ran away from Mister's compound. Your father, Chito, waited in his jeepney. He grinned when he saw me. "Ready to elope with me now?"

Not a baby like you, but still a child, I climbed in, sat next to him, and never looked back. My first time was that night with Chito. He couldn't wait. We went to a love motel. My thighs, streaked with blood, moved him to tears. I stayed with Chito long enough to discover that he already had a common-law wife and a year-old son living somewhere in Bulacan. By then I was carrying you in my belly.

Nevertheless.

Will you miss me one day as I miss my mother? Mama, Nanay, Candelaria. I miss Sputnik. I miss him—Mister Señor Zamora. Why, I don't know. Can Mama or Mister ever forgive me for run-

ning away? If they had seen me dancing naked in front of all those
men ...   ↳ shame

    Nevertheless. I am no longer Jinx, and it doesn't matter anymore.

One day I will see Mama. One day I will tell her everything. About
Papa. About Mister Señor. About Chito. About Vincent. How I
came back to this place and brought you to Aling Belén. Yeye, my
Yeye.

You stir. Open your lovely black eyes (eyes of my dead father). I
pick you up, carry you to the window. Look! No more shitty days.
The sun is out. Monkeys screech in the trees, pigs grunt in their
pens, the fool rooster chases after the nasty, obstinate hens. Look—
he's caught one! Climbed on her, fucked her. It is over in a second.
He hops off, clucking and preening. Fool rooster. Fool hen.

The sound of my voice, the rooster clucking and the monkeys
screeching make you gurgle and coo with delight. You grab a fistful
of my hair, gaze at me with your sweet, sleepy eyes. Yeye, my Yeye.
Do you know who I am? Look at me hard, daughter. Remember
this face.

Graveyard

is driver, Nap, spotted her first. A slender brown figure in a red dress walking purposefully on the side of the road. She held a folded newspaper over her head to shield herself from the noonday sun.

"There she is, boss."

The mayor grunted, pleased. Nap slowed the car down so Mayor Fritz could speak to her. The girl turned her head toward them. She was exquisite, long black hair pulled into a single braid down her back. "Lina," the mayor called to her. "It's Lina, isn't it?"

Her nod was reluctant. She kept walking.

"Would you like a ride?" The mayor's tone, light and jovial. Lina knew enough to be polite and not enrage him. Mayor Fritz was all too familiar—a man very much like her father, arrogant and thin skinned. She saw it in the paranoid glint of his darting eyes, the way he'd looked around the table at Pierce's dinner party, sussing everyone out.

There was no one on the road. It was Sunday; all the townspeople were at church. Eyes straight ahead, Lina walked a little faster. Should she say something? Vincent was asleep at the house the movie people had rented from the man in the slow-moving car. He'd been up all night, waiting to shoot a scene with Sebastian Claiborne. A scene that never happened. Claiborne had kept Tony Pierce busy, both men holed up in the director's tent—arguing, analyzing, and rewriting the scene while Vincent and the crew sat around waiting. Vincent was driven back to the house at six in the morning, too wired to sleep, brandishing a bottle of potent *lambanog*. The fiery white nectar of coconut—all he could find in the house at six in the morning. "If I weren't such a pussy, I'd get back to L.A. as fast as I could," he kept mumbling. He consumed half the bottle before finally passing out.

"Did you hear what I said?" The mayor again, grinning.

She was too young and skinny for Nap, who preferred the fleshy curves of much older women. But Mayor Fritz was different. He liked and appreciated them all. Fat and skinny, old and young. And being with an ex–*bomba* queen like Dolly—who never gave him any trouble and still looked good in spite of bearing those children— wasn't enough for him. Mayor Fritz was a man of intellect and prodigious appetites. Nap was proud to work as his driver and bodyguard. There were several like him in the mayor's employ— earnest young men, unswerving in their loyalty and devotion. Their lives revolved around the mayor and his whims; there was no other future for them. But Nap was different. He didn't drink the night away in dismal beer gardens like the others did on their days off. He didn't blow his salary on flashy clothes and dreary whores. Nap was saving his money for a trip to Manila, a city he had never been to but often daydreamed about. There he would win first prize in any one of the many TV talent shows hosted by giddy starlets and cruel, has-been comedians. Nap was blessed with a crooner's velvet voice, the kind of smooth, aching voice that drove women crazy. The mayor and Dolly often demanded that he sing and entertain their guests at fancy parties. Mayor Fritz enjoyed teasing Nap in front of other people. "You've got a homely face but a handsome voice," he'd say with a great deal of affection. Nap would laugh in good-natured response. He loved the mayor and Dolly; the mayor and Dolly were like family.

Nap considered himself lucky to be living underneath the boss's big house—the only house in town with a record player, cassette deck, and television set. Actually, the mayor owned two. The twenty-seven-inch color Motorola was locked in his bedroom. But an ancient black-and-white portable with a broken antenna that Dolly had ordered thrown out was rescued from the trash by Nap and installed downstairs. He watched TV nonstop on his days off. *You're a Star!* was Nap's favorite show. He imagined himself singing something bouncy like "Do You Know the Way to San Jose?" and could visualize the exact moment when the host would slap him on the back and yell, "Congratulations, Napoleon Padilla! You're a star!"

Nap slowed to a halt, idling the engine. The radio was on. A commercial extolling the miracles of Camay soap. "Don't be shy," Mayor Fritz was saying to the girl, who stood poised as if in midflight, still holding the folded newspaper over her head. "I heard about what happened to you. How your father and those little twin brothers of yours drowned in the sea. *Mga kawawa naman.*" You're a survivor, Mayor Fritz murmured. I admire that about you.

On her right arm, Nap noticed, was a large oval keloid. Probably from a bad burn that had healed. The girl squinted at the men in the car. "Where in God's name are you going anyway? You're walking *away* from town," Mayor Fritz continued cheerfully, "and headed for the cemetery. Is that really where you want to go?"

The girl bit her lower lip and blinked.

"You have family buried there, I suppose?"

Lina shook her head. A moment passed before Mayor Fritz said, "Well, I do. Funny, but I was on my way there just now." He was lying, which made Nap nervous. The last time things didn't turn out so well. The mayor was on a roll, though. Making it up as he went along. "I go every Sunday, to pay my respects. My beloved mother is buried right next to my grandfather." Mayor Fritz opened the passenger door. "Would you like a ride? The cemetery's a long way off. There's a nice beach right next to it. You know this, of course. You may have already taken your actor friend there. White sand. And the water—well, the water is clean and . . . *undefiled.* I told those location people they couldn't use it for their movie. It's virgin territory, off limits to Hollywood." He chuckled, waiting.

It was hot. The hottest time of day. Lina longed to climb into the backseat of the air-conditioned car, lean against the plush velour cushions, and close her eyes.

"Are you afraid of me?" Mayor Fritz looked pained by his own question. He moved over and patted the seat beside him. Lina took a deep breath and climbed in. She looked into the older man's dark, impenetrable glasses as if daring him to hurt her.

The car began moving again.

"And how is Mr. Moody—your actor friend? I enjoyed our discussion the other night." Mayor Fritz took her hand, holding it as if it were a fragile bird captured between his own small, but powerful hands. As if she already belonged to him. She decided not to pull away, closing her eyes so she wouldn't have to look at his face, the face that reminded her of . . . *Nevertheless*. The driver, a slightly cross-eyed young man, hummed along with the song on the radio. Mayor Fritz caressed her hand. It was all she could do to stay calm and not jump out of the moving car. She wondered if it was her turn to die. He wanted what they all wanted. An image from her recent childhood flitted across her mind. Mister Señor sitting in the bathtub smoking a cigar. A goat nailed to a cross.

The car stopped moving. Lina peered out the window. Gnarled coconut trees, bent by ocean winds, offered no respite from the blazing sun. The rural cemetery had its own stark beauty. White wooden crosses marked each grave, the names of the dead painted in black on every cross. The sea was calm, a few waves lapping the shore. Seagulls squawked. Not a fisherman or *bangka* in sight. Mayor Fritz helped Lina out of the car. "What a beautiful day!" he exclaimed, to no one in particular. Lina slipped off her sandals, her blistered feet burrowing into the warm sand. The driver had disappeared, perhaps behind a grove of coconut trees to smoke a cigarette. He seemed harmless enough, a bumbling, sympathetic oaf. But Lina knew she could be wrong.

"Are you going to hurt me?" she suddenly asked Mayor Fritz.

"Why would I want to hurt a lovely young girl like you?"

"Who knows?" Lina said. "Maybe I make you angry."

His expression became incredulous. "Angry? *Dios ko,* do I look angry, Lina?"

Lina took note of the mayor's smooth brown face, the carefully trimmed sideburns and mustache, the manicured fingernails. "Take off your sunglasses," she said.

Mayor Fritz laughed, excited by her boldness. She stepped forward and pulled the Ray-Bans off his head, catching him off guard. His eyes were red rimmed and bloodshot. She wondered if he was drunk, wondered why she had gotten in the car with him, wondered where the driver was, if they were going to take turns with her. Mayor Fritz probably had a gun. Surely the driver did. Rizalina thought of Vincent fighting his way out of sleep. Wondering where she was and calling her name. He loved her—it had taken her a long time to believe him. They all said they loved her; the word "love" came cheap. Lina threw the Ray-Bans to the ground. She knew that Mayor Fritz would have to bend over to retrieve them—they were much too expensive to lose. It was her only chance to escape. She turned and ran. She could run fast, even while barefoot on burning sand. The one thing she could count on were her spindly gazelle legs, leaping over the humble graves and crude wooden crosses, over the names of the dead and buried, the tenant farmers, fishermen, and market vendors—their wives, daughters, and sons. Her feet barely touched the ground, littered with the split-open husks of young coconuts and dried branches of withered palms. She headed for the road. Perhaps a passing truck would stop, a lone farmer on a *carabao.* She knew she was a foolish girl, born reckless. And now she was going to pay for her foolishness. Her sins.

Vincent called her "my one true love." She imagined him going from room to room barking out curses. *I am fucking pissed off where are you don't fuck with me, Lina!* Funny how she could dance naked or sell her body to some potbellied cop, yet words like "fuck" or "piss," especially in English, had the power to make her cringe.

Lina gasped at the sight of Napoleón Padilla, emerging from behind the trees. He grabbed her as she ran past him, holding her so tight she could barely breathe. Mayor Fritz appeared a few seconds later, smiling. Lina tried to break free of Nap's arms, but he tightened his grasp. Mayor Fritz reached over and touched her hair.

"Where do you think you're going?" Mayor Fritz stroked Lina as if she were some wild horse he was attempting to tame. She tried turning her head to bite his hand, but Nap's snug embrace was much too formidable.

"This one, Nap, is well worth the trouble," Mayor Fritz said.

Nap wasn't sure what the mayor meant, but he nodded as if he understood and agreed. Well worth the trouble. Nap wasn't so sure about that. What was the big deal with her anyway? She was just a teenage girl, slightly prettier than most, but so what? Plus, she smelled of salt breeze, sweat, and coconut oil. Smelled ordinary and poor. Mayor Fritz's wife, Dolly, smelled of perfume. She was refined and truly desirable, with her pale skin, remote gaze, and narrow, upturned nose. But this one? Squirming and struggling in his arms. Trying to break free. Nap scrutinized the mayor's face for answers but got none. Mayor Fritz was obviously thinking. Stroking the girl's head over and over again while considering his options. The sunglasses were back on, hiding his eyes. In the distance two figures—one holding an umbrella—were slowly approaching.

"Boss," Nap warned in a low voice.

Mayor Fritz was unfazed. He could simply sigh and say, "Let her go, Nap. I'm done playing." Or gesture toward the car and not say anything. It would be clear to Nap what needed to be done. The girl would be bound and gagged, then taken to a little cottage the mayor kept not far from the beach. There Nap would help the mayor tie her down to a bed, spread-eagled, of course, so the mayor could have his way with her. But first the mayor would sit in a chair facing the bed and talk. Nap would be asked to stay and listen, perhaps contribute to the one-way conversation with a few words of his own. "Yes" or "no" was preferred. Mayor Fritz usually expounded on history, tossing out morbid tidbits that Nap always found fascinating. Like the story of the nine hundred Jews who committed mass suicide at Masada rather than face the prospect of being conquered by the Romans. Or Mayor Fritz's favorite—the Balangiga massacre of 1901. Native insurgents, under the leadership of guerrilla general Vicente Lukban, were said to have disguised themselves as women to gain entry to U.S. colonial military barracks in the small port town of Balangiga, Samar. They caught the American soldiers by surprise, hacking them to death with *bolos*. All the officers were killed. Mayor Fritz was careful to add gruesome new details and extra little flourishes whenever he told the story, so that Nap never tired of hearing it.

"It was one of those rare instances," Mayor Fritz once said, "when we Filipinos outfoxed and outnumbered the Americans. But, oh, how we paid! We paid and we paid and we paid. . . ." He paused for dramatic effect. "The lives of all those officers were much too precious to waste, you see. So vengeance came in the person of General Howlin' Jake Smith. Have I ever told you how he got his name?"

"Not really, boss," Nap had answered, though he'd heard the story hundreds of times.

"The Americans were outraged; they couldn't get over the fact that their docile little brown brothers had managed to be so creative and pull off an act of stealth and vicious aggression. Indeed, that we could be so vicious at all. Do you comprehend the meaning of the words 'stealth' and 'aggression,' Napoleon?" Mayor Fritz chuckled at the expression of woe on Nap's face. "*Ay naku*, Nap. Relax *lang*. You know I love the English language, don't you? In spite of its surprising limitations."

Nap nodded. Stealth and aggression. What was all that about? The boss was always throwing shit his way, testing his knowledge. Nap at least knew what the word "aggressive" meant. Something to do with being forceful. Bodyguards like himself were expected to be aggressive, for example. But "stealth"? Were they somehow connected, and was that a good thing?

" 'I wish you to kill and burn,' " Mayor Fritz declared, mimicking the dark imagined growl of the bloodthirsty commander. " 'The more you burn and kill, the better it will please me.' General Smith ordered the island of Samar, Leyte, transformed into a 'howling wilderness.' Hence his name," Mayor Fritz explained. "The systematic killings took six months. Every male over the age of ten was slaughtered by American soldiers. After that, nothing but a terrible silence." Mayor Fritz sighed. "Samar, to this day, has never quite recovered."

Would this be the same story he told today, to the feisty young girl named Lina? "You think I'm going to hurt you?" Mayor Fritz was asking her. "You think I'm a savage like all your other men?" The girl was spilling angry tears. They were inside the car—Nap in the driver's seat, the mayor in the back with the girl. "Stop crying," Mayor Fritz muttered.

The slow-moving figure turned out to be Aling Belén, carrying Yeye in her arms. Next to her was Boyet, holding an umbrella over the old woman's head and carrying a *bayong* packed with offerings for the dead. Aling Belén hobbled toward the car, staring at the dazed young girl in the backseat. Mayor Fritz rolled down his window and flashed a million-dollar smile. "Good afternoon, Aling Belén. My, my. What a beautiful child."

"Get out of that car," Aling Belén said, beckoning to Lina. Yeye, recognizing her mother, held out her arms and started to cry.

"What now, boss?" Nap asked.

"What now? What now? What do you think, Nap? What exactly do you think we should do?"

Nap stammered, embarrassed. "I . . . I don't know, sir."

Mayor Fritz turned to Lina. "Until our people learn to take the reins and lead themselves out of this cycle of dependency, mediocrity, and despair, then we are truly lost. What about you, Lina? Are you lost? What exactly do you think we should do?"

"Let me go," she said.

"What's stopping you? You've always been free to go," Mayor Fritz said.

Napoleon Padilla couldn't believe his ears. He glanced furtively in the rearview mirror. The girl had her hand on the door, a skeptical look on her face. "Go ahead," Mayor Fritz was saying. "Be my guest." The girl bolted from the car and took the child from the old woman. They hurried toward the cemetery, Boyet scrambling to keep up with them.

Nap started the engine. "You want me to follow them, boss?"

Mayor Fritz rolled the window back up. "What for? Turn around and head back to town. We're going to Mass."

Aling Belén knelt before a grave marked "Inocencia Garay." From her *bayong* she pulled out several homemade rice cakes wrapped in banana leaves, a couple of tangerines, a packet of lemon drops, and several red plastic roses.

"You hope thieves won't come along and steal this, but they do. They always do," Aling Belén said. "They can resell my flowers. You know, plastic flowers don't come cheap."

Lina and Boyet stood at a respectful distance, silent. Yeye sucked on a thumb, content in her mother's arms.

Aling Belén made the sign of the cross, clasped her hands in prayer, and began reciting Hail Marys. Lifting her head as she finished, Aling Belén seemed surprised to find them still there. "Those men didn't hurt you, did they?" she asked Lina.

"No."

Aling Belén was unconvinced. "You should get away from here. I'll take care of Yeye, but I can't help you anymore—you're much too stubborn and never listen to anything I say. A bad thing, that movie. All it does is bring trouble to our town. You don't agree with me, do you?"

"No."

Aling Belén directed her sharp gaze at Boyet. "And you, skinny boy. What do you have to say?"

Boyet hung his head, confused and embarrassed by the old woman's attention.

"Well, you're both young. What do you care? None of the young people in town agree with their elders. You all think this movie is going to change your sorry lives. Is he going to marry you?"

"Who?"

"Your *Amerikano* movie star."

Lina shrugged.

They walked on the side of the road that led back to town. Aling Belén leaned on Boyet's arm, holding up one side of her long skirt to keep from tripping. Boyet held the battered golf umbrella over both their heads. A bus packed with too many people barreled past them, honking and belching thick clouds of black smoke. Aling Belén fished a hanky out of her pocket and covered her nose and mouth. They stopped to rest under a *balete* tree. Aling Belén, surprisingly agile, sat back on her haunches and once again reached into her pocket for betelnut leaves. She began chewing, spitting the red juice onto the dusty road. Lina leaned against the wide, sturdy trunk of the tree, Yeye asleep in her arms. Boyet stood nearby with his umbrella, waiting. For what, Lina wasn't sure.

"Is my mother still alive?" Lina asked Aling Belén.

"Of course she is."

"But how do you know this?"

"If you doubt me, don't ask."

"Is Mr. Zamora López de Legazpi alive?"

"Of course he is."

"Thank you for saving me from those men."

"I did nothing," Aling Belén said. "Why were you in that man's car?"

"I don't know," Lina said. After a pause Lina continued, "I keep dreaming about a tiger. What does my dream mean, Aling Belén?"

"I don't know," Aling Belén said, chewing. Without any assistance she slowly got up from her squatting position. "We should go," she murmured.

It was late afternoon by the time Lina reached the house. Moody was on the veranda. She could tell he was high. He lay back on a tattered plastic lounging chair, shirtless and barefoot. Months of exposure to the relentless tropical sun had turned his skin an angry pink. He sat up a little straighter at the sight of her. Lina dreaded what he might say but waved to him as if nothing were out of the ordinary. She climbed the wooden stairs. The house was unusually quiet. No piercing guitar music blaring from Isaiah Waters's room. No imported whores or stoned party girls from Manila wandering around half naked in the *sala*.

"Where you been?" Moody asked.

"For a walk with Aling Belén and Yeye."

"I was worried," Moody said.

"Nothing to worry about," Lina said.

"How's the baby?"

"Yeye's good," Lina said.

"Promise me you won't disappear again like that," Moody said.

Lina was silent. Moody took her by the hand and pulled her toward him. He gazed into her face. Tried to read it but couldn't.

The Tiger

The tiger was a muscular Bengal male named Shiva, after the Hindu god of destruction. His huge face, framed by tufts of snow-white hair, glowed with ferocious beauty and power. The movie people flew him in by special cargo plane from California. It was impossible to keep his presence a secret from the townspeople. Not one among them had ever seen a real tiger, not even the worldly Mayor Fritz. As word of the creature's presence spread, the tiger began to assume supernatural powers and dimensions—more thrilling and mysterious than all the *kapres*, *aswangs*, *tikbalangs*, and malevolent *duendes* who roamed the caves and valleys of Lake Ramayyah late at night. Mayor Fritz did nothing to squelch the rumors or put a stop to the townspeople's mounting excitement and hysteria. The tiger, like the Vietnam war movie, made life seem less slow, petty, and provincial.

Mayor Fritz claimed to have seen the tiger, claimed that it was at least ten feet long and weighed two tons. The creature's preferred diet was supposedly children, especially girls under the age of seven, whose flesh was considered sweeter than the flesh of boys. Parents in Ligaya and Sultan Ramayyah used this bit of lore to their advantage, threatening to feed their unruly children to the tiger if they misbehaved.

❦

The script called for the character played by Kevin Cassells, while on patrol with Moody near the Cambodian border, to be attacked and killed by the tiger. Pierce was against using a stunt double because of the tight, close-up style in which Franco Broussard had decided to frame the confrontation. Cassells, a man who hated animals, was terrified but tried not to show it. As usual, he wanted to please Pierce.

The handler insisted on a closed set, with as few people present and as little artificial lighting as possible. Pierce's family and the starstruck Mayor Fritz would be the only visitors allowed. But Lina didn't let this stop her; she longed to see the tiger in the flesh. "Please ask Mr. Pierce, Vince. Tell him I know how to be very, very quiet," she said.

"I can't do that. When Big Man says no, he means no."

"Nevertheless. If you are too scared, then I will ask him myself."

The day before the scene was to be shot, Moody approached Pierce during a break.

"Sorry to bother you, man. But it would mean the world to Lina if—"

"Lina?" Pierce looked impatient.

"My girlfriend."

"Ah."

"She wants to know if . . . well, if an exception—"

Pierce groaned. "Oh, jeez. Not the goddamn tiger again!"

"She's been dreaming about it," Moody said.

Pierce chuckled. "Dreaming about it? Sorry, Vince. No can do. The tiger's a jumpy sonuvabitch, and I've already got too many—"

"Tony, please. It's just one more person. I've never asked you for anything," Moody added, hating himself.

Before sunrise the tiger, alert in his metal cage, was driven to the foot of Mount Taobo in a covered truck. The townspeople were warned to stay away, but Pierce took the extra precaution of hiring soldiers from the nearby Philippine constabulary barracks to guard the location. Boyet and a few of the more daring young men from town, under cover of darkness, scrambled up the towering coconut trees, where they could watch the filming undetected.

Inside a huge tent, makeup artist Jay Donnelly and his assistant, Suki Blake, were busy working on the faces of Moody and Cassells.

"Did you see the size of that thing?" Cassells asked Donnelly.

"He's a big kitty," Donnelly murmured.

"I just wanna know what happens if it freaks."

"He ain't gonna freak," Donnelly said.

"How do you know?" Cassells nervous, unconvinced.

"Pierce won't let him." Donnelly smeared green clay on Moody's forehead and cheeks.

Cassells frowned.

Lina poked her head into the tent. "You're not supposed to be in here, dear," Donnelly said. Ignoring him, Lina entered and waved at Moody.

"Jay and Suki, meet Lina." Moody smiled.

"Oops. Sorry, hon. I didn't know." From one of the secret compartments in his makeup kit, Donnelly removed a glass vial with a tiny spoon attached. "Want a quick pick-me-up, doll?" he asked Suki, who shook her head. "What about you, Vince?"

"Not today, thanks."

"Any takers?" Donnelly held up the vial. "My, my. I'm impressed. We're all being very disciplined." Donnelly took a couple of toots before putting the vial away. Energized, he went back to work, swiftly transforming Moody's face into a mask of forest green camouflage. He added a raccoon strip of black across Moody's eyes as a finishing touch.

"You look like an Injun!" Lina marveled, coming closer. She reached out to touch Moody's cheek but was stopped by Donnelly's shrill voice. "Sweetie, please! Don't mess up my art!"

"I can't stop thinking about it," Kevin Cassells suddenly blurted out.

"Scared of that cat, hon?" Donnelly asked, sympathetic.

Cassells nodded. Poor bastard. Moody noticed that the worried actor was perspiring heavily, which was odd. Night and early-morning temperatures were especially chilly because of the elevation. Everyone in the tent, except for the sweaty Cassells, wore layers of clothing.

"Animals smell fear from miles away," Moody teased. "For fuck's sake, Kevin. I gotta do this scene with you. Will you take it easy?"

Janet Pierce glanced at Lina with friendly curiosity, then turned away. Dante and Jesse stood beside her. Dante tugged at the hem of her skirt. "Where's Papa? Where's the tiger?" He was sleepy and miserable. Janet took Dante's hand.

"Let's go to Papa's tent so you can lie down," she said.

"I don't wanna lie down. I wanna see the tiger."

Janet's voice was kind but firm. "That's enough. If you don't do as I say, we're going home."

The boy's face lit up. "We are? We're going to California?"

"Man, you are stooo-pid!" Jesse Pierce sneered. Janet swatted his butt with the palm of her hand. Not too hard, but hard enough. "You don't ever, ever talk to your brother like that. Understand?" Jesse swallowed his tears, stunned. Janet ordered him to STAY RIGHT HERE DON'T MOVE UNTIL I COME BACK. She and Dante walked away. Lina observed Jesse standing with his head bowed, humiliated. Should she comfort him? Mayor Fritz sidled up next to her.

"*Magandang umaga*, Lina. How are you?"

She moved a few inches to her left. The mayor's tone, nonchalant. "*Aba*. Are you trying to avoid me?"

Lina was relieved to see Janet Pierce return. "Why, Mayor Magbantay. How nice to see you," Janet greeted him warmly.

"You know I would not miss this for the world, Mrs. Pierce."

"None of us would."

"So you are here for the tiger?"

"Absolutely," Janet Pierce said. "The infamous tiger."

Jesse: "Mom, I'm hungry."

"Run over to the food tent and see what you can scrounge."

"But, Mom. The tiger—"

"Have you said hello to the mayor? Say hello to Mayor Magbantay."

"Hello," Jesse mumbled.

"It's gonna be a while until they start, Jesse. Go get your breakfast," Janet urged her son, who skulked away.

"What a good-looking boy!" the mayor declared. "Just like his father. Very *guwapo!*"

Lina rolled her eyes.

The mayor strutted and preened, hands in his pockets, little chest puffed up. After all, he was on the closed set of a Hollywood movie. He heard the tiger, somewhere nearby, growling softly in his cage. Mayor Fritz shuddered with delight. What a day. Plus, the director's wife was flirting with him. Not bad looking, though he preferred women with bigger breasts and longer hair. He took to calling her "Jan," which she seemed to find amusing. Such a friendly *Amerikana*, obviously neglected and lonely. If only his uncle, the president, could see him now!

Janet Pierce smiled at Lina. "How are you?"

"Fine, ma'am."

"Not 'ma'am.' Please. Call me Janet."

"Quiet on the set!" someone yelled.

Moody and Cassells rehearsed one more time, walking through the bush in tense silence. The tiger was to leap out at them midway through the scene. Cassells would fall back. Cut to: a close-up of Cassells's face as the tiger pounced on him. The way the script was written—which of course could always change because Pierce loved to fuck with things just to fuck with things—Moody/Cowboy momentarily freezes, paralyzed by awe and his own fear. By the time he shoots the tiger, it would be too late. Cassells's character would already be dead.

Lina craned her neck, jockeying to get a better view. The actors rehearsed their scene without the tiger. Pierce had been warned that Shiva—fierce and impressive as he looked, worth every dollar the producers coughed up for him—was strictly a one-take animal.

"Exactly how do you want us to do this?" Moody asked Pierce.

"Do just what you're doing," Pierce answered. "Walk slowly and carefully. Hold your guns up like so. Looking, listening for anything. You're both wound tight. Scared. You're on patrol in enemy territory, for fuck's sake."

"But what about the tiger?" Cassells, clammy, nervous Cassells.

"What about it? The tiger's a surprise. You don't hear him at all. You don't feel his presence until—" Pierce grins.

"But, Tony. What if it freaks?" Cassells, shaking, trying to smile back.

"Don't tell me you're *nervous*, Kevin?"

"Nah. I'm just cold."

"Of course he's nervous," Moody said. He could feel Janet Pierce's curious eyes. Lina, looking at him. "That tiger—"

Pierce, annoyed. "Excuse me, Vince. Was I talking to you?"

Franco Broussard walked over to them, slowly shaking his head. "I don't like this, Tony."

Pierce sighed. "What now, Franco?"

"That tiger is—well, how you say—" Broussard hesitated. "Beeg?" The men laughed. Even Cassells, who looked sick. "I got idea," Broussard said. "How to fix."

Pierce crossed his arms, not pleased. "Shoot."

"We do tiger first. Boom! He jumps out of bushes. Perfect.

Finito. Cut! Take tiger away. Then we do Vince and Kevin. More acting for them, but much safer, no?"

"You think this is really necessary?" Pierce asked.

"Necessary? Absolutely, *si.* That animal is too beeg, too—*come si dice?*—unpredictable."

"I want unpredictable," Pierce said.

"Not like this, Tony. Please. Someone might get hurt. We try my way. If not work, okay, we try something else."

"My way or nothing," Pierce said. "Cinema verité."

"Okay. I'll do it," Cassells said quietly.

"No, no, Kevin. Is not safe," Broussard insisted.

"I said I'll do it!" Cassells shouted.

Pierce threw an arm around him. "Kevin, I knew you wouldn't disappoint me."

A hush came over the set. Even Tony Pierce held his breath. The tiger peered out from its hiding place in the bushes. A dragon's face, magnificent and dreadful. Ready to spring, the tiger's rear legs and massive padded feet pressed beneath its powerful body. Lowered tail twitching. Lina gasped at her first glimpse of the beast. Mayor Fritz clicked his tongue in appreciation. If only his real father, the one he killed, were alive to see this. If only his mother. Mayor Fritz found it difficult to enjoy such moments alone. If only Nap, his faithful bodyguard and driver, had been allowed on the set with him. Nap would surely comprehend the significance of the occasion.

The tiger snarled softly, sniffing the air. The actors walked into the camera's view. Off camera, a man named Sven crouched down, holding on to the tiger's nearly undetectable chain leash. The animal's handler, ready for anything. Moody heard an almost inaudible hum coming from Cassells. The hum of fear. On cue the tiger leaped out at them. Kevin Cassells screamed. Moody, trembling, aimed his gun and pulled the trigger. A perfect take.

"Cut!" Pierce shouted. Cassells lay collapsed in a faint.

"Hey, man. You dead?" Moody poked gently at Cassells with the toe of his boot. It was over, thank God. Cassells stirred.

The daring boys perched high in the coconut trees couldn't contain themselves any longer. "*Tigre! Tigre!*" They cheered. The gleeful, exuberant sound of their voices drifted down from the trees. Pierce looked up. "Get those little bastards out of there," he ordered one of the soldiers.

"Is that it?" Lina overheard the boy called Jesse ask his mother in a thin, incredulous voice.

"I'm afraid so," Janet answered.

"Aw, phooey," Jesse Pierce said. "That was lame."

Lina stared at the tiger, riveted. She was looking for a sign. Anything at all, to explain all those dreams. To point her in the right direction. Shiva was a god—Vincent had said so. Gods knew the way, could help her make a decision. To stay or to go? To leave Yeye behind or take her along? The tiger gazed back at Lina, languid, indifferent. His work was done. The handler cracked his whip. "Come, Shiva." The handler's voice commanding and sharp, like his whip. The tiger blinked its amazing eyes and roared. As if to say, Yes, yes. It's about time! Will you feed me? Lina felt a great joy. The handler, tugging once on the thick chain leash, led the unresisting tiger back to his cage.

Amor, Solo

3rd person
Lina & Moody

The colors of the tiger—Day-Glo orange fur, jet-black stripes—disturbed every waking moment, every attempt at sleep. In her dreams his scowling face peered out at her from his hiding place in the bush. Was she going mad? She began drawing the beast in childish, stick-figure fashion. Then more assuredly as the days went by. She drew him with her eyes closed. Her right hand, sometimes her left, moved the stubby pencil around the paper's surface as if she were guided by some spirit. Tiger in motion, leaping out of the bush or out of water. Ready to attack. Graceful and sinuous, every muscle outlined.

"Let me see," Moody said.

Lina covered the drawing with her hands. "I don't show nobody, Vince."

They were alone in the house. Moody, up the night before shooting the final scene with Sebastian Claiborne, wandered out of his room to find Lina bent over the kitchen table. He collapsed into the chair across from her, groggy with sleep. Lina closed her eyes and began drawing on a fresh sheet of paper. Only the tiger's face this time, its jaws open in a growl. Fangs, tongue, penetrating eyes. Moody watched her, afraid to speak and break the spell. When she was done, Lina stood up and took his hand. She led Moody back to his room. Moody's heart beat wildly as she locked the door behind them. He held his breath as she slipped out of her dress and lay back on the bed. Moody kissed the keloid on her arm, heard her soft gasp. His hand enormous on the slope of her slender back. He tried to be gentle, but he felt too excited and afraid of her, afraid of their mutual silence. His job on the movie was over. What would happen to them now?

Moody kissed her mouth. God, he loved her. Her eyelids fluttered, then opened wide. Tigers danced on the walls and ceiling, on the bed of tangled sheets on which she and Moody thrashed and moaned. Pagodas of tigers, floating islands of tigers. Pouncing, roaming, prowling. Out of a sea of tigers rose her tiger-faced mother, father, and twin brothers. Rose a glaring Zamora López de Legazpi. As hard as she tried to distract herself, Lina was unable to shake her mind free of its multiplying visions. Tigers in trees, trees of tigers. Tigers within tigers.

"I love you," Moody murmured. "I love you, Lina." But she could not hear him, lost as she was in her nightmare of tigers. The sound of cars pulling up out front. Footsteps. Voices from the living room. Billy Hernandez's raucous, distinctive laugh. Isaiah Waters said something funny, made a woman screech. More laughter. Something jazzy-funky by Roy Ayers was piped through the sound system.

Moody sat up in bed, tense.

"Are you in there, my little lovebirds?" Billy Hernandez banged on the door with his fist. "Come on out and join the pah-tee!"

Moody slipped on his jeans. Tiger in his body of tigers. Lina grabbed his right arm, taking him by surprise. She dug her nails into his arm. He gazed down into her face, shimmering with what he mistook at first for beads of sweat, then realized was some sort of caul. Stretched taut like a second skin over the delicate surface of face, her face—Lina who was not Lina now but something or someone else. A mirror to myriad other female faces—Lori, Sandy, and Marian, his mother. *Are you in there, Vince?* Billy Hernandez's gruff voice jolted Moody from his reverie. His arm was bleeding. He started to pull away, but Lina tightened her grip.

"Yeah," Moody answered. "We're in here, yeah."

"You asleep? Heh-heh." Hernandez's speech already slurred.

"Yeah."

"Sorry, bro. Music too loud?"

"Nah."

Someone turned the volume way up, then just as abruptly turned it down. The unmistakable scent of burning marijuana wafted into Moody's bedroom. "Maybe we should join them," Moody whispered. Lina pulled him back down onto the bed. She covered his body with hers. The pupils of her eyes large, dilated. The caul over her face unearthly. He would lose himself forever if he didn't look away. But he wouldn't. Couldn't. His body immobilized by hers. And he, lost forever. She made no sound. A child not a child. Mother to Yeye. And he a sinner, an actor by accident. By destiny. By the sheer force of divine talent. Understanding the joke of it all. *The earth seemed unearthly.* The party grew louder and wilder in the other room. Moody thought he recognized Tony Pierce's voice rising above the din. Or was it Mayor Fritz?

"Shall I stay here with you and Yeye?" Vincent Moody asked Rizalina Cayabyab. He knew she might not answer, but he asked her anyway. "What do you want?"

She finally spoke. "Maybe I go back to Manila. Maybe I go with you to the States."

"I don't know if I'm ever going back," Moody said.

Kaibigan

script

— why? —

— little feeling —

PEPITO: You're leaving?

PAZ: I'm leaving.

PEPITO: I'm going to miss you, *chica*.

PAZ: I'm going to miss you, too.

PEPITO: When are you coming back?

PAZ: I don't know.

PEPITO: You don't know? What about your papa?

PAZ: He'll be fine. Too bad I didn't get to see your movies. Maybe next time?

PEPITO: Maybe.

Excerpts from
Janet Cattaneo Pierce's Diary

1st person

This morning I found a snake in the kitchen. A pretty, pale green thing, but apparently quite poisonous, so one of the maids cut its head off with a cleaver. Dante was extremely upset. It's been a hard time for all of us because of the foul weather. Rain, rain, and more rain. We're trapped indoors while Tony's gone most of the day and night. They're trying to shoot in spite of the typhoons. And the roads are so bad sometimes Tony doesn't bother coming back into town at all. So the boys and I are stuck with each other. This past week Jesse's been sick on and off with stomach flu. I feel like the wisest thing for us to do would be to get on a plane, but somehow I can't. Not ready yet to leave. Not sure why.

Dante and Jesse have learned some Tagalog and a bit of (B?) Visayan from their tutor, Mrs. Javier. They've made friends with village boys their age, barefoot skinny things who hang about the driveway gawking at everything. They seem terrified to enter the house. The servants try to shoo them away, but I've warned them about this. Horrified them by inviting the boys to eat "merienda" with Dante and Jesse. Servants unhappy about serving one of their own. Made faces when they thought I wasn't looking. Strange country.

✦

Because of the civil war in Mindanao, we've been having troubles. Every day the government sends Tony different helicopter pilots, pilots Tony hasn't rehearsed with, so he has to start all over again, and the next day the same thing happens. It's frustrating for the actors and costing us thousands and thousands of dollars. Today one of the air force generals got skittish and called six of the helicopters away while Tony and Franco were setting up a complicated shot. According to Menching, Tony lost his temper and cussed the general out. One of the general's flunkies threatened to shoot him— it was a pretty nasty situation. Mayor Fritz was called in to smooth things out. Menching was pretty shook up when she told me about it. She said Mayor F. calmed everyone down by cracking jokes. Probably money was exchanged—that's Tony's usual style of "managing" things, which I don't approve of at all. Tony claims in a place like this bribes are necessary evils. No big deal, I suppose. I should open my eyes "be a REALIST, Jan, for fuck's sake!" (to quote my dear husband), but it bothers me nevertheless. I remember when we did that other movie in Mexico. It was pretty much the same situation. Tony paid off the middlemen and fixers, the cops, guerrillas, and whores—whoever needed to shut up and go away.

I am not a cynic. I believe in the basic goodness of man, and I think this amuses my husband. Perhaps he finds my lack of cynicism compelling. Perhaps it is why he stays married to me.

Menching explained that the MNLF rebels ("Moro National Liberation Front"—*Moro* for Moors?) are up in the hills only ten miles away from us. The air force guy needed his helicopters for some kind of little "bombing" mission on MNLF territory. We're in the middle of a real war, which makes me tense and uneasy but seems to excite Tony. He wonders why I haven't broken down and left yet. While I wonder which frisky bunny he's fucking now. There are a cute bunch who flew in with Claiborne on his private jet. Tenacious party girls with amazing stamina. Hang out all day on the set, stay up all night with the actors, snort coke, smoke weed, and drink like longshoremen. Tony invited the girls over to the house. One of them actually introduced herself to me as "a budding starlet." How long are you staying? I asked her. Underneath all the paint and hardware was a sweet and friendly young woman. I don't really know, she said. When she was a little drunk and more comfortable with me, she asked in a low voice, *What's it like, being married to a man like Tony Pierce?* Pretty pedestrian, I said. Which seemed to baffle her.

And there was that other one. Gary's skinny little druggie named Claire. It gives me goose bumps to think what might've happened to her. Is she dead? Was she murdered? I dreamed her at the bottom of some ravine. Tony won't discuss it. Neither will anyone else. He's lost a lot of weight since we've been here. It's the heat and the stress and this thing with the missing girl. He doesn't look good. He's irritable with the boys, which I don't appreciate. Told him so, but he's so preoccupied he can't even give a decent response. The movie's nowhere finished, and everyone is watching, waiting. Coming at him nonstop. A reporter from *Esquire* flew in for an interview. Smarmy man with a fake English accent, terribly polite. Or maybe he was just a smarmy Englishman. "Mr. Pierce, there have been rumors of spectacular delays." Tony coolly assured him, "Well, we're a little behind, but not really. This project is what you'd expect. Like a great war in itself."

When Tony thinks I'm asleep, he slips out of bed to hang out on the balcony. Then he starts to pace, muttering a paranoid mantra to himself from some long-forgotten movie. *What if I can't tell it isn't any good? What if I can't tell?* Once I thought I heard him say to himself, "But I have no ending." There was wonderment in his voice. Then he began to sob.

Yet they all love him, admire him. They are willing to die for him, for this fucking movie. All these actors, young and old, enthralled by his genius. Except for Sebastian Claiborne, who is only enthralled by the genius of himself. Do I doubt my husband or his so-called genius? Most days *I hate this movie*. The power it has over him. Over all of us.

I should at least take the boys to Manila for fun. Check in at the Manila Hotel. Take long, hot showers. Watch TV and order room service. Shop for stupid stuff. Souvenirs. The weather can't be this bad in Manila. A few days of luxury and Jesse should get over his flu just like that.

Will tell Menching to make arrangements. Book us a flight to Manila a.s.a.p. God, when is this rain going to stop?

Sebastian Claiborne is fat as a . . . what? Walrus? Sea lion? An aging Japanese madam? Fat as a girl! With his shaved head and all those robes and tunics he favors, there's something soft and girly about him. I am in awe of his hugeness. We all are. Huge as a house! Crazy as a loon, yet still the king! He threw a party the last week he was here and invited the entire town, cast and crew. Rather sweet. Plus some Himal people showed up. After a lengthy process of negotiation that involved Tony, Menching, Mayor Fritz, and a respected elder named Aling Belén (rumored to be a healer and witch), the Himal have agreed to play Montagnard tribesmen in the movie. They demanded horses, carabou (sp?), and cash in exchange for their work. The horses and oxen more important than the money, it seems. Tony said yes to everything. The Himal have never seen a movie, nor do they seem interested. A lovely, proud people who came down from the mountains to attend Claiborne's grand fiesta. At Claiborne's behest Menching hired entertainers from Manila—an excellent band that sounded exactly like Chicago or that other one ... Blood, Sweat & Tears. Uncanny. Also various slick crooners, disco dancers, and a dwarf magician. The Himal looked bored with all the hoopla, but they were absolutely fascinated by the clever little magician.

Claiborne's become Tony's nitpicking demon, his worst nightmare, combing over every inch of the script before anything can happen. While the other actors stand around and fume. This precious script—"*Napalm Sunset.*" "*Jungle of No Return.*" "*Emperor X*"—which no longer belongs to Tony but to everyone. Sebastian Claiborne in particular. And it's all Tony's fault.

Claiborne—"the greatest living actor in the English-speaking hemisphere"—stormed off the set as soon as the helicopters were called away again. (Or should I say he waddled off?) Obese, enigmatic, and imperious. He shouted, "I can no longer think up any more dialogue for your movie!" Poor Tony.

The boys and I will miss Lake Ramayyah. After we're done here, it's on to a location up north. Wonder what that's going to be like? Tony says the new terrain will add a whole other texture to "my" documentary. (Ha-ha.)

Mi Último Adiós

1st person memoir / script

A year before her death, my mother started dictating a rambling, out-of-sequence memoir into a tape recorder. Everything she could recall about her life went into that machine. She got too sick and didn't get very far, of course. Plus, she was stoned out of her mind those last few months. On some of the tapes, my mother's voice slurs and her words are unintelligible. But my father went ahead and had Mrs. Locsin transcribe and type up what she could. After the funeral my father handed me a bound, neatly typed manuscript. "Your mama's final gift. It's addressed to you, Paz." He also gave me a bag of cassette tapes.

In her druggy, dreamy state and with her usual flair for irony, my mother had decided to call her memoir *"Mi Último Adiós."* My last farewell—a nod to José Rizal's famous poem, probably.

I cried while reading it on the plane going back to the States. I cried for the most selfish and sentimental of reasons—because I felt guilty for not being there for my mother while she was sick and while she was dying.

My favorite part will always be the beginning, which goes:

MI ÚLTIMO ADIÓS
by Pilar de los Santos Marlowe

I married your father, Enrique "Henry" Marlowe, in a civil ceremony on April 16, 1940. Of course I was preg-

nant! Big scandal. My mother, your Lola Truding, refused
to speak to me. Wouldn't even let me in the house. Your
Lolo Gordo threatened to shoot your father and disin-
herit me. So many accusations, so many tears. Your Lola's
sisters, Tiya Ampao and Tiya Mary, came all the way from
Cotabato to negotiate some sort of settlement and save
face. They were pillars of Manila society and had great
influence on the family.

Church wedding: July 5, 1940.
Enrique Joseph Marlowe Jr., born Dec. 10, 1940. Died
    Nov. 5, 1941.
Enrique Joseph Marlowe Jr., born Dec. 20, 1942. Died
    Dec. 28, 1943.
Enrique Joseph Marlowe Jr., born Feb. 5, 1945.
Pascal Maria Marlowe, born Oct. 6, 1949.

DAILY LIFE
Getting up early in time to go to the first Mass.
It didn't matter what day of the week.
Tuesdays were St. Anthony's day. (?)
Wednesdays were novenas to (?)

In the old walled city of Manila. *Intramuros!* That's
where we went. WHO WOULD GO? ALL OF US. Your Lola Truding, your Lolo Gordo, Ampao, Mary, my brother Joselito,
and me. Rain or shine, that's where we went. There were
different churches for different days of the week. Sundays we went to San Augustín, of course. Saturdays we
attended Mass at Our Lady of Lourdes Church. Aren't you
lucky I never forced this upon you? Your brother, Ricky,
has made his own choices, of course. He loved the splen-
dor of church even as a child, loved reading stories and
looking at images of tortured saints. What was his favorite? That saint holding a little tray of eyeballs—
well, they're her own eyeballs, and her head is tilted

up toward heaven—it's all very sweet, unbloody, unreal.
There's a bit of the martyr streak in your brother. He
probably takes after your Tiya Ampao and should've been
born a girl. Ricky longs for a flaming, glorious death.
But not you. Oh, no, not you.

The smell of burning candles and hot, humid churches.
I remember it as if it were yesterday. Sundays dedicated
to Our Lady of the Rosary, in the cathedral right near
Fort Santiago. Sundays were special, even more stifling
and forbidding. I could not wait to escape that gloomy,
termite-ridden house.

But why am I telling you all this? How I wish you were
here. I imagine you here by my side, Paz. Asking questions about—

What exactly would you want to know? Everything, I
suppose.

Tiya Ampao and Tiya Mary were both old maids. After
Tiya Mary almost died from being bitten by a rabid dog,
they came to Manila from Cotabato to live with us. They
were my mother's elder sisters, devout Catholics and
strict disciplinarians. Tiya Ampao was born without
beauty, a tragedy in the Philippines, especially back in
those days! Whereas Tiya Mary may have been quite plump
and pretty in her youth but had grown bitter by the time
she and Ampao came to live in our house on San Gregorio
Street. Those two carried a lot of secrets around inside
them—you could see it in their steely eyes and pursed
lips. Such tightness and control! My God, I was so terrified of them. What were they holding back? What were
they hiding? Praying and praying and praying, that's all
they ever did.

Tiya Ampao would walk around with a ruler in her
dress pocket. At the dinner table, she'd bring out her
ruler to measure the distance between the silverware
and the plates. Then she'd scold the servants.

Tiya Mary mumbled prayers throughout the day, wandering the hallways and spying on me. Well, that's how I saw it—she was "spying" and hoping to catch me in some unmentionable act. What could I possibly be doing? I was never left alone. There was always my *yaya* hovering about, fussing over me. What was her name? She was pretty young, I remember that. Your Lolo Gordo was putting her through school. Cora or Dora, I think. Anyway, Tiya Mary was suspicious, always muttering about the men running off with servant girls. And Tiya Ampao was even worse. Accusing them of stealing. When those two women lived with us, most of the servants left. My mother was appalled, but what could she do? These were her older sisters, and she had to respect them. *Ay!* Imagine—this happened almost forty years ago, and I still get upset. And I wonder what you are going to do with all this information. What you call "family history," Paz. Little scenes I re-create in my mind, clear as day. I can even smell the mothballs in the closet, the lavender eau de toilette your Lola Truding wore. And of course the old maids had their own peculiar scent—sweat mixed with baby powder and too many layers of clothes in that steamy climate. We did not have air-conditioning, not in those days. Your Lolo Gordo had some family money and a good name. We had to watch it, though. We lived frugally, and of course it didn't help when I ran off with some good-for-nothing Cuban Irish American. Good-for-nothing, that's what they called your father. A man with a shady past and not much money. He was all those things they said, and I loved him.

HOW I MET YOUR FATHER
Purely by accident. I was making *pasyal* with my *yaya* in Luneta Park. My cousins Ludy and Conching were with me. They were older and quite flirtatious. They spotted your

father first. He was by himself, walking along the boulevard. *"Ay! Qué guwapo!"* The girls started giggling and
making goo-goo eyes. *Dios ko,* my poor *yaya* was too
young and naive to control them. Ludy approached him—
she was pretty bold—and asked him if he had the time.
I almost died of embarrassment. But your father was
quite amused by our silliness, and probably flattered by
all the attention being paid to him by such pretty girls.
Did I tell you how pretty Ludy and Conching were? You'd
never guess that now—they're such cranky battle-axes,
but they were pretty pretty pretty in their youth. I was
about fifteen, then. Ludy was seventeen, and Conching was
eighteen. Conching was engaged to Dr. Ocampo's brother,
but that didn't stop her from batting her long lashes
at your father. Did I mention how pretty she was? Not
as mestiza-looking as Ludy, but taller and more . . .
graceful.

Isn't it funny how things turn out? Your father only had
eyes for me. I used to sneak out and meet him late at
night after everyone had gone to sleep. This was all
done with my *yaya's* help, of course. *Naku!* I still feel bad
about what was done to that poor girl. My father beat
her with his cane when he found out what was going on,
and then he fired her. And I still wonder whatever became of her. Cora . . . Dora . . . Flora! That's it. Flora
Galuman! She was my age, you know. Helping to support
her family with those meager wages—my father was such
a tightwad, and he paid the servants nothing. And because of my selfishness, because Flora couldn't say no
to me . . . *Ay,* Paz. Over forty years later, and I'm still
ashamed.

Too much death in my life, *di ba?* First the war, then
so many children lost. You know there was a miscarriage

in between you and your brother. A girl who only lived
for a few days. She had your name. No one else mentions
it, but I remember her. Your father was anxious and disappointed in me. After all, two of his sons and a daughter died! He never said it out loud—he was much too kind
to say so. But you'd better believe men care about that
sort of thing.

Why am I telling you this? You wander the planet, Paz—
seeking answers to questions without any answers, like
some cosmic detective without grounding or direction,
or an explorer who isn't really interested in discover-
ing anything new. Or am I wrong? Perhaps I should take a
more Buddhist approach. What are those clichés that
artists are always spouting? "It's the process that's
important." "It's the journey that's worth taking." Pretentious homilies I used to spout myself, when I was
painting. But now I am sick with this stupid cancer, and
I am in a hurry all of a sudden. I feel helpless, Paz.
I worry about you and your brother and the damnedest
things.

PART THREE

Requiem for a Prodigal Son
1997

3rd person
&
journalist notes

The procession makes its way past the churches of Quiapo, Baclaran, and San Agustín, the little girls resplendent in their rhinestone tiaras and satin gowns, clutching satin rosettes, burning candles, and rosaries. The lucky man, the chosen one costumed as Christ, grunts and groans under the weight of his wooden cross. His wailing disciples follow close behind. Men, stripped to the waist, flagellate themselves with homemade bouquets of tiny, razor-tipped whips. Flesh and blood glint in the midday sun. The children chirp bittersweet hymns in Latin, in Tagalog, in Bisayan, Ilocano, and English, miniature kings and queens perched on thrones of wood and tin. They wave stiffly to the crowds from flower and sequin-bedecked floats snaking down Taft Avenue, across United Nations to Roxas Boulevard. What time was Jesus actually crucified? What time did the Virgin Mary die? This is not Ash Wednesday, this is not Good Friday, this is not Easter Sunday. This is the funeral of Zamora López de Legazpi, only son of Don Flaco and Mary the American.

The women inch across Padre Faura on scraped and skinless knees, across Ongpin Street, across Buendía, across Ortigas Avenue, across Escolta, across Claro M. Recto, across Mabini, across M. H. del Pilar, across Epifanio de los Santos, crossing and crisscrossing the avenues of bloody history in spite of the stink and heat and traffic.

Don Flaco declares: It is a crime for a father to have to bury his only son.

His mother, Mary Garrison López de Legazpi, declares: God's will. *Bathala na.*

His father is at war with God and at war with his wife.

His father is baffled by everything but money.

His father's daughters, *his older sisters*, are flying in just for the funeral. They are not staying long, and they don't matter as much, of course. Only their brother, his only son, matters now.

From the glorious markets of Divisoria to the noodle emporiums of Binondo and the shoe factories of Marikina, they come together to pay homage and sing. Manila alive with the sounds of 30 million voices lifted in prayer, in hope, in desperation and forgiveness, voices celebrating Zamora and his astonishing tribe of innocents, voices singing for no reason at all, for the sheer joy of singing. Zamora the playboy explorer, stuff of *chismis*, dark myth and legend. These are the processions and the pageants as his father Don Flaco orchestrates them, utilizing his own money, his millions and billions, stocks and bonds, leverages and buyouts, World Bank and IMF loans, black-market scams, kickbacks, and ransoms, his share of Yamashita's gold.

More children appear, costumed as miniature virgins, angels, and saints. The procession snakes through the narrow streets, streets swarming with packs of dogs and mobs of the pious and starstruck, all gripped by hysteria and ecstatic longing. Bodies succumb to the unbearable heat, fainting and falling at an incredible rate, trampled upon by oblivious hordes of believers. The procession creeps along, unsure of its final destination. Perhaps Rizal Park, perhaps Intramuros, perhaps Malacañang Palace. Everyone moves forward, pushing and shoving and surging ahead, keeping up as best they can. Tinny loudspeakers blare undecipherable hymns and overwrought love songs. The miniature virgins, angels, saints, kings, and queens are trapped in their lavish floats. They maintain somber expressions, these children with the faded eyes of old people.

All this pomp and spectacle to honor Don Flaco's only son! A reviled man, a ruined man, a forgotten man. Once admired, feared, and envied, once the butt of too many jokes, once the shining star of sordid *chismis*, but deserving of honors, nevertheless. And his three elder sisters, María Amparo, María Azucena, María Angelita, are flying in for the funeral from Madrid, Palma de Mallorca, and Miami Beach. Perfumed, paranoid, filled with regrets, they fled Manila as soon as they could, as soon as he was born. They understood that their lives were over, saw it all coming. And on the day he dies, skeletal, covered with violet lesions, vomiting black phlegm and begging for mercy, his overdressed sisters are driven from the airport separately in their Mercedes-Benz, Nissan, and Lexus sedans. They arrive on the front steps of their brother's house flanked by polite bodyguards in stylish *barong* shirts, bodyguards brandishing walkie-talkies and guns. *Is he dead yet, our brother?* Our dear brother, Junior. *Sí, sí, sí.* He is dead. The sisters purse their lips in grim disapproval. They've been away too long, no longer used to the sweltering heat, the crowds, the chaos, and snail-paced traffic. They are furious; they've just missed their brother's last rites. They fan themselves, murmuring I told you so, I told you so, I told you so. The monkeys and macaws in the garden screech in sympathy.

Mary stumbles down the hallway into her son's private, air-conditioned chapel. He lies in his closed coffin, his once fine, feral face now the waxen, puffy face of a mannequin or fool. Not her son at all, not her beloved boy child. Mary bolts the chapel door from the inside, collapses facedown on the marble floor, hard and cool to the touch. Her sinewy arms are spread out in a crucifixion of sorrow. She mourns prostrate before the coffin, before her son's corpse awaiting his resentful sisters and baffled father, before the statue of the black, bloody Nazarene and the statue of her namesake, the Holy Virgin Mary. Her son is dead, and none of it is any use, no comfort whatsoever.

From her hiding place within the confessional booth, the servant Candelaria Cayabyab observes Mary the American. Candelaria who is a stout old woman now, cursed with chronically bloodshot eyes and a bellyful of tumors. She studies Mary with the detached curiosity the poor sometimes have about the rich and the rich never have about the poor. *Aha, aha, aha. So this is how the crazy bastard's mother mourns her son.* Candelaria takes note of the plain black shoes. The plain, calf-length, black crepe dress. The veil, the black pearls. She dozes off and dreams of her daughter, Rizalina. Gone now, for . . . what? Twenty years? Had Master Zamora driven her away? She had warned her about him. The one they all bowed down to and addressed respectfully as *Sir. Boss. Master. Mister Señor.*

Insistent banging and knocking. The anxious, insistent voices of Mary's husband and daughters come through the thick, medieval wooden doors: Let us in, Mama. Let us pray with you. The funeral must begin! Don't shut yourself in there like a madwoman!

Mary the American remains frozen in her crucifixion of despair. Candelaria, roused from her sleep, giggles softly to herself. At last Master Zamora is dead. At long last. Her feet ache, her bellyful of tumors aches, but she feels a strange peace. The confessional's velvet cushions are plush and inviting, stuffed with kapok and hand-stitched by Candelaria herself. She surrenders to twenty years of servitude, leaning back against the soft pillows to doze off once again. Oblivious to the servant in the confessional, Mary the American recites the rosary of bitter lament, never lifting her head off the stone floor. Her penance will last for hours, the rosary repeated until Mary's vocal cords hemorrhage and Candelaria awakens to the violent sounds of axes breaking down doors.

But that is yet to come.
NOW
even under the closed lid of the coffin, Zamora's embalmed corpse begins to stink. The sweet, sickening odor seeps from under the bolted doors and into the hallway where his sisters and father wait

in vain. Don Flaco refuses to be defeated by his stubborn wife and calls an emergency meeting. His attorneys, his flock of priests, family physician, family mortician, his entire public-relations staff, and the *comandante* of his private army are summoned. He postpones the funeral. More processions, commemorative pageants, and arbitrary fiestas are planned. Press releases are faxed throughout the world: Zamora López de Legazpi Jr., discoverer and protector of the Stone Age Taobo tribe, is dead after a long, undisclosed illness.

Outside the gates of the Casas Blancas compound, several foreigners, photographers, and journalists insinuate themselves into the front ranks of the swelling crowd, pointing cameras and taking notes while whispering furtively into microcassette recorders.

Note: SO HOT! Not too big of a crowd, but not too little. Usual morbid gawkers and passersby. Few celebs. Grieving starlets in tacky outfits. Old loves? Paid mourners? Recognized one or two scholars and bureaucrats (maybe the controversial anthropologist Dr. Cabrera?) standing next to an unidentified woman.

Note: Respectable enough turnout, considering.

Note: ZLL died of "undisclosed," "unconfirmed," "mysterious ailment." HA!

Note: Where is mother? Rest of Legazpi family? Aunts, uncles, etc.? Ex-wife and children?

Note: Where are Taobo?

Note: The crowd, orderly so far, waits hours in the sun. "How about some goddamn water?" Foreigner with red hair shouts in English. (His faithful friend and defender, Ken Forbes?)

Note: One of two angry guards points a gun at (maybe) Forbes. Mocks foreigner: Talking to me, SIR? Foreigner, sheepish, backs off.

Note: Old man, probably Don F, spotted briefly on balcony. Waves.

Note: Zamora López de Legazpi, dead at age 59.

Today's date: May 22, 1997.

Lost Tribes

3ʳᵈ Person

Z amora's obituary in the *New York Times* was a shock to Paz. She stared at his photograph and read the obituary over again, filled with a weird combination of restlessness, sorrow, and elation. Nothing had ever come of that article she'd tried to write about him back in 1977, but the long, awkward day she spent with Zamora was burned into her brain. Paz decided it was time to find Ken Forbes. She wasn't sure why, but she knew it was important. Could he possibly still be living in San Francisco? Paz dialed San Francisco information and found he was the fifth "K Forbes" listed in the directory. She was stunned that it was so easy, that he actually answered the phone when she called. "You're a journalist?" Forbes asked in a brusque but not unfriendly voice.

"Not anymore."

"I don't talk to journalists. But if you're not, then why—"

"I knew Zamora as a child. I tried interviewing him a long time ago. He wasn't very cooperative. Then, as you know, he disappeared. I feel like I've got to finish the story, Mr. Forbes. Even if it's just for myself. But, honestly, I totally understand if you don't want to see me."

"I'll see you," Ken Forbes said.

Uncle Jorge and his new wife picked Paz up at the airport. Uncle Jorge was her father's older brother. He and Paz had never met. He had left Manila when Paz was still a baby, living first in Boston, then Seattle, then finally San Francisco. All Paz knew was that he had outlived two wives and was close to eighty years old. Wife number three was Marilyn, a fortyish, hefty bottle blonde who worked at Wells Fargo Bank.

"Just look at you," Uncle Jorge murmured, smothering Paz in a vigorous hug. "Just . . . look . . . at . . . you!" There were tears in his eyes, but he couldn't stop smiling. They drove to a Vietnamese restaurant in the outer Mission with iron bars on the windows.

"Your Uncle Jorge loves Vietnamese food. Don't you, hon?" Marilyn patted his arm.

Uncle Jorge kept his gaze on Paz. "Do you miss your papa, Paz? You look just like him, you know. That nose—"

"Jorge, hon," Marilyn said.

Uncle Jorge ignored her. "First your mother, then my poor baby brother. Everybody's dead. And me, with my heart ticking! Boom! I'll probably outlive all of you."

"Don't brag," Marilyn said. She addressed Paz. "Did you come all the way out here just to visit us?"

"Sort of," Paz said.

"Sort of?" Marilyn looked baffled.

Uncle Jorge hummed and stared out the barred windows. It started to rain. They finished the rest of the meal in silence.

Forbes opened the door. Paz had been waiting on the steps of his two-story town house for at least ten minutes. She rang the doorbell and knocked, calling his name. She knew he was home, having had sense enough to call from a gas station to make sure she was headed in the right direction. She had rented a car.

"Oh," he had said on the phone, "you're really here?" Now he stood in the doorway, flustered and uncertain. Paz thought of a mole emerging blind from some dark, subterranean tunnel.

"Thanks for agreeing to see me, Mr. Forbes," Paz said.

"Come in," he said, not missing a beat. "Nobody calls me 'Mister.' Just Ken, please."

Paz apologized for dripping water on the carpet as she handed him her jacket. "Should I take off my boots?" Forbes shrugged. *Not necessary.* He led her through the cozy living room, filled with books and mementos from the Philippines. His elegant, black-and-white photographs of the Taobo hung on the walls. "I guess you've got your own little museum," Paz said.

Forbes cracked a faint smile and gestured toward the thick stack of papers next to the laptop on his desk. "My manuscript. Over a thousand pages, and I'm not finished yet. Think anyone will want to publish a new book on the Taobo?"

"Big books are in," Paz answered. He glanced at her sharply, not sure if she was making fun of him. She followed him into the tidy kitchenette, at ease in his presence.

"You're a coffee drinker, I take it?" Forbes was grinding coffee beans and fussing with cups and saucers. He pulled out a Saran-wrapped peach pie from the refrigerator. "This is darn good. It's from the Portuguese bakery around the corner." His domesticity surprised Paz. They sat at a fold-out kitchen table.

"You have a family?" she asked.

"Yup. It didn't last long, but I've got two grown kids. They're great. What about you?"

"A daughter. She's fifteen."

"Where do you live?" he asked.

"New York."

Paz helped herself to a slice. The peaches were canned and too sweet, but Forbes was right. The pie was good. "Tell me about your book."

"My book is about the truth," Forbes said, suddenly energized. "The Taobo are real. How could people say they were actors, faking everything? Goddamn. Was I just dumb and blind?"

Paz took the tiny tape recorder out of her bag. "No," Forbes said, agitated. "You can take all the notes you want, but absolutely no taping."

He waited until she put the recorder away before he continued talking. "How could you not know? How could I not know? *I was there.*" Forbes got up from the table. The rain beat against the windows. A drab, chilly grayness had seeped into everything. Paz hunched her shoulders in the kitchen gloom, wondering if Forbes would take notice and turn on more lights. He paced, voice quivering with a mounting excitement. "People accused me of conspiring with Zamora and the others. Why would I do that?"

"But what about Zamora?" Paz asked. "Do you think he was capable of masterminding such an elaborate hoax?"

The silence was palpable in the memento-filled rooms.

"No," Forbes said, when he finally spoke. "Absolutely not, no. I don't believe Zamora staged any of it."

"Did you attend his funeral?"

"You bet," Forbes said. "I still considered him a friend, though I hadn't seen him in years."

He disappeared behind a curtain and emerged a few seconds later carrying a large box of photographs. Forbes cleared the table and spread the photographs before her. Without saying a word, Paz walked over to the kitchen sink, flicked on the light switch, and sat back down.

"Do you remember Bodabil?" Forbes asked.

Paz nodded, gazing at the image of Bodabil as a ten-year-old boy—laughing, long hair flying, swinging from a vine. There was another image of Bodabil clinging to Zamora by the neck. Playful, affectionate. Zamora squinted at the camera, clearly enjoying himself, surrounded by naked children and bare-breasted women. It was a legendary photograph, the same one used in the *Times* obituary.

"Were they actors?" Forbes repeated. "Were we all fools?"

"I wanted to believe it," Paz said. "I saw what I wanted to see."

"Hindsight," Forbes muttered. "Everything in hindsight."

He stood before the large bay windows that looked out into the street. Wind and rain pummeled against the panes of glass. It was an impressive winter storm minus the snow, no doubt about that. Yet oddly warm and tropical, as if San Francisco had been transformed into a Southeast Asian metropolis. Paz had rented the cheapest car available, a pint-size, no-frills Dodge Neon that barely got her to Forbes's house on the outskirts of the city. Where the fuck was she? Paz wondered. She hoped she could find her way back to her hotel in the south of Market.

"Do you mind if I smoke?"

"Go right ahead," Forbes said.

There were no ashtrays, so Paz settled for the lid of an empty mayonnaise jar. Forbes watched as she lit up and inhaled. Paz had the distinct feeling that he hadn't had any visitors for quite a while. Isolation: the curse of having been touched, in one way or another, by the late Zamora Legazpi.

"Nobody I know smokes anymore," Forbes said.

"I'm determined to defy the odds."

Forbes blushed. He was . . . what? Close to sixty? Freckled, still boyishly earnest and compelling. Straight out of a Norman Rockwell illustration, except for the melancholy eyes. "I was supposed to stay in Mindanao for only two weeks," he said. "Document the expedition for Zamora and get the hell out. But after that first visit to the caves, I couldn't leave. I kept postponing my departure. It was glorious. The kind of thing that makes you question everything. I mean, the Taobo people had no word for war."

"Right," Paz said. "That was the most quotable thing about them."

"You think Zamora made that up, too?"

"It was a great sound bite." Paz regretted sounding so cynical. Forbes looked sick. "Are you sorry you let me come here?"

"No." Forbes stared at the clock on the wall, an innocuous Felix the Cat novelty thing with a wagging tail and moving eyes. "If you aren't a journalist, what is it exactly that you do?" His tone turned harsh.

"I work in television." Paz looked around. Did he even own a TV? "I'm a story editor. For a dramedy."

"A what?"

"Combination drama-comedy. Get it?"

Forbes grinned. "Jesus. What would the Greeks think?"

"They'd probably love it. The main character's a neurotic gangster. It's not a bad show, actually. I'm lucky," Paz said.

"You make a lot of money?"

Paz shrugged. "It's cable."

"I don't know what that means." Forbes stared at the thick stack
of papers on his desk, a man possessed. "A thousand pages! Some
days I just can't believe it. I never thought I'd have this much to say.
And I'm nowhere finished."

Do you remember?

Did you hear the one about?

He sat down and began to talk. Paz listened and tried to make
sense of his precious memories. A dimly lit tunnel with rooms on
either side. A hokey metaphor, but literally what she saw as Forbes
told his stories:

whose voice ?

Zamora, shirtless, stands on a stool in his baggy karsonsilyo, *railing about
something or other, probably Imelda. He always railed about Imelda and her
antics, expertly mimicking the first lady's girlish affectations and gooey voice.
He dressed in drag, putting on makeup and one of his wife's traditional
gowns—what do you call those things? With the butterfly sleeves. He pretended to be Imelda and made us all laugh. Zamora surrounded by anxious
aides and servants, his captive audience. Hands gesturing flamboyantly. Get
me my shirt, he'd bark. Celia, you know which one!*

"Did you ever meet Celia or that little one, Sputnik?" Forbes asked.

"No. Wait—I remember that time I tried to interview him, this
little person served us drinks."

"That's her, that's Sputnik!" Forbes chuckled, pleased.

*Celia, shaking with nervousness, scurries to the closets that make up one
whole side of the room. Zamora was a clotheshorse. Closets just for shoes,*

closets just for pants, for shirts, for leisure wear and formal wear. Closets organized to the point of insanity.

Celia: You mean the white one, sir?

Zamora, screaming: I own thousands of white shirts! Which white one do you think I mean?

All the shirts look the same. Celia shaking harder. The new one, sir?

Celia hurries over with the correct shirt of Egyptian cotton, which she slips over his hairy arms and buttons deftly with icy fingers.

Thank you, Celia, Zamora says in English.

"He could be rough on those servants. But then," Forbes said, "Zamora would surprise you with his kindness and generosity. He sent them all to school, you know. Paid for everything." He caught Paz glancing at Felix the Cat. "Are you worried about the time?"

There was the roller rink Zamora had installed on the first floor of his house, after Ilse left him. Zamora loved to dance, did you know that? He loved to watch other people make fools of themselves on the dance floor. The wilder the better. To dance is a deeply spiritual thing, he would say in all seriousness. Look at the Santería and Candomble practices of Cuba and Brazil, the "voodoo" rituals of Haiti and New York City. To lose yourself like that is to get closer to God. Dance, dance, dance!

"Have you seen or heard from Ilse or his children?" Paz asked.

"Ilse wasn't at the funeral," Forbes said. "Did you know her?"

In the tunnel of memory, a silver disco ball hangs in place of a chandelier. Zamora rollerskates to "It's Your Thing" by the Isley Brothers, with Miss Spain, Miss Texas, Miss Aruba, and Gigi Fontaine along for company. Beauty queens and movie stars. Boy, did he love 'em! They skated up and down the slippery ramps of what had once been the living room of his house, grooving to the disco beat provided by Zamora's personal live-in DJ.

Paz laughed, astonished. "A live-in DJ?"

"Zamora knew how to have fun," Forbes said.

The relentless rain and descending darkness made Paz uneasy. "It's getting late," she said. "I should go. I'm worried about finding my way back."

"All right," Forbes said.

"Thank you for your time, Ken. Good luck with your book."

Forbes cracked another faint smile. He walked Paz to the door and helped her on with her jacket. "Be safe, Paz Marlowe," he said, meaning it.

Back in the car, Paz thought about what she had seen on TV years ago. It was either 1971 or 1972. She was in her apartment in Los Angeles. Her then husband, Stefan, was out gallivanting with his actor friends. Stefan had a lot of friends. Vain and ambitious, hard to tell apart. They were always around and wore her out. But on this particular night, the place was all hers. She poured herself a glass of cheap Gallo red and turned on the funky TV—the colors were off and she had to keep adjusting the rabbit-ears antenna to get a clear reception. Paz was just in time for some PBS documentary called "Forgotten Tribes of the Philippines." She gasped—the actual opening shot was of Zamora López de Legazpi standing on the side of a mountain, squinting hard at ominous, billowing clouds of smoke. It was all so dramatic. The sounds of gunfire and the voices of angry men erupted from the fields of tall grass below. The men emerged from the tall grass, waving *bolos* and rifles. Zamora remained calm as they approached, shouting in a language Paz did not understand.

An American actor of some repute narrated the documentary in a solemn voice. The music on the soundtrack soared just as Zamora's helicopter soared above the fertile, breathtaking terrain.

Zamora spoke to an off-camera interviewer in the restless, impatient tone of a man who was used to ordering people around and not having to explain himself. "I will not allow the forest or these great people to be destroyed," Zamora said. "We have to keep lumber companies out of here. I have spoken to the president, and it's as simple as that."

The helicopter hovered over a clearing. There were people waiting on the ground. The men spread their arms to receive him, smiles of welcome lighting up their eager faces. Zamora López de Legazpi jumped out of the helicopter into their open arms. He was agile, with the sharp, bearded face of a fox. A white yachting cap sat on his head of dark curls. The women winced at the grinding sound of the helicopter hovering noisily above them, unsure whether to laugh or scream at the sight of the hairy, pale-skinned man. *Tao Puti, Amo Data, Great Father.* They stepped aside as the men hoisted him above their shoulders. Father from the sky, the men called out. You have come back! The women observed Zamora with grave demeanor. They lagged behind the parade of men wending their way down the zigzag mountain path. The rhythmic, mournful clanging of *kulintang* echoed through the green mist. Heavy sticks beat on brass gongs and drums, announcing the arrival of Zamora into a village in the valley of clouds, where the elders waited.

Father from the sky has returned! the men called out.

Zamora held out his arms, ready to give as well as to receive. He was a long-lost king, a glorious saint, a triumphant savior. *Our hero, our villain.* His performance was sublime. He smiled down at his devoted supplicants, a stern man who had never smiled as freely as this. The scene was well rehearsed, yet it rang true. Zamora meant every inch of his reluctant smile. His heart ached to be home at last.

To give is to receive.

How they loved him! How he loved them.

We have never heard of the Philippines. Datu Blen, the eldest elder, renowned killer of several men and proud father of twenty-two children, spoke in a raspy voice. He wore a towering headdress to signify his authority, decorated with beads, tiny brass bells, shards of bone, and wild rooster feathers. In deference to their chief, the rest of the villagers lowered their gaze as he spoke. His language sounded like the warbling of certain birds. A wizened man named Duan translated into Tagalog for Zamora's benefit.

"The Philippines is where you live," Zamora said to Datu Blen, amused. Duan translated back into the warbling language. Datu Blen seemed perplexed but also amused.

"I live in the valley of clouds," Datu Blen declared.

"The valley of clouds is part of the Philippines," Zamora said.

Datu Blen, unimpressed, barked an order at a young woman nearby. She was a village beauty of some stature, adorned with bracelets and dozens of earrings, her teeth filed razor sharp, her lips stained red-violet. Perhaps she was one of the *datu*'s many wives, or a daughter. Her name, Duan informed Zamora, was Itek. Itek hurried off and returned with another woman, pulling her by the arm. The woman was mortified at being singled out. She knelt on the muddy ground before Datu Blen, Duan, and Zamora, her bowed head covered with a woven cloth that concealed most of her face. Itek spoke in an urgent tone to Datu Blen, who was indifferent and gestured impatiently toward Zamora. Itek surprised Zamora and Duan by speaking in Tagalog. She pointed to the kneeling woman.

"Her husband was murdered two nights ago," Itek said.

"Who murdered your husband?" Zamora asked the kneeling woman. Itek translated the question.

The woman, trembling, could not bear to look into Zamora's eyes or answer his question.

"Speak!" Datu Blen commanded her harshly.

"Who murdered your husband?" Zamora asked again.

Itek prodded the woman with her foot. The kneeling woman finally lifted her head but kept her eyes closed. "The loggers," she whispered.

"The loggers," Itek translated for Zamora.

The woman whose husband was murdered grasped Zamora's hand and wailed. Her covered head remained bowed. Her desperation was painful and embarrassing to watch. Zamora seemed to forget he was being filmed and allowed the world to glimpse his un-ease as the wailing woman tugged at the fingers of his hand. "What can I do?" he asked, helpless. "What do you want me to do for you?" The woman whimpered and sobbed. Exasperated, Zamora turned to a big man carrying a rifle and wearing a straw cowboy hat. Sonny Limahan. "Gather some men. See what you can find out," Zamora said to him.

The kneeling woman was beside herself with gratitude and threw her arms around him. Zamora surrendered, pulling her close. The villagers, except for Datu Blen, smiled in appreciation at this public show of affection. Staring at the TV screen, Paz was overcome by a sudden torrent of feelings. Sharp pangs in the pit of her stomach, a strange dread that choked the air out of her lungs. She lay on the floor taking slow, deep breaths. The voices on television droned on. The documentary came to an end; Paz turned the TV off. She felt, was, sick with longing. Homesick for gaudy spectacles and contra-dictions, the anxious sound of her mother's and father's voices. "*Paz, Paz . . . Puñeta! Dónde estás?*"

In the blinding rain, Paz drove slowly and carefully to the hotel south of Market. She prayed she wouldn't end up in an accident, or take the wrong turnoff leading to . . . *nowhere*. Paz had to laugh. She had no idea where she was. The night and fierce rain had swallowed up Ken Forbes and his house. On a road back there, somewhere be-hind her, the nice, kind man and his house receded into the pitch-black night. Gone, forever. Her mother, Pilar. Her father, Enrique. And now Zamora. It was all so long ago, Paz thought. But the mongrel dogs kept howling, calling her home.

Joke's on Us:
The Sacred Mysteries of the Taobo*

by Prof. Amado G. Cabrera

(Ph.D., Sorbonne)
Department of Anthropology and History,
University of the Philippines
Diliman, Quezon City

Ladies and gentlemen, distinguished colleagues. Back in 1971 a man named Zamora López de Legazpi introduced the world to a small band of paleolithic cave dwellers known as the Taobo. Supposedly they lived in the remote Mindanao rain forest, isolated from other tribes and the rest of civilization. The media hailed his discovery as the "ethnological find of the century." Was it, in fact, the *hoax* of the century? Twenty years later we are still not sure. I laugh, somewhat painfully, at the chutzpah** involved. *Tao* or Taobo? Performance or real life? Is there a difference? I was going to show some slides and excerpts from several pertinent videos, but no image or series of images can really, in my mind, convey the scope and ramifications of this . . . *controversy*. So I'm going to talk instead.

---

*Dear reader: I apologize in advance for writing this speech—this paper—in English, my second language. You may have also gleaned that, in spite of everything, I was rather fond of Zamora Legazpi. I will undoubtedly be branded, now and forever, as a traitor to my race, a post-neo-neo-neocolonialist. *Que será, será.* Or, as they say in our country, *bahala na, que sira-sirang ulo!* My life has been a kick. Exhilarating, complicated, and rich. I am not afraid to die. All infuriating puns intended.

** Chutzpah (hootz-pah)—origin: Yiddish, colloq. 1. Shameless, brazen impudence.

❧

The ethnographic evidence is nil. We have all been made fools. The Taobo were a marvelous prank cooked up by our very own notorious mestizo trickster, the late Mr. Zamora López de Legazpi Jr., aka "*El Segundo.*" Who exactly was this man? We know a few colorful things about him. That he was the iconoclast playboy son of tycoon Zamora López de Legazpi Sr.—one of the five richest men in the Philippines. That Zamora Jr. was a champion swimmer in his youth, a pelota and polo player in his middle age, a villain to some and a do-gooder to others. After all these years, I am as confused as anyone else about what to believe about the man. He died a mystery. But I do have my theories, which is why I've finally decided to stick my neck out and invite you all here. My distinguished colleagues, my friends and peers. Here goes: The Taobo exist, but are fake. PIMPF was a money-laundering scam. Zamora López de Legazpi Jr. was a gangster, a poet, and an exploiter of our dreams.

There. I've said it.

No doubt I will be dismissed as just another envious, small-time academic, someone who's way out of his league. But I strongly believe that the implications of my "discoveries" are quite damaging to the anthropological—no, make that the global community as a whole. And I am perfectly aware that there are those of us who are still afraid to speak up, though Zamora is dead and we suspected things were not right as far back as 1971. Yet because of the powerful Legazpi name and the fear of having one's tongue, *bayag,* or *susu* hacked off by goons, we have said nothing. Who can blame us, taught from childhood to fear and respect the supernatural and the superreal? And of course there is the omnipresent specter of the president himself. Reduced to a mummified corpse in an air-conditioned tomb in faraway Hawaii, yet still capable of casting a long shadow over those of us who remember. Nineteen seventy-one. O wonder of the world, enchanted forest! How can we forget?

Never mind who's in office now. It's all just a ploy to make us think things have changed for the better. As always, when we least expect it, the crocodiles will return, hungrier than ever.

I never denied working for him. I was young, conscientious, and eager, fresh from my sojourn in Paris. I was thrilled to be part of those early expeditions to the caves. Who among you wouldn't be? I collected data, scribbled my field notes, made my observations, did as I was told. From the start I had my reservations, but kept my mouth shut. As you know, there were three of us who later resigned and voiced our suspicions. Dr. Eng was one—Dr. Philip Eng, the distinguished ethnobotanist from the University of Australia in Sydney. And Vivian Miller from Stanford. They regret not being able to attend this symposium, but I cannot tell you how excited I am that they have given us permission to publish their papers in our forthcoming anthology.

Anyway, back to the gaps and holes in the story. From day one there were just too many of them. Who was Duan, really? A man who came out of nowhere yet seemed to be everywhere back in those days. He claimed responsibility for teaching the Taobo everything—from making simple tools to farming and hunting. And that bit about rice—*rice*, ladies and gentlemen! The Taobo were supposedly perplexed by rice. They sniffed it, they chewed it raw, they spit it out in disgust. But later someone—I can't remember who—caught them sneaking sacks of rice into the caves. And what about those caves? So clean, so bare, so suspiciously devoid of human waste and detritus.

Paleolithic. Oh, it was an audacious scheme, all right. Brilliant! Entertaining! But let's face it: A lot of people who dared to come forward are now dead. Just as Zamora, our notorious mestizo trickster, is now dead. Meanwhile, we so-called regular folk scratch our heads and try to make sense of his *kalokohan*. Let sleeping dogs lie, they warn us. What's past is past. Blame it all on the excesses of a mummified dictator and his insomniac wife. The fake primitive Stone New Age is upon us. Let the healing begin!

Kalokohan. Origin: probably Malay (*ka*), Hispanic (*loco*), Chinese (*han*). Your guess is as good as mine.

One of the first things I asked myself was, why? Why would Zamora do it? A man this rich, smart, handsome, this set for life— why bother? And of course I knew the depressing answer almost as soon as I asked the question: because he could. The simple arrogance of it all is beautiful, *di ba?* So inventive, outrageous, playful, and inherently Filipino! And that is what I liked best about him, why I continued to work with him despite all my misgivings.

Just think, ladies and gentlemen. Zamora, the president, and the first lady cooked up this elaborate scheme just so they could get their hands on forty thousand acres of primo rain forest. In the process they gained international cachet as environmentalists and protectors of indigenous peoples. *Now, that's visionary!*

Rizalina Santa Monica

S onny Limahan spotted her as soon as he walked in. She wore a backless dress the same color as her skin and stood before a painting. The painting, which took up one entire wall of the gallery, was of a gaunt Jesus carrying a massive wooden cross. Near Christ were a crowing rooster and a pile of skulls. Four corners of the canvas were decorated, as if in afterthought, by sloppily rendered swastikas. What the fuck was she looking at? Limahan wondered as he approached her.

Lina. He called out her name, just loud enough for her to hear and turn her head. The gallery was intimidating—a vast industrial space in downtown L.A., empty except for the two of them and the young man with a shaved head and an expensive-looking suit stationed behind a desk in the reception area. Wall after wall was covered with angry paintings by the same artist. The crude, unbeautiful images irritated Sonny Limahan. He felt out of his element. Why couldn't he appreciate these pyramids of skulls, these decapitated priests and cartoonish conquistadors in hats and suits of armor? The artist's ghoulish sense of humor was evident. Why did he take such offense? *I'm just getting too old for this shit*, Limahan thought.

Meeting at the gallery had been her idea. "Shall I pick you up?" Limahan had asked her on the phone, hoping.

"No. Not necessary," Lina replied. She was surprised to hear from him. "How did you find me?" she asked, vaguely hostile.

"I ran into your actor friend at a bar in Malate," Limahan said. "We were talking and—your name came up. Small world, *talaga*."

Lina giggled. "Where I live is his place in Santa Monica. Can you believe? Vince gave me keys to his old house."

Limahan was nervous and excited to see her. He broke into a sweat although it was a cool day in Los Angeles. Bright, yet strangely cool. Lina seemed genuinely pleased to see him. "Long time no see, *di ba?*"

Limahan grinned back at her. "Long time. What a funny place to meet." He wondered if she found his exhausted face and spreading paunch shocking or sad.

"The artist is Filipino," Lina informed him.

"Ugly work," Limahan muttered. "Profanity without the talent."

Lina moved away to study another painting. Limahan regretted his bluntness, his priggishness. He hesitated before walking over to where Lina now stood. The savage, incomprehensible images screamed out at him. Two wizened rats squabbled over a gigantic hypodermic needle. More sloppy swastikas adorned the painting. "Why are you here, Sonny?" Lina asked him in Tagalog.

"Zamora's dead. I was in Manila for the funeral. I thought you'd want to know. I saw your mother, and she asked me to find you." *Ang inay mo.* When the silence became too uncomfortable, Sonny Limahan said, "*Tayo na*, Lina. Let's get out of here."

They walked down the block to a café sporting a French name. Bon Appétit or Bon Pain or Bon something or other. The linoleum floor was sticky, and the display of pastries meager and unappetizing. "We can go somewhere else," Limahan said. "Somewhere nice. *Sigé na*, I rented a car."

Lina sat down at a table. "They let you smoke here." She rummaged in her shoulder bag for a pouch of tobacco and Bambu rolling papers. Limahan watched her roll a perfect cigarette. "You want one, Sonny?"

Limahan shook his head. "How old are you now?"

She shrugged, impatient. "Old. So. How did Mister Señor Zamora die?"

"Cancer. Other things. His family wouldn't say. You know, he wasn't even sixty yet."

"You with him when he die?"

Sonny Limahan nodded. He met Lina's gaze, felt her take it all in.

A startling goth of a woman with short, spiky, dyed black hair and black lipstick sauntered over. "Ready?"

"I want one of those." Lina pointed to a large croissant in the display case.

Limahan ordered an American coffee for himself. Lina smeared the croissant with jam and butter as soon as the waitress set it down in front of her. She smoked as she ate. "Funny how I have been thinking about the boss. Wondering if he is okay. And suddenly here you are. How is my mother?"

"Candelaria wants you to come home," Limahan said. *Ang nanay mo.*

Lina waited. Smoking, eating. Another person entirely than the one he had expected to see. "Your mother is not well," Sonny Limahan said. He wanted to ask Lina about the daughter she left behind, but he didn't. Zamora had known about Yeye, now living and going to school in Davao. Zamora, on his deathbed, had ordered money deposited into a bank account in Yeye's name. *For her education.* A grandiose and showy gesture, befitting the contradictions of Zamora's legend. Sonny longed to tell Lina about it.

Lina rose from the table. "I must go now."

"What? But you haven't finished—"

"You came here to tell me he was dead. That my *nanay* is sick. Nevertheless—" She gathered her things. "I must go now. *Salamat.* Thank you, Sonny. Thank you, thank you. You're a good man. Please do not follow me."

Lina hurried out of the café without once looking back. Sonny Limahan knew she didn't drive, that she took buses everywhere. She had said so on the phone.

"People make fun of me. They ask how can I live here without a car!"

Limahan had laughed in sympathy.

"Where do you live, Sonny?" Lina asked.

"San Diego. You need a car there, too."

"I like riding the buses in L.A.," she said. "The buses here are clean and not so crowded, like back home. I sometimes ride them from one end of the city to another."

He was supposed to ask. Candelaria had insisted. "Do you have enough money? Everything okay?"

Lina nodded. "I have a job. Everything okay."

She was mysterious about the job; she refused to tell him exactly where she lived. "I stay near the beach," was all she said. "I am happy now. I want to stay happy."

From the window of the café, Sonny Limahan watched Lina cross the wide boulevard to a bus shelter. Her black hair streamed down the bare back of her sundress. She had grown into quite a woman, more beautiful than ever. Limahan wished that there was some way he could have assured her that she was safe from his meddling. He would not chase after her; he was too tired. He had made a rash, reckless decision only thirty-some hours ago. Changing his ticket at the last minute for LAX instead of flying home to San Diego. To find her. *Rizalina Cayabyab.* The child who was part of his memories, his life in the Philippines with the Taobo and Zamora. But with Zamora's death, all that was over now. The jet lag and fatigue made his hands shake. He would drive to San Diego in the rented car, use the time to decompress. His family would be happy and relieved to see him. It was different now that he was always home. He was a different man. Mr. Middle-Class Anonymous. Helpful neighbor, avid churchgoer. An asset to the growing, prosperous community of Filipinos in Mira Mesa, a suburb of San Diego. Fondly referred to by insiders as "Manila Mesa." He was no longer someone's servant. No longer a thug or goon on Zamora López de Legazpi's payroll. Terms of contempt people in Manila used to call him—behind his back, of course. Those were the days. When he was privy to secrets and he was feared. But things were different now. He was a different man.

"Miss?" Sonny Limahan looked around the dreary café. After a few moments the goth waitress emerged from a back room looking flustered. He wondered if there was anyone else in the café—some *duende* in the pantry perhaps. "Check?" the waitress asked, giggling. Sonny Limahan shook his head and ordered a double espresso with a twist. He would stay a little longer, long enough for Rizalina to board that bus and disappear from his life for good.

The Shark's Lament

The bitch queens of the world—Miss Bolivia Newton-John, Miss Coastal Rica, Miss Arriba Aruba, Miss Nicaraguagua, Miss Natahiti, Miss Sri Langka, Miss Walang Malaysia, Miss Japantasya, Miss Puerto Ricopuno, Miss Grease, Miss Roast Turkey, and Miss Hungry—the *baklas*, *chismosas*, poison-tongued *brujas*, and devilish *doñas* of Manila pack the pews of the Holy Cross Mortuary Chapel on a humid Saturday night. They are unpaid extras, a flamboyant chorus assembled to portray sobbing mourners at a funeral. Rainbow Reyes (a former Miss Philippines) stars as Magda Lena, the sultry proprietor of a Boracay beach resort who meets her gruesome end in the jaws of a ferocious shark. Vince Moody plays Mike, the American marine biologist who tracks the shark and eventually kills it.

The queens of the world fan themselves with sandalwood *abanicos* and woven *pye-pyes*, sipping lukewarm Cokes through dainty straws while retouching their makeup and awaiting their cues. Director Pepito Ponce de León, he of the hissy fits, big hips, stinky French cigarettes, and bushy ponytail, huddles with cameraman Tirso Aranas. Pepito figures it out as he goes along. This is a ten-day shoot, a one-camera operation, no storyboards necessary. Pepito likes to work fast, hates wasting money. *Tagboy ng Pating (The Shark's Lament)* is a combination *Jaws* and *Deep Blue Sea*, Filipino style. The extravaganza of sex and gore features a colossal female shark who goes on a vengeful path of destruction when her shark pups are captured by Japanese tuna fishermen.

Vince Moody comes up with the original idea—he hadn't starred in all those shark movies back in the States for nothing—but he couldn't care less when Pepito offers to share screenwriting credits. *Just gimme my money and I'll say the lines. In English or Tagalog, whatever you want.*

You can't blame Moody for being crass; he's lived in this country long enough to learn a few lessons. Cash up front, none of the usual "percentage of the profits" shit. *Let's keep things simple,* that's what Vince Moody says. Smiling that shy, self-effacing smile, *Nothing personal, man, just business.* Which is why Pepito continues to hire him, why the *doñas* and *brujas* find it all so entertaining. Plus, his son is cute. Alex Moody is visiting the set today. All the way from California! Friendly and cute, Alex is a taller, huskier version of his popular father. He hovers on the sidelines, next to a man with stringy hair and gold teeth named Bong. Bong is Vince Moody's driver, bodyguard, and friend.

Rainbow Reyes plays dead in a fancy, satin-lined casket. Only her head and upper torso are visible—the lower half of her body having been supposedly bitten off by the grieving shark in an earlier scene, while she swims naked. Pepito will worry about the censors later. Rainbow was/is always game for anything, flaunting that voluptuous, immortal body of hers, which defies gravity.

Vince Moody whispers in Rainbow's ear, *You're beautiful, babe. Even in that coffin.* Rainbow giggles but keeps her eyes shut. She longs for a cigarette but reminds herself to stay in character, that only one lovely half of her exists and that she is dead.

Pepito knows he's got another surefire hit on his hands. The formula was effective; the terrifying story tried and true. For who could resist the lure of the vast, beckoning, fathomless ocean? Shark. *Pating*. Mother. Outraged monster creature of the deep. Lonely, cunning predator of voracious appetites. Hell hath no fury, dark stuff of dreams. *"Sigé, Direk."* The producer, Menching Lázaro, calls out to the director.

The bitch-queen *baklas*, the *brujas* and *doñas* are ready for their close-ups, Mr. Ponce de León. *Abanicos* and *pye-pyes* flutter in the stifling heat. The candelabras are lit. Cameraman Tirso Aranas is ready to roll. The hordes of devoted fans and curious street children who have been pressing against the barricaded doors of the mortuary chapel all night—hoping for a glimpse of their beloved, sexy Rainbow or handsome Vince—are momentarily quiet at last. Pepito and Menching pray that the bitch-queen extras will weep and wail with abandon, that Rainbow Reyes won't start giggling, that Vince Moody won't blow his lines, that the power won't go out, and that this will be the one and only take.

Epilogue

Zamora in the Year 2000

/

I have no nose, but I can smell. No eyes, but I can imagine. No
ears, but I hear everything. I am sick of this stifling darkness,
the metal odors permeating my ashes and bones, all this nothing. Shall I try to tell you how much fun it was? Fun. A blunt word,
perfect in its brevity, the exactness of one's upper teeth lightly touching down on the lower lip, resulting in a soft hissing airy phffff . . .
sound. Phfffun. I taught Bodabil that English word and how to say
it, which made him laugh. I loved his laugh. Pure, bubbling energy.
He was a Taobo, and the Taobo understood fun.

Not one anthropologist has bothered to consider the significance
or importance of fun in my life, the pleasure and satisfaction I de-
rived from helping my tribes. My Taobo. So obvious, isn't it? *Coño*, I
can feel your eyes roll back with disdain at the mere mention of my
name. *Zamora sounds like such a typical colonial! So patronizing, so arrogant, so glib.* Your withering contempt powerful enough to penetrate
the bronze, Grecian-style urn displayed on the marble mantelpiece
in the *sala* of my daughter's condo in New York City.

Consider this: I was a small man, five feet five inches in height,
weighing 132 pounds while alive, compact and strong. Consider this:
I took five and a half hours to burn down to ash and bits of bone,

gravelly white as the bleached coral and virgin sand of a tropical beach. Two strapping young men wearing surgeon's masks and rubber slippers presided over my cremation. They shoved my bloated body into the incinerator, stoked the fires, kept the pop music going, made sure my distraught family didn't come too close. Oh, how they loved their unholy work! Singing along with the catchy refrains on the radio, lowering their voices, and cracking obscene jokes at my expense. And when it was all over, at exactly five in the afternoon, the strapping young men—taking great pains not to inhale—took their little whisk brooms and carefully swept the dust of my former self into a handy Ziploc pouch, zip-zip—then stuffed the pouch into an urn. Pathetic. All that is left of me, *yo, ako,* I, Zamora López de Legazpi Jr.: not much more than a sandwich bag, *puñeta kayong lahat!*

My ex-wife, Ilse, mother of my children, did not attend my funeral. But everyone else turned up, which was a relief. Forbes, whom I hadn't seen in years, flew in that morning and made it just in time. Dependable Forbes, decent and loyal to the end. I guess I could have treated him with more respect, but I knew he loved me for being exactly the *cabrón* that I was.

You've probably noticed that I refuse to refer to myself as a "corpse." I prefer the neutrality of "body" instead. "Corpse" is clinical and unappetizing; even now, resigned to my Ziploc and the stifling darkness of my urn, I cannot bring myself to accept mortality or use that word. They say I am dead. But I have not gone to heaven, hell, or purgatory; I do not know any more than you do; I have not met God or Allah or Bathala—whoever and whatever is supposed to be in charge. My heart stopped beating, but there was no white light, no tunnel, no line of joyful, dancing buddhas or ethereal choir of angels. Just the urn and a plastic bag. *Puñeta kayong lahat!*

I heard the hiss and crackle of fire, felt the dull thud as my body—worn down to nothing by my diabolical virus, my cancers, my non-immune system—slid from metal tray to fiery furnace. Snap crackle pop! Heard the jokes and inane love songs, heard myself sizzle and explode, a charred slab of meat on a grill—yet, mercifully, mercifully, I felt nothing. Not a thing. Mercy in death, the only absolute I can guarantee you, dear reader.

In life I was not afraid of anything except fire. My dear wife used to tease me about being terrified of heights and flying, which of course was absurd. If it were so, I never would have bought my Alouette. My elegant, smooth Alouette. Helicopter of helicopters, sleek demon bird from the sky. *Le Petit Prince* I called it. Rather predictable of me, but so what. *Que se joden todos.* Back then I could afford to be as predictable and pretentious as I wanted or needed to be.

In death my once sallow mestizo complexion turns black as a "Hawaiian emperor" (Papa's own words). The mortician, armed with his Stateside pedigree and eager to please my father, slathers on pancake makeup as thick as cement but finds it impossible to conceal the lesions. He rouges my lips and cheeks a ghoulish red in desperation. My sisters faint when they see the painted wreck of me, an obscene doll laid out in the coffin. Thereafter referring to me as "that." *Who is that? That is not our baby brother.*

Papa made a decision. Papa made a crucial decision to have me cremated at the last minute. Arrangements were made for the strapping young men to haul my body away to Manila Memorial Park, before the public and the media caught a glimpse of scary me. *Ay, Dios ko! Bad karma. Horror of it all.* In death as in life, I dare anyone to pity me. *Fuck you putang ina ninyong lahat.*

Mama begged my father not to go through with it. She was my mother, after all, and understood the irony of what was about to happen. Cremating Junior is sacrilege, she cried. But Papa ignored her, as usual.

Burn, baby, burn!

Mama, eaten alive by pessimism and despair, died a month after I did. And here I am. Powdery residue. Sand on a beach. Furious at my father, who is still alive. Nearly a hundred years old, vigorous and vicious as ever, his elephant's memory intact. My son, Zamorito, now runs the empire under his tutelage. My daughter, Dulce, has exiled herself to New York. Financially secure for the rest of her days, sweet Dulce toys with the idea of taking a thankless job at some homeless shelter for women. She paces the living room of her luxury condo night after night, too lonely and anxious to watch TV or movies, unable to sleep. She has grown into a lovely, overly compassionate young woman—a chain-smoker, binge eater, and budding alcoholic. Martyrdom runs deep in her blood.

But where is Ilse? Failed love, source of my agony. I keep hoping she'll show up one day at our daughter's door. And that Dulce will invite her into the *sala* and offer her a cup of hot chocolate—Ilse's favorite beverage—thick hot chocolate made from bitter Mexican cocoa tablets, gobs of milk and sugar, a stick of cinnamon added at the last minute. Ilse will hesitate as she always does, being careful and reserved, then say yes after she sees the unhappy expression on our daughter's face. When Dulce leaves the room, Ilse collapses on the sofa and wonders why she ever bothered showing up. She has not seen Dulce in years. I won the battle, remember? Ilse took the

children with her back to Germany when she left, but I sent my men out to wrench the children from her loving arms and bring them back to me. I convinced the judge that my foreigner wife was certifiably mad for leaving me the way she did.

I imagine Ilse starting to cry when she sees Dulce as a grown-up woman. But she is allergic to tears and stops herself, immediately. My wife—my "ex"—has always been good at this. Tears dry up in an instant; you'd never know her heart was breaking.

She glances around the room, curious and bemused by our daughter's tasteful furniture and pricey knickknacks, which have been selected and arranged by an equally pricey interior decorator. Ilse notices that some of the paintings on the wall used to hang in our old house. A flood of memories threatens to engulf her; she is tempted to flee. Dulce, unsuspecting, babbles from the kitchen. *Want some churros, Mama? There's a new Spanish bakery on the Upper East Side. Not exactly like Manila, but . . .* "Manila," capital of desire and longing, that loaded word, hangs in the air. Dulce realizes her mistake and starts to apologize, but her mother rescues her. *I never expect anything to be exactly like Manila, Schatzi.* Then Ilse sighs. *How I've missed you.*

A black-and-white image of Bodabil in the jungle, clowning for th camera, catches Ilse's eye. The mounted eleven-by-seventeen phot graph, taken by Ken Forbes, is propped up on the mantelpiece n to my urn. My urn that is so discreet it looks like just another tique *tchotchke*, the kind of infuriating, meaningless object wo and homosexuals love to scatter around their apartments ju "fun." And speaking of fun, I was hoping that at the precise m Dulce walks back in with her tray of colonial treats, Ilse's gre would fall on me. Me by way of urn and Ziploc, that is. A

Dulce would notice her mother staring at the urn, fascinated. And that Dulce would say, in that playful tone I know so well, Guess who *that* is?

But of course, this never happens. Dulce is much too excited by her mother's surprise visit to point out the urn and reveal the me contained inside it. Instead they sit on the sofa for hours, slurping cocoa and chomping greasy churros, catching up on international *chismis* and laughing at each other's feeble jokes. Ilse inquires about our son. He is doing so well! Dulce marvels. Ilse sighs again, this time with relief. Mother and daughter ask each other's forgiveness, making vague promises to see each other again as soon as possible. Not once does my name come up. No mention of my glamorous photo and the lengthy obituary published in newspapers around the world.

(Rizalina, do you ever wonder if I have forgotten you? Do you care? *Sampaguita, waling-waling, glory of saints. . . .* No, *mi paloma,* no. I have not forgotten you.)

Here, helpless. Heap of dust,
heap of ash, dirt, bone, dung.
Zamora López de Legazpi Jr.
Fuck me.
Fuck you.
Putang ina ninyong lahat.
Que se vayan todos a la mierda!

Sun goes up, sun goes down. Ex-wife and beloved daughter continue to chat and chew. A bottle of Merlot is uncorked for Ilse. *Vant a little wine, Mama?* Ilse nods, says something in German. The

bottle of Flor de Manila rum, half full, set in front of Dulce. She's got cases of it stashed away in the pantry. Glug-glug. My daughter's happy now, lost in the warmth and glow of my rum and her mother's radiant smile. I smell cigarettes burning, hear bursts of laughter and the murmur of their drunken voices through layers of bronze. The girls are having fun. And not once does my name come up. Not once.

Acknowledgments

For their care, patience, feedback, and support, many heartfelt thanks to Jane von Mehren, my editor, and to my agent, Harold Schmidt. Thank you to Jennifer Ehmann for her insights, and to Brett Kelly and the team at Viking Penguin.

The characters in this novel speak and dream in many languages. *Danke, salamat, grazie, y gracias* to Ulrich Baer, Mia Katigbak, Jaime Manrique, Ralph Peña, and Angela Reid, for their good cheer and help with the tricky business of translations.

My thanks to Neal Oshima and Angel Velasco-Shaw, and the many gracious people, both here and in the Philippines, who were generous with their resources and contacts, their wisdom, humor, kindness, and hospitality: you know who you are.

My gratitude to the John Simon Guggenheim Foundation for a 2001 Fiction Fellowship, which made it possible for me to travel to the Philippines, conduct research and interviews, and complete the writing of this book. Last but not least, *maraming salamat* to my fearless and delightful traveling companions—Ching Valdes-Aran and Zack Linmark—who made the journey with me.

Permissions

Dream Jungle

Two seemingly unrelated events occur in the Philippines—the discovery of the Taobo, an ancient lost tribe living in a remote mountainous area, and the arrival of an American, celebrity-studded film crew, there to make an epic Vietnam War movie. But the "lost tribe" just might be a clever hoax masterminded by the brooding wealthy iconoclast and the Hollywood movie seems doomed as the cast and crew continue to self-destruct in a cloud of drugs and their own egos. *Dream Jungle* evokes the desperate beauty and rank corruption of the Philippines from the height of the Marcos era in the mid-1970s to the end of the twentieth century.

ISBN 0-14-200109-0

Dogeaters

A wildly disparate group of characters—from movie stars to waiters, from a young junkie to the richest man in the Philippines—becomes caught up in a spiral of events culminating in a beauty pageant, a film festival, and an assassination. In the center of this maelstrom is Rio, a fiesty schoolgirl who will grow up to live in America and look back with longing on the land of her youth. In a world in which American pop culture and local Filipino tradition mix flamboyantly, gossip, storytelling, and extravagant behavior thrive in this "surrealistically hip epic of Manila" (*San Francisco Chronicle*).

ISBN 0-14-014904-X

The Gangsters of Love

Rocky Rivera arrives in the U.S. from the Philippines on the day that Jimi Hendrix dies. So begins a blazing coming-of age story suffused with the tensions of immigration that find Rocky moving from the counterculture in the 1960s San Francisco to the extravagant scene in Manhattan of the 1980s. *The Gangster of Love* tells the story of the Rivera music family as they make their new life in the States all the while haunted by the memory of the father and the homeland they left behind.

ISBN 0-14-015970-3

Charlie Chan Is Dead 2: At Home in the World
An Anthology of Contemporary Asian American Fiction

More than a decade after its initial publication, the groundbreaking anthology *Charlie Chan is Dead* remains the best available source for contemporary Asian American fiction. Edited by acclaimed novelist and National Book Award nominee Jessica Hagedorn, *Charlie Chan Is Dead 2: At Home in the World* brings together forty-two fresh, fascinating voices in Asian American writing. Sweeping in background and literary style, from pioneering writers to newly emerging voices, these exceptional works celebrate the full spectrum of Asian American experience and identities, transcending stereotypes and revealing the strength and vitality of Asian America today.

ISBN 0-14-200390-5